Praise for The Secret, Book

T0023470

"Lovers of reading and strong
this entertaining cozy packed with mystery, romance, and
sisterhood."
—*Kirkus Reviews*

"Delightful . . . Adams has a knack for creating endearingly
imperfect characters. Cozy fans will be well satisfied."
—*Publishers Weekly*

"The third book in the Secret, Book, and Scone Society series
serves up an appetizing dish for mystery lovers who enjoy
books about bookstores, small towns, and female friends."
—*Booklist*

"A love letter to reading, with sharp characterizations and
a smart central mystery."
—*Entertainment Weekly*

"Adams launches an intriguing new mystery series, headed
by four spirited amateur sleuths and touched with a hint of
magical realism, which celebrates the power of books and
women's friendships. Adams's many fans, readers of Sarah
Addison Allen, and anyone who loves novels that revolve
around books will savor this tasty treat."
—*Library Journal* (starred review), Pick of the Month

"A perfect read . . . four women whose divergent lives
intermingle due to their shared passion for books, good food,
and, ultimately, friendship, become unwittingly embroiled in
a murder investigation. The deep, dark secrets each of them
carries provide the suspense in this admixture of cozy small-
town life and perplexing mystery with the right amount of
pathos to garner the reader's sympathy."
—*The Cape Cod Chronicle*

Also by Ellery Adams:

The Secret, Book, and Scone Society Mysteries:

Book Retreat Mysteries:

THE VANISHING TYPE

A SECRET, BOOK, AND SCONE SOCIETY NOVEL

ELLERY ADAMS

Kensington Publishing Corp.
www.kensingtonbooks.com

KENSINGTON BOOKS are published by

Kensington Publishing Corp.
119 West 40th Street
New York, NY 10018

Copyright © 2022 by Ellery Adams

All rights reserved. No part of this book may be reproduced in any form or by any means without the prior written consent of the Publisher, excepting brief quotes used in reviews.

All Kensington titles, imprints and distributed lines are available at special quantity discounts for bulk purchases for sales promotion, premiums, fund-raising, educational or institutional use.

This book is a work of fiction. Names, characters, businesses, organizations, places, events, and incidents either are the product of the author's imagination or are used fictitiously. Any resemblance to actual persons, living or dead, events, or locales is entirely coincidental.

To the extent that the image or images on the cover of this book depict a person or persons, such person or persons are merely models, and are not intended to portray any character or characters featured in the book.

Special book excerpts or customized printings can also be created to fit specific needs. For details, write or phone the office of the Kensington Sales Manager: Kensington Publishing Corp., 119 West 40th Street, New York, NY 10018. Attn. Sales Department. Phone: 1-800-221-2647.

The K and Teapot logo is a trademark of Kensington Publishing Corp.

ISBN: 978-1-4967-2646-9 (ebook)

ISBN: 978-1-4967-2645-2

First Kensington Hardcover Edition: May 2022

First Kensington Trade Paperback Printing: April 2023

10 9 8 7 6 5 4 3 2 1

Printed in the United States of America

To the artists who see a story's soul and create a home for it in their book design.

To my favorite book designers and book cover designers:
Hugh Thomson
William Morris
Margaret Strong
Elbert Hubbard
Mr. Boddington's Studio (Rebecca Schmidt Ruebensaal)
Coralie Bickford-Smith
Hülya Özdemir

Even as a small child, I understood that woman had secrets, and that some of these were only to be told to daughters. In this way we were bound together for eternity.
—Alice Hoffman, *The Dovekeepers*

"What must I do, Mother, what must I do to make a different world for her? How do I start?"

"The secret lies in the reading and the writing. You are able to read. Every day you must read one page from some good book to your child. Every day this must be until the child learns to read. Then she must read every day, I know this is the secret."
—Betty Smith, *A Tree Grows in Brooklyn*

The Secret, Book, and Scone Society Members

Nora Pennington, owner of Miracle Books
Hester Winthrop, owner of the Gingerbread House Bakery
Estella Sadler, owner of Magnolia Salon and Spa
June Dixon, thermal pools manager, Miracle Springs Lodge

Relevant Miracle Springs Residents

Sheriff Grant McCabe
Deputy Jasper Andrews
Sheldon Vega
Tyson Dixon
Miles and Meredith Comfort
Lea Carle

Persons connected to The Lady Artist Books

Elmore Freeman—Author
Sadie Strong—Book Designer

Chapter 1

*Oh, my girls, however long you may live, I never
can wish you a greater happiness than this!*
—Louisa May Alcott, *Little Women*

Nora Pennington dropped multicolored marshmallows into a
mug of hot chocolate and then smothered them with whipped
cream. As she added a dusting of rainbow sprinkles to the tur-
ret of cream, she felt eyes on her.

Deputy Jasper Andrews stood at the ticket agent's booth
window, gazing at the Disney *Fantasia* mug with unconcealed
longing.

"No wonder the kids think your Harry Potter hot cocoa is
magical."

"You're never too old for rainbows." Nora jerked a thumb
at the pegboard of mugs behind her. "Want one? That new *Star
Trek* mug has your name on it."

Before Andrews could answer, a ginger-haired boy appeared
at his side. Pointing at the *Fantasia* mug on the counter, he said,
"That's mine."

Andrews raised his hands in surrender. "You're a lucky kid."

The little boy took in Andrews's black boots and snow-
dusted sheriff's department coat and forgot about his drink.

"I got my teeth pulled. I can't bite apples anymore. Not until my big teeth grow in. See?" He bared his teeth like a wolf cub and stuck his tongue through the gap between his lateral incisors. "Mom's buying me a book because I was brave and didn't cry. Any book I want!"

Nora and Andrews exchanged grins as the boy stood on his tiptoes and reached for the handle of the mug. The movement caused sprinkles to slide down the slope of whipped cream and fall onto the counter.

Andrews looked around for the boy's mother. She wasn't sitting in the Readers' Circle or perusing new releases in the North Carolina Authors section. And because Nora's shop was a labyrinth of book-lined shelves, it was impossible to see much past the Hot Enough to Melt Snow display at the beginning of the Romance section.

"Brian's mom is in the Children's Corner with a two-year-old and a newborn," Nora explained. "Brian wants to drink from a mug like his dad, and since he was so brave at the dentist, I said I'd carry his not-too-hot hot chocolate for him."

Andrews looped his thumbs through his belt. "How about this, Brian? I'll put your drink on that coffee table and hang out with you for a bit." He lowered his voice to a conspiratorial whisper. "I want to know if the marshmallows *really* taste like magic."

"Me too," Brian whispered back.

Suppressing a smile, Nora handed Andrews a compostable spoon. She watched the tall, lanky deputy with the boyish face escort Brian to the Readers' Circle and made a mental note to tell Hester Winthrop, owner of the Gingerbread House bakery, and one of Nora's closest friends, that her boyfriend was a very sweet man.

Ten minutes later, Andrews returned to the ticket agent's booth.

"Brian's got his eye on a book about policemen. Kid's got

good taste. Now, *I* need to find something to read." Blushing, he added, "I also need your help with something. Something really important."

Nora stepped out of the narrow room, where an agent had once sold tickets to people traveling by train to cities like Asheville, Raleigh, and Charlotte.

Trains still ran to Miracle Springs. Once a day, passengers would arrive at the new station. They'd roll their suitcases across the shiny marble floor while studying the departing passengers. They wanted to see a crowd of healthy, well-rested, energetic people. They wanted to believe that Miracle Springs was true to its name.

Every day, the sick, stressed, and soul-weary traveled to a place that promised to soothe and rejuvenate. The little berg in western North Carolina had hot springs, beautiful vistas, and dozens of businesses catering to visitors from all over the globe.

And when the powers-that-be decided to build a train station rivaling the beauty of Grand Central, the old station building was put on the market. It sat there for a long time, waiting.

"Waiting for me," Nora always said.

She'd turned the neglected station into Miracle Books. Now the buttercup-yellow building with the periwinkle shutters was the heart of the town. And Nora, who'd been lost and lonely before she became a bookseller, tried to help every person who came into her store.

And here was Deputy Andrews, asking for her help. She touched his arm and said, "Is everything okay?"

"Yeah. Sure." His expression didn't match his tone, so Nora waited for him to elaborate. "Can we talk in the Sci-Fi section?"

Sheldon, Nora's only employee, had already gone home. When she was alone in the bookshop, Nora usually flitted back and forth between the checkout counter and the ticket agent's booth. But since it was five o'clock on a cold and drowsy winter afternoon, Nora knew she could give Andrews her undivided attention.

The Sci-Fi section was a narrow, book-lined alcove tucked between Fantasy and Young Adult. String lights shaped like tiny stars hung from the shelves, and a Doctor Who mobile dangled down from the ceiling. A shiny blue telephone box spun lazily in the air, endlessly chased by glittering Daleks.

Andrews paused in front of the new releases.

"What are you in the mood for?" Nora asked.

"Something like that last Bradbury. I like comparing the book to the movie."

Nora laughed and pointed at a ceramic plaque that said: THE BOOK IS ALWAYS BETTER.

"I guess, but I like seeing how a really good story translates to the screen. So far, I've read and watched *Ender's Game*, *Dune*, *Fahrenheit 451*, *The Martian*, and *Starship Troopers*. That one was so bad that I want to see it again. It's a guy thing. We like to watch bad movies multiple times."

This last bit didn't register with Nora because she was already hunting for books with movie adaptations. She took a copy of *2001: A Space Odyssey* off the shelf and showed it to Andrews.

"The movie puts me to sleep. I need something with more action, so unless the book is *way* different, I'll pass."

Nora tapped her finger to her lips as she skimmed titles. "I'm thinking *Minority Report* or *The War of the Worlds*. I don't know how you feel about Tom Cruise, but he stars in both movies."

"Hester isn't a fan, but I like him. I don't need an Oscar performance from an action hero. Plus, he broke his ankle doing a stunt. That's dedication. I think I'll try *The War of the Worlds*." Andrews chose the hardcover over the paperback and read the blurb on the back cover. When he was done, he closed the book and held it to his chest.

"Is that the one? Because I could come up with a few more."

Glancing down at the book, Andrews said, "It's the one. I know what I want right away. It was like that with Hester. I knew she was the one the first time we met. Which is why . . . I'm going to ask her to marry me."

Nora wasn't surprised. Andrews and Hester, who were both in their mid-thirties, had been dating for two years. Hester had spent Christmas with Andrews's family, and many people believed the couple would be engaged by New Year's. Though Andrews hadn't popped the question in December, he was clearly ready to do it now, at the start of a new month in a new year.

"That's wonderful!" Nora squeezed Andrews's free hand. "I'm so happy for you both."

Andrews responded with a shy smile. "Thanks, but I don't think I can do it without your help. I mean, I know what I want to say, but I don't want to get down on one knee in some fancy restaurant or have her see the question on a stadium scoreboard. I want to ask her when she's surrounded by her closest friends." He gave Nora an imploring look. "You, Estella, and June are the closest things she has to a family. I'm hoping you'll help me come up with the perfect time and place to ask her the most important question of my life."

Andrews sounded so nervous that Nora hurried to relieve his anxiety. "Of course, we'll help." When his shoulders sagged in relief, she added, "But there's something you need to hear first—about marriage—starting right now, with this proposal."

"What's that?"

"A marriage is the union of two imperfect people, which means you need to go into it knowing it'll never be perfect. Open up your mental window and throw that word out. Relationships are many things, but they're never perfect. And that's okay."

Andrews shifted on his feet. "Um . . . okay . . ."

Nora smiled at him. "Don't worry. June, Estella, and I will do everything we can to make your proposal amazing. We have a book club meeting tonight, so we'll put our heads together then. Do you have a ring?"

"Yeah. My grandma's. She left it to me to give to my future wife. It's a ruby surrounded by little diamonds. It's kind of star-shaped. And what's really cool is that Hester and my grandma were both born in July. They have the same birthstone."

"It sounds perfect," Nora said with a wink.

Later, after the bookstore had closed for the day, the members of the Secret, Book, and Scone Society filed in through the delivery entrance.

"I hate the winter," grumbled Estella, owner of Magnolia Salon and Spa. She sank into her favorite chair in the Readers' Circle, hugging the throw pillow embroidered with JUST ONE MORE CHAPTER.

"Would coffee help?" Nora asked. "Or a shot of whiskey?"

Estella released the pillow and reached up to pat her hair. Satisfied that her soft auburn waves were as they should be, she sighed. "Honestly, I just want to complain. I have to be perky and sweet all day long, even when I don't feel perky and sweet. If my clients don't have a positive experience, they might not come back. I listen to their problems. I sympathize. I smile until my cheeks hurt, but it's such a relief to be with you gals because I can finally be myself."

Hester, who'd carried one of her delicious homemade desserts into the ticket agent's booth, called out, "Same here!"

"Honey, we all have to play nice for a living." With one hand, June Dixon unwound the scarf she'd knitted over the course of three relatively sleepless nights while digging into a grocery bag with the other. Pulling out a bottle of champagne, she flashed Estella a wide grin. "Are you too cold for a glass of bubbly?"

Estella jumped to her feet and leaned over to hug June. "You got the promotion!"

Beaming, June said, "You are looking at the new Guest Experience Manager of the Miracle Springs Lodge."

Nora, Estella, and Hester clapped, whooped, and gave June congratulatory hugs.

"Are you happy with the terms?" Nora asked.

"Yes, and that's partially thanks to you," said June. "Because of the books you recommended, I was prepared to ask for what I deserved. And I *got* it. All of it! The job, the salary, *and* the benefits."

Hester perched on the arm of June's chair. "What were these incredibly empowering books?"

"I read three of the five on Nora's list. *Lean In*, *Grit*, and *Secrets of Six-Figure Women*. I almost gave up on that last one when the author wrote something about how women believe in the nobility of poverty. *Puh-lease!*" June cried. "I grew up in a Black neighborhood in the Bronx, and I can tell you that we didn't think there was a damn bit of nobility in being poor."

"I'd rather be a rich degenerate than noble and poor," said Estella, picking up the bottle of champagne.

June pointed at her. "I hear you. Still, I won't quit reading a book because I disagree with a single point. Good thing too, because I took that author's advice to heart. I walked into that interview with the swagger of a first-round draft pick. I knew exactly how to convert my skills and experience into a dollar amount."

Estella opened the champagne, filled the four mugs she'd taken from the pegboard, and distributed them. Hester got the hot-pink BOSS BABE mug, June received the Wonder Woman mug, and Nora's was white with black text that said: NEVER CROSS A WOMAN WHO READS STEPHEN KING. For herself, Estella chose a mug featuring four women with different skin tones and hair colors. The text marching around the rim said: WELL-READ WOMEN ARE DANGEROUS CREATURES.

Nora raised her mug. "Congratulations, June. Here's to your seat on the rocket ship."

"That's from the Sandberg book," June explained to Estella and Hester. "It goes, 'If you're offered a seat on a rocket ship, don't ask which seat! Just get on.'"

"May your star keep rising," Hester said.

After sipping champagne and chatting for a bit, the women loaded their plates with a cheesy chicken casserole and green salad from the ticket agent's booth, grabbed napkins and flatware, and returned to the Readers' Circle.

While they ate, they discussed Kristin Hannah's *The Nightingale*. As usual, certain scenes prompted the sharing of personal anecdotes. These stories led to discussions on a whole range of topics, until, finally, the focus circled back to the book.

By the time Hester served slices of chocolate hazelnut tart with a salted shortbread crust, the group's analysis of fictional characters had given way to casual chitchat. Between bites of tart and sips of decaf, the women traded tales of mutual acquaintances, as well as the juiciest morsels of town gossip.

Nora loved talking books. Her face shone like the sun whenever she had the chance to share her thoughts on characters, plot, setting, title, or quoteworthy lines. She took in every part of a book, from its cover design to its copyright page. She read every word, including author notes, dedications, and biographical info.

The fact that her book club spent only a small portion of the evening talking about the book didn't bother Nora. She cherished these weekly meetings for the food and fellowship more than the actual book discussion.

Nora, June, Estella, and Hester hadn't always been friends. Several years ago, the death of a stranger had brought them together, and before they even realized it was happening, the fiercely independent, distrustful women began to rely on one another. Eventually they sat in this circle of chairs and released their darkest secrets into the coffee-laced air. This was how the Secret, Book, and Scone Society was formed. Four strangers had become a sisterhood.

Their book club meetings didn't have an official end time, but when Estella yawned and got up to carry her dirty dishes to the sink, the rest of the women followed suit.

When the kitchen was clean, Hester buttoned up her peacoat, pulled a knit hat over her honey-hued curls, and waited for her friends to bundle up. She didn't realize that June and Estella planned to stay behind to talk over proposal ideas with Nora.

"Go on without me," June told her. "I need to visit the ladies' room."

Estella grimaced. "Me too. Coffee."

Nora beckoned at Hester. "Come on, I'll hold the door and watch you walk to your car."

"It's too cold to walk. I'm going to run." Hester fished in her pocket for her keys and yelled, "Good night!" before heading outside and jogging across the parking lot.

As soon as Hester was safely inside her car, Nora let the heavy metal door slam shut and hurried to the checkout counter to join June and Estella.

"Can I tell you how hard it was to act normal tonight?" Estella put a hand over her heart. "Andrews is going to propose!

To our own darling Hester. And after that, there'll be a wedding. A *wedding*! Isn't it wonderful?"

"Not according to my ex-husband," June muttered.

Nora elbowed her in the side. "I have one of those too, but we're not talking about failed marriages right now. This is about Hester. Sweet, generous Hester. A woman who loves vintage everything."

Estella smiled. "You have an idea, don't you?"

"Maybe."

Nora walked over to the large display table in the fiction section. "Oscar's Theater opens in a few weeks. I bumped into Oscar at the hardware store right after Christmas, and he told me that he'd be showing the movie adaptations of these books and plays from January to the beginning of March. Hester likes everything from the forties and fifties, so if she's into one of these movies, Andrews could take her to the theater and—"

"There could be a technical problem and the movie would suddenly stop playing. And *that's* when Andrews could propose!" Estella cried. She surveyed the books on the table. "It has to be a romantic movie. He can't propose in the middle of *Twelve Angry Men* or *Old Yeller*."

June laid her hand on a book. "This is the one."

"*Little Women*?" Estella frowned. "That's not romantic. What about *A Streetcar Named Desire*? Marlon Brando is sexy as hell in that movie. Or *The African Queen*? Humphrey Bogart. Katharine Hepburn. Talk about chemistry. Oh, and there's *Father of the Bride*. You can't beat that."

Crossing her arms, June said, "None of those can hold a candle to Hester's favorite book. She reads *Little Women* every year. You've seen the framed quote in her bakery, right?"

" 'I'd rather take coffee than compliments just now,' " said Nora.

"Once, on the way home from book club, Hester told me about this set of dolls she had when she was little. She wasn't allowed to play with them. Her mom said they were collectible and weren't to be touched. *Ever.* I remember her saying there was an Alice in Wonderland, Scarlett O'Hara, a bunch of princesses, and Marmee, Jo, Meg, Beth, and Amy. Of all the dolls, Hester liked Amy the most. She and Amy had the same color hair, and Hester loved the doll's gingham dress. After reading *Little Women*, Hester wanted to be like Amy in every way."

"I've never seen the original movie," said Nora.

Estella's phone was in her hand. As she stared at the screen, her eyes widened. "The original is from 1933 and featured Katharine Hepburn, but in the 1949 version, Elizabeth Taylor played Amy. She's a blonde! See?"

Nora and June peered at the tiny screen with interest.

June grunted. "They're supposed to be awkward teens, not pinup models."

"Lucky Liz. I've been trying to look like a pinup girl since I was eleven years old." Estella touched her cheek. "I guess I can't call myself a girl, now that I'm forty."

June chuckled. "Honey, you're the same redheaded bombshell at forty that you were at thirty. There isn't a man in town who doesn't get whiplash when you walk by."

Nora wasn't listening to her friends. She was mentally skimming the novel in hopes of recalling a scene to complement Andrews's proposal. A sweet scene that included Amy.

Suddenly she snapped her fingers.

"You just had a eureka moment," said Estella.

Grabbing a copy of *Little Women*, Nora began turning pages. "There's an exchange between Amy and Jo. It's the perfect place to stop the film and give Andrews the chance to go down on one knee or whatever he plans to do." After making sure the lines were as she remembered, Nora read the scene to her friends.

When she was done, June wore a dreamy expression. Smiling to herself, she said, "Hester will be sitting in the theater, totally focused on the movie and the bag of popcorn she's sharing with Jasper, when the screen suddenly goes black. The house lights come up and folks start murmuring. Mr. Oscar walks into the theater to tell everyone—Oh, Lord! I just thought of something."

Nora and Estella exchanged worried glances.

"It's nothing bad," June was quick to assure them. "Actually, it's really good. Tyson's ready to work full-time, and he applied for a job at Oscar's Theater. I never dreamed that he'd want to live in the same town as me, but we've come a long way over the past year." Her eyes grew misty. "When he asked if he could take me to church on Christmas Eve, I felt like I was in a Hallmark movie. Having him beside me and hearing him sing 'Silent Night' was the miracle I'd been praying for since I left New York."

"You made that miracle happen," said Nora. "You stood by Tyson when he hit rock bottom and moved mountains to help him get back on his feet."

June nodded. "But it's time for him to stand on his own. Lots of men his age are married with their own kids. Those damned drugs stole fifteen years of his life. I sure hope he gets this job."

"Me too," Nora said.

As the women bundled up in coats, gloves, and scarves, they tossed around more ideas for Jasper's movie night proposal. Estella thought it would be cute if he hid the ring inside a box of Twizzlers.

June's mouth twisted to one side. "I don't know. We don't want her to end up in the ER."

Nora switched off the floor lamp in the Readers' Circle and

followed her friends into the Children's Corner. They paused at the edge of the colorful animal alphabet floor rug and waited for her to turn off the lamps stationed at opposite ends of the tallest bookshelf.

A waterfall display topped with the sign IT'S A NEW YEAR, BABY was positioned slightly in front of the shelves, and the light from the Paddington Bear lamp fell directly on the row of board books.

Nora's gaze skipped over DK's *Baby Faces*, Hayley Barrett's *Babymoon*, Helen Oxenbury's *Say Goodnight*, and Jimmy Fallon's *This Is Baby*, to rest on *I Love You Like Crazy Cakes*, Rose Lewis's heartwarming story about adoption.

"You okay?" Estella asked.

Without taking her eyes off the book, Nora said, "There's a possibility we haven't considered. What if Hester says no . . . or isn't ready to say *yes*? He's going to propose in front of an audience. That's a lot of pressure. And Hester's already under pressure."

June and Estella didn't respond. They just stared at the baby books.

All three women were thinking about Hester's secret. She'd shared it with them years ago. They were the only ones privy to it. She'd never told the man she loved. She was always waiting for the right time.

Her friends were suddenly aware that the time had come.

The silence suddenly felt heavy. The shadows, banished to the corners during the day, now seemed to stretch and grow.

Nora was the first to move. She turned off the Paddington Bear lamp and walked over to the Winnie-the-Pooh lamp on the other end of the shelf. She noticed how its light landed on the eyes of the plush animals and puppets, making the toys look eerily sentient.

Nora glanced down to find that she was standing on the letter *S*.

A snake formed the letter's spine, its elliptical pupil and wobbly grin looking more sinister than goofy in the dimness. Nora felt compelled to step off the rug.

"Maybe Hester's secret can stay buried," June said without conviction. "Maybe she and Andrews will be okay."

Estella shook her head. "It'll come out. And then what'll happen?"

"It will destroy them," Nora whispered.

Chapter 2

Names have power.
    —Rick Riordan

Two weeks later, Sheldon Vega held out a package of silver stars.

"I know you have post-traumatic glitter stress from the holiday window, but I promise to vacuum every single sparkly speck after we take this display down."

"It's true what they say: All the crazies go to Walmart after midnight." Nora pointed at the bags piled behind Sheldon. "Is that a disco ball?"

Sheldon's mouth curved into an impish grin. "It *is*. And guess what? It *rotates*. We can hang it over the books we're dressing up like movie stars. And for the final movie premiere touch, I got *this*."

He pulled a square of velvety red fabric from a bag. As he unfolded it, dozens of twinkly flecks landed on his pants and over the books lined up near the window.

"Oops, I did it again," he said, glancing at the mess without a hint of remorse. "Just call me Britney."

"I'm never letting you go to Walmart alone again."

Pushing the bag to the side, Sheldon mumbled, "I should probably leave the feather boas in here for now."

Nora scowled. "If you didn't make such good coffee, I'd fire you."

Sheldon smiled so widely that the tails of his mustache kissed his cheeks. "This place wouldn't be the same without me. I'm irreplaceable."

"That's true," Nora agreed. "Who else would come in late, leave early, forget to put the lid back on the Nutella jar, swear under their breath in Spanish, buy decorations covered in glitter for every occasion, play matchmaker to the members of the Blind Date Book Club, and frighten small children during storytime?"

"I didn't mean to! I had no idea that *Sleep, Black Bear, Sleep* had a picture of hibernating snakes." Sheldon shuddered. "I'm like a half-Cuban Indiana Jones. I saw that pit of snakes—that nasty tangle of tails and scales—and I could almost *see* them moving. So I freaked out."

"When I heard the shrieks, I thought it was one of the moms. For a man with such a low voice, you can reach some high notes when you see snakes."

Yesterday's storytime had been a disaster. She'd been at the checkout counter prepping the online orders for pick up when she'd heard Sheldon's barn owl screech followed by the wails of a dozen children.

Eventually Sheldon had finished the book and shown his pint-sized audience how to make a bear cave. After the activity, the parents and sitters didn't linger to browse or chat over coffee, as was their habit. Nora didn't ring up a single title from the hibernation display. In fact, the only thing she sold to that group was the board book *When I Feel Scared*.

Thinking back on the hasty exodus of the storytime crowd, Nora had to laugh.

She often laughed around Sheldon Vega. He had that effect on people. He also had a knack for recommending books, the ability to listen very closely, and gave the world's best bear hugs. He favored bowties and sweater vests, Nutella on toast, and rearranging the shop's inventory until every book or vintage accessory was exactly where he felt it should be.

Sheldon had inherited his love of reading and his ability to put people at ease from his Jewish mother. He got his self-possession and devotion to delicious food from his Cuban father. A tall man in his sixties, he had silver hair, a tidy goatee, and a jaunty mustache. He also suffered from chronic pain, and there were days when his osteoporosis and fibromyalgia refused to let him function. The pain in his joints and nerve endings was unpredictable. Sometimes it was mild. Sometimes it was crippling, forcing him to arrive late, leave early, or not work altogether.

Nora didn't care that he was an unreliable employee. She loved him just as he was.

"No more snake books for you," she said with a smile. "Okay, I'm going to hang the disco ball. You decide which books will walk the red carpet."

Sheldon scanned the rolling cart. "This won't be easy. I always like the book better than the movie."

"This Printed Page to Silver Screen display is our way of supporting Oscar's Theater." Nora picked up the disco ball and spun it around. "After people see our display, maybe they'll buy the books *and* go to his theater to see the movies."

While Nora hung the disco ball and Sheldon attached glittery stars to a midnight-blue backdrop, they discussed which books to put in the window. They agreed on *To Kill a Mockingbird, The Godfather, L.A. Confidential, Like Water for Chocolate, The Color Purple, Crazy Rich Asians, The Maltese Falcon, Pride and Prejudice, Lonesome Dove, The Namesake, The Remains of the Day, No Country for Old Men, The Silence of the Lambs,* and *The Wizard of Oz.*

Nora surveyed their choices. "We need another two, maybe three, more."

"*Cloud Atlas* was unwatchable." Sheldon looked at the book cover and frowned. "I hate movie tie-in covers. They're like the worst dressed at the Oscars. Whoever came up with the idea to replace cover art with what's basically a movie poster should be exiled to Mars."

Nora glanced at the offending cover. "As much as I love Tom Hanks, I don't want him on my book cover. Especially not *that* version of Tom Hanks. It doesn't even look like him."

"How about this?" Sheldon held up Kazuo Ishiguro's *Never Let Me Go*.

Nora pulled a face. "The person who designed that movie poster clearly didn't read the book. They made a dark, gripping, beautifully-written dystopian novel look rosy and warm."

After reviewing the next group of books in the cart, Nora and Sheldon had enough titles to fill the transparent ledges floating among the silver stars.

"Time to pick our main attractions," Sheldon said, draping a gold feather boa around Nora's neck. "No movie tie-in cover for our red-carpet couple. They should be the best-looking covers in the window."

"What about *Rebecca*? The anniversary edition by Virago Modern Classics is pure elegance. It's totally white with gold font."

Sheldon rummaged around in yet another plastic bag. "White with a hot-pink boa. Done! This is for the male lead." He showed Nora a tiny top hat.

"That's adorable."

Sheldon spun the hat around on his finger. "It came with a doll called Magic Show Barbie, though her outfit makes her look more like Strip Club Barbie."

Nora laughed. "This, I need to see. Where is she?"

"Actually, she was a knockoff Barbie. But she had pretty hair and a fabulous pair of boots, so I asked the woman in line behind me if her little girl wanted the doll, minus her hat. The girl definitely wanted it, and that's how Pole Dance Paula found a home."

This had them both roaring.

"Okay, no more Walmart stories," Nora said. "We need to pick the leading man."

Sheldon glanced around. "Harry Potter's too young to be Rebecca's date, and I can't see Forrest Gump or Dracula as her plus one. Robin Hood? Sherlock Holmes? I bet she'd have a lovely evening with the Count of Monte Cristo."

Nora checked their inventory of Dumas novels. "Nada. If only we had the Penguin Clothbound edition, we'd be all set." Suddenly she brightened. "Coralie Bickford-Smith, the artist who designed those covers, created gorgeous Art Deco covers for another series."

Crossing the room to the lawyer's bookcase next to the checkout counter, Nora retrieved a hardback with a gold-and-cream dust jacket and showed it to Sheldon. "I present to you the debonair, devilish, and always dazzling Jay Gatsby!"

Sheldon grinned. "*The Great Gatsby* and *Rebecca*. Two icons."

He slid the books into the clear holders affixed to the middle of the red carpet. Then he draped the boa around *Rebecca* and positioned the top hat on *The Great Gatsby*.

"Turn on the disco ball, boss. Let's see if our display makes the cut. Ah, the puns never end."

At that moment, someone knocked on the front door.

"Pizza!" Nora cried happily. "I'll grab our pies while you find a book to go in that empty space next to *The Lord of the Rings*. We'll light everything up after we eat."

Hurrying to unlock the door, Nora greeted the young man holding a pair of pizza boxes.

"Hey, Ji-hun."

"Hi, Ms. Pennington."

Nora relieved him of the boxes and asked if he wanted to

come inside and warm up for a few minutes, but he politely declined.

"I've gotta get to my next stop *fast*. This customer always tries to score free food by saying that it's cold. Even if steam is coming out the sides of the box, he'll say it was cold when I gave it to him. And he *never* tips."

Nora doubted the customer knew that Ji-hun worked two part-time jobs to help support his family or that he hoped to study genetic engineering one day. Whenever Nora ordered pizza, she asked for Ji-hun by name and tipped him generously.

"Don't let him get to you," she said, handing Ji-hun some cash and telling him to keep the change.

He glanced at the bills and smiled. "Thanks, Ms. Pennington."

He was halfway up the block before Nora saw a wallet on the front mat. Leaving the pizzas on the floor, she ran after him.

The blare of a car horn kept him from hearing her shouts, but she managed to catch him before he crossed the street.

"Oh, man! I'm sorry, Ms. P.! Now *your* food's going to be cold."

"It won't take me *that* long to get back inside," Nora said with a laugh.

She'd just turned toward the store when a man looking down at his phone walked right into her. The collision knocked his phone from his hand and sent it clattering to the sidewalk.

Cursing, he grabbed it and examined the screen.

"Are you blind?" he shouted at Nora. "Everyone knows women can't drive. Now you can't walk either?"

"*You* ran into *me!*"

"Aw, cry about it to your MeToo friends." And after muttering, "dumb bitch," he walked away.

Inside Miracle Books, Nora told Sheldon about the encounter.

"What'd the gorilla look like?"

Though Nora was fuming, this made her grin. "Honestly, it was like bumping into Donkey Kong. The guy isn't local. If I'd seen him before, I'd remember. His beard had seriously uneven cheek lines and was at least two shades too dark. He must be grooming himself in the dark."

"He clearly doesn't respect the art of facial topiary."

When Nora stopped laughing, she asked Sheldon if he was ready to eat.

"Start without me. I have to get something first."

A minute later, Sheldon appeared in the Readers' Circle, carrying a stack of paperbacks.

Nora took a bite of pizza and moaned. "Are you reorganizing the Book to Movie display *now*? Do you not see the pizza?"

"I had to take these off the table," he said.

Nora gave him a quizzical look. "Why?"

"Because they're damaged."

The pizza boxes occupied most of the coffee table, so Sheldon balanced the stack on an empty chair. Before sitting down, he grabbed one of the books and passed it to Nora, back cover side up.

Reluctantly Nora lowered her pizza slice to her plate and wiped her hands. As she turned to take the book from Sheldon, she caught a glimpse of the back cover. Her initial impression was that it had been a victim of the box cutter. She rarely cut so deeply when opening a box that she damaged its contents, but it did happen.

But this book hadn't been neatly sliced in one place. It looked like someone had taken a vegetable peeler to the blurb. Bits of cover had been scraped off like potato skin, revealing the white flesh underneath.

As her eyes traveled over the mutilated plot summary, Nora saw that words had been carved out in a possibly random pattern.

Only it wasn't random. And it wasn't a word. It was a name. That of the main character.

"What the hell?"

"The whole stack looks like that," Sheldon said. "Why would someone do this? *Qué loco.* So you don't like Hawthorne. Okay. We get it. But why vandalize every copy of *The Scarlet Letter*? Did someone fail high school English because of this book? Did seeing Demi Moore in the movie adaptation send them over the edge? Because that's relatable."

Nora flipped through the copy in her hands and then stared at the stack of books.

Sheldon touched her arm. "I'm sorry. I should have waited until we finished eating. You're upset now. I am too. It's criminal to abuse a book, but it was probably some stupid kid. Come on, *cariño*. Eat your pizza before it gets cold."

"I need to see the rest," Nora said.

With a sigh, Sheldon moved the books from the chair to Nora's lap. While she examined every copy, he washed his hands and started eating. He managed to gobble down an entire slice before noticing the stricken expression on Nora's face.

"What's wrong?" he asked.

"Every book is the same. Someone scraped off Hester Prynne's name. Except they didn't remove the Prynne. Just the Hester." She laid her hands over the cover, hiding it from view. "It feels like a message, a creepy one. Andrews is proposing to her tomorrow. Maybe someone knows this and is unhappy about it?"

Sheldon shook his head. "Like a jealous ex? If someone wanted to cause problems between those two, this seems like a really complicated way to go about it. Don't let this ruin our TGIF vibe," Sheldon said. "Our window looks amazing. And we have pizza."

Nora put the book on the top of the stack. "You're right, but we might need music to help us get our groove back. Your Friday night playlist?"

Sheldon's eyes twinkled. "That's the spirit!"

While Sheldon pulled up the playlist on his phone, Nora carried the damaged books back to the stockroom. She and Sheldon finished eating to the energetic beat of salsa music, and since Sheldon wanted to futz with the window some more, Nora offered to clean up.

Carrying their plates to the sink, she ran the water until steam rose from the basin. She held her cold hands over the steam, hoping the heat would dispel the tingling sensation in the space above the knuckle of her pinkie finger. The space once occupied by the rest of her finger.

She'd lost the top half the same night she'd been burned. The puckered scars swam like jellyfish over the back of her right hand, along the length of her arm, and up the side of her neck. Half of her face had also been scarred, but a magician of a plastic surgeon had erased most of the damage.

The car fire she'd caused after driving while impaired happened nearly a decade ago. By now, Nora was so used to her scars that, other than applying sunscreen to the affected areas, she barely noticed them. Neither did the residents of Miracle Springs. They looked past Nora's scars and saw her for what she truly was: a compassionate purveyor of books. Her shop was a haven of stories and serenity, of coffee and comfy chairs, of discovery and delight. In a chaotic world, it was an oasis of calm.

Like most people, Nora's heart was scarred too. The night of the car accident had forever changed her. And one of those changes had been the sudden onset of a ghost tingle in her ruined finger. Not unlike an animal's sixth sense—the pins-and-needles sensation was an omen. It meant something bad would soon happen.

When the hot water failed to end the tingling, Nora turned it off. Her gaze swept over the various coffee mugs hanging from the pegboard and came to rest on the mug Hester had used at their last book club meeting. Goosebumps erupted all over Nora's body, and she felt chilled to the marrow. It was as if a fragment of glass from the evil mirror in Hans Christian Andersen's "The Snow Queen" had pierced her heart, and there was nothing she could do to stop the cold from spreading.

Miracle Books was always busy on Saturday, and though Nora reveled in the high foot traffic and robust sales, she practically chased the last customer out of the shop at closing time. She skipped most of her end-of-day tasks and left the store in a state of disarray. The shelves needed restocking, the tables were disorganized, and the Children's Corner was a flat-out mess, but if Nora wanted to make it to the seven o'clock showing of *Little Women*, she had to hurry home.

Luckily, home was a two-minute walk across the parking lot. Nora lived in a tiny house that had once been a working train car. She'd spent most of her savings converting the red caboose into a livable space. Every inch of the bedroom, bath, kitchen, and living room had a purpose, as did the furniture. Most of the pieces doubled as storage units, and she'd added bookshelves wherever she could.

From the outside, the caboose looked the same as it had when it was first built. The only alteration was the set of stairs leading to a small deck. Whenever the weather allowed, Nora would start her day at her little café table. She'd sip coffee and gaze out at the wooded hills rising above the train tracks marking the edge of her property line.

No train whistles welcomed her home that Saturday. On weekends, the freight trains chugged through late at night and the passenger train had already come and gone.

The new batch of visitors would be having dinner or drinks at the lodge or one of the many B&Bs in town, and if they happened to wander to Oscar's Theater in hopes of seeing a movie, they'd be turned away. Next week's grand opening would be for the public, but tonight's event was restricted to a small crowd. Andrews had made arrangements with Oscar to host a private screening in the guise of a soft opening. Without Hester's knowledge, invitations had been issued to their closest friends and to several members of the sheriff's department as well.

Nora showered, dressed in dark jeans and a wool sweater with a pomegranate hue, and ate a salad with grilled chicken for dinner. At six forty-five, she jogged back to the parking lot, where June was waiting for her, the engine of her old Bronco idling.

"Are you ready for a night to remember?" June asked when Nora slid into the passenger seat.

"I sure am. I'm also ready for popcorn and candy."

From the backseat, Sheldon said, "Let's split a tub."

Nora shook her head. "You know I like butter on mine."

Sheldon pretended to gag. "There isn't a drop of butter in that chemical-laced soybean oil."

"It can't be any worse than those cheddar and sour cream potato chips you love," Nora teased. "Neon orange is not a natural color."

"Okay, children. Stop bickering," June chided. "Tonight is doubly special for me. Not only is Andrews proposing to our sweet Hester, but my son is also running the projector. I am so proud of him I could burst."

"Is he nervous?" asked Nora.

"Not a bit. Tyson is crazy excited about this job. He doesn't care if he'll be sweeping floors, popping popcorn, or tearing tickets. He's a pig in mud working for a man like Mr. Oscar. Over dinner last night, Tyson told me that Mr. Oscar knows all there is to know about Black directors, actors, writers, and musicians. He's taught Tyson more about our people's history this past week than he ever learned in school."

Sheldon spied a parking spot half a block from the theater,

but June didn't think her new Bronco would fit in such a tight space.

"There's plenty of room. Don't you want to show off those New Yorker parking skills you're always bragging about?"

Muttering that she was going to evict Sheldon and find a better housemate—preferably a mute one—June maneuvered the car into the parking spot.

"You do have mad parking skills," Nora said when they were out of the car. "Can I buy you a box of Milk Duds for saving me from a very cold walk?"

June threaded her arm through Nora's. "Milk Duds will rip out my fillings, but I'll take a box of Reese's Pieces."

"Since you're buying, I'll have Sno-Caps," Sheldon said, taking Nora's other arm.

The outdoor ticket window was closed, so the trio went inside, where Tyson was selling tickets from a narrow space that looked like a coat closet.

June leaned over the half door separating the closet from the lobby and hugged her son. "You're looking sharp tonight. Mm-hmm."

Tyson had his mother's golden-brown eyes and close-cropped black hair, but the similarities ended there. June was all soft curves and had been blessed with luminous skin that had people thinking she was in her forties instead of her fifties. Drugs and alcohol had prematurely aged Tyson's face, and no matter how much he ate, he remained lean and wiry.

They also had contrasting personalities. June was energetic and loud, while her son was a quiet man of few words. She could talk to anyone, stranger or friend, about almost any subject. Tyson avoided people he didn't know well, and since he'd just moved to Miracle Springs, that included just about everyone.

At least Tyson was comfortable around Nora and Sheldon. He welcomed them with a smile and told them that Mr. Oscar was currently operating the concession stand.

"Just so you know, he goes a little crazy with the butter."

Nora shot a look at Sheldon and said, "Good."

They walked through the lobby, marveling over its elegance. Light from a series of small chandeliers bounced off the gilded tin ceiling tiles. The carpet was a deep scarlet with a pattern of gold diamonds and was thick enough to muffle footfalls. The movie posters lining the pale green walls featured Black actors from the Golden Age of Hollywood to the present.

"Stop drooling over Idris Elba," Sheldon scolded his female companions.

"That's like asking us to stop breathing," Nora said.

Because the movie was scheduled to start in five minutes, the line at the concession stand wasn't long. Nora, June, and Sheldon got in line behind several officers from the sheriff's department and discussed whether they should stop calling Andrews by his last name and start calling him Jasper instead.

Seeing Hester at the front of the line, Nora put her finger to her lips. They'd have to table their discussion for another time.

Hester paid for her soda and tub of popcorn and walked over to her friends. She kissed the air near their cheeks and cried, "Isn't this place gorgeous?"

"Not as gorgeous as you," said Sheldon.

Hester beamed. "I've been looking for an excuse to wear this skirt. It's from the sixties."

"Only you could pull off that plaid without looking like a Scottish clansman or a curtain panel," said June. "Where's your man?"

"He just came out of the men's room." She smiled. "Will you look at him? I don't know why he's so impatient. It's not like we need to beat off a crowd to get the good seats. Well, see you in there!" She collected her food and was about to walk away when she stopped to look at Nora. "Hey, after the movie, remind me to tell you about this strange book I found in the bakery this morning."

"It wasn't *The Scarlet Letter*, was it?" A chill tiptoed up Nora's spine as she thought of the paperbacks with the ruined covers, and of how the removal of a name had left those books with jagged white scars.

Hester cupped her ear, but before Nora could repeat the question, an upbeat xylophone chime danced out of the speakers.

Suddenly Andrews was there. After a quick hello, he grabbed Hester's hand. "Come on, hon. We'll miss the previews."

As Andrews led her away, she turned and shouted, "Remind me to tell you about the book I found!"

But Nora wasn't going to remind her. If Hester thought the book in the bakery was strange, then it might be damaged—just like the books in Nora's stockroom. If those books were meant to be a warning—or a threat—Nora wanted them to stay where they belonged.

In the dark.

Chapter 3

*His soul swooned slowly as he heard the snow falling
faintly through the universe and faintly falling, like
the descent of their last end, upon all the living and
the dead.*

—James Joyce

Despite the warning chimes, the red curtains covering the
screen were still closed when Nora, Sheldon, and June took
their seats.

Only half of the theater was occupied, so there was plenty of
room to spread out. Nora had just put her coat on the empty
seat when another coat landed on her lap, nearly spilling her
popcorn.

"Don't give me the death stare," Sheldon told her. "I need to
sit on the end so I can stretch my right leg out. I'm immuno-
compromised, remember?"

June snorted. "Mentally compromised is more like it. You
took the end seat to make sure no one from my knitting circle
could sit next to you."

Sheldon rolled his eyes. "Well, they refuse to accept me for
who I am. They think they can reverse my asexuality by flirting
or making me double-fudge brownies. If they don't ease up on
the baked goods, I'll be wearing tracksuits to work."

"You could always give the brownies to Tyson," June said.

"*Yes!* I love the idea of them focusing on your son instead of me." Glancing up at the projection booth, Sheldon said, "I just threw you under the bus, Tyson. Sorry, not sorry."

Nora was too curious to see who'd been invited to tonight's event to pay attention to her friends' good-natured bickering. As she pivoted in her seat to survey the audience members behind her, she caught sight of Sheriff Grant McCabe and waved.

His hands were full, so he couldn't wave back, but he smiled widely and made his way to her row.

"Is this seat taken?" he asked, using his elbow to point at the seat next to Nora.

She narrowed her eyes. "That depends. Do you look at your phone, cough loudly, or slurp your soda?"

He laughed. "None of the above."

"In that case, I'd love to share an armrest with you."

McCabe put his food on the floor and moved the coats over to the next empty seat. He sat down with an audible sigh. "When the lights go out, I might fall asleep. I've nodded off during movies with lots of chitchat before, so if I start snoring, just punch me in the arm."

Nora said, "I won't let you fall asleep. You can't miss the special action scene."

"There's a gleam in your eye," McCabe whispered, his breath tickling the baby hairs on Nora's neck. "What's this private screening really about?"

As Nora mimed zipping her lips, Morgan Freeman's doppelganger appeared on the small stage in the front of the theater. He walked up to the microphone stand and tapped the speaker. The audience quieted down immediately.

The man's smile was like a spotlight. It lit up the whole room and everyone in it.

"Welcome, my friends!" he said in a voice as bright as his smile. "Welcome to Oscar's Theater. I'm Oscar James Langston Hughes. Quite a mouthful, eh?" He chuckled. "I was named after Oscar Micheaux and Langston Hughes because my mother couldn't decide which of them she admired most. Lucky for her—and for me—the man she fell in love with just happened to be a Hughes."

His laughter rumbled like a train.

"You might think I named this theater after myself, but that honor belongs to Oscar Micheaux. When I was a boy, I loved everything about the movies. I was very young when Oscar Micheaux became my hero. He is still my hero today. This man, who had the same color skin as me, wrote novels, directed, and produced films. Mr. Micheaux has a connection to North Carolina too. He breathed his last in Charlotte. Tyson, tell these fine people what's written on his tombstone."

Nora twisted in her seat but didn't see Tyson anywhere.

Suddenly the red curtains behind Oscar parted. A single line of text appeared on the massive screen: *A man ahead of his time.*

"May we all be people ahead of our time," Oscar continued, stretching his arms as if he wanted to embrace everyone in the room. "If our dreams make the world better, then we should never stop chasing them. This place is my dream, and it's my pleasure to be able to share it with you."

Oscar gave a little bow and the crowd responded with enthusiastic applause.

June sniffed and asked Nora for a napkin. "I had my own, but Sheldon stole them."

Pressing several napkins into her friend's hand, Nora whispered, "I have a feeling you'll need more later."

"I might need them the whole time. Just thinking about my son up in that projection room, doing something that makes his heart sing, has me all choked up. My baby's come so far in the last year." She paused to collect herself. "I thank the good Lord every day for giving us both a second chance."

"You never gave up on your son," said Nora. "He was the dream you were chasing."

Sniffing again, June shook her head and murmured, "Get it together, woman."

At that moment, the house lights went dark, the curtains opened even wider, and the film began to roll.

"So much for the previews," Nora whispered to June.

"Fine with me. We'll get to the good part faster."

Sheldon leaned forward to shush them, and June elbowed him in the ribs. Five minutes later, they were sharing candy and giggling like two teens on a date.

Nora hadn't seen a movie in a theater in ages and was spellbound by *Little Women* in no time. She'd always felt a kinship with Jo March because of her independent spirit, and though she had to suspend her disbelief that thirty-one-year-old June Allyson was a moody, rebellious, outspoken girl of fifteen, she was still charmed by the film.

June and Sheldon were just as captivated, but Sheriff McCabe was fast asleep. His fatigue was probably due to the extra shifts he'd been working because one of his deputies had abruptly quit. It was also why he'd canceled their lunch date this week, much to Nora's disappointment. She enjoyed Grant McCabe's company. He was never dull. Over the course of a meal, he might share all kinds of fascinating topics from the destruction his two cats had wrought, to the audiobook he was currently listening to, to a particularly frustrating case.

Nora and the sheriff had been friends for several years, but the more time they spent together, the more difficult it became to define their relationship. Grant McCabe glowed whenever Nora entered a room. And Nora reacted the same way at the sound of McCabe's voice. He did his best to send tourists to visit her bookshop. She wouldn't let anyone talk trash about him.

Their feelings for each other were deeper than their occasional lunch date implied, but Nora wasn't exactly sure what those feelings were.

Nora looked at the sleeping sheriff. She wasn't used to being this close to him. She watched light and shadow dance across his face, alternately highlighting and hiding the lines around his eyes and the creases in his forehead. She noticed how his salt-and-pepper hair was longer than usual—he favored military buzz cuts—and he had more than a day's worth of stubble on his cheeks and chin. His lips were parted, and she could hear air whistling through them. She wanted to lay a soft blanket over his body and brush his brow with her fingertips—a wordless wish for his pleasant dreams.

She didn't know how long she'd been staring at him when June suddenly nudged her arm and murmured, "This is it."

Onscreen, Jo was saying good-bye to Amy before she left for France. At the door, Amy turned back to ask Jo if she had a message for Laurie.

Smiling, Jo said, "I wish he'd find a beautiful girl and settle down."

Amy beamed with happiness. At last, she had the chance to be with the man she loved.

The film came to an abrupt pause, the frame stuck on Elizabeth Taylor's lovely face. When a minute passed and the movie remained frozen, people began whispering and shifting in their seats.

The house lights came on. The sudden brightness was a shock. Beside Nora, McCabe startled awake.

"What'd I miss?" he mumbled.

Oscar Hughes appeared from a doorway near the stage and strode up the aisle between the middle section of seats and the seats hugging the right wall. He was carrying a microphone. Two rows back from the row where Hester sat, he stopped to say, "Sorry for the inconvenience, folks. We've had a technical hiccup."

This news elicited a fresh round of whispers from the audience.

"Hold on now." Oscar raised a hand. His voice, infused with

a blend of warmth and authority, captured everyone's attention. "There's nothing wrong with our equipment or our projection-ist. Love is responsible for this intermission. Love is ready to step into the spotlight. And who am I to stand in its way?"

On cue, Andrews walked down the aisle from the back of the theater.

"What's going on?" McCabe whispered close to Nora's ear.

She replied without turning away from Andrews. "Just watch."

Andrews took the microphone from Oscar. His hands were shaking. And when he spoke, his voice shook too.

"This is my girlfriend's favorite book, but the movie doesn't show her favorite part." He turned to face Hester, who looked both curious and more than a little confused. "When Amy and Laurie are together in that boat, Amy notices that they're row-ing in synch. I think she says, 'How well we pull together, don't we?'"

A baffled Hester managed a nod.

Andrews went down on one knee. Then he reached under his seat and withdrew a toy rowboat. He opened the lid of the jewelry box tucked inside the boat.

"'How well we pull together . . . ,'" he said to Hester. "'So well that I wish we might always pull in the same boat.'" He paused, creating a space between Alcott's message and his own. "Will you travel through life with me, Hester? As my friend and partner? Will you be my wife?"

Hester looked from her man to the ring box inside the boat. Her face was raspberry red, her eyes were round as moons, and her hand was clamped over her mouth.

The silence in the room was absolute, and Nora wondered what everyone around her was thinking. Were longtime cou-ples recalling the heady rush of their early days together? Did they clasp hands or smile at each other as they waited for Hes-ter's answer?

What about those who'd had a painful breakup recently? Or were in the middle of a messy divorce? Was the sight of the two lovers hard to bear?

Nora had an ex-husband, but she rarely thought of him. She didn't know where he was or what his life looked like. She truly didn't care. He belonged to the past. This theater and the people in it were Nora's present and future, and she felt only anticipatory joy as Hester jumped out of her seat and opened her arms to Andrews.

"I love you so much!" she cried. "Yes! Yes! Yes!"

Andrews gathered Hester in his arms and kissed her. The theater erupted with cheers and applause.

Sheriff McCabe laid a hand on Nora's shoulder. "You had something to do with this, didn't you?"

"Not much," she said. "Andrews and Oscar planned this whole private screening. All he needed from me was a little help with the *Little Women* part. He's a good man. I'm glad he and Hester found each other."

When McCabe removed his hand, Nora missed its weight and warmth. But he kept his head close to hers and quietly asked, "Seeing them—does it make you wish Jed had stayed?"

She looked directly into McCabe's eyes and said, "No. He and I are both exactly where we're supposed to be." After holding his gaze for a few seconds, she grabbed McCabe's wrist. "Come on. Let's go congratulate the happy couple."

The following morning, Nora saw the kiss of frost on her window glass and knew it would be too cold to go for a hike until later that afternoon. In warmer months, she'd comb the paper's classified ads in search of yard sale listings. In the winter, the best she could hope for was an estate sale or a link to an online auction featuring books or unique vintage knickknacks.

She scanned the ads, and when it became clear that there was no point in leaving her snug house until the flea market opened, she refilled her coffee cup and settled on the sofa to continue her re-read of Eowyn Ivey's *The Snow Child*.

Later, after finding nothing at the flea market, Nora spent hours scouring Etsy and eBay listings in search of bargain book or vintage accessory lots. Unfortunately, bargain prices meant the items were also in poor condition. By three o'clock, she'd purchased two items. The first was a large set of Boxcar Children books in excellent used condition. The second was a lot of vintage soup bowls with lids. The blue-and-white stoneware bowls were perfect for winter and all four were in excellent condition. Even better, Nora bought both items from the same seller and had qualified for free shipping.

"This will hardly fill the gaps on my shelves," she mumbled to herself.

After a quick glance at the current temperature, Nora laced up her hiking boots and pulled on her lightweight down jacket. She pocketed her phone and a small water bottle, but left her walking stick behind. It was too cold for snakes or spiderwebs.

As she descended the grassy hill behind her house, her thoughts turned to last night. After everyone finished congratulating Hester and Andrews, Oscar invited his guests to sit down and enjoy the rest of the movie.

Nora had tried to give *Little Women* her full attention, but McCabe's question about Jed had thrown her off balance. By the time she got home, she'd been too tired to analyze her feelings about the man she'd dated for two years. Instead, she'd gone to sleep.

But as she approached the trail leading into the stark, quiet woods, there was nothing to distract Nora from thinking about her ex.

She felt no anger toward Jedediah Craig. He wasn't the type of person who made others angry. He was quite the opposite, in fact. Jed was a friendly, easygoing man with a ready smile. He was devoted to his job as a paramedic and to his mother, who was the only family he had.

Nora and Jed's mother were both burn victims. And while Nora had been hospitalized for an agonizing month, Jed's mother had sustained more serious injuries. Her lungs, for example, would never again function at full capacity and she would always be more susceptible to infection. As a result, she was always in and out of the hospital.

Last fall, she'd caught a cold that morphed into pneumonia. A very worried Jed had dropped everything and driven to his hometown on the North Carolina coast. Love had spurred him onward. And guilt too. It was Jed's fault that his mother had been burned in the first place, and even though she forgave him, he couldn't forgive himself. Year after year, he refused to come to terms with his guilt and shame. He'd waved away the books Nora had recommended and claimed that he didn't have extra time or money to waste on counseling.

Nora had never pushed the issue. She cared about Jed. She wanted him to be healthy and happy, but she was aware of the limits of their relationship. From the start, Jed had been torn between his life in the mountains and his life at the coast. And though he'd never said as much, Nora knew that he'd return home eventually.

And when Jed's mother recovered from the pneumonia, only to fall and break her hip a month later, Jed did exactly that. He quit his job, packed up his belongings, and said good-bye to Miracle Springs. And to Nora.

"You could come with me," he'd said.

Nora remembered how he'd stood in her living room. He hadn't taken his coat off and his cheeks were flushed from the cold. When he'd reached for her, his hands had been so cold that she'd cupped them in hers until they were warm again.

"You could open a bookstore," he'd continued with a smile.

Nora had wrapped her arms around him and held him. He'd sighed into her hair. They'd stood this way for a long time because they both knew it would be the last time they held each other.

"I understand why you have to go," Nora had whispered. "But I'm going to miss you. I'll miss your laugh, your work stories, our weekend coffee ritual. I'll miss how you warm up the bed and how you smell when you're fresh from the shower. It's going to hurt, being without you, but I'm so glad that you came into my life."

Jed had buried his face in her shoulder. "I wish I could be in both places at once. I wish Miracle Springs wasn't six hours away." He'd held Nora tighter. "I wish I didn't have to go. But she needs me, and I owe her."

Nora had forced him to look her in the eye. "Jed. I've never met your mom, but she doesn't want you to feel guilty for one more second. Take care of her *and* take care of yourself. Okay?"

"Okay. But can we still talk? I mean, maybe we could—"

Nora had stopped his words with a kiss. It was a farewell kiss, and when it was over, and Jed walked out of her house, she knew that she'd never see him again.

In the stillness of the winter woods, Nora now relived that good-bye. Yes, she missed Jed. When they were together, she had laughter and kisses and cider donuts. They'd gone out for meals and movies. They'd stayed in to watch TV or play cards. They'd made love without falling in love.

As Nora began to ascend the narrow path that would later merge with the Appalachian Trail, she didn't feel sad or lonely. She was fine on her own. Actually, she was better than fine. She had her bookshop, her tiny house, and the truest friends a woman could have.

She was also surrounded by beauty. Every day, she woke to the sight of unspoiled forests and the peaks and ridges of the Appalachian Mountains rising into the sky. She loved hiking the stretch of Appalachian Trail that skirted around Miracle Springs. Even now, with the sharp air pricking her lungs and her leg muscles burning, she was happy to be exactly where she was.

Pausing to catch her breath, she glanced up at the sky. It was a rainy-day gray with an undertone of pale pink. Weather forecasters were calling for snow later that night, and the locals were certain that there'd be enough to clothe the drab hills in a gown of a glittering white by morning.

At the top of the first rise, Nora stopped for a drink of water. She expected to run into other hikers or see flashes of color from their coats on the trails ahead. It was too cold for through hikers—a term for the intrepid adventurers who walked the full length of the AT—but not for day-trippers. On weekends, Nora was used to encountering people with dogs, children, or both. And the lodge offered daily hikes from noon until sunset. So, why did the trail feel deserted?

Nora rounded a bend and came to an intersection. The trail to the right led to downtown Miracle Springs. The trail to the left ventured deeper in the woods. If Nora remained on her current course, she'd be in for another uphill stretch. It was longer and steeper than the ascent to the first rise, but the view was worth the effort. Once she reached the top, Nora could sit on a flat boulder and stare at an expanse of open sky and blue peaks that seemed to go on forever.

As she deliberated, she heard a muffled shout bubble up from the trail leading to town. This was followed by a second shout.

Unconcerned, Nora took another sip from her water bottle.

After the third shout, she began to wonder if someone—a man, judging by the sound—was in trouble. People got hurt on the trails all the time. They tripped on roots or slipped on wet rocks. They lost their footing, falling hard on unyielding ground. They broke bones, strained muscles, and twisted ankles. And help could be a long time coming.

Years of budget cuts meant fewer park rangers. All too often, injured hikers had to rely on the kindness of strangers.

This thought prompted Nora to turn right.

Walking as quickly as she could, she headed toward the bridge spanning a small gorge.

After five minutes of brisk walking, she caught voices on the wind. She couldn't make out specific words, but the urgent tone was unmistakable.

Nora increased her pace, rounding the final bend that led to a break in the trees. From this vantage point, she could look down at the bridge.

At least a dozen people were moving around down there. Uniformed people. Firefighters, EMTs, and officers from the sheriff's department were fanned out along the edge of the gorge. Fifty feet below, an EMT waved to the group above. The EMT wasn't alone at the bottom of the gorge. A park ranger squatted beside a person in an orange coat.

Nora couldn't see much from her vantage point, but something was wrong with the way the person in the orange coat was positioned.

Is this a rescue or recovery operation? she wondered.

Her curiosity and concern propelled her forward, and by the time she drew level with the bridge, a stretcher had been lowered to the EMT.

"Hey!" someone barked. "Hey, you! *Ma'am!*"

Nora's gaze jerked from the action at the bottom of the gorge to the group of emergency responders. As she searched for the speaker, a familiar figure stepped out from behind a burly firefighter. Sheriff McCabe paused to say a few words to the firefighter before heading over to Nora.

He touched the brim of his hat and said, "Cold day for a hike."

The tip of his nose was red, and Nora wondered how long he'd been here. "What happened?"

McCabe glanced back at the gorge. "He fell. Or jumped. We'll have to wait and see what the ME finds."

"What a terrible way to go." Nora's voice was soft with sympathy. "Is he a local?"

"We don't know who he is. No one recognizes him and he had no ID, no phone, and no keys. He had one thing on him. It was in his pocket, and I don't know why he'd carry it to the woods in the dead of winter."

Nora watched the stretcher rise into the air, foot by foot. The orange coat was garishly bright against the backdrop of dark stones. All eyes were on that coat. Except for McCabe's. He was staring at Nora.

Feeling the weight of his gaze, she turned to him. "What was in his pocket?"

Someone called McCabe's name. He held up a finger, his eyes never leaving Nora's, and said, "A book."

Chapter 4

I wasn't scared; I was just somebody else, some stranger, and my whole life was a haunted life, the life of a ghost.

—Jack Kerouac

A finger of cold air worked its way under Nora's coat collar and she hunched her shoulders at its icy touch. Glancing skyward, she saw that a fleet of dark gray clouds had moved in, muting the light and chasing off all vestiges of warmth.

Nora wished she could magic herself back home. She wanted to cocoon her body in blankets and wrap her hands around a steaming mug of tea. But she knew she couldn't go anywhere yet. Not after what the sheriff had just said.

"What book?" she asked him.

He pointed at the stretcher, which had been pulled out of the gorge and was now resting on a patch of ground halfway between the cliff's edge and the tree line. Two firefighters were detaching carabiners and removing slings while the EMTs looked on.

"I don't know yet. Ranger Ryland was first on the scene. He searched the man's pockets in hopes of finding an ID, but found a book instead. I'm going over there now. Could you hang out here for a few minutes? In case I need to show you the book?"

"Of course."

Even if McCabe hadn't asked her to stay, Nora wouldn't have been able to walk away. She'd have spent the rest of the day wondering which book had kept the man company as he moved from one world to the next.

McCabe approached the stretcher and stood still, staring at the man's body. A paramedic holding a clipboard spoke to him, as did one of his deputies. The sheriff nodded, keeping his eyes on the man in the orange coat. Following a moment of silent contemplation, he squatted down and removed his hat.

The buzz of conversation and movement stopped as everyone watched the sheriff lay a gloved hand on the dead man's arm. Nora knew that this gesture was McCabe's promise. Friend or stranger, sinner or saint, the sheriff would see that this man would be treated with dignity and respect.

Donning his hat again, McCabe conferred with the paramedic. The younger man pointed to various places on the dead man's body. As they talked, McCabe pulled on gloves and looked at the man's hands. He then exposed the dead man's wrists, but the paramedic shook his head.

Nora understood the gesture to mean that the man wasn't wearing a watch.

The sheriff checked the man's pockets next. Satisfied that there was nothing to find in his shirt or pants, he focused on the orange coat. The pocket in the lining was empty, as was the first outside pocket. Finally he withdrew a rectangular object from the second outside pocket.

The book.

Nora took an involuntary step toward it.

McCabe stared at the front cover for a long moment. Cradling the spine, he then let the book fall open in his hands. After flipping through a few pages, he closed it and got to his feet.

He paused to speak to one of his officers, drawing a circle in the air above the dead man's boots before returning to Nora.

"I don't think this'll help us ID the guy, but I'll show it to you anyway." Catching sight of Nora's fleece gloves, he added, "I'd better hold it. Just in case. Tell me what you want to see."

The book was in bad shape. The light green cover had partially separated from the body of the book and its corners were rubbed and bent. The green cloth was also pockmarked with dark stains. It was old and battered and probably couldn't stand on its own.

In her mind, Nora was already repairing the book. It was beyond the point of restoration, but she could stitch, glue, and clean it until the lovely design on its cover would eclipse the rest of its faults. Picturing the repair kit she kept at home, she started reaching for the book.

Checking herself, she frowned at McCabe. "Just in case?"

"His fall wasn't an accident."

If the book ended up in a sealed evidence bag, this might be her only chance to examine it.

"Is there any writing inside? An owner's name or an inscription? A price or notes in the margins?"

McCabe showed her the inside front cover, which was blank, before continuing on to the heavily foxed copyright page.

"*Miss Delphinium* by Elmer Freeman. Published by Charles Scribner and Sons in 1918. I've never heard of this author, but this must be a novel." Nora waved a finger. "Can you show me the cover again?"

Closing the book, McCabe moved closer to her.

"The title is almost too faded to read, but I can see flowers. They might be delphiniums, but I don't know what that flower looks like. I do know that this is an Art Nouveau design. The columns, medallions, and swags framing the flowers are so detailed. This book must have been beautiful once."

"Is it valuable?"

Though Nora was reluctant to cast a negative light on the old book, she answered honestly. "Probably not. It's in rough shape, which wouldn't matter as much if we were dealing with an original Shakespeare folio, but I'm guessing *Miss Delphinium* is a pretty obscure title. Is it illustrated? Are any of the passages underlined? Any bits of paper or dried flowers tucked between the pages? Maybe the man had it with him for sentimental reasons."

"There are illustrations. All of the same lady."

He gently turned pages until he landed on a black-and-white image of a woman in Victorian dress standing in front of an easel. The woman was about to touch the tip of her paintbrush to the blank canvas on the easel. The caption read: *Miss Delphinium could paint anything she saw.*

Another coil of wind swept down from the mountain peaks. It ruffled the book pages, stung the tip of Nora's nose, and made McCabe's eyes water.

"The rest show her painting, dancing, drinking tea—that sort of thing." McCabe let Nora see a few more examples before lowering the book to his side.

"Unless he's a painter or is close to a woman who is, I can't see an obvious reason to carry this around. Sorry I couldn't help."

"Thanks for trying." He jerked his head in the direction of the path. "Go home and get warm. And make sure you have enough wood for your stove. Ranger Ryland said we're getting way more snow than what the weather people predicted, and when it comes to snow, his word is gospel."

McCabe turned to see a procession of firefighters, EMTs, and deputies heading their way. Four men carried the stretcher bearing the man in the orange coat. While Nora and McCabe had been examining the book, the EMT team had zipped the dead man in a black body bag and secured the bag to the stretcher. With his orange coat out of sight, the world resumed its palette of dull brown and gray.

Nora dipped her chin in respect as the stretcher passed by. The assembly crossed the bridge and continued along the footpath leading to town. Within minutes, the men and the stretcher were gone—hidden by rocks and trees.

"I saw you point at his shoes," Nora said quietly.

McCabe looked down at his boots. "They weren't like these. They looked like steel-toe boots. Like construction workers wear. Except for the coat, the rest of his clothes weren't right for this. For these trails." His gaze swept over the area. "Why did he come up here?"

Nora looked from the bridge back to McCabe. "Do you think he jumped?"

"I don't know, but I'll do what I can to learn his story." The sheriff put a hand on Nora's shoulder. "Why don't you come with us? It's a much shorter trail and I can drive you home on the way to the station. I'd hate to think of you getting frostbite or being chased by a ravenous bear."

Nora smiled. "Thanks, but I'm okay. It's all downhill from here."

Someone called out to McCabe. He withdrew his hand and Nora turned and started making her way toward the woods and the deepening gloom.

"Call me if you learn anything about that book," McCabe yelled after her. "Or send me a text—just so I know the bears didn't get you."

Nora gave him a quick wave before disappearing into the trees.

As she returned to the isolated trail, she couldn't stop thinking about the Art Nouveau book cover. She saw its columns in the trunks of trees, its flowers in a cluster of pinecones, and its medallions in every circular rock.

She didn't know why she was so captivated by the old book. She'd seen plenty of vintage books with beautiful covers. In fact, she had several lovely books with Art Nouveau covers in her shop and would sell the lot of them without regret.

But, of course, those books hadn't been found on the broken body of a stranger. *Miss Delphinium* was the only possession the man in the orange coat had when he embarked on his final journey.

In Nora's mind, this elevated the book from bedraggled novel to well-loved keepsake, like a child's favorite teddy bear. Maybe the book had been a comfort object. Or belonged to someone the man loved. The book had fallen from that bridge too. And now, both man and book were damaged beyond repair.

Hours later, when Nora was in bed with the comforter pulled up to her chin, she watched the snowflakes swirl outside her window and thought about the man in the orange coat.

If he hadn't been found this afternoon, his body would be snow-dusted right now. By dawn, he'd be shrouded in white. And when the sun rose over the mountains, the skein of frost that had hardened around him like a cocoon would be painted with light. His would be a peaceful grave. He wouldn't be alone, either. The trees and birds would keep him company. He'd have his book too. It would sleep inside his pocket until, drop by drop, the melting snow broke it into pieces.

On Monday, Hester sent a group text thanking Nora, June, and Estella for helping Andrews with his proposal. She attached a photo of her left hand, zoomed in on her engagement ring, and then added a second message: **I'm making dinner for Jasper's parents tonight. They'll probably ask a million questions about the wedding, but I don't have any answers. I'm still getting used to having a ring on my finger! Talk soon! xoxo H**

Nora was glad that Hester hadn't mentioned the dead man. She'd told her friends about him in a group text hours after his body had been found. Nora had been on her sofa trying, but failing, to read. Eventually, she'd put down her book and picked up her phone. Hester, who'd already heard about the incident from Andrews, said that no one at the station recognized the man in the orange coat.

Though Nora wondered if the sheriff's department had identified the man since last night, she didn't ask. She didn't want to dim Hester's happiness by raising such a grim subject.

The season's first big snow had cast a spell of lassitude over Miracle Springs, leaving Nora plenty of time to think about the stranger and the book he'd been carrying. She didn't mind the quiet, but the lack of sales was a concern. Like every other small business in town, Nora depended on the lodge guests and other visitors. The locals didn't shop frequently enough to keep her afloat, and plenty of them—too many by Nora's count— had never stepped foot inside Miracle Books. And while Nora understood the desire to save pennies by shopping online, she wondered if her neighbors realized that the Goliath they supported was destroying all the Davids of the world.

With nothing else to do, Nora cleaned every inch of the store. That done, she spent the afternoon reading. The sleigh bells hanging from the front door remained stubbornly mute, and when the streetlights flickered on at five o'clock, Nora locked up and went home.

On Tuesday, she walked to the Gingerbread House on sidewalks that had been shoveled and salted. Bright sunshine took the edge off the cold and coaxed people out of their houses. Joggers and dogwalkers resumed their daily routines, and the streets were bustling with weekday traffic.

After knocking twice on the back door of Hester's shop, Nora let herself in. Every day, either she or Sheldon stopped to pick up an assortment of book pockets to sell their customers. These book-shaped pastries, which had the light and flaky dough of a croissant and dark chocolate or raspberry fillings, were often gone by lunchtime.

The bakery's kitchen was a haven of warmth and delightful aromas. Cinnamon, maple syrup, and butter were the most pervasive scents, and when Nora peered into the ovens, she saw pies with apple cutouts in the top crust. To the left of the ovens, loaves of bread were neatly lined up on the cooling racks.

"It's maple oatmeal," said Hester, breezing into the kitchen from the front room. She placed a birthday cake with teal frosting on the counter and reached for a piping bag. "I saved you a heel. It's on the butcher block. Help yourself to butter."

The door chime dinged and Hester shouted, "Be right with you!" before piping a message on the cake with sure, deft movements.

Nora was captivated. "I don't see how anyone can write with icing."

"I've had years of practice."

"Did you ever write the wrong thing?"

Hester laughed as she eased the cake into a box. "Oh, yeah. I still wince when I think about the first one. Back in college, I had a part-time grocery store gig. It was a Saturday morning in June, and we were *really* behind on cake orders. Someone called in sick, and there was a line of people waiting for cakes." She taped the sides of the box and began securing it with twine. "I was writing 'Happy Birthday' and 'Congrats, Grad' as fast as I could. I was on autopilot, which is why I wrote 'Weeding Blessings' on a cake and boxed it up."

"No!" Nora cried.

"Yep. Not only that, but the *L* on a cake that said 'Good Luck, We'll Miss You' looked like it had a tail, so people thought it was an *F*!"

Hester carried the cake box to the front. When she reentered the kitchen a few minutes later, Nora asked, "When did the customers spot the mistakes? Were they still in the store?"

"Nope. The woman who ordered the 'Good Luck' cake called from her house to complain. I told her to freeze the cake for fifteen minutes and then scrape off the tail with a toothpick." Hester grabbed two pot holders and started transferring the pies in the ovens to the cooling racks.

"Are they all apple?"

"No. I made three variations of apple and dried fruit. Apple and fig, apple and currant, and apple and cherry."

Nora had already breakfasted on a bowl of yogurt and granola, but that didn't stop her from gobbling the piece of maple oatmeal bread or from wishing one of the pies had caved. She didn't want Hester to have a baking disaster, but if one happened naturally, she'd be glad to taste-test any of the pies.

"What about the 'Weeding Blessings' customer?"

"Oh, no one spotted that mistake until the cake was put on the table a few minutes before the newlyweds were supposed to show up. The mother of the bride was livid." Having finished transferring the pies, Hester slid half-a-dozen muffin pans into the oven. "My manager chewed me out *and* deducted the cost of the cake from my paycheck."

"Even though you were doing the work of two people? Ouch."

Hester set a timer on her watch and sat down across from Nora. "I didn't care about the money. All I could think about was that I'd ruined that couple's magical day. I kept imagining the bride bursting into tears after seeing my cake, so that night, I went home and made a new one. The mother of the bride was hosting a brunch for the newlyweds, and you should have seen her face when she saw me on her front porch, holding this superheavy cake."

"Do you remember what it looked like?"

The chime sounded and Hester jumped up. "I'll show you as soon as I come back."

When she returned, she placed a photograph in front of Nora.

"This is beautiful!" Nora traced the spray of tropical sugar flowers curving down the front of a three-tiered cake frosted in Caribbean blue. A pair of fondant suitcases at the base of the cake featured luggage tags reading MR. and MRS.

Hester smiled. "Thanks. I was pretty proud of it. And the mother of the bride was thrilled. She ended up being my first client. I started making cakes for her friends and their families. After that, I never had to work in a grocery store again."

"I guess everyone will be asking about your wedding cake now."

Hester rolled her eyes. "Jasper's parents were worse than the Spanish Inquisition. I thought they'd never leave."

The door chime rang. Hester slipped the photo in her apron pocket and pointed at the large bakery box on the counter opposite the cooling racks. "That book I wanted to tell you about? It's in the box, under the pastries. I thought you might want to see it. I'll give whoever left it here a week to claim it. Otherwise, it's yours."

"Hester?" a woman called. "Are you back there?"

"Gotta go," said Hester. In the front room, Nora heard her say, "Good morning, Mayor. Your usual?"

Nora was tempted to dig the book out of the box and examine it then and there, but if she didn't get going, she wouldn't have time to finish her opening tasks.

Snowmelt pellets crunched underfoot as she hurried down the narrow alley behind the stores. As she approached the bookshop's delivery door, a UPS truck pulled into the loading zone.

"Oh, boy, Ms. Nora! I've got a boxload of bricks for you!" Arlo, the driver, hopped down and jogged to the back of the idling truck.

While she waited, Nora pictured how she'd sever the packing tape with a box cutter and fold back the cardboard box flaps to reveal a row of colorful spines. Whose logo would stare up at her from those spines? Penguin? Knopf? Macmillan? Kensington? Or had the distribution center sent her a mix of imprints?

Arlo lowered a large box onto his handcart.

"This one's full of cannonballs. The next one has the bricks," he said, easing a second on top of the first. When the third box was in place, he asked, "What's in this one?"

She and Arlo played this game all the time. Nora smiled and said, "Billiard balls."

"Oh, so you're a pool shark. Good to know."

Nora held the door for Arlo. "Everyone needs a side hustle."

"You got that right. Hey! You should watch *The Hustler*. It's got Paul Newman and Jackie Gleason and won two Oscars." Arlo turned his cart to the wall and eased the box tower onto the floor. "Got any books about playing pool?"

"Sorry, no. I think you're the first person to ask for one."

Arlo made a check mark in the air as he walked back to the truck. "That's a point for movies. You know I'm keeping score."

This was another game the two of them played. If Arlo raised a subject, no matter how bizarre, and Nora had a book on that subject, then she got a point. If she didn't have a book and Arlo could name a movie about the same subject, then he got a point.

"'I'll get you, my pretty,'" Nora yelled before the heavy metal door slammed shut.

She was halfway down the hall when the life-affirming aroma of coffee hit her.

Coffee. Boxes of new books. Sunshine after a snow. A good start to the day.

Nora entered the ticket agent's booth in high spirits. She put the box of book pockets on the counter and, seeing that the coffee was still brewing, hung her coat in the stockroom.

Next she loaded the stack of boxes Arlo had deposited in the hall onto her handcart and wheeled it into the stockroom. She'd just sliced through the tape of the biggest box when Sheldon appeared in the doorway. His face was puffy, his eyes were bloodshot, and his canary-yellow bow tie was crooked.

All thoughts of new books forgotten, Nora walked over to her friend and straightened his tie. She then gently took hold of his left hand and examined it. His knuckles looked like grapes.

"You didn't get much sleep last night. Why don't you go home and get back into bed?"

"I'm sick of bed. I want to see people. I want to talk about books, news, the weather—anything. I watched ten seasons of *Married at First Sight* in the last twenty-four hours. My brain is mush."

"Okay, but if that flare-up gets worse, I'm sending you packing." Nora returned to the box, opened the flaps, and removed the packing slip. "George R.R. Martin, Sarah J. Maas, and Steve Martini. Oh, good. We can finally fill in our cozy mystery section. We got titles from V.M. Burns, Lauren Elliott, Margaret Loudon, Leslie Budewitz, and Kathleen Bridge."

Sheldon made a gimme gesture. "Let me see the list. I get such a kick out of those titles. You know I love a clever pun."

Nora waved at the box. "Dig in. I'm getting coffee."

"I'll start restocking the shelves. I've been dying to rearrange the Mystery section and put out those vintage teacups you bought." Sheldon glanced around. "Where are they?"

Nora pointed at the Crown Royal box peeking out from behind the stepladder. "I haven't washed or priced them yet. I was saving them for you."

"Best boss ever." Sheldon smiled. "Get your coffee and put some music on for us. Can you find a playlist that says, 'There's nothing better than a bookstore'?"

"That's a tall order, but I'll try."

Coffee cup in hand, Nora turned on the lights and powered up the register. She selected a bossa nova playlist and nodded in satisfaction as the catchy rhythm and upbeat melody of the first song danced through the empty shop.

At ten, she flipped the wooden sign in the window from CLOSED to OPEN and unlocked the front door. She'd barely reached the checkout counter when the sleigh bells rattled and half-a-dozen red-cheeked women entered.

"My four kids were climbing the walls yesterday. My house is a total wreck, but that's nothing new. I just need four or five cappuccinos. That should give me *just* enough energy to do the laundry," said a blonde in a maroon parka.

She waved hello at Nora as her friend, a brunette in a black coat covered in dog hair, complained that her children had spent most of their snow day playing video games.

The rest of the women said "Good morning" to Nora on their way back to the Readers' Circle.

Nora was happy to see the Monday Morning Moms on a Tuesday. Not only did the women order coffee and pastries every week, but they usually bought handfuls of books too.

The Monday Moms could be loud. They were often shushed by other customers, but Nora let them be. Between their jobs, families, volunteer work, and caring for aging parents, the six women had little time to socialize. Week after week, they spent a precious hour at Miracle Books. And week after week, Nora and Sheldon made sure the Monday Moms felt at home.

As three more customers filed in, the phone rang. It was June, calling from the lodge.

"I hope you've had your Red Bull because I'm sending a hundred bored guests your way. So many people signed up for the midmorning shopping outing that we had to add two more trolleys!"

Nora said, "Good. I barely sold a thing yesterday."

"Well, keep an eye on Sheldon. I heard lots of muttering coming from his room, and he wasn't talking to book characters."

"He talks when he reads?"

June chuckled. "All the time. He says stuff like, 'You know you can't trust her' or 'This isn't going to end well.'"

An elderly man came into the shop, list in hand, and Nora told June she had to run.

"And so it begins" was June's gleeful reply.

Nora helped the man locate five of the six books on his wife's wish list, but when she offered to carry the books to the checkout desk, he asked her to find one more book.

"My wife is a wonderful cook. I don't know how many meals she made for our family over the years. How many birthday cakes. She's turning eighty next week, and the kids and grandkids are coming over. I want all of us—the whole family—to cook for her this time." Lowering his voice to a whisper, he added, "But I don't know where to start."

Nora gave him a reassuring smile and said, "We'll figure it out together."

Twenty minutes later, the man left with a bag of books for his wife and one for himself. Nora had recommended several cookbooks, including *How to Cook Everything* and *How to Bake Everything* by Mark Bittman, *The Complete Cookbook for Young Chefs* by America's Test Kitchen, and Yolanda Gampp's *How to Cake It: A Cakebook*.

Nora told him that two cookbooks would be a great place to start, but he bought all the books she recommended, as well as Joy Howard's *Disney Eats: More than 150 Recipes for Everyday Cooking and Inspired Fun*.

"Can you manage those?" Nora asked the man.

"I'm tougher than I look," he replied with a wink.

Nora was about to check on the Monday Moms when a young woman with wavy brown hair balancing a toddler on her hip placed two potty-training books on the counter. Nora recognized the pair as they rarely missed a storytime. She remembered the little boy's name, but not his caregiver's.

"Jefferson, right?" she asked the toddler.

The towheaded boy hid his face in the young woman's shoulder. She smiled, readjusted her glasses, and said, "That's right. And I'm Lea Carle. Lea without an *H*. I'm Jefferson's nanny."

Nora pointed at the books. "Exciting."

"We're going to surprise his mom," said Lea. "She doesn't think he's ready, but he totally is."

Nora wished them luck and rang up the books. As soon as she was done, the Monday Moms were ready to check out. Then the first group of lodge guests streamed in.

In between locating, recommending, and ringing up books, Nora stole a few seconds to ask Sheldon how he was doing.

"I'm okay," he said, sounding surprised. "The extrovert in me needed this."

"I get that, but I don't want you to overdo it. You should knock off at two."

Sheldon created a cinnamon-sprinkle heart on a crown of foamed milk and called, "Large Wilkie Collins for Wendy! Made with love!"

As he grabbed another mug from the pegboard, he said, "I'll leave at three, but only if the after-school rush is manageable."

It wasn't. Parents and grade school kids were followed by teenagers, most of whom traveled in packs. Sheldon was so busy making Harry Potter Hot Chocolates that Nora had to handle the food orders. Since the book pockets were long gone, she made plate after plate of Nutella on toasted Cuban bread.

People were still waiting in line when Nora told Sheldon to go home.

"Sleep in tomorrow," she said. "Or take off the whole day. Just promise me you'll rest."

"Like the dead" was his weary reply.

When Nora finally closed the shop that evening, she was beyond hungry. Other than a handful of nuts, she hadn't eaten since breakfast, and the lunch still sitting in the refrigerator was calling her name.

Standing over the sink, she devoured her salami sandwich. It was only when she reached for a paper towel to wipe mustard off her chin that she noticed something tucked behind the paper towel holder. It looked like a book wrapped in wax paper.

It took Nora a moment to connect the wrapped book to Hester. Sheldon must have moved the book out of harm's way while he unpacked the pastries. They'd had such a busy day that he probably forgot all about it.

"I certainly did," Nora murmured.

After unwrapping the book, she stared at it for a long moment. The cover was instantly familiar. The cobalt-blue cloth was old, but the gilt Art Nouveau floral designs were mostly bright, as were the gold letters of the title.

"*Miss Daffodil,*" Nora whispered.

This book was very similar to the one found on the dead man. The same author had written it. Its cover was decorated with the flowers mentioned in its title. Inside, there were illustrations of another young lady. There were no markings, no notes, and no clues as to why it had been left at the Gingerbread House.

Without warning, Nora felt a prickling sensation start at the base of her ruined pinkie finger. It moved upward to the space above her knuckle, to where she shouldn't have been able to feel anything at all.

Nora dropped the book and balled her hand into a tight first, but the tingle refused to subside.

Two books. The first was in a dead man's pocket. The second was left where Hester could find it.

Nora wouldn't normally assign such significance to a pair of old books. But after holding those copies of *The Scarlet Letter*, she felt like the Elmer Freeman books also conveyed a message. And though she didn't know what that message was, Nora felt inexplicably scared.

Not for herself, but for Hester.

Chapter 5

A new book smells great. An old book smells even better. An old book smells like ancient Egypt.
—Ray Bradbury

Nora knew she had to research Elmer Freeman more thoroughly. The night after she'd seen the dead man in the ravine, she'd gone online to look for information on *Miss Delphinium*. She'd found only a brief plot description of a Modernist novel about a charming young woman who dreamed of becoming a renowned painter. It had very few reviews, most of which were lukewarm. Fans of Edith Wharton or Virginia Woolf seeking a similar read were disappointed by the lack of substance in Freeman's novel.

Nora knew there had to be more to Elmer Freeman and his works than short plot summaries and a handful of reviews. If she could learn all she could about the old books, she might understand why they'd suddenly appeared within hours of each other.

"A dead man's pocket and a bakery table," she murmured as she trudged across the near-empty parking lot behind the bookshop.

She couldn't see a connection. *Miss Delphinium* and *Miss Daffodil*. A painter and a weaver. A dead man and a baker.

Hester.

If it hadn't been for those copies of *The Scarlet Letter*, Nora might dismiss the book in the bakery as coincidence. She had no concrete reason to feel uneasy, which is why she decided not to mention the vandalized books to The Secret, Book, and Scone Society members just yet.

At home, she shucked off her clothes and stepped into the shower. The hot water released the tension from her muscles and washed the pervasive scent of books and coffee from her hair.

Bundled up in flannel pajamas and a robe, Nora flopped on her bed, picked up *Miss Daffodil*, and opened to the copyright page. The information was the same as *Miss Delphinium's* except for the year of publication. This book had been printed several years earlier, in 1914.

Nora began gently turning pages. Foxing, water stains, small tears, and creased corners indicated that it hadn't sat on a shelf. It had been read more than once. The book hadn't been mistreated. It had simply been marked by time.

Nora counted six illustrations, five of which were of Miss Daffodil at her loom. In the sixth, she stood next to a completed project. Staring at the young woman's proud bearing and triumphant smile, Nora whispered, "Nicely done."

The caption read: *Miss Daffodil wove flowers of every shape and hue into her rugs.*

"Flowers again."

Nora's hair was still wet. She needed to dry it, move her dirty clothes to the hamper, and turn off the lights in the kitchen. But she did none of these things. She turned to Chapter One and began to read.

When her alarm sounded the next morning, the light shining on her face confused her. Slitting her eyes, she saw that she'd fallen asleep with her lamp on. When she fumbled for the switch, a pain shot up the left side of her neck. Her fingers brushed the collar of her robe before traveling over her head. Her hair was matted to her skull. Her comforter was heaped in a pile on the floor and her extra pillow was suffocating *Miss Daffodil*. Nora had obviously gotten too hot in the night.

"I hope you weren't too squished," Nora told the old book, which seemed no worse for wear.

She got dressed for work and packed her lunch. With *Miss Daffodil* tucked under her arm, she entered the bookshop and started the coffeemaker. While it was brewing, she took out yesterday's trash and hung the clean mugs on the pegboard.

Before heading out to get the book pockets, Nora placed *Miss Daffodil* next to the register in case she had time to do more research on Elmer Freeman later in the day.

She was reaching for her coat when Sheldon whipped the door open and lurched inside. In his arms were three bakery boxes instead of the usual two.

"Never fear, your devoted barista is here!"

Nora took the boxes from him. "You're supposed to be sleeping."

"I slept like Rip Van Winkle." Sheldon hung up his coat and followed Nora to the kitchen. "How about you?"

"Mine was more of a Princess-and-the-Pea sleep, but with two peas. A book and a big, puffy robe."

Sheldon winced. "Oh, that's bad. I'm going to heat up my neck wrap this second. It'll fix you right up."

Between Sheldon's ministering and a strong cup of Cuban coffee, Nora was able to finish her opening tasks with fifteen minutes to spare. She powered up her laptop and began to type.

"Okay, Elmer Freeman. Let's see what else you wrote."

Nora's favorite online book source offered millions of books by independent sellers, including books by Elmer Freeman. Scrolling down the results page, Nora saw titles like *Miss Rose*, *Miss Iris*, *Miss Tulip*, and *Miss Buttercup*. The eight books listed were all published between 1914 and 1922. Only the originals were for sale. There were no reissues that Nora could find. No paperback, ebook, or audiobook versions. They were never reprinted in hardback with eye-catching dust jackets or bundled into a thick tome of collected works.

Certain series captivated generation after generation of readers, but Freeman's wasn't one of them. Nora thought this was a shame, especially since the covers were so lovely. From the few images she could see, all of the books in Freeman's Lady Artist series featured elaborate designs and colorful flowers on every clothbound cover.

A Lady Artist book in very good condition could be purchased for ninety dollars. Most of the available books were in good condition and, on average, sold for closer to fifty dollars.

According to a description written by a very thorough bookseller, the artists in the series included a potter, weaver, writer, fashion designer, composer, sculptor, illustrator, and painter.

From the outset, the series sounded quite appealing.

Were the books poorly written? If so, why would any publisher continue putting out new books in the series?

Nora opened a new browser window and ran a search on Elmer Freeman.

She scrolled past reviews of his books until she found a link to Modernist authors. When she clicked on Elmer Freeman's name, she was directed to an article, "'His' Words Were Written by a Woman."

"A pseudonym?" Nora was instantly intrigued.

Catching movement out of the corner of her eye, she looked up to see a customer peering in through the window.

Nora glanced at her watch and muttered, "Crap."

Darting out from behind the checkout counter, Nora unlocked the door.

"I'm sorry," she told a woman whose lips were blue from the cold. "I was lost in my own world."

"Happens to the best of us." The woman smiled and pulled

off her leather gloves. "I've been in your shop before, but not as often as my son, Jefferson. He's a regular. You do such a wonderful job with your storytime. Thursdays are his favorite days because he gets to come here."

"I'll be sure to pass the compliment on to Sheldon. Storytime is his baby. He has just as much fun as the kids—probably because he loves to read aloud. I think he was a voice actor in another life."

The woman shoved her gloves in her pocket and offered Nora her hand. "I'm Meredith Comfort. Jefferson comes in with our nanny, Lea." After the women shook hands, Meredith continued, "Lea thought you were the right person for me to talk to about my mother's books."

Everyone in Miracle Springs knew Meredith Comfort. If not personally, then by name. She was the orthodontist of Comfort Orthodontics and Dentistry. Her husband, Miles, was the dentist. The Comforts had a thriving practice, but were also known for their acts of philanthropy. They sponsored soccer teams, after-school programs, and summer camps. The local paper was always advertising their latest food, coat, or toy drive. They organized litter cleanup events and mailed care packages to the troops. Nora had always wondered if the Comforts were really that nice, but now that she was talking to Meredith, she thought it highly possible.

"Are you looking to have the books appraised?" she asked.

Meredith shook her head. "My mom passed away recently. I kept the books I wanted, but I'd like to sell the rest. There are boxes and boxes. They're all stacked in the bonus room right now, and I'd really love to get that space back. If you'll take them off our hands, you can name your price. Is this something you do?"

Before Nora could reply, Meredith pointed at a vintage porcelain figurine of a woman reading and said, "I have a few boxes of things like that too—figurines and little teapots and such.

My mom's shelves were so stuffed with books and knickknacks that they got warped over the years." Meredith's eyes went misty. "Her books made her happy, and I want them to end up with people who'll love them like she did. Most of my books are loaded on my ereader. Same goes for my husband."

"Did your mother live in Miracle Springs?"

"Connecticut. That's where I'm from." Meredith's face clouded with guilt. "After Mom passed, I cleaned out her house and put it on the market, which is why I now have a truckload of stuff to sort out."

Nora hated how guilt and regret were such common side effects of loss. Grief was heavy enough as it was, and Nora could see the way it bore down on Meredith's shoulders. Though she couldn't erase the pain in the other woman's hazel eyes, Nora would do her best to chase it away for now.

"I'd love to take a look at your mother's books. If any or all of your mom's collection ends up in my shop, her books will go to homes all over the country. What made her happy will make others happy too."

Meredith put a hand over her heart and smiled. "What a lovely thought. It sounds just like something my mom would have said. Lea was right. You were the person I needed to talk to about this. She also said that you're always here, no matter when she comes in, which makes me think we work similar hours. Do you have a free evening this week?"

"Actually, tonight would work. I have dinner plans, but I could come by after. Around seven thirty?" said Nora.

Other than book club or the occasional dinner with a friend, Nora spent most of her evenings at home. She was perfectly content with her own company and had given up trying to convince people that they needn't feel sorry for her. To them, Nora was a woman with no partner, no children, and no pets, so she must be lonely.

Of course, Nora had moments of melancholy, but they were few and far between. It was when she was feeling her worst that a book would come along to remind her that she was perfectly fine. As long as she kept learning and growing as a human being, she was exactly where she was meant to be, doing exactly what she was meant to do.

Books reminded her that she was never alone. How could she be when the world was full of stories waiting to be read? Of characters waiting to introduce themselves?

Sometimes Nora could get herself out of a funk just by looking at a list of upcoming releases. And she lived for moments like this—when she was able to give someone the help they needed.

"Really? That's perfect!" Meredith's voice was infused with gratitude.

She wrote her address on the back of a business card, handed it to Nora, and rushed off to see her next patient.

Nora was unable to continue her Elmer Freeman research until after lunch. She managed to learn an interesting tidbit about the Lady Artist author moments before the after-school rush began.

It was edging toward the time Sheldon usually called it a day when Sheriff McCabe walked through the front door. He closed it very slowly, so as not to rattle the sleigh bells.

A wave of wintry air crashed into Nora and she said, "Are you trying to share my heat with everyone on the sidewalk?"

McCabe issued a hapless shrug. "I know how much Sheldon hates those bells. I don't want to make him mad. I need a cup of his coffee."

Hands on hips, Nora feigned offense. "But it's okay to make me mad?"

"You don't hold a grudge. Sheldon still fusses about that *one time* I showed him the grounds floating around in my mug." McCabe took off his hat and waved it at the Fiction section. Completely deadpan, he asked, "Care to join me? My treat."

Nora laughed. "How could I resist such an offer?"

Minutes later, they carried their mugs of coffee to the Readers' Circle.

"Sheldon, do you go out of your way to give me emasculating mugs?"

Sheldon batted his lashes and said, "Doesn't everyone love unicorns and rainbows? Or is the *I Still Read Fairy Tales* text the emasculating part?"

Smiling, McCabe took a sip of coffee.

Sheldon gestured at Nora with the milk-frothing pitcher. "She'd never pick that mug. *Maybe* the mug picked *her*."

The text on Nora's mug read: ALL I NEED ARE CATS, BOOKS, COFFEE.

"We should switch. You're the one with the cats," she told the sheriff.

He shook his head. "Steak would top my list. It tastes great and doesn't shred my furniture."

In the ticket agent's booth, Sheldon hummed as he washed the dishes. Hearing all the unnecessary splashing, Nora knew that he was trying to give her a little privacy.

"Were you able to identify the man in the woods?" she asked McCabe.

He frowned. "Not yet. His prints aren't in the national database and we got no hits from facial recognition systems. We can't figure out how he got to Miracle Springs. We've watched hours of security footage from the train station without a single sighting. If he came by car, then we can't find it. There's no record of a man with his description registering at an area hotel either. All we have is that book."

Seeing the question in McCabe's gaze, Nora said, "I know a bit more about it, but I'm not sure if what I learned will help. *Miss Delphinium* is part of a series called The Lady Artists. One woman's a painter, another's a sculptor, et cetera. All the main characters are named after flowers."

"I found a plot summary online, but it tells me nothing about our John Doe. Maybe his first name is Elmer or his last,

Freeman. Maybe he knew someone who loved delphiniums. I'd never heard of them, but I now know that another name for delphinium is larkspur. That might win me a point on trivia night, but it doesn't get me any closer to identifying our stranger."

Settling deeper into his chair, McCabe relaxed his shoulders.

In contrast, Nora sat ramrod straight as she pictured the various flowers from Freeman's book titles. "The flowers he used are all different. Shapes, color, habitat—there's no common thread."

"Maybe our stranger was a florist. Or a botanist. Maybe *Miss Delphinium* belonged to someone he loved." McCabe's voice tightened in frustration. "Or it's just a random book that isn't going to help us find what we need to know."

"I don't think it's a random book and neither do you. There's more than meets the eye when it comes to this book," said Nora. "For example, Elmer Freeman was the pseudonym of a woman named Enid Elton. When she wrote these books in the early 1900s, it wasn't unusual for women to use a pen name because critics tended to judge writing based on gender first and quality second."

"Wasn't the series a flop, anyway?"

Nora was quick to defend Enid Elton. "It didn't sell because critics trashed the books as being frivolous, which was their way of condemning the progressive ideas Freeman presented. To them, a female character interested in pursuing a career was not only absurd, it also threatened the structure of their society. A woman focused on a career couldn't see to the needs of her husband or their children and household. The very fabric of society would unravel if women chose a career over family after reading Enid's books."

"But it's '*Miss*' Delphinium," McCabe countered, using air quotes to emphasize the Miss. "There's no husband or kids in the picture, so what's the problem? Why can't she be a painter? Or a bookshop owner?"

Nora smiled at him. "Enid Elton wrote about women living

during Victorian times. During this period, a young woman's number one goal was to make an advantageous marriage. If this wasn't possible, she was supposed to find a respectable occupation. She could be a governess, for example. Few parents would approve of a daughter who made a living by selling art."

McCabe mulled this over for a moment before saying, "When my sister was in high school, she told our parents that she wanted to play guitar in a rock band. I remember my dad's answer to this day. He said, 'Music's a hobby, not a career.'"

"Did she keep playing?"

"For a year or two. During my last visit to Missy's place, I asked if she still had that guitar, but she'd sold it twenty years ago." He shrugged. "My sister didn't end up with the life she dreamed about in high school, but who does? At least she's happy with the life she got. *I'd* be happier if I could ID my John Doe, and I don't think Enid Elton can help."

"I don't know why he had that book, but it has to matter. No one keeps every book they read, which means the ones we *do* keep are important. A person's library is like a fingerprint. The books on their shelves are a collection of memories and wishes. They're as unique as a snowflake."

McCabe stared into the middle distance. "I wonder what mine says about me."

"It says that you have lots more books to buy." Nora grinned at him. Setting her coffee cup aside, she said, "I want to show you something."

"In my line of work, that's never a good thing."

Nora had left *Miss Daffodil* in a cubbyhole next to the register. She carried it back to the Readers' Circle and handed it to McCabe. "This was left on a table at the Gingerbread House. Hester's never seen it before and doesn't remember any of her customers reading it."

"*Miss Daffodil*, eh?" McCabe took his time examining the cover before opening to the copyright page. After scanning what was printed there, he slowly turned every page, pausing only when he came across an illustration.

When he was done, he closed the book and looked at Nora.

"What was your initial reaction to this?"

Nora hesitated. She wanted to be honest with McCabe, but since she didn't want to mention the ghost tingle in her finger, she said, "It felt like a message. Not a good one either."

"I don't like it," he said.

The sleigh bells rang, but Nora kept her eyes on McCabe. "What if the man in the orange coat is somehow connected to Hester? Like, I don't know, they have something in common."

McCabe gave her a searching look. "What makes you say that?"

"I need to show you something in the stockroom. And before you ask, it isn't good."

Nora got to her feet just as two kids rounded the corner of the Fiction section.

"Mom said we can have hot chocolate. The marshmallows will make you feel better," the little boy told his sister.

The little girl's long face indicated that marshmallows wouldn't help.

Realizing that Sheldon had gone home, Nora leapt to her feet.

"You'll see copies of *The Scarlet Letter* on the table to the right of the door," she told McCabe. "Turn each one over and you'll understand why I'm worried about Hester. Unless you think it's a prank—some kids messing around."

Nora entered the ticket agent's booth. She was tying her apron strings when a harried-looking woman appeared on the other side of the pass-through window.

She mustered a smile and said, "Hi, Nora. I'd like to order two Harry Potters, a Jack London, and a book that'll stop kids from picking on other kids."

"I'd like to sell an adult version of that book. Sounds like someone could use an extra helping of rainbow marshmallows."

After making sure her kids were out of earshot, the woman said, "Two days ago, my daughter fell off her bike, face-first. She landed on the sidewalk."

Nora winced.

"Yeah, it was a nasty fall. We thought she'd lose one of her front teeth, but it's going to be okay. The thing is, it's totally gray right now. Nadia's so embarrassed that she won't open her mouth. She hid in the nurse's office during lunch and doesn't want to go back to school. With her overbite, it's hard for her to hide her teeth. She's getting braces next month, but she told me today that they'll just make things worse."

"Do kids make fun of her teeth?"

The woman sighed. "All the time. And the stuff they say is really mean. It breaks my heart to see how much their words hurt her." She covered her mouth with her hand until she'd mastered her emotions. "I'm sorry. I didn't mean to put all of that out there. But when you're a mom, you try to fix everything. Even things that can't be fixed."

Nora placed the Jack London and two not-so-hot Harry Potter hot chocolates on the counter and said, "I have a book you might be interested in. It won't stop your daughter's classmates from teasing her, but it might make her feel less alone. It can be a comfort to know that someone else understands exactly what she's going through. Feeling seen can be empowering."

"If it can help her get out from under that black cloud for a little while, then I need that book."

Nora headed into the stacks and returned with a copy of Raina Telgemeier's *Smile*. She handed it to the woman and said, "See what you think. I'll be back in a minute."

In the stockroom, Grant McCabe stood with his arms crossed, staring down at the two books lined up on the table.

"I don't know what this means." There was a sharp edge to his voice. His eyes were dark and troubled. "But this isn't a prank. This is a deliberate destruction of property. It targets a specific name. Hester. Add this to the fact that the book left at her bakery is from the same series as the one found on a dead man and I know a message is being sent. But damn it, I don't understand what it is!"

He slapped *The Scarlet Letter* against the table. The noise startled Nora, causing her to jump back.

McCabe was instantly contrite. "I'm sorry," he said, walking over to her. "I know you're trying to help. I just can't see the forest for the trees."

He passed his hands over his face. Before he could lower them again, Nora caught them in hers.

The moment she made contact, the air in the room shifted.

As Nora looked at McCabe, she felt the static of an electrical storm fill the space between them. Seeing the want in his eyes, her skin flushed with warmth. She parted her lips, inviting him to come closer. To touch her in a way he never had before.

McCabe's hands turned in hers, capturing her wrists.

"Um . . . hello?" a young woman's voice echoed down the hallway.

Releasing her, McCabe let out a huff of frustration. He walked back to the table and scooped up a damaged paperback. "Can I bring this to the station? I need to show it to Andrews."

Though Nora was flustered, she tried not to show it.

Out in the hall, the restroom door slammed and someone called her name again. The moment between her and McCabe had passed.

"Help yourself," she said. "Do you want to take the other book too?"

At McCabe's nod, Nora led him back to the Readers' Circle. *Miss Daffodil* sat on the coffee table.

Nora was just about to pick it up when a teenage girl poked

her head around the corner of the cookbook section and said, "Hey. Sorry, but my friend's in the bathroom and she needs, um . . ." The girl darted a glance at McCabe and went bright pink with embarrassment. "Can you just come with me?"

The girl ran toward the restroom and Nora followed behind. When she turned to say good-bye to McCabe, both he and the book were already gone.

Chapter 6

I've had more honest satisfaction and happiness collecting books than anything else I've ever done in life.

—Peter Ruber, *The Last Bookman*

Instead of going straight home after work, Nora hopped on her moped and drove to the Pink Lady Grill to meet June and Estella. Hester had plans with Andrews and wouldn't be joining them.

The diner was warm and noisy. A line stretched from the door to the host stand and all the seats in the waiting area were taken.

Nora said hello to several people as she walked to the front of the line.

"Hey, lady!" The hostess waved a laminated menu. "You're the last table by the window. Estella put your order in already."

"Can she put mine in too?" a man at the counter joked. When his server placed a cheeseburger and fries in front of him a few seconds later, he glanced over at Estella and murmured, "Well, if that doesn't just dill my pickle."

Nora maneuvered around the wait staff, customers shrugging out of coats, and a busboy balancing a dozen dirty plates to the booth where Estella and June waited.

"The joint is jumping," she said, taking a seat on the hot-pink vinyl cushion next to June.

Estella glanced up from her phone screen. "Sorry. Jack's home sick, so I'm asking if he wants me to bring him anything to eat. Dating the owner of a diner means that we rarely get to go out on Friday or Saturday nights, but it also means that I never have to cook, even when my man isn't feeling well."

June said, "The flu is going around. We've been short staffed at the lodge all week. Take your vitamins, wash your hands, and keep your feet warm, ladies."

"Aren't you going to warn us about going out with wet hair?" Nora teased.

Putting her phone down, Estella said, "Believe it or not, some of my clients ask me to put them under the dryer *after* their blow outs. Just in case I missed a few strands. 'I'll catch a cold if my hair's wet!' is what they say. Do I explain that colds come from viruses? Nope. I do what they ask because they're coming to me for pampering, not a science lesson."

"Those old women know what they're talking about," said June. "You don't see folks running around without coats, do you? Who'll catch the virus faster? The person who's warm and dry or the one who's wet and shivering from cold?"

The arrival of their server put an end to the discussion.

"All right, ladies! I have three bowls of jambalaya, a basket of biscuits, and three unsweet teas with lemon. Enjoy!"

Nora stirred her jambalaya with a spoon. The andouille sausage, shrimp, and vegetables shifted, releasing a burst of steam smelling of onions, garlic, cayenne, and smoked paprika.

June passed the basket of buttermilk biscuits to Nora. They were still warm from the oven, so Nora pried hers open, deposited a pat of butter in the middle, and quickly replaced the top. Within seconds, melted butter trickled down the sides of the biscuit and pooled on the bread plate.

"A perfect dinner for a winter's night," she said.

Estella jerked a thumb over her shoulder. "The place is packed because people from around here know about tonight's special. Visitors won't get a table until eight, and only if they're lucky."

Taking a bite of buttery biscuit, Nora felt very lucky indeed.

"I can't wait to hear all about Meredith Comfort's house," said Estella. "She's one of my clients, and I really like her. It's hard not to. It's also hard not to feel like a slug of a human being when she's around. When I'm not working, I flop on my couch and read or watch movies with Jack. Meanwhile, Meredith's out there, feeding the hungry, sheltering the homeless, and rescuing kittens and puppies. If she and her husband weren't so busy fixing everyone's teeth, they could put an end to climate change in a month or two."

June squeezed lemon into her tea. "I don't know Meredith, but Miles is a fine man. A few years ago, I broke a crown. My dentist was off on a two-week cruise, but I couldn't wait that long for it to be fixed. Dr. Comfort stayed late to take care of me, and he was patient and gentle."

"What do they want to sell?" asked Estella.

"Books that belonged to Meredith's late mom. Boxes and boxes, apparently. That's all I know." Nora glanced at her butter-stained napkin. "I just hope they're in good shape. I've been to house calls before where all I saw were warped and yellowed paperbacks. Some people think an old book is automatically valuable, no matter its condition. I wish that were the case. I wish every book would find a home on someone's shelf."

When their server stopped by to check on them, Estella asked for chicken noodle soup in a take-out container.

"Good thing Jack has someone looking after him. Keisha said he sounded real bad when she talked to him on the phone," the server said, referring to the diner's day manager. "You tell Jack everything's under control here and he needs to put all his energy into getting better."

After smiling warmly at Estella, the server walked away.

"Has Jack ever taken a sick day?" June asked.

"Not since I've known him," answered Estella. "But there was no way he could work today. He has a fever and can't keep anything down. The man is as weak as a newborn kitten. As soon as they bring his soup, I'd better go."

Fishing around in her handbag, Nora said, "Me too. But I need to talk to you about Hester first."

"About the wedding?" asked June.

Nora placed a paperback on the table. "I'm afraid not. This is one of the books I told you about—the ones that were damaged right before Hester got engaged." She pushed *The Scarlet Letter* closer to June. "In time, I would have forgotten about these. I'd chalk them up as a loss and move on. But now, I want to know who did this. Let me explain why."

She told her friends about the book found on the dead man and went on to describe the book left at the Gingerbread House.

"Might be coincidence," said June.

"True. The fact that someone carved out Hester's name from a whole stack of books in my shop may have nothing to do with the book she found at the bakery," Nora said. "But what if there's a connection?"

Estella picked up *The Scarlet Letter* and ran her fingertips over the slashes in the back cover. "Hester's such a sweetheart. What could she have done to make someone this mad? Given them a donut filled with custard instead of jelly?"

June shook her head. "If a customer told her off, she would've told us. Crazy customers are one of our favorite stories to swap at book club."

"Maybe someone is unhappy about her engagement," Nora suggested.

Estella considered this for a moment before saying, "I could see a jealous ex behaving badly, but I don't think Andrews had a serious relationship until now."

June held up her hand, palm out. "The books were cut up *before* Andrews proposed. The jealous-ex theory doesn't fit."

Nora couldn't argue with this logic. "No, it doesn't fit. None of this makes sense. I can't think of anything connecting the dead stranger, the old books, and Hester, but I still feel uneasy. So does McCabe."

The server stepped up to the silent table, Jack's soup in hand. Seeing the unfinished bowls of jambalaya, she asked, "How's everybody doing?"

Estella flashed her an apologetic smile. "We started talking about that poor man who died in the woods. Guess we lost our appetites."

"And nobody knows who he is or where he came from." The server tut-tutted. "It ain't right. He shouldn't be sitting in a drawer like a package of cold cuts. He needs to be laid to rest." As she cleared the table, she added, "I heard a dog howl the night before he was found. You're supposed to turn over a shoe when a dog howls at night. I can't remember if I did or not."

The server wore a Mickey Mouse watch, and when Nora noticed the position of Mickey's gloved hands, she tossed her napkin on the table and began pulling on her coat.

"I'm going to be late," she told her friends. "Can I pay someone back next time we meet?"

June gave her a friendly shove. "We got this. Good luck wheeling and dealing."

Nora didn't argue. She buttoned her coat on the way out of the diner, shoved her helmet on, and drove as fast as she could up Mountain Loop Road toward Wildflower Way.

* * *

Because the Comforts lived close to the lodge, Nora hadn't needed directions. She wasn't worried about finding the right house, as there were only twelve in the exclusive neighborhood. All of the large, elegant homes had stone facades, oversized windows, and expansive decks.

When Nora's headlight illuminated a white mailbox with a sunflower design, she turned into the driveway and continued to wind her way uphill.

In the darkness, it was hard to see where the asphalt ended and the woods began. To Nora, the air felt colder up here. The stars felt closer too.

Coming to a stop in front of the house, Nora took off her helmet and gazed upward. The stars pulsed like bioluminescent jellyfish suspended in a midnight ocean.

The front door opened, spilling golden light over the flagstone path. As Meredith waved Nora inside, she asked, "Did you find us okay?"

"I did. Sorry I'm late."

Meredith smiled. "Not at all. You're just in time for dessert."

Nora put her palm to her stomach. "I don't think I have room. Not after the jambalaya I had at the Pink Lady."

"Did you hear that, Miles? Jambalaya!"

Miles was bent over, rearranging the plates and pans in the bottom rack of the dishwasher. "We *need* to try that," he told Meredith. Turning to Nora, he asked, "Can I get you something? Hot chocolate, decaf coffee, herbal tea? Or a piece of this edible work of art made by Lea and Jefferson?"

Nora stared at the giant, cookielike thing in the center of the table.

Sensing her confusion, Meredith laughed. "Jefferson is in love with Mo Willems books. He wanted to make the cookie from *The Duckling Gets a Cookie!?*"

"It had to be big enough to share with everyone," Miles added.

"And half-yellow, half-green. The green side has nuts and is for the pigeon. The yellow side is for the duckling." Meredith broke off a piece. "It tastes better than it looks."

"Not really," Miles whispered.

Meredith popped the piece in her mouth and grinned at him. "You're going to sneak down here in a few hours and eat the rest of the green side."

"Me? Never! I'm a dentist!"

Lowering her voice, Meredith told Nora that they should give Miles and the cookie some privacy and led her out of the kitchen and down a long hallway. The walls were lined with family photos, a hand-drawn family tree, and framed works of needlepoint.

"My mom made this when she was ten," Meredith said, pausing in front of a needlepoint of a bluebird perched on a cherry blossom branch. "She was incredibly artistic, but I didn't get that gene. I can't even draw a stick figure. It's a good thing Jefferson has Lea because she's an amazing artist."

Nora admired the needlepoint. "This is beautiful. I can barely sew a button."

"Buttons are overrated," Meredith said. She opened the door at the end of the hall and flicked on the lights. The room was full of moving boxes and an eclectic assortment of furniture that included two church pews, a pie safe, a painted fire screen, and a tall case clock.

Nora tried to contain her excitement. "Did all of this come from your mom's house?"

"It sure did." Meredith ran her hand over the arm of a church pew. "I've already taken what I wanted from these boxes. The rest is all yours if you want it."

Nora wished she could comb through the contents of each

box in private, but she'd been to enough house calls to know that Meredith probably wouldn't leave her alone with her mother's things. People tended to hover while Nora examined the books they wanted to sell. They watched her face for signs of interest or outright desire, but Nora was always careful to conceal her feelings.

To her surprise, Meredith pointed at the door. "If you don't need me, I'm going to tuck Jefferson in. Depending on how many stories I end up reading him, I'll be back to check on you in twenty minutes or two hours."

Nora couldn't believe her luck. "Is it okay if I put books on the floor so I can get a better look at them?"

"Absolutely! Make yourself at home. There's a packing list in each box too. I love making lists. In another life, I might have been an event planner or a professional organizer." Glancing around the room, she grinned ruefully. "In another life, I might actually use my gym membership. But I don't. Neither does Miles. We made a resolution to turn this space into a home gym. So you're really doing us a favor by taking these books off our hands."

Nora waited until Meredith was gone before opening the first box. She scanned the packing list and murmured, "Whoa."

The box was filled with leather-bound limited editions from Franklin Library. Meredith's mother had collected mostly first editions from the quality press, but there were some signed editions too.

Nora unpacked books and laid them on the carpet. Other than red, the covers tended to be black, brown, dark blue, or forest green. The lettering and spine stamps were gold and the pages had gilt edges. Every volume was in very good to fine condition, and Nora was pleased to see that most of the titles were by recognizable authors. Even though Mailer, Vonnegut, and Faulkner weren't Nora's favorites, the books would sell.

The books by Joyce Carol Oates, Wallace Stegner, Jessamyn West, and John Updike would move faster, but Nora knew that they were all saleable. She had no idea how much these specific signed editions were worth, however, and spent a few minutes checking prices on her phone. Ray Bradbury's *Death Is a Lonely Business* was selling for eighty dollars, while a near-fine copy of Philip Roth's *The Anatomy Lesson* brought closer to forty.

Nora felt dejected. If every box was like this one, a fair offer on the whole collection might be beyond her means. She was careful with money, but she was still making mortgage payments on the Miracle Books property, and the monthly insurance and utility bills for her business and home seemed to be increasing all the time.

The next box held more quality press books. These were a mix of box sets from Easton Press and the Folio Society, and even though most of the slipcases were scuffed, Nora knew she'd have no problem selling the beautifully illustrated editions by popular authors like Tolkien, Lewis, Austen, Dickens, Trollope, and Alcott.

The third box was filled with early twentieth-century treasures. To Nora's delight, every book was a collection of fairy and folk tales or nursery rhymes. At the very bottom of the box, she found a series of books that took her breath away.

"Oh, wow," she breathed as she peeled back a sheet of white paper to reveal a bright blue cover showing a witch riding a broomstick.

Nora stared at the copy of *The Blue Fairy Book* for a long moment. Andrew Lang's Fairy Books were known to most booksellers, but Nora had never held one of the originals. The book in her hands was from 1889, but had aged very gracefully. The spine was faded. There was edge wear, foxing, and minor tears. No major problems, though, and Nora could barely contain her delight when she unwrapped *The Crimson Fairy Book*.

She was so captivated by the illustrations in *The Lilac Fairy Book* that she didn't hear the door open until a soft voice said, "Hi."

Nora looked up to see Lea standing in the doorway.

"Can I come in?" she asked.

"Of course. After all, you're the reason I'm here." Nora gestured at the circle of books around her legs and laughed. "I've made my own fairy ring."

Lea dropped to her knees next to Nora. "I thought those were made of mushrooms."

Nora touched the cover of *The Olive Fairy Book*. "I'd rather have these than a crate of the world's most expensive truffles."

"I'm not much of a book person," Lea admitted. "But I love reading to Jefferson. I like kids' books because I like the illustrations. I'd love to do that for a living."

"Sounds like a fun job."

Lea's face clouded. "Yeah, but who knows if I'll ever get to do it. It costs a ton to go to art school, and this job pays way more than any of the entry-level graphic design jobs I applied for, so here I am, finger-painting with a toddler. And I can't even be bitter about it because I love Jefferson. His parents are awesome too."

"He's a lucky kid. I've seen you two at the bookstore. You're good with him." Nora shook her head in wonder. "I don't know how you do it. Do you have younger brothers or sisters or were you an unofficial member of the Baby-Sitters Club?"

A light danced in Lea's brown eyes. "I remember those books—from the Scholastic Book Club sheets our teachers used to hand out. Courtney, this girl in my class, looked exactly like the blond girl from those books." Lea puckered her lips. "I looked more like one of the other characters. Ally? Addy? Something like that."

Nora pulled up an image of one of the books and showed it to Lea. "Must be Abby. You two have the same dark hair and eyes. You're both lovely, but I like you better because you recommended me to Meredith."

Lea laughed and picked up a book of Chinese folk tales. "It just made sense. Meredith won't feel guilty about selling this stuff if someone else can use it."

"I'd love to take this off her hands, but I don't have the funds to offer her a fair deal." Nora traced the gold title letters on the cover of a collection of nursery rhymes. "Some of these books are valuable, and Meredith could make more money by selling them online."

Lea shook her head. "Doesn't matter. She wants *you* to have her mom's books, and one way or another, she'll make sure you get them."

Since Lea knew Meredith far better than Nora, she didn't argue. As she began repacking the Fairy Books, Lea scooched across the carpet to help.

"Are you still on the clock?" Nora asked.

Pointing at the door, Lea said, "No, but I live in the apartment over the garage. Even though I'm done at five, I eat dinner with the family a few nights a week. Tonight I stayed to help Jefferson make a cookie pizza and to see what you thought of the books."

Meredith appeared in the doorway in time to catch the end of Lea's sentence. Looking at Nora, she said, "What *do* you think?"

"Your mom had great taste and she treated her books well. The thing is, I can't afford to buy them. Not if I want to turn around and sell them in my shop, which I do." Nora held up *The Grey Fairy Book*. "Collectors would pay you hundreds of dollars for this book."

Meredith joined the two women on the floor. "Why? I mean, it has a really pretty cover, but what's so special about it?"

Nora thought for a moment before answering. "People collect books for different reasons. Some treat them as investments. Others want to own titles from their favorite authors or genres. Most of the book collectors I know want to fill their shelves with the books that moved them in some way. Childhood books, books that comfort, books given to them by a loved one. As for these Fairy Books? People want these because they're beautiful. Who wouldn't want a rainbow of magical stories on their shelf?"

"You sound like my mom," Meredith said wistfully. "She organized her books by color. It drove me crazy! But she had an artist's eye. Like our Lea. You should see her drawings and paintings."

"I'd love to," said Nora.

Lea hopped to her feet. "Maybe some other time. You two have stuff to talk about and I need to watch *Stranger Things* before I hear spoilers. See you at storytime."

After saying good night to Lea, Meredith put one of the Fairy Books on her lap and ran her fingers over the cover. "If you took these books, you'd be doing me two favors. You'd be selling them to people who'll cherish them, like my mom did. That would help *me* let them go without feeling guilty. And when this room gets cleared, I can cancel my gym membership. I'll be saving money. See? That's two favors."

"But there's no way I can offer you a fair price."

Meredith pushed the book toward Nora. "You'd be offering me peace of mind, which means more to me than money. Tell me what you can comfortably afford, and we'll go from there."

Nora gave her an honest reply and finished repacking the box. When she was done, she stood up and said, "Thanks for letting me look at these."

"No, thank *you* for coming up here on such a cold night."

Meredith got to her feet and pulled out her phone. "Both Miles and I drive big cars, but he thinks we can fit everything into my minivan. We're taking a half day on Friday because we're both heading out of town for the weekend. I have a women's retreat at a supercute country inn, and Miles is doing a men's wilderness retreat, but I'm leaving my van with Lea and hitching a ride with a friend. We could pack it and drop the boxes off at the bookstore before we go. Does that work?"

When Nora didn't reply, Meredith touched her lightly on the shoulder. "You're hesitating because you don't think it's a fair offer, but it is. Seriously, I feel a thousand pounds lighter already. And Mom? She's giving me a thumbs-up from heaven. Some things are just right, even if they don't make sense. So, how do you feel about Friday?"

Nora smiled. "I feel like I'd better clear a big space in the stockroom."

She drove home with stars shining above her and the lights of town spread out below. On such a silent night, the golden glow from all the windows created a Christmas card scene.

Nora couldn't remember the last time she'd felt this happy, and she wanted to hold on to the moment as long as she could. When she got home, she didn't turn on the television or pick up the novel on her nightstand. She made a cup of chamomile tea, lit a scented candle, and stretched out on her sofa. She sipped tea and thought about the people and the books she'd interacted with that night.

Her mug was half-full when her eyes grew heavy, but she wasn't ready to call it a day yet. Happiness was like a firefly in a jar, and she didn't want it to slip away while she slept.

Eventually she went to bed, but didn't sleep. Her mind refused to shut down. Thoughts bounced around like a pinball caught between bumpers.

She wondered how Jed was doing. She remembered the look

on McCabe's face in the stockroom. She thought of Lea, the artistic nanny who'd led her to an amazing book collection. She should find an art book to give Lea as a thank-you. Nora pictured the Art section in Miracle Books. As titles moved through her mind, she started drifting off.

When sleep finally came to claim her, she was smiling.

Chapter 7

A life with love will have some thorns, but a life without love will have no roses.

—Dr. Seuss

Estella studied the sheet of paper in her hand. "Since *Villette* is a classic *and* a novel about an orphan, does that mean we can check off two boxes?"

"Nope. One book per reading goal," said Nora.

June, who was making drinks in the ticket agent's booth, pointed the cocktail shaker at Estella. "You're the one who wants to read *Anne of Green Gables*."

"Because she's a redhead. My personal goal this year is to read a book about a redhead every month," replied Estella.

Hester said, "Maybe I'll read about curly-haired blondes. Except I can't think of a single curly-haired heroine. Can you, Nora?"

"There's Cathy from *Wuthering Heights*."

Hester grimaced. "I'll pass. Cathy has anger issues and Heathcliff is abusive. I didn't like them as a couple when I read about them in high school. I'd probably like them even less now."

Over the rattle of the cocktail shaker, Estella said, "The Brontë gals loved a brooding male lead. I prefer my book boyfriends to be more upbeat. Adding a joke or snarky comment every now and then wouldn't hurt."

A few minutes later, June emerged from the ticket agent's booth and put a tray laden with two cocktail shakers and four martini glasses rimmed with black sugar crystals on the coffee table. With great ceremony, she poured the contents of the cocktail shakers into the glasses and dropped a cherry into each glass. The cherries sank like stones in a garnet-red sea.

"Speaking of boyfriends, how's yours feeling?" June asked Estella.

Estella grimaced. "He can't shake his fever and all he wants to do is sleep. When he's awake, he moans about missing work. But will he go to the doctor? *No.* He thinks green tea and another day of rest will do the trick. I made him promise to go to Urgent Care tomorrow if he still has a fever in the morning. If he looks any worse, I'm going to drive him straight to the emergency room."

It seemed like everyone in town was talking about the flu. She'd sold several books on holistic medicine that day and had had to order more family health titles.

"Are you feeling okay?" she asked Estella.

"Perfectly peachy. And if I have germs I don't know about, a martini or two should take care of them. I have no idea what you put in this drink, June, but I know I'm going to like it."

"I'm just the mixologist. Hester invented tonight's literary cocktail."

Hester raised her glass. "This gothic black-cherry martini is for you three. Because book friends are the best friends and I can't think of a better way to spend a Saturday night."

After a single taste, everyone agreed that the Jane Eyre cocktail was a winner.

Nora studied Hester out of the corner of her eye. There was something off about her tonight. Even though she sounded like her chipper self and looked absolutely adorable in a fifties-style cardigan embroidered with pink flowers and pearlized buttons, she was unusually fidgety. She kept twisting the same button with such intensity that Nora wouldn't be surprised if it popped off.

"Are you okay?" asked Nora.

The question took Hester by surprise. "Yeah, sure. Why wouldn't I be? *Oh!* Because of those books. I don't think they have anything to do with me. It just proves that other people besides me hate *The Scarlet Letter.*"

Estella motioned to indicate herself, June, and Nora. "It bothers us. Wouldn't you be worried if Estella was the only word gouged out of a pile of *Great Expectations*? Or if every June was scratched out of *The Secret Life of Bees?*"

"I'd think it was a kid's prank," said Hester.

"What kid?" June countered.

Hester sighed. "Some hormonal teen. A few weeks ago, a bunch of them came to the bakery before school. You know how they travel in packs. I was crazy busy, but I heard them griping about how they were going to be late. When they tried to cut in front of old Mrs. Perry, I told them to be polite and patient or leave. They weren't polite, but they stayed. Later, a customer showed me an Instagram post of one of my donuts. There was a hair in the icing."

"Uh-oh," Estella whispered.

"Anyone with half a brain could see that it wasn't mine because it was short and black, but lots of people saw that post." Hester took a generous swallow of martini before continuing. "At first, I was furious. But after a few days, half of those kids were back, ordering their usual donuts and cookies as if the post never happened. I guess the others are still mad, so maybe one of them ruined your books. If that's true, I'm sorry that I ever said anything to them."

June made a noise that meant she had her doubts about Hester's theory, but wasn't going to challenge it. "What about the other book? The old one?"

"I'll tell you what I told Jasper. Just because someone left an old book at my bakery doesn't mean it has anything to do with me. People leave stuff all the time. Keys, purses, small children . . ."

She arched her brows, waiting for her friends to smile and move on to a new subject. When they didn't, she drained the last drops of martini from her glass and stared at the bloated cherry. Suddenly tears pooled in her eyes.

Nora reached for her friend's hand. "You don't have to fight it, sweetheart. It's just us. Nothing leaves this circle unless you want it to."

Hester pulled her hand free and pivoted it under the light, making her engagement ring shine like a small star. Staring at it, she said, "I love Jasper, and I want to marry him. But when I think about a wedding—about vows and church and witnesses—I just shut down. I can't see myself in a white dress. I know I can't stand at an altar and promise to be something I'm not."

The button she'd been ruthlessly turning around and around finally gave way. Hester closed her hand around it like an oyster refusing to part with its pearl.

Nora, Estella, and June traded worried glances. It had been years since they'd listened to Hester share the secret she'd been guarding for half a lifetime. It had been years since the four of them had been brought together by another stranger's death. The bond they'd formed in this Readers' Circle was stronger than ever. In the silence, they all felt it.

June was the first to disturb the quiet.

"I just assumed he knew by now."

She spoke softly and without recrimination, but color rushed into Hester's cheeks and she lowered her gaze.

Estella smacked the table. "There's no shame, Hester. Push it away. We know the truth and it didn't stop us from loving you. We might even love you more because of it."

Hester kept her eyes fixed on the coffee table. "It was so

hard—telling you what happened. It wasn't even the whole story. I couldn't let it all out. I felt like I could never be who I want to be if I told you all of it." She took a deep, shuddering breath. "I tried telling Jasper so many times, but the words get stuck. Every time. And when he finds out what I've been keeping from him, he'll ask for his grandma's ring back. Why wouldn't he?"

Her friends didn't respond. They couldn't predict how Jasper Andrews would react. All they could do was support Hester.

Nora leaned close to her and said, "What if you practiced with us? If you add the parts you left out, you might have a breakthrough."

"You can take all the time you need," Estella added.

Hester looked to June, who gave her an encouraging nod.

"You already know the important parts," Hester began. "When I was a junior in high school, I met a boy named Elijah Lamb at our local library. I fell for him the second I bumped into him in Fiction, *W* to *WH*." A smile tugged the corners of her mouth. "For months, we met at the library. For months, we were just friends. But when I wasn't with Elijah, I was thinking about him. Later, he told me that he was thinking about me too."

Hester's expression softened, and it was easy to picture her as a love-struck teenager.

"It's sweet that you met in the library," said Nora.

"*He* was sweet. And smart and funny. I'd never been so happy." Sorrow darkened Hester's eyes. "Fast-forward to Easter. I was helping my mom cook dinner when the smell of the ham made me sick to my stomach. I was tired and queasy for days after that. My parents thought I had a virus, so I stayed home from school."

"I hate ham." Estella shivered in revulsion. "Do you know

what we had for Christmas dinner every year? SPAM and baked beans. I'll never eat real or fake ham again."

"That's because you haven't had my honey and brown sugar–glazed ham," said June, picking up Hester's empty glass. "You ready for a refill?"

"After I finish the next part," said Hester. "A week went by and I didn't feel better. I also realized that I'd missed at least two periods. I bought a pregnancy test from the drugstore, and when that plus sign started forming in that little circle, I wanted to die. Honestly. At that moment, I thought it would be the easiest way out."

June's face creased in sympathy. "Thank God you didn't hurt yourself."

"My parents probably wished that I had." Hester seemed to shrink into her chair as she spoke. "I'd always been a disappointment to them. I wasn't beautiful, charming, or popular. My job was to smile prettily, talk softly, and serve my family and community. I didn't do any of it right."

"Sounds like your folks were trapped in a time warp," June said.

"It was more than that. They criticized me and showered praise on my brother. He was brash and good-looking. An honor student and star athlete. From birth, he was groomed to take over my dad's company when my dad retired. My job was to marry the first man who'd have me."

Nora was irate on Hester's behalf. How could her parents make her feel unwanted and unworthy? Why hadn't they recognized her potential? Hester didn't get married. She went to college, worked various jobs, and started a business. And despite being belittled or ignored by her family, Hester was still the kindest, most cheerful person Nora knew.

"I'm amazed you kept in touch with them after how they treated you," said Estella.

Hester shrugged one shoulder. "I haven't called home for years. After we became friends, I didn't need their approval anymore. They haven't reached out to me since."

"I knew that you'd been talking to them less and less, but I didn't realize that you'd stopped altogether. So no communication at all? Not even a Christmas card?" asked Nora.

"Nope." Hester looked at her engagement ring. "Jasper knows about my family, but I never told him why things went from bad to worse. When my parents found out I was pregnant, they locked me in my room until they could figure out how to 'fix my mess.' I was literally a prisoner in my house for ten days."

Estella shook her fists. "I swear, I'd like to slap the stupid out of those people. It wouldn't work, but I'd give it my best effort."

Hester rewarded her with a small smile before continuing. "My parents drove me to a little town in Westchester County to live with my great-aunt Mary. I'd never even met her before, but I'd heard my mom talk about her when she thought no one was listening. She called her a sour, miserable old woman who was rotting away in her Victorian mansion and would probably leave all her money to a cat sanctuary. My job was to cook my aunt's meals and keep her house clean until my time came. I was scared. I was ashamed. And since I thought I deserved to be punished, I did whatever my aunt asked."

Nora held out her hand in silent invitation and Hester took it.

"Two weeks before my due date, my aunt dropped me off at this church-run adoption center. I stayed in a dorm with other girls like me. All minors. We gave birth in secret, surrounded by strangers. As soon as they were born, our babies were given to their new moms and dads. I heard my baby cry. I caught a glimpse of her body as they wrapped her in a blanket. Her tiny head and dark hair. But I never saw her face. I'll never know if she got Elijah's brown eyes. The shade always reminded me of Fall. Acorns and caramel apples."

Hester gazed into the middle distance. She was no longer sitting in the Readers' Circle with her friends. She'd traveled back in time to that delivery room, to that fleeting glimpse of her newborn daughter. The memory was over twenty years old, but Hester could recall every detail as if she was there now.

Nora, June, and Estella wished they could ease Hester's pain. They wished someone had been there to comfort her when her baby was carried out of the room and out of her life.

"You're doing great, honey," June whispered.

Hester pointed at her empty martini glass. "Can I get that refill? It feels like my mouth's full of sand."

June was on her feet in an instant. "Anyone else?"

Nora and Estella politely refused. Minutes later, Hester had a fresh black-cherry martini. After two sips, she seemed fortified and ready to go on.

"When I told you this story before, I didn't talk about Elijah." She let his name linger for a moment. "I can't imagine what went through his head when I disappeared without a word. There was no way to contact him before I went to my aunt's. And after I left the adoption center, I was totally numb. I never told Elijah about the baby. I just tried to forget and move forward."

The others nodded in understanding. They'd all experienced a trauma-induced numbness.

"Did you go back home?" Estella asked.

Hester recoiled at the thought. "Never again. My aunt let me stay with her. She wasn't a nice person, but we got used to each other. She liked my cooking, and to my surprise, I liked cooking for her. After dinner, we'd read in the library. This was my favorite time of the day. By the time I finished college, I was closer to my aunt than I was to anyone else in my life."

Nora asked, "And Elijah? Did you ever cross paths?"

"There was no chance of that happening." Hester let out a

humorless laugh. "Elijah was a Mennonite. His world was his hometown, his farm, and his church. I wanted him to move on—to be happy—so I stayed out of his life."

June pointed at her. "You deserve happiness too. Write that on a sticky note and put it somewhere you'll see it every day."

"Do you have one?" Estella asked.

Catching the mischievous gleam in Estella's eyes, June reached over and stole the cherry from her glass. "Yes, I do. There's a Maya Angelou quote taped to my computer. It says, 'A wise woman wishes to be no one's enemy; a wise woman refuses to be anyone's victim.'"

"And what does a wise woman do when someone steals her cherry?" Estella demanded.

June wagged her finger in warning. "We are *not* going to talk about who took your cherry tonight."

Hester giggled, which eased the sense of heaviness in the room.

"Do you have more to say?" Nora asked. "Or are you ready to get out of the hot seat?"

"I am *so* done. Can we please focus on something else?"

Nora stood up. "Who wants to see the collection I bought from Meredith Comfort?"

June raised her hand. "Me! Sheldon won't shut up about The Haul. I want to see if it's all that—and a bag of salt and vinegar chips."

Nora led her friends to the stockroom and pointed at the bookcases hugging the back wall. "This collection belonged to Meredith's late mother. I still have two boxes to unpack, but the books are here."

"In all their glory," whispered Estella.

Hester made a beeline for the shelf of fairy-tale books. "These covers! The colors remind me of the marshmallows in Lucky Charms."

Nora waved at the shelves. "Have a closer look. They won't break."

Estella selected a copy of *Grimm's Fairy Tales*. The cover featured a young woman with long red hair. She turned to the list of illustrations and smiled. "Rapunzel was always my favorite. Big shocker, right? But I loved that her hair was strong enough to hold the weight of a man. It didn't matter that he was a prince. What mattered was that someone tried to lock her away, but she escaped. The key to her freedom was her own body. I thought that was so cool."

"I liked Hansel and Gretel," said June. "Gretel saved her brother *and* roasted that nasty witch like a turkey. That girl was fierce."

Hester pulled a copy of *Perrault's Fairy Tales* off the shelf. "I love them all. Except for *Peter Pan*. I thought Peter had a screw loose. Why would he want to be a kid forever? I couldn't wait to grow up. I couldn't wait to go to work and drive a car. And have my own house."

Estella returned her book to the shelf. Without looking at Hester, she said, "I guess Jasper's moving into your place, then."

"That's the plan. If he's still speaking to me." Hester turned to Nora. "These books are beautiful, but I'm too worn out to appreciate them. I'm going to head out."

Estella and June decided to leave too. Estella was eager to check on Jack, and June wanted to stop by the theater to see Tyson before calling it a night.

At the door, Nora hugged her friends. She held Hester a little longer—and a little tighter—than usual.

She knew she wouldn't be able to read with Hester's story echoing in her head, and she was too restless to be confined to her tiny house, so Nora carried her laptop to the stockroom and worked on pricing and cataloguing her acquisitions.

As she checked recent sales on eBay and Abe Books, she

considered creating a display encouraging customers to buy a beautiful book for their valentine. The books couldn't go in the window because people needed to see them up close, but neither could they be left on a table in the middle of the store. They needed to be handled with care, which meant keeping them away from mugs of coffee and chocolate-filled pastries.

The rare first-edition and signed books were displayed near the checkout counter, but that shelf was already full. She needed a small but unique bookcase. Something colorful and eye-catching to temporarily replace the spinner rack of bookmarks.

"If the flea market doesn't have something, I'll hit the thrift stores," Nora said, addressing the books in the stockroom.

Her gaze landed on the two boxes of shelf enhancers. She'd promised Sheldon that he could price and arrange the contents, but saw no harm in unwrapping the items and lining them up for him.

As she cut through tape and peeled off layers of Bubble Wrap, she silently berated Hester's family, conjured images of Elijah, and wondered what had become of Hester's baby.

Hester had never tried to find her child. She didn't think it would be a kindness to her daughter, or to her daughter's adoptive parents, to interfere in her life.

Nora was in no position to pass judgment on Hester's decision. After all, she'd put all the people from her former life into a mental box and pushed that box into the darkest corner of her mind.

Only one person had escaped that box. Roberta "Bobbie" Rabinowitz, Nora's college roommate, was a woman who played by her own rules. She'd tracked Nora to Miracle Springs and showed up on her doorstep with a bottle of wine. Nora had invited her in and the two friends had talked as if they'd never been apart. And though Bobbie had returned to New York, she was only a phone call away.

"I could use a dose of Bobbie right now," Nora told a Peter Rabbit figurine. "I should call her when . . ."

The rest of her thought dissipated as she stared down into the box. Removing Peter Rabbit had created a gap between the other objects.

And through that gap, Nora saw a book.

It had an oxblood cloth cover and was decorated with loops of barbed wire. Peering closer, Nora saw that it wasn't barbed wire, but a wild rosebush. A riot of thorns garlanded crooked branches. Here and there, a rose emerged from the tangle of thorns and leaves, with petals shaped like arrowheads.

Nora reached into the box to move the sphere-shaped object obscuring the book title, but when her fingers closed around it, she felt a sharp pain, as if she'd been stung by a wasp.

Realizing she'd just grabbed a pincushion, Nora jerked her hand out of the box. She saw a bead of blood welling on the tip of her thumb and swore under her breath. As she pressed tissue paper to her finger, she sat back on her heels and looked at the bookshelves. Staring at the row of fairy-tale books, she thought about stories with pricked fingers. All were dark. And violent.

And there was always a curse.

Nora snatched the Lady Artist book from the box and grabbed her coat. She locked up and, bracing herself against the cold, turned toward home.

As she crossed the parking lot, a couplet from *Macbeth* crept into her head: *By the pricking of my thumbs, Something wicked this way comes.*

Chapter 8

Nothing is swifter than a rumor.

—Horace

Nora leaned over her phone and said, "Bobbie, I've got another book problem."

Hearing a symphony of city noises in the background, Nora felt transported to another place and time.

Sirens wailed, someone called for a cab, and the ever-present honking of horns took her back to her college days. At the time, she couldn't imagine living anywhere else. Yet here she was, in a small Southern town that couldn't be more unlike Manhattan.

"Sorry!" Bobbie panted. "I had to get out of the wind. It's so damn cold. My lips are as blue as a Smurf and, I swear, there are tiny icicles hanging from my eyelashes. Oh, my Gawd! My phone is stuck to my gloves!" She laughed. "I just popped in the Strand. I can defrost while we talk. Did you mention books? Because this is an excellent place to talk about books. Am I right?"

Nora had Bobbie on speaker, and her friend's brassy, Brooklyn-accented voice surged into the room like a marching band.

An ache of longing spread in Nora's chest. Bobbie had es-

caped the cold by ducking into one of the most amazing bookstores in the world. The Strand. Six miles of books. Shelf after
shelf of glorious books. It had been one of Nora's favorite
haunts during her tenure as a New Yorker and she could picture herself meandering through the stacks as if she'd been
there yesterday.

"Bobbie, I have another book mystery."

"Music to my ears. Unless someone else left a grimoire on
your Welcome mat. In that case, you're better off calling a
priest."

Even though Bobbie couldn't see her, Nora shook her head.
"It's nothing like that. These books seem harmless."

"Ha! People say that about *The BFG* too—a book about a
giant who kidnaps a little girl and snacks on cats."

"I said they *seem* innocuous. And you know I love *The
BFG*, so leave him out of this. Let me tell you what's been
going on around here."

Bobbie listened closely as Nora told her about the man in the
orange coat and the book found in his pocket. Nora then described the book left at the Gingerbread House, as well as the
one she'd just discovered in the box of shelf enhancers that had
belonged to Meredith's mother.

"Wait a sec. The third Lady Artist book was part of this
woman's collection? And she was from Connecticut?" Bobbie
whistled. "That's pretty weird."

"Yeah. These books are showing up, out of the blue, in different places around town. And they've all appeared within the
last week or so. I feel like they're a message. But I don't know
what they're saying. Did this woman from Connecticut happen
to own one of these books? Or did someone put it in the box
for me to find?"

Bobbie said, "I can't answer those questions, but by this time
tomorrow, I'll know everything there is to know about the
Lady Artist series. In fact, I know the rare book guru of the

Strand. If he's around tonight, I bet he'd be glad to help. I'll also see what the chair of the English department has to say. Modernist lit is her specialty."

"It's good to have brilliant friends."

"Are you talking about me or the English chair?" Bobbie asked.

Nora smiled. "You, of course. Roberta Rabinowitz, Empress of Columbia University's Rare Book and Manuscript Library, Queen of Narnia, Princess Dragonrider of Pern, and—"

Bobbie cut her off by saying, "As of this morning, I have a *new* title. I'm officially a divorcée. The *bubbes* at my synagogue will be dining on this juicy tidbit for weeks."

"Oh, Bobbie. I'm sorry."

"Me too." Her sigh held decades' worth of grief and regret. "I'll be okay. Stan and I were very mature about the whole thing. The kids have been great too. I just never thought I'd be puttering around, alone, in the house we lived in as a family." Suddenly brightening, she said, "But I took your advice and rented the studio apartment to one of our visiting scholars. His name is Marcel and he's an astronomer from Oxford."

"Will you have him over for dinner?"

"He's coming on Wednesday. I've ordered a brisket and made an appointment to have my hair straightened and my eyebrows waxed."

Nora grinned. "My, my. If you're serving brisket, you must be into him."

"I didn't think I would be when we first met, but he's so interesting. These days, that's more important to me than a handsome face. A lively mind is sexier than a hot bod. And Marcel is a master conversationalist. He's smart, funny, and sophisticated. He's not a snob either. He's sweet."

"Maybe you should pull out all the stops and serve him chocolate-raspberry *babka*."

Bobbie shouted, "Not on your life! That *babka* is for emergencies only!" Lowering her voice, she said, "I'm getting shushed. Can you believe it?"

"You are the loudest librarian I've ever met. Don't ever change."

After promising to touch base when she had information about the books, Bobbie said good-bye.

In the silence that followed, Nora heard the wind rattle the trees outside her window. She'd felt chilly the whole time she'd been on the phone, so she took a hot shower. Even after wrapping herself in the knit blanket June had given her, she wasn't entirely warm.

"I can't get sick," she told the teakettle. "I just can't."

Twenty minutes later, she was asleep on the sofa. Her unfinished cup of chamomile tea sat on the table and Elmer Freeman's *Miss Rose* was splayed open on Nora's chest. It moved in time with her breath, rising and falling like a ship at sea.

The next day, Nora had a crick in her neck and bags under her eyes. Even though two cups of coffee did little to shake her fatigue, she dressed in jeans and her heaviest sweater and prepared to face the day. After retrieving the cash she kept inside the hollowed-out copy of *The Bonfire of the Vanities*, she pulled on every piece of outerwear she owned and drove to the flea market.

The parking lot in front of the renovated barn was almost full, and Nora chided herself for dawdling. She liked to be there when the doors first opened. This was her best chance to view the vendors' wares and do some bargaining.

It was now midmorning, and the aisles were clogged with strollers, wheelchairs, and locals who'd come to chat, not shop.

Just relax, she told herself.

She still had two boxes of shelf enhancers to price and put out for sale, so she wasn't desperate for inventory. For once, she could take her time browsing her favorite booths.

With Valentine's Day fast approaching, items featuring hearts or flowers were prevalent. Though Nora wasn't interested in Cupids, red roses, or lace doilies, she did want to buy a number of pink and red vintage curios for her shelves.

She'd barely entered the barn when she spotted a small red suitcase. To her delight, it was lined with red toile. The paper was stained in several places, but this didn't bother Nora because she planned to fill the case with red and pink books. She turned to the vendor and asked for his best price.

Because they expected their customers to haggle, the flea market vendors typically inflated their prices by 10 percent, which is why Nora never hesitated to ask for a discount. And when the suitcase vendor made her a fair offer, she accepted it, paid him in cash, and headed deeper into the barn.

The candle booth was always popular, but Nora was willing to wait her turn to sniff the newest scents because she knew she could sell anything this vendor made. Her candles came in Mason jars decorated with gingham ribbons. They burned evenly and were never overpowering.

"I have more strawberries and cream in the truck," the vendor said when Nora carried a box of red candles to the checkout area.

"I still have a few of those, thanks. Could I have a dozen rose water and a vanilla lotus blossom?"

While she waited for the vendor to tally her purchases, Nora picked up a candle called Candy Hearts and gave it a sniff.

"Doesn't that smell exactly like those little hearts with the words?" asked someone standing behind Nora.

Nora turned to see Jefferson Comfort asleep in a stroller. His nanny held its handle with one hand and raised a candle to her nose with the other. She shuddered and quickly replaced the lid.

"You might want to pass on this one," she whispered.

Nora pointed at Jefferson. "I wish I could sleep like that."

Lea smiled down at the little boy. "He was missing Mom and Dad last night. I read half the books in his room before he finally conked out. He was fussy when he woke up too, so I decided to get him out of the house. He loves coming here to see the wooden-puzzle guy. All of his puzzles have a marble trapped inside. Jefferson loves to turn them around and watch the marbles move. He must have six marble mazes already, but he'll get another one today."

"Do you know when Miles and Meredith will be back? I wanted to ask Meredith about something I found in one of her mom's boxes."

Lea pushed her glasses higher on her nose. Behind the thick frames, her eyes were golden-brown and wide set. With her smooth skin and heavy curtain of straight bangs, she looked like she could still be in high school.

"I don't know about Miles, because the schedule for the men's retreat is pretty vague. A weekend of bonding in the wilderness? That's so not my idea of fun. The women are staying at a B&B with amazing food and a spa. Smart." She tapped her temple. "Meredith should be home in time for Jefferson's dinner. She's catching a ride with a friend, so I won't know when to expect her until they're on the road. Should I ask her to call you tonight?"

Nora shook her head. "That's okay. It can wait until Monday."

Jefferson stirred in his stroller, and Lea put her finger to her lips and stage-whispered, "He needs to sleep a little longer. I've gotta go. Bye."

Nora paid for the candles and packed them in her red suitcase. She then headed across the aisle to see what treasures her favorite vendor had to offer.

"Was that the Comfort boy's nanny?" Bea asked by way of hello.

Bea knew most of the residents of Miracle Springs by sight,

and if she didn't, someone in her extensive family did. Nora didn't think of her as a gossip but as an information broker. Noteworthy news was a form of currency in her family, which meant Bea was always looking for a story to trump the ones her siblings or cousins shared during Sunday dinner.

Nora was fond of Bea. She was an honest, hardworking woman with a weathered face and brittle blond hair. When Nora had first moved to Miracle Springs, Bea was one of the few people who'd looked at her burn scars without flinching.

"It was," Nora said. "She and Jefferson come to the bookstore every week for storytime. He adores her."

"I've seen her with him. For such a young thing, she sure knows what she's about." Bea kept talking as she repositioned items on her table. "You might wonder why a pretty gal like that hides behind those glasses. She looks like Velma from *Scooby-Doo*. 'Course, Velma was the only one with brains in that bunch."

"I had a soft spot for Fred," Nora admitted.

Bea went on as if she hadn't spoken. "The last nanny was a real knockout. She turned heads wherever she went. Why would any woman invite a girl like that to live in her house? What's a coyote to do if you dangle a steak in front of his face?"

"Is Miles Comfort the coyote?"

Bea shrugged. "My mama used to say that it's easy to make a man happy. Keep 'em fed and keep 'em warm in bed. Anything else is gravy on their biscuits. That's true for most of them, but not all."

"Was there talk?" asked Nora. "About Miles and the nanny?"

As if she hadn't heard the question, Bea pointed at a cranberry glass vase with a ruffled rim. "This would look good on your shelf. I've got a whole box of glass. Wanna see?"

"Definitely."

Pleased, Bea bent down to retrieve a rubber bin from under the table. "It's wrapped up, so you might as well come around and look for yourself. Put the pieces you want next to the cookie jar."

Nora knew she wouldn't get more out of Bea until she committed to buying several items. Luckily, Bea had a wonderful eye, and it was a rare Sunday that Nora walked out of the flea market without having purchased something from her booth.

After selecting two bowls and four vases, Nora pushed the bin back under the table and returned to the customer side of the booth to examine the rest of Bea's wares. It didn't take her long to add an Art Deco flapper figurine, a heart-shaped powder jar with a silver lid, a heart-shaped hand mirror, brass lovebird bookends, and a pair of pink ballet slippers displayed in a shabby chic frame to her pile.

"You did okay," Bea said, flipping to a fresh page in her receipt pad.

Other than gathering intel, there was nothing Bea liked better than a robust haggling session.

Nora planned to give her both.

"I can't mark the cranberry glass much higher than what you've got on it, or it won't sell." Without taking her eyes off the pieces, Nora added, "I went to the Comforts' house the other night. Meredith asked me to take a look at her mother's book collection."

"Don't they live in one of those mansions near the lodge?"

Bea's casual tone didn't fool Nora. She was hooked, which meant she'd trade information. Nora wanted to learn more about Miles and Meredith Comfort than what she read about in the paper. Maybe she'd find a connection between them, the Lady Artist books, and the man who'd died on the mountain trail. She knew it was a stretch, but she had nothing to lose by hearing what Bea had to say.

"Is the new nanny livin' with them?" asked Bea.

Nora crossed her arms and said, "You haven't answered my question yet."

Bea dipped her chin and moved closer to Nora. "I'll repeat what I heard, but I have no idea if it's true. The word is that Miles got too close to the last nanny and Meredith found out. Folks say they saw the girl on a Wednesday, at the park with Jefferson. That Thursday, she was gone."

Nora went very still. "What do you mean, *gone*?"

"She went back to her people, I guess. She wasn't from around here."

"How old was she? Same age as Lea?"

Bea shrugged. "There about. We all thought Meredith would pick someone older the next time. A granny nanny. Guess she didn't."

"Do you remember the girl's name?"

"Candace." Bea gave Nora a quizzical look. "Why do you want to know about her?"

Nora watched the crowd for a moment before saying, "You heard about the man found on the trail?"

Bea's brows rose a centimeter. " 'Course."

"There was an old book in his pocket. A book about a lady painter. It's not the kind of book most men would own—let alone carry around in their coat pocket."

Nora told Bea about the other Lady Artist books, and where each book had mysteriously appeared.

"I'm trying to figure out if they mean something," she said. "I wouldn't be worried about Hester—or myself—if the first one hadn't been found on a dead man. That's why I'm asking about the Comforts, even though I like them. They seem like genuinely nice people, but even nice people have things to hide."

Bea surveyed her booth. Without looking at Nora, she said, "What I heard about Miles and the nanny isn't gospel, but since it's my turn to host the family tonight, I'll put the question to them. The whole clan'll be there. Somebody will know somethin'."

A man edged up to the booth, looked over the items on the middle table, and frowned. "Did you sell the cranberry glass vase?"

"Put your number on my receipt pad. Just in case I need it," Bea told Nora before walking over to the man. "I'm sorry, hon. Somebody bought it."

He held up a take-out cup. "That's what I get for going to the snack bar. I just can't resist those biscuits, but my wife would've loved that vase."

Bea's mouth curved into a cat-with-cream smile. "Those biscuits would tempt the devil himself. But we'll find a gift for your wife yet. I've got a few more pieces of cranberry glass under the table. Wanna see?"

Having written her cell number on the receipt pad, Nora waved at Bea.

Bea waved back without breaking eye contact with her customer. "It's a rare man who can shop for his wife. You know what's even rarer? A man who buys somethin' special for his mama. Valentine's Day is the time to remember who taught us about love in the first place."

Marveling over Bea's ability to upsell, Nora headed for the exit.

Outside, she strapped the suitcase to the rack on her moped, shouldered her backpack, and drove to Miracle Books. After depositing her purchases in the stockroom, she locked up the moped and went home to make lunch.

The contents of her pantry and fridge were a major disappointment. This was the case every Sunday because she'd gone through all of the food she'd bought for the week by now and needed to restock. Still, she didn't want to eat what she had left.

"Pathetic," she grumbled, reaching for a can of tomato soup and a package of crackers that were nearly, but not completely, stale. While she ate her unsatisfying lunch, she made a grocery list. Fantasizing about the delicious treat she'd have with her afternoon tea, she left her soup bowl in the sink and headed to the grocery store.

On the way, she conjured images of various baked goods. Croissants, madeleines, brownie bites, warm chocolate chip cookies, buttered rolls, two-bite fruit tarts with lemon curd—Nora wanted them all.

She'd just passed through the automatic doors when her phone rang. Sheriff McCabe's name appeared on her screen.

Feeling a twinge of guilt because she hadn't told him about *Miss Rose* yet, Nora answered by saying, "I was going to call you. You beat me to it."

"Oh, yeah? What's up?"

Stepping away from the doors, Nora moved to the relative quiet of the Florist section and told McCabe about the collection of books and shelf enhancers she'd bought from Meredith Comfort.

"It belonged to her late mother, who mostly collected books in a particular series rather than single titles. So when I found one of the Lady Artist books in a box of bookshelf décor, it bothered me. There were other books with Art Deco bindings in her collection, but none in that series. And I keep wondering, why was this one book packed with the figurines?" She paused for a moment before saying, "It still feels like these books are being used to convey a message. And I still have no clue what that message is."

"I'd like to see the book."

Nora looked down at the cellophane-wrapped bouquets. Her gaze landed on the roses. Unlike the flowers on Freeman's cover, these barely had any thorns.

"When?"

"Do you have dinner plans?"

As she scooted out of the way of another customer, Nora said, "No. Did you have a place in mind?"

"I know we usually go out, but how about coming to my house instead?"

Nora's cheeks grew warm. She and McCabe went to restaurants together. That was their thing. Even when she was dating Jed, she'd gone out to lunch with McCabe once or twice a month. Jed wasn't the jealous type, and he knew that Nora and the sheriff were just friends. That's what Nora had believed too, though she had to admit, there were times when she wasn't sure what they were.

There had been moments—brief, brilliant flashes—when sparks had danced between her and Grant McCabe.

She'd felt those sparks when she'd been close to him in the movie theater and again in the woods. She felt them when she heard his voice on the phone. Their friendship was turning into something else. The thread connecting them was shrinking in size, pulling them closer together with every encounter.

"That'd be nice," she said, feeling like a girl who'd been asked out for the first time. On impulse, she put a bouquet of white chrysanthemums in her cart. "Are you cooking?"

McCabe chuckled. "Yes, but don't worry, I have two working fire extinguishers . . ." Another phone rang in the background. "Can you hold for a sec?"

"Sure." Nora pushed her cart toward the bakery.

When McCabe came back on the line, he sounded like a different man. "I need to go. The Comforts' nanny was in an accident. Her car went off the road and into a ditch. Apparently, the car's in bad shape. EMTs are heading there now. So am I."

Nora stopped in front of the cake display, but she didn't notice the colorful confections. All she could see was Lea and a chubby-cheeked little boy, fast asleep in his stroller. "Was Jefferson in the car?"

"I'm afraid so," said McCabe.

After promising to call her later, he hung up.

The bakery clerk smiled at Nora and asked if she needed anything from the case.

She shook her head and kept walking. Aisle after aisle, she mindlessly added things to her cart. She couldn't stop worrying about Lea and Jefferson.

In the checkout line, she waited behind a mother of two. Her son was too mesmerized by the candy bars arranged next to the credit card machine to move, while her daughter sat in the front of the cart, swinging her legs and cramming pieces of dry cereal into her mouth.

Meeting Nora's eyes, she smiled and held out her snack container. "Elmo."

The little girl's dimpled cheeks reminded Nora of Jefferson Comfort. At the end of every storytime, he'd leave his spot on the carpet, cross the alphabet rug, and lay a hand on Sheldon's shoulder. Standing on his tiptoes, he'd whisper, "I wuv you."

Nora's throat tightened and tears came to her eyes.

He has to be okay. Lea has to be okay.

She turned to the magazine racks, but the smiling, airbrushed faces of celebrities offered no comfort.

At home, she unpacked her groceries, started a load of laundry, and sat at the kitchen table, waiting for the phone to ring.

Chapter 9

The best doctors in the world are Doctor Diet,
Doctor Quiet, and Doctor Merryman.

—Jonathan Swift

Around three in the afternoon, the rain started.

It lightly tap-danced on Nora's roof, keeping her company as she folded laundry. Thirty minutes later, as she was putting the kettle on for tea, the sound of the rain changed timbre. The spritely patter was replaced by a more forceful rhythm.

Sleet, Nora thought, turning to her kitchen window.

She watched ice pellets gather on the sill until her kettle whistled.

Her fingers had just closed around the handle when someone knocked on her door.

For a moment, Nora didn't move. She rarely had unexpected visitors. But then it dawned on her that whoever had come to see her in this weather was probably soaked to the skin, so she hurried to the front door.

Estella stood on the WELCOME mat, shivering in a too-thin raincoat. Her sneakers and jeans were damp, her hair was dripping, and her face was moon-pale.

"You must be freezing!" Nora pulled her friend inside and positioned her next to the woodstove. She helped her out of her coat and draped her throw blanket around her shoulders. "Sit on the sofa. I'll be right back."

Nora hung the sodden raincoat from a hook in her shower. She returned to the living room with a pair of clean socks and told Estella to kick off her shoes. She placed the shoes by the stove and added another piece of wood to the fire.

"I was about to have tea. Wanna join me?"

"Please," Estella answered in a small voice.

They didn't speak again until Nora carried a tray with two steaming mugs of tea and a plate of fudge shortbread cookies into the room.

Estella wrapped her hands around the warm mug and let the steam rise into her face. She was the picture of misery.

Nora adjusted the blanket around her friend's shoulders and waited for her to speak.

Estella took a tiny sip of tea and said, "Cinnamon?"

"Hot cinnamon. It'll warm you all the way down to your bones."

After a second sip, Estella made an appreciative noise. Then she lowered her mug and turned to Nora.

"Jack's in the hospital."

"What?"

Tears sprang into Estella's eyes and her chin quivered as she said, "You know Keisha, right? The day manager?" At Nora's nod, she continued. "She needed Jack to sign checks. The staff was fine with their pay being a day late, but three days was too long. Keisha wanted to show up at work tomorrow with everyone's checks in hand, which is why she decided to pop by Jack's place after church."

Nora tensed, fearing what Estella would say next.

"She rang the bell, but no one answered. Jack's car was in the drive and she knew he was sick. She tried calling me"—her voice began to hitch—"but I didn't pick up. She was worried because of how bad Jack had sounded on the phone the last time they talked, so she banged on the back door and peered in the kitchen windows. That's when she saw Jack. He was on the floor. And he didn't move, no matter how hard she hammered on the window."

"Oh, Lord."

Estella continued as if Nora hadn't spoken. "Keisha's husband was there. He kicked in the back door and tried to rouse Jack. But he was unconscious. They called an ambulance. And guess what I was doing while all of this was going on?"

Nora waited for Estella to answer her own question.

"I was cleaning out my closet. Yeah. I took everything out and spread it on the bed. I had my music on and was organizing things into piles. Keep or donate or whatever. It felt *so* good because I've been putting this off for way too long, but I was finally doing it. Keisha's over at Jack's, trying to tell me that he's in an ambulance, and I'm congratulating myself for sorting my clothes. My phone was dead. Of course. Five minutes after I plugged it in, I looked at the screen and . . ."

Nora took her friend's hand. "You drove to the hospital like a bat out of hell."

"Yeah. By the time I got there, I was shaking. I could barely say Jack's name when the woman at the info desk asked if I needed help. When she told me that he was in the ICU, I ran. I thought that if I could just get to him, he'd know I was there and everything would be okay. *He'd* be okay. How dumb is that?"

"It's not dumb. You were telling Jack that you loved him in the only way you could right then."

Tears slipped down Estella's cheeks as she nodded. "But it didn't matter how fast I got there. The ICU nurses wouldn't tell me *anything*. Just that he was being treated and I'd have to wait for the doctor. They also asked if I was family. The emergency contact on Jack's medical profile hasn't been updated for years. His sister's name is still on there."

"Jack has a sister?"

Estella pulled a face. "Yes, but you'd never know it. When Jack's parents got divorced, Jack's sister moved to California with their dad. Jack hasn't seen her since his dad's funeral. That was years ago. They haven't had much contact since then."

"That's sad."

Anger sparked in Estella's eyes. "I used to think so too, but Ishi—that's his sister's name—is mean to Jack. The last time they talked, she said that his business was an embarrassment to their family name."

"What? That's ridiculous."

"You know what's even more ridiculous? Ishi will hear what's wrong with Jack before I will! She probably couldn't pick him out of a crowd, but they'll call her first!"

Nora made a sympathetic noise. "So you waited for the doctor. Then what happened?"

"She said that Jack has a serious infection. They're giving him fluids and medicine and keeping him sedated. No visitors until tomorrow morning." Estella picked up her cup and gulped down the rest of her tea. "After I cancel my appointments and talk to Keisha about the diner, I'm going back to the hospital. I just needed to see a friend first. I needed to see you."

After giving Estella her best Sheldon-style bear hug, Nora brought their tea things into the kitchen. She'd just put the tray on the counter when her phone rang. Leaning over the screen, she frowned.

"Telemarketer?" asked Estella.

"Yep. I was hoping it was the sheriff."

Estella seized on the chance to focus on something else. "Calling to ask you out? On a real date?" When Nora averted her gaze, Estella gasped. "He already *did*. Tell me *everything*."

"We're supposed to have dinner tonight, but that's probably off now. Grant was called to the scene of an accident."

Nora hoped Estella wouldn't ask for details. Jack's illness already had her friend twisted up in knots. She didn't need to worry about Lea and Jefferson too.

"First there was Jed. Now the sheriff. You have a type, Nora." Estella smiled wryly. "I like a man in uniform as much as the next girl, but I'll stick to my sexy firemen calendars. The whole hero thing sounds great until an emergency ruins your plans for the umpteenth time. I'd rather date my accountant."

Nora grinned. "Bernie Winkler? He wouldn't last five minutes with you."

"Ha! That man's a firecracker. Most people celebrate their eightieth birthdays having cake with family or friends. Bernie spent his running a half marathon, and he's making plans to turn eighty-one on some mountain peak." Estella gestured at Nora's phone. "Getting back to your date with the sheriff— how did he make it clear that it was a date?"

"Usually, we go to lunch at Pearl's or another restaurant. We're always surrounded by people. But tonight Grant was going to cook me dinner at his place."

Estella raised her eyes to the ceiling. "It's about damned time. Everyone knows the man is smitten with you, but I guess he wanted to be sure you were over Jed." She cocked her head. "Are you over Jed?"

Nora nodded. "It took a little time, but yes."

Estella slid her hands under Nora's elbows. "Did you love him?"

"I cared about him. A lot. But I wasn't in love with him. He wasn't in love with me either."

"I liked Jed. We all did. But he always felt like an understudy." The corners of Estella's eyes crinkled. "I think your leading man is tired of waiting in the wings. He's ready to take center stage."

Nora laughed to cover her discomfort. There was no way she could think of Grant McCabe as her leading man. The thought of an intimate evening alone with him was unnerving enough.

"All the theater metaphors are a sign that I'm losing my mind and should get going." Estella glanced out the window. "The sleet's let up, so I'll make a break for it while I can."

Estella's jacket hadn't had time to dry, but at least it was no longer dripping. Nora carried it to the living room and held it out for Estella. She slipped it on and turned around.

"I hope the sheriff calls you soon."

Nora pulled Estella's hood over her head. "Will you be okay?"

"Yeah. But if anyone tries to keep me from seeing Jack, they're going to get a dose of the infamous Sadler temper. And if Jack's sister thinks she gets to be in charge of his care, I'll just have to tell her that my daddy's in the slammer for murder, and that I'm a chip off the old block."

Estella's anger, which had never been far from the surface, reignited.

As Nora pulled Estella in for a hug, she said, "Whatever's going on with Jack, you'll handle it. You can handle anything as long as you remember that you have friends who love you."

Not long after Estella disappeared into the gray gloom, McCabe called. Nora was almost afraid to answer the phone. She was shaken by Estella's news and wanted more time to process everything, but she couldn't ignore McCabe. She was worried about Lea and Jefferson. And for him too.

"How are you?" were the first words out of her mouth.

"I'm fine. So is little Jefferson."

Nora exhaled in relief.

"He's got some bumps and bruises, but they're minor," McCabe added.

"And Lea?"

McCabe waited a heartbeat before answering, which was enough to tell Nora that Lea hadn't been as fortunate as Jefferson.

"The ER doc says her head hit the side window pretty hard.

They're keeping her asleep while they run more scans. Her left arm is broken and she has a bunch of cuts from the shattered glass—none deep enough to require stitches. Meredith Comfort is with her. Miles took Jefferson home."

Nora couldn't imagine how terrifying it must have been for Miles and Meredith to hear that their son and his nanny had been in an accident while they were still miles away from home. Since they were on separate retreats, they weren't even together when they learned what had happened, but Nora had no doubt that they immediately raced to the hospital—fear coiling in their chests as they closed the distance between themselves and their child.

How they must have cried out in relief when they saw their little boy. After covering his cheeks with kisses, had they examined his bruises, gently touching his hands and face, his hair—even his small, socked feet? Nora could picture Meredith holding Jefferson, while Miles expressed their gratitude to the doctors and nurses.

"I'm glad Meredith stayed with Lea. How did she end up in that ditch, anyway?"

"At this point, it's unclear. Something made her lose control. Could be a deer shot out of the woods and spooked her. She swerved hard and couldn't regain control. The ditch was on the other side of the road, which is why Lea's side took the brunt of the impact. Jefferson was strapped in his car seat, nice and tight, in the back, right-side bucket seat. If not for some loose items bouncing off his legs, you wouldn't know he'd been in an accident."

"He must have been so scared," Nora whispered. "The crash would have been bad enough, but then Lea didn't say anything. He had to sit in his car seat until a stranger came and took him out."

"Luckily, he didn't have to wait long."

McCabe explained how a lodge employee was on his way

home from work when he heard the shriek of tires followed by a crash. He pulled behind the minivan, called 911, and did his best to comfort Jefferson until help came.

"Jefferson's young enough to forget all about this in a few months. The rest of us find other ways to cope. We distract ourselves. I usually watch TV and drink a beer or two. But tonight I'd rather be with you."

Warmth spread through Nora's core. "Then I'll be there."

When McCabe opened his door a few hours later, Nora presented him with a candle.

"There was a bow on it when I left my house. Guess it's somewhere on Main Street now," she said, stepping inside.

McCabe read the label on the Mason jar. "'The Wood Paneled Library. Smells like oak, old books, and masculinity.'" He laughed. "No one's ever given me a candle before. Thank you. I'll light it while I read books from your store."

Nora flushed with pleasure.

Unscrewing the lid, McCabe inhaled the scent of the cream-colored candle. "I wonder if it can mask the smell of cat food. But even if it does, I still have to fine you for littering."

"Oh, I'm sure we can work something out."

McCabe laughed again and took Nora's coat. "Tell you what. I'll give you community service instead. Your assignment is to pick out the wine."

In the kitchen, Nora found no evidence of cooking. There were no pots on the stove and the oven was off. The counters were clean, as was the sink. Puzzled, she asked, "What are we having?"

Looking sheepish, McCabe gestured at the table in the adjacent room. "I didn't have time to make the meal I had planned, so I hope you like charcuterie."

There were three cutting boards on the table. One held sliced meats, the second held cheese and crackers, and the third had a colorful array of berries, dried apricots, and sliced veggies. In addition to these boards, McCabe had placed small bowls filled with pickles, olives, nuts, hummus, and various condiments around the table.

Nora couldn't have been happier. The casual fare was more her style than a fancy, multicourse meal.

"It's perfect."

McCabe rewarded her with a warm smile, and when she said that beer would suit the meal better than wine, his smile broadened.

"You're making this too easy. It's been a while since I've . . ." He stopped and started again. "I've only had people from work over. We order pizza and watch the ballgame. Or we order pizza and play cards. That's why I wanted to make you something special."

"You did."

McCabe opened two bottles of craft beer. He knocked the neck of his bottle against Nora's and said, "Cheers."

As Nora titled her head to drink, she noticed an unoccupied cat tree in the living room. Pointing to it, she said, "Are your cats asleep?"

"Nah. They're probably sharpening their claws on my pillow. I promised them a piece of ham if they behave. I doubt they will, so have as much ham as you want."

They helped themselves to the items on the cutting board before passing the small bowls to each other. While they ate, Nora asked if Lea had shown any signs of coming around.

"Not yet, but her doc thinks it'll happen soon." McCabe touched his temple. "The swelling in her head is gone."

Nora said, "I hope that means she's out of danger. I was going to call Meredith tomorrow to ask her about the book I found with her mother's things, but after today, I can't. She must be beyond exhausted."

McCabe's gaze sharpened. "Where's the book now?"

"In my coat pocket."

It was clear that McCabe wanted to see it, so she pushed back her chair and walked to the coat closet. As her hand dipped into her pocket, she thought of the man in the orange coat. Had he put a Lady Artist book in his pocket because he meant to show it to someone?

In her brief absence, McCabe had removed their plates and wiped off the table.

"I didn't want to find out what you'd do if I got mustard on a book."

"I'm in no position to judge. Not when I almost bled on it." Holding out *Miss Rose*, Nora recounted how she'd pricked her finger on the antique pincushion.

"Another flower and another lady artist." McCabe sounded disheartened. "Could something be hidden in the binding? Or under a cover?"

Having already examined the book closely, Nora said, "I don't think so. The spine's loose. If there was anything hidden in the binding, we'd have seen it. As for the inside of the covers, they're smooth and the glue is intact."

McCabe began turning pages.

"No one's come looking for our John Doe. His prints aren't on file. He has no identifying features or possessions. All we have to go on are his clothes. The orange coat looks brand-new, but the rest of his clothes are comfortably worn. Gray pants, a dark blue shirt, cotton socks. Plus, the workman's boots. To me, two things don't quite fit with the rest. The orange coat and the book. And then there's what the ME said about his hair."

"Which was?"

McCabe laid a hand over the salt-and-pepper bristles on the crown of his head. "The scalp was irritated around here, and the hair in that area wasn't as healthy as the hair at the base of his neck. The ME's seen this before in men who wear hats on a daily basis for many years."

Nora thought about this for a moment. "Maybe his job called for boots and a hard hat."

"That's what we're concentrating on now," said McCabe. "Our John Doe isn't giving us much else. He's in his late thirties, wasn't wearing contacts, and never had a cavity filled. No tattoos or piercings either. He has more than his fair share of scars—most of which are on his hands. His hands are rough and calloused. Very little body fat. The guy was all lean muscle. He worked hard."

"And wore a hat."

Having paged through the book, McCabe closed it with a sigh. "I'd like to show this to Meredith on the off-chance it's connected to our John Doe. I'm guessing I'll see her before you do."

"I think so too," said Nora. "And if she doesn't know anything, there's still hope. I've asked the world's best book detective, aka Bobbie Rabinowitz, to do some digging."

McCabe chortled. "Bobbie! She burst into my office like she owned the place and told me exactly what she wanted. I knew I'd never get her out of there if I didn't agree to her demands. Has she always been such a force of nature?"

Nora shared a few anecdotes from her college days, which led to a story about McCabe's roommate from hell. They were both in stitches by the time he got up to fetch the dessert board.

"I didn't cook, but I'm hoping for bonus points for my presentation."

He set down a small cutting board covered with pieces of dark and white chocolate, carefully arranged in a checkerboard pattern.

Nora said, "It's beautiful."

"Better with wine, though. Don't you think?"

Before Nora could answer, McCabe's phone rang.

He pointed at the kitchen. "I should see if that's the hospital."

"Yes, go! I'll stuff myself with chocolate while you're not looking."

McCabe smiled sweetly and gave her hand a quick squeeze before hurrying into the kitchen.

From where she sat, Nora could hear McCabe's end of the conversation. She knew their date was over when he said, "Excellent. Is she clearheaded?"

She collected her coat and was waiting by the front door when McCabe ended the call.

"Lea's awake," he said, coming to stand close to Nora. "She told her doctor that it wasn't a deer that forced her off the road. It was another car. She remembers the make and model too. If we're lucky, we can track down the driver by the end of the night."

She smiled at him. "Then you'd better get going."

McCabe brushed her cheek with his knuckles. "I'm sorry—"

Nora silenced his apology with a kiss.

Chapter 10

Love is friendship set on fire.

—Jeremy Taylor

As Nora got ready for work that Monday, she replayed her kiss with Grant McCabe over and over.

It had surprised her. In the past, she'd waited for the man to make the first move. But she'd been undone by McCabe's crestfallen expression over having to cut their date short. It wasn't just the one look either. All night, whenever his mouth was occupied with other things, his eyes had smiled at her. The look made it plain that he delighted in her. It made her glow inside.

There was no way she could leave without kissing him.

It was a brief kiss, but full of promise.

It was a prelude.

When she pulled back, she saw the yearning in his eyes. And in his hands. His fingers reached forward, curling around empty air, before reluctantly falling to his side.

"Next time, I want to start off where we ended," he'd said.

Now, as Nora packed her lunch, her emotions swung from giddiness to uncertainty.

Am I ready for this? a tiny voice questioned.

Another shouted, *Hell yes!*

The voices continued battling as she prepped Miracle Books for the day.

She was changing a lightbulb when Sheldon bellowed, "Where are you, *bella dama*?"

Nora removed the lampshade in the reading nook dividing YA and Fantasy and called out, "Between *A Game of Thrones* and *Throne of Glass*."

She heard whispers. Then Sheldon said, "You'll never guess who came in for a dose of Doctor Sheldon's Magical Elixir."

It was Hester. Nora knew without looking. No one else perfumed the air with the scent of homemade dough and melted chocolate.

"Have you been baking on your day off?"

Hester brushed at a spot of flour on her jeans. "Just book pockets and teapot cookies. I asked Sheldon to pick them up so I could walk over with him. I knew he'd interrogate you the second he got here, and I want to hear you spill the tea."

"Spill the—"

Sheldon elbowed Hester aside and stood in front of Nora. "It's probably what the cool kids are saying on TicTac and Shatchat. It's not important."

The women giggled. Sheldon loved to create alternative names for social media platforms. He found it extremely amusing to ask the high school students if they were on Instascam or YouCube. The teens would roll their eyes and refuse to engage, but that didn't stop Sheldon from coming up with a new list of silly names every time he saw them.

Sheldon took Nora's hand and pulled her toward the ticket agent's booth. "Okay, boss. Hester will put the pastries away while I brew pots of liquid energy. Your job is to stand there and tell us about your date. We want details."

"How'd you know? Did you talk to Estella?"

Sheldon put a filter in the coffee machine. "She called Hester who called June who told me."

"She really called to tell us about Jack," added Hester. "She didn't bring up your secret rendezvous with the sheriff until the end."

"It wasn't secret," Nora muttered.

Hester put the last book pocket in the case and moved to the sink to wash her hands. "Estella said that McCabe might have to cancel, but he didn't. How do we know? Because even though it was cold enough to cure heartburn, June went out for a walk last night."

Nora shook her head in wonder. "I don't know how she does it. My teeth were chattering so hard that I thought I'd chip a tooth."

"Yeah, yeah. It was cold enough to freeze balls off a pool table. Now tell us about the date!" Sheldon commanded.

"Give Hester a hit of coffee first," said Nora.

Sheldon filled the NO SHELF CONTROL mug for Hester and the orange Penguin Books mug for Nora. After handing Hester a carton of half-and-half, he selected one of the newest additions to their wall of coffee mugs.

"I don't think you've seen this one yet," he said, showing the mug to Hester.

"The guy in the glasses looks like Freud." She read the mug's text aloud, "WHEN YOU SAY ONE THING BUT MEAN YOUR MOTHER."

Sheldon's booming laugh filled the ticket agent's booth. "Gets me every time!"

When everyone had doctored their coffee, Nora beckoned at Hester and Sheldon to follow her to the stockroom.

"Might as well work while we talk. Sheldon, we need to price the new goodies and decide what should go on the floor and what should be held back."

"This is my favorite part of the job," Sheldon told Hester. He was practically humming with excitement.

Hester said, "Do you even need caffeine?"

"Yes. For medicinal purposes." Seeing Hester's dubious

look, he said, "I'm serious. More bean juice equals less inflammation. Less inflammation means less pain, which gives me a fighting chance to get through the workday."

Hester was instantly contrite. "I never see you on your bad days, so I sometimes forget about them."

"That's because I hide in my room like a cave troll. It's not just the physical pain. I don't feel good on a cerebral or emotional level either. I can handle a little reading or a few hours of TV, but that's it. And whatever I watch has to be upbeat. Anything dark or overly complex makes me feel worse. If June's home, she'll sit with me for a bit and listen to me complain. Sometimes that's the best medicine of all."

It was shaping up to be one of those days when Sheldon's chronic pain couldn't touch him. He danced into the stockroom and made a beeline for the items Nora had already unwrapped. After a cursory examination, he set to work unpacking the rest of the contents from the open box.

Nora sat on a stool and began to explain how the date with McCabe had come about. She filled out price tags as she talked.

"A man who offers to cook for a woman is putting himself out there," Sheldon said. "That's not a standard first date. More like third or fourth. But since you two have been friends for *years*, inviting you over for a meal is Sheriff Smooth Operator's way of saying that he wants out of the friend zone."

"What did he cook?" asked Hester.

"He didn't cook. What he did, instead, was just perfect."

Nora explained why McCabe had created a charcuterie because he'd been short on time. When she got to the part about the accident, Sheldon froze.

"Lea and Jefferson?" he cried. "No! They're two of my story-time regulars!"

Hester looked shell-shocked. "They come to the bakery every Thursday too. I can't believe it! What happened? Please tell me Lea wasn't on her phone."

"She wasn't. Jasper didn't tell you anything about this?"

"We didn't talk yesterday."

Nora caught the shift in Hester's tone. Something was going on between her and Jasper, but her closed expression made it clear that she didn't want to talk about it.

"Our date came to a sudden end because McCabe needed to get to the hospital to see Lea. She told her doctor that someone ran her off the road—that there was no way she could have avoided going into the ditch."

Sheldon ran his hands down the front of his sweater vest. "*Mi amor*, you packed a week's worth of telenovela drama into one night. When's your next date? Can we buy tickets? I want a front-row seat."

Ignoring him, Nora turned to Hester. "I thought about visiting Lea after I close—assuming she's up for it. I want to give her an art book as a thank-you for recommending me to Meredith, but maybe I should wait."

"Why don't you call your man and ask his opinion? You can put the phone on speaker." Sheldon waved between himself and Hester. "We'll be super quiet. Promise."

Nora scowled. "He isn't *my* man."

"You're no fun. Okay, Hester. How about *your* man? He might know how long Lea has to be in the hospital."

Hester jumped to her feet. "I can't call him now. He's in the middle of something. I'm going to make a treat basket for Jefferson and his family. Nora, if you end up seeing Lea at home, let me know. You can deliver goodies for me."

Nora sensed that Hester's departure had less to do with making treats and more to do with her fiancé, but she couldn't let Hester dash off without telling her about *Miss Rose*.

"Before you go, see that box behind Sheldon? It was full of shelf enhancers and one book. I'd show it to you, but McCabe has it." Nora briefly described *Miss Rose*. "This is the third book in the same series to pop up in or close to town, and since you found *Miss Daffodil*, I thought you should know."

Hester gazed warily at the box. "What's with these books? Were they all part of this collection? Because if the books belonged to Meredith's mom, the Comforts must know something we don't. Why else would someone deliberately run their nanny off the road?"

Nora remembered what Bea had said about Jefferson's last nanny—how she'd been there one day and gone the next. Why had she left so abruptly?

When she told her friends what she'd heard at the flea market, Sheldon let out a groan.

"Why do people hire beautiful young girls to watch their kids? *Why?*" he spluttered. "How many marriages have gone up in flames because Daddy got it on with the nanny? Have some common sense, people. Don't hire Helen of Troy to change your baby's diapers. Hire Ursula the Sea Witch."

Nora grinned. "Bath time would definitely be interesting."

"I wish *I* had eight arms. My to-do list is so long. I'm going to grab my coat and head out." Hester pasted on a smile. "Thanks for the coffee."

Sheldon waited a few seconds before whispering, "She hasn't been her sweet, bubbly Anne of Avonlea self since she got engaged. I was ready to dazzle her with my *Princess Bride* wedding ideas when she first came in, but it's obviously not a good time to bring up the future groom's name."

"I bet lots of couples fight after the engagement. I mean, two individuals now have to figure out how to mesh their lives together. Where will they live? Whose stuff will go where? Will they share a bank account? And all the wedding planning and—"

"Stop! You're stressing me out."

Hearing footsteps in the hall, Nora put her finger to her lips.

"Hand over those price stickers," Sheldon demanded. "I want to get the cranberry glass on the floor before we open."

Hester didn't pause as she passed by the stockroom. She just waved and kept right on walking.

* * *

Soon after the back door slammed shut, Nora's phone rang. Seeing McCabe's number on the screen, she didn't hesitate to answer.

"Can I buy you a cup of coffee?" McCabe joked.

When McCabe was off duty, he'd often stop by Miracle Books and offer to buy Nora coffee. It was his way of saying that he'd like to sit and talk if she had the time. If she wasn't too busy to chat, she'd say, "Coffee's on the house," and join him in the Readers' Circle.

"Sheldon just brewed a fresh pot of rocket fuel. Are you on your way?"

"I'm already here."

When Nora opened the door, McCabe was partially hidden behind a big bouquet of flowers. The fluffy blue hydrangea and bright sunflowers smelled like springtime and looked like a summer sky.

"Because I ran out on you last night," he said, handing her the flowers. "And because you gave me something to smile about on the drive to the hospital."

Nora felt that shy teenager feeling again. Her face didn't used to flame when she saw McCabe, and she found it frustrating to have so little control over her body.

Since she couldn't think of anything to say, she buried her nose in the bouquet and inhaled the sweet perfume.

When she looked up, her eyes were bright with pleasure.

"They're beautiful. Blue and yellow is my favorite color combo."

McCabe took out his pocket notebook and flipped to a page. "That's not entirely accurate, Ms. Pennington. It's a mix of purples, blues, and yellows."

Stunned, Nora reached for the notebook. "What else do you have on me?"

"Are you attempting to assault an officer of the law?" Laughing, McCabe showed her the blank page he'd been pretending to read. "So. How about that coffee?"

When Sheldon saw Nora's bouquet, he whistled but refrained from teasing her.

"I'll put those in water for you," he said gallantly, taking the flowers and disappearing down the hall.

Nora poured coffee into a Batman mug with the text I'M NOT SAYING I'M BATMAN, I'M SAYING THAT NO ONE HAS EVER SEEN ME AND BATMAN IN THE SAME ROOM. After adding a splash of milk, she placed it on the pass-through window ledge and said, "Can I get you anything to eat?"

McCabe put a hand on his stomach. "No, thanks. I'm trying to keep my middle-aged spread from crossing state lines."

"Happens to the best of us," Nora said, patting her hips in commiseration.

Though she'd never said as much, Nora was more comfortable with McCabe's subtle paunch than she'd been with Jed's washboard abs. Jed was younger than Nora and far more active. Ever since she'd hit forty, her skin wasn't as taut as it used to be and her soft places had grown even softer.

These signs of aging hadn't bothered her until Jed came along. There were times when dating a man whose body looked like a Michelangelo sculpture amplified her insecurities.

McCabe was a few years older than Nora. His hair was peppered with silver and his face was etched with small lines. Women didn't cast admiring glances his way, as they had with Jed. Most people didn't see past his sheriff's uniform. It was rare for someone to really look at the man wearing it.

Nora had. She knew that McCabe had a crescent-shaped scar on his forehead from the time he'd slipped in the bathtub when he was a child and that his brown eyes revealed filaments of green and gold in the sunlight. She could trace a line from the small mole on his right cheek to the one on his earlobe and point out which tooth needed a cap after he'd chipped it on an ice cube. She'd seen him bearded and clean-shaven. She knew his facial hair was the color of aged pewter and coarser than the hair on his head, which was as soft as goose down.

Nora had seen Grant McCabe from the beginning, and she liked what she saw.

"How's Lea?" Nora asked him as she sat down.

McCabe took a sip of coffee and sighed in satisfaction. "Banged up, but okay. Her broken arm is being set and the swelling in her head is completely gone. Her scans are clear, and she had no problem telling me everything she could remember."

"Can you tell me what she saw?"

He snorted. "If it was in my budget, I'd take out a front-page ad asking people to keep an eye out for this truck. Ford pickups are a dime a dozen around here, but this one was *all* black. Not just the body—the wheels, grille, and front bumper were black too. Lea said that she knows cars and, to her, the truck was from the late eighties. It had a rectangular grille and a dented bumper."

Nora was astounded by the level of detail Lea had recalled. "What happened exactly?"

"Lea could see far enough ahead to get a sense of how fast the truck was coming down the mountain road. She was already leery of it before it reached her, but there was nothing she could do about it. There was no place to pull over or turn around, so she kept going."

Imagining that stretch of road, which was tree-lined and curvy with a very narrow shoulder, Nora said, "What a terrible feeling."

"I know. Poor kid. When the truck was less than two car lengths away, it crossed into her lane. She was left with two choices."

Nora imagined the bared teeth of the truck's grille rushing closer and closer, Lea's white-knuckled grip on the steering wheel, and the horrifying realization that there was no escape. She could either let the truck run into her or swerve so sharply that she'd end up in the ditch on the opposite side of the road.

"Talk about presence of mind. From where I'm sitting, Lea did all she could." Nora shook her head, clearing away the unnerving images. "Did she see the driver?"

"Just a glimpse of a man." Looking aggrieved, McCabe added, "He had a beard. And he was smiling."

Nora inhaled sharply.

"It's why she's so sure this was a deliberate act. The driver of that truck was going to hit her or force her off the road."

"What kind of person does that?"

McCabe grunted. "Lea doesn't think it was road rage. She never saw the truck before, and she hasn't done anything to incite so much as a honk from another driver since she started working for the Comforts."

"But can she really be sure? It would be hard to notice an all-black truck at night. Maybe she cut him off without meaning to or something like that."

"I wondered the same thing, but Lea avoids nighttime driving. She doesn't see well in the dark, but doesn't know why. She can't remember when she last had her eyes checked. I mentioned this to her doc and he said that someone from the eye clinic would evaluate Lea before she's discharged."

Nora didn't like to drive at night either. Because of the astigmatism in her left eye, headlights were too bright and star-shaped instead of round. Twenty years ago, it had been a minor annoyance, but her condition had worsened with age.

"How are Meredith and Miles doing?"

"When I showed up at their house at seven thirty this morning, they both looked worn out. I don't think they got much sleep last night. Neither of them remembers seeing a truck like the one Lea described."

Nora grabbed McCabe's arm. "I just realized something!

Lea was driving Meredith's van. What if the driver of that truck was gunning for Meredith?"

"I brought that up to Meredith, but she can't name a single enemy or think of anyone she'd offended or unintentionally angered. And even though she was upset, I went ahead and showed her the Lady Artist book before I left." He slipped on a pair of reading glasses and opened his notebook again. "'Meredith's mother lived in her Greenwich, Connecticut, house for fifty years and owned over a thousand books. Meredith was never much of a reader and would only recognize a handful of titles. Since her sister is more familiar with the collection, Meredith will ask if she remembers *Miss Rose* or any of the other books in the series.'"

While Nora debated whether she should mention the sudden departure of the previous nanny, Sheldon poked his head through the ticket agent's pass-through window and said, "Sorry to interrupt, but I can't find the Blind Date Book Bash flyers and Arlo wants to hang one up at work."

"Arlo's our favorite UPS driver," Nora explained to McCabe. Chewing her lip, she tried to remember if she'd left the flyers at the checkout counter or under the pile of books waiting to be moved into the window. Today was the day she and Sheldon had planned to switch out the movie-themed displays for an array of love themes—a task more easily accomplished when there were no customers.

As if sensing her shift in focus, McCabe stood up and placed his empty mug on the window ledge. "How many tickets are left?"

Sheldon said, "As of yesterday, ten. Tell your people to buy theirs before they're gone." Lowering his voice, he added, "Tell them they're welcome to bring handcuffs to the party."

"Traditional metal, plastic zip ties, or both?" McCabe asked without missing a beat. Over the sound of Sheldon's laughter, he said good-bye to Nora.

* * *

After McCabe had gone, Sheldon picked up the flower vase and said, "I'll start clearing the window if you want to work on the Love Over Forty display."

"We're not doing a—" Nora broke off and glared at him. "Oh, very funny."

In the stockroom, she sent Bea a text, asking if she'd learned anything more about the sudden departure of the Comforts' previous nanny. She then loaded books about young love onto a cart. As she took in the colorful covers of *The Sun Is Also a Star*, *Eleanor & Park*, *The Fault in Our Stars*, *To All the Boys I've Loved Before*, and *Simon vs. the Homo Sapiens Agenda*, she decided that a romantic display featuring mature couples was an excellent idea.

Nora's phone buzzed while she was adding picture books about love to the waterfall display in the Children's Corner. There was a new text message from Bea, and it was disappointingly short: **No one in my family knows why Candace left. I don't think the Comforts talked to anybody about what happened except their preacher. Maybe you can find the girl online. My cousin said her last name is Heikkinen. He works at the post office and is real good with names.**

Nora sent a quick reply thanking Bea and decided to do exactly as she suggested, but poking around online in search of Candace Heikkinen could wait. Right now, Nora was more interested in searching the Romance shelves for books with older couples. She had novels from Elin Hilderbrand and Jojo Moyes in her hand and was about to add a Kristen Ashley title to the stack when the sleigh bells rang.

A few minutes later, a man from Sheldon's book club approached the ticket agent's window.

"Tyler!" Sheldon cried. "You look like a human Popsicle."

"I should've worn my heavy coat." Tyler rubbed his hands together so fiercely that it looked like he was trying to start a fire. "Can I get a large Ernest Hemingway and a chocolate book pocket to go?"

The men chatted about the upcoming Blind Date Book Bash, and Nora smiled when Tyler told Sheldon that his book club was the highlight of his month.

"No one in our group expects me to be something I'm not," he said. "Can I tell you how refreshing that is? I mean, my parents want me to get married because they want to be grandparents. My boss wants me to be more of a team player. My roommate wants me to hit the gym and play poker with his buddies. Book club is the only time I can relax and be myself."

By this point, Nora had enough books for an endcap display. As she began swapping them for the books currently occupying the space, Sheldon called out, "I was only kidding about the over-forty thing."

Nora flashed him a smile. "But it's a good idea. Love isn't just for the young and beautiful."

Tyler pulled a face. "Tell that to the people who make the jewelry commercials. Man, I hate Valentine's Day! It's bad enough if you're not in a relationship, but it's the absolute worst for single men. Single women have the whole Galentine thing. They'll get together, eat some food, drink some drinks, and have fun. Where's the guy version of that?"

Sheldon nodded. "You're right. We need our own thing. We need . . . a Malentine's Day!"

"*Yes!*"

As he and Tyler exchanged fist bumps, Nora murmured, "Looks like I'm adding another display."

As the morning wore on, Sheldon steamed milk, poured coffee, and served pastries to a steady crowd of heat-seeking customers, while Nora put together a small Malentine's table of books featuring male friendships. So far, she'd selected *The Kite Runner, Brideshead Revisited, The Outsiders, A Separate Peace, The Song of Achilles,* and *The Nickel Boys.*

A woman carrying a stack of books approached the table. Taking a book off the top, she held it out to Nora. "You should add this one. If all men were forced to read this gem, the divorce rate would go way down."

Nora thanked her and found a place for *The Bromance Book Club* on the table.

By midafternoon, Miracle Books had become Julia Roberts from *Pretty Woman*—a breathtakingly beautiful woman in a red chiffon gown and white opera gloves.

As Nora took in all that she and Sheldon had accomplished, she felt a surge of pride.

"We definitely dialed up the romance today," said Sheldon. "The question is, can we compete with the jewelers, the chocolatiers, and the florists? Will our customers find what they need here?"

A slow smile crossed Nora's face. "A bookstore is the perfect place to fall in love again and again and again. Every day is Valentine's Day when you're surrounded by books."

Chapter 11

How many desolate creatures on the earth have learnt the simple dues of fellowship and social comfort, in a hospital.

—Elizabeth Barrett Browning

Nora finished her closing tasks and plopped down in a chair, hoping to catch up with Estella. When she didn't answer her phone, Nora sent her a text.

She repeated the same process with Bobbie.

Frowning at her phone, Nora thought about the random assortment of groceries she'd bought the day before and decided to order comfort food from the Pink Lady. On a cold Monday night, Jack's chicken parmigiana would hit the spot.

The phone rang three times before a woman answered.

"The Pink Lady, Keisha speaking."

Nora was surprised to hear Keisha's voice. As manager, she helped run the diner from her office behind the take-out counter, but she didn't work nights. When she'd interviewed for the job, Keisha had made it clear that she had to be waiting when her four kids got home from school.

Jack had never hired a night manager. He was always there for the dinner service and liked to fraternize with the customers when he wasn't cooking.

Nora placed her order and then asked after Jack.

"Nobody knows!" Keisha cried over the din in the background. "Hang on a sec. I can't talk out here."

A door slammed and the noise abruptly ceased.

Keisha said, "I'm in my office, digging around for Tylenol. I've got about a minute before I need to get back out there, so tell me, what's the news from Estella?"

"I haven't talked to her since yesterday. She told me how you found Jack. Thank God you did."

"But that was yesterday!" Keisha spluttered. "I sure as hell expected an update by now. Last night, Estella said that Jack had a real bad infection. He was sedated and they wouldn't let her see him. I figured she'd have spent all day camping out at that hospital."

Nora was sure that's exactly what she'd done. "I'd bet my store that she's there right now."

Keisha sucked in her breath. "Then it's gotta be real serious. Oh, Lord. I can't stand this. Jack is such a good man—one of the best I know. I'm going to call my cousin Jasmine. She's a nurse at that hospital. I wasn't going to get her involved because she just started working there, but I have no choice."

Before Nora could reply, someone yelled, "Keisha! We've got a situation. This guy's Visa keeps declining, but he says to keep trying. Says we'll make it work if we wanna get paid."

"Gotta go," Keisha said.

When Nora entered the diner ten minutes later, she saw Estella and Keisha standing together in the office doorway.

Without waiting for permission, Nora joined them.

"Hey, you," she said, placing a hand on Estella's back.

At Nora's touch, Estella visibly sagged.

Nora slid her arm around her friend's waist and wordlessly guided her into the office. When she was settled in a chair, Keisha stepped into the room and closed the door.

"I swear, this Monday is a week long," she said. "Anyone who likes Mondays is either retired or two sandwiches short of a picnic." Keisha fixed her gaze on Estella. "Have you eaten anything today?"

Estella flicked her wrist, a dismissive gesture. "I had a protein bar."

Keisha and Nora exchanged glances.

"I'll split my chicken with you. It's too much food for one person, especially with that salad and garlic bread. Can we eat in here, Keisha?"

"You sure can. I'll get some water and silverware."

As soon as Keisha left, Estella said, "I'm not hungry."

"You look like a gust of wind could knock you over. You need to get some food in your belly."

Estella responded in a flat, lifeless voice. "How can I eat when Jack's food is coming through a tube?"

Nora covered her friend's hand with hers. "Has there been any improvement?"

Estella shook her head. Her eyes were dull and ringed with black mascara smudges.

She's in shock, thought Nora.

Keisha returned, carrying a tray. She put the plates of food and glasses of water on her desk and pressed a fork into Estella's hand.

"You eat, or I'll tell Jack how you added to my worries by going on a hunger strike."

Nora waited until Estella started on her salad before turning to her own plate. She poked her fork through the molten melted cheese draped over the chicken. Steam escaped through the vents, so she tore off a piece of garlic bread and popped it in her mouth. The bread had a crisp crust and a soft, buttery middle, but Nora was too concerned about Estella to truly enjoy it.

"Is he still in the ICU?" she asked softly.

Estella twirled noodles around and around her fork. "Yes. He's hooked up to all these machines. I don't know what half of them are for. He has all these tubes and lines. It's like something from *The Matrix*. Monitors track his pulse, his breathing—I stare at the lines and try to understand what they mean. Everything makes noises. And he's there, in the middle of all of it."

"Did they tell you more about his infection?"

For the first time since Nora's arrival, Estella became animated. "They don't know exactly what's causing it, so they don't know exactly how to treat it. That's scary enough, but I have this feeling they're holding something back." She started sawing her chicken with her knife. "I can tell it's serious, but I don't know why. When people hear that I'm a hairstylist, most of them assume I'm dumb. Or that I'm not tough. They don't know that I grew up fending for myself. They look at me and see a woman who's good at hair and makeup. They think I grew up playing with Barbies instead of scrounging for food and fighting off my mom's boyfriends."

By this point, Estella had cut her chicken into tiny pieces, but her frenetic energy was far from spent. Releasing her knife and fork, she grabbed the garlic bread. As she started tearing it into chunks, the door swung open.

"June!" Nora shouted in relief. She didn't think she'd ever been so happy to see her.

June sent a smile Nora's way before walking over to Estella and wrapping her arms around her shoulders. "How you doing, baby?"

Estella's only response was to close her eyes.

"She's scared and frustrated," Nora said, gesturing at Keisha's chair.

June listened while Nora summarized all she'd been told. When Nora was done, June glanced from the phone on Keisha's desk to Estella.

"Do you have his doc's number?"

Estella gave her a confused look.

"Come on, woman. Snap out of it!" June's voice was like a

whip crack. "This is your man we're talking about! Don't you want to know what's happening? Are you going to be intimidated, or are you going to put up a fight?"

When Estella stammered something incoherent, June shouted, "What would you do for him?"

"Anything!" Estella shrieked, bolting to her feet.

June nodded. "Okay, then. Let's have that number."

Handing her phone to June, Estella pointed at her recent call list. June selected the number and put the phone on speaker. The call was answered by a woman who listened as June explained that she was calling for an update on Jack Nakamura's condition.

"Are you a family member?" the woman asked.

June replied in a saccharine-sweet tone. "I'm a close friend, but I'm here with Estella Sadler, Jack's partner. Mr. Nakamura's mother has passed. Estella is his family now."

After a lengthy pause, the woman said, "Ms. Sadler has been receiving regular updates about Mr. Nakamura's condition, so—"

"We were hoping to hear the most current update. I worked in an assisted-living facility for years and dealt with all kinds of illness, and I'd like to understand how a man in excellent health is suddenly so sick. Estella said he had a bad flu case. What is his condition right now?"

"Mr. Nakamura's flu developed into pneumonia and sepsis. Are you familiar with that condition?"

The woman's tone was becoming increasingly condescending, but June refused to be baited.

"Sepsis is how the body reacts to an infection. Usually, it's an extreme reaction. Is Jack breathing on his own?"

"He's intubated."

June stiffened. "What about seizures?"

"Two."

Seeing the fear in June's eyes, Estella's face drained of all color. "What does that mean? How bad is this? Is there a chance he could die?"

The woman said, "Unfortunately, that is a possible outcome. We're going to do all we can to help him fight this, but you should know that even if he does recover, he may never be the same. Sepsis can lead to long-term effects requiring rehabilitation. He may experience muscle weakness, insomnia, decreased cognitive function, organ dysfunction—it might be a long road. It's too early to tell at this point what will happen."

Despair swept over Estella. Nora hated how her friend seemed to shrink. She felt so powerless to help. This intense sense of powerlessness made her angry, and without thinking, she shot to her feet. Standing tall, her chin raised in defiance, she looked larger than life. And when she spoke, her voice was a mixture of softness and steel.

"I know Jack," she said, addressing the women in the room. She didn't care about the woman on the other end of the call. "He's healthy and strong. And he can be incredibly pigheaded. Do you know what that combination of traits means? It means he can fight this and win."

As if Nora hadn't spoken, Estella said, "It's my fault. He had a persistent fever. Chills. Excessive sleepiness and clammy skin. He wasn't getting better. I tried to get him to call his doctor, but he wouldn't! I was going to take him, and if I'd known his flu had turned into pneumonia . . ."

June quickly thanked the woman and hung up. Taking Estella's hand, she said, "Jack isn't sick because you're a beautician. He isn't sick because you're a small-business owner. He's sick because he let his flu get out of hand. He's a man, not a child. You cannot beat yourself up over this and you can't wear yourself out either. I think I know how to get you some help."

"What do you mean?"

"Tyson's girlfriend can check on Jack. Not only is this lovely young lady a nurse, she's also Keisha's cousin. I came here tonight to have dessert with Tyson and Jasmine. Keisha's out there now, explaining everything to her."

A few minutes later, a young woman cracked open the door and peered into the office. Catching sight of June, she entered the room. Tyson stepped in after her and shut the door.

"Hey, Mama," he said. "Hey, Ms. Nora. Ms. Estella."

June walked over to the young woman and put a hand on her shoulder. "Ladies, this is Jasmine Jones."

At first glance, Tyson and Jasmine seemed like a mismatched couple. He was tall and lean while Jasmine was short and curvy. Tyson's eyes and skin were dark brown. His hair was close-cropped. Jasmine's eyes were peridot green and she had fawn-colored skin. Her braided hair was swept up into a thick bun, and as she slipped her arm around Tyson's waist, the top of her bun kissed the bottom of his chin. He smiled down at her with a mixture of tenderness and pride, but her attention was fixed on Estella.

"Keisha told me about Mr. Nakamura," she said. "He's in good hands, I can tell you that. And I'll check on him every shift."

Estella's eyes lit up with hope. "You don't know what this means to me. Thank you."

June turned to Jasmine. "I know you won't to do anything to put your job at risk, and I also know that Estella will drive straight to the hospital as soon as we're done here. Will she be able to see Jack?"

"I think so, but only for a few minutes. Visiting hours will be over soon," said Jasmine. "Since you'll probably be visiting a lot, it wouldn't hurt to bring something to the nurses. Everybody loves pie. I'll call the floor and let them know a friend of mine is coming in with treats."

"I'll buy all the pie the diner has! Thanks again." Estella kissed Jasmine on the cheek and hurried out of the office.

After Tyson and Jasmine said their good-byes, they also left.

"We should go too," Nora said to June.

She nodded. "You read my mind."

Ten minutes later, Nora and June were on the highway in a silent car. The radio was off and neither woman felt like talking. After a while, Nora said, "We should call Hester."

"If she answers, I'll put her on the car speaker so we can both talk to her."

June pushed a button on her steering wheel and issued a verbal command to call Hester's cell phone.

Hester picked up right away. "I'm on the other line with Jasper. They think they found the truck that forced Lea off the road. Hold on. Let me tell him to call me back when he knows for sure."

Nora looked out her window to where the asphalt gave way to grass. It was too dark to see the ditch that ran parallel to the highway.

"It *is* the truck," Hester said, her voice shrill with excitement. "It's a big pickup with a crew cab. Half of the sheriff's department is checking it out. Guess where they are?"

June said, "I'm in my car and Nora's with me. If you tell us where the truck is, we'll tell you why we're on the highway right now."

"What?" After a brief pause, Hester said, "The truck's at the train station. It was parked next to an RV, and whoever checked the lot the first time didn't see it. The sheriff walked around the whole lot on foot, so he spotted it. Okay, your turn."

June glanced at Nora. "Go on. I'll focus on driving."

"We're following Estella to the hospital. She's in her car with a boxload of pies."

Nora described the scene in Keisha's office. She barely had the chance to finish when Hester exploded.

"That woman sounds like my brother—that judgmental, self-centered, stuck-up bastard!" she snarled. "Even when he was in high school, he'd talk down to women. Waitresses, flight attendants, grocery store clerks. He'd talk trash about anyone who didn't own a jock and a set of golf clubs."

The venom in her tone surged through the speaker. Nora wasn't sure why Hester was so focused on her brother, but she had no idea how to respond. Apparently, neither did June.

Hester saved them the trouble by saying, "Sorry. I'm such a mess these days. I should be in the car with you. I've been too wrapped up in my own stuff lately. You, June, and Estella are my best friends. I want to help."

June shook her head. "Honey, you get up before dawn. There's no sense in your driving to the hospital when we don't even know if Estella will be able to see Jack or for how long. I'll call you when we get there, okay?"

"Okay."

Hester sounded so dejected that Nora had to say something to make her feel better. "Hester? You're allowed to be wrapped up in your own stuff. You could sail to the other side of the world and we'd be here, waiting. We're the lights at the end of your dock. We're the Daisy Buchanan to your Jay Gatsby."

"Thanks, Nora."

After Hester hung up, June said, "She still hasn't told Jasper, has she?"

Nora looked out the window at the pinpricks of light coming from a farmhouse perched atop a dark hill. "No, I don't think she has."

Eager to change the subject, she asked how Tyson and Jasmine had met. June was more than happy to talk about her son and the goings-on at Oscar's Theater. When those topics were covered, she grilled Nora about her date with McCabe.

By the time the hospital sign came into view, they were exchanging theories on how *Miss Rose* ended up in the box in Nora's stockroom.

"Anyone could have stuck it in there," June said, pulling into the parking garage. "It's not like you and Sheldon follow your customers to the restroom. Is the stockroom ever locked?"

Nora said that it wasn't.

"You don't worry about shoplifting?"

"No. Most of the new releases are in sealed boxes until their sale date, and if someone goes in there to steal back stock, they could shove a book or two in a bag, under their shirt, or down their pants. But most people wouldn't bother. Did you know that back when I was a librarian, the Bible and the *Guinness World Records* were stolen more than all other books?"

June snorted as she pulled into a spot and killed the engine. "The Bible? Guess those folks didn't know about the Ten Commandments."

"Do you know which book people steal the most from my shop? It's *The Book Thief.*"

"No!" June's shout bounced off the walls of the parking garage.

Heads bent and shoulders hunched, the two women made their way into the hospital. They found Estella sitting in the ICU waiting area, her face hidden in her hands. Her muffled sobs were heartbreaking.

"Oh, Estella," Nora whispered, putting an arm around her friend's quivering back.

June yanked tissues from the wall dispenser and sat down next to Estella. She leaned over, lightly pressing her shoulder to Estella's shoulder.

"We're here, honey. We're right here."

Estella raised her head. Her face was wet and puffy. Red blotches had bloomed on her neck and cheeks.

"What good am I to him? All I can do is talk to him and hold his hand."

"He needs that from you," Nora said, her vision blurring with tears. "The medicine, the doctors and nurses—they'll treat his body. But his heart? It's only going to listen to one person. You. You're the person who loves him the most. No matter what you see or don't see, he can hear you. He can feel the touch of your hand."

June was crying too. Her chin trembled as she said, "I know what we need to do now."

She pulled Estella and Nora to their feet. Then she opened her arms, gathered them in close, and lowered her head.

As June began to pray, Nora closed her eyes and tightened her hold on her friends.

In this intimate huddle, they found comfort.

Chapter 12

Human society, the world, and the whole of
mankind is to be found in the alphabet.

—Victor Hugo

The next morning, Nora saw that she'd missed calls from Bobbie and McCabe. She'd muted her phone at the Pink Lady and had left it that way for the rest of the night.

Bobbie had also sent a text: **Where are you? I have info on your mystery books.**

Nora carried a mug of coffee to her kitchen table, booted up her laptop, and called Bobbie.

"It's about time!" Bobbie bellowed. "Do you know how much I wish you still lived in the city? I'd love to drop by your apartment with a bottle of wine and some Thai takeout. I'd love to meet up for coffee and a massive book-buying session. Just think of all the things we'd be doing if you were here."

"I wish we lived closer too," Nora said. "Why don't you take early retirement and move to Miracle Springs? We could run the bookshop together."

Bobbie groaned. "Don't tempt me. I have a budget meeting this afternoon. I was supposed to make cuts, but I'm asking for more money instead."

"You'll get it too. You could sell water to a drowning man."

Bobbie chuckled. "My dad used to say that I could sell ham at a Bar Mitzvah."

Their mingled laughter erased the distance between them. They could have been back in college, talking late into the night about everything and anything.

"If you ever want to get away, you know I'd love to see you. You could book the same room at the Inn of Mist and Roses," said Nora. "But we can talk about that later. What'd you dig up on the Lady Artist books?"

"First of all, I want you to be impressed by my thoroughness. I talked to not one, not two, but *three* experts. I can practically write a dissertation on gender roles in Modernist literature, women who wrote under male pseudonyms, and female characters in American literature from Reconstruction to the Interwar period."

Nora was confused. "What about the connection to British lit? The characters and setting are British."

"My decisions to focus on the American aspect has nothing to do with the content of the books and everything to do with the cover design." After pausing to let this sink in, Bobbie said, "How many different Lady Artist covers have you seen?"

Nora said, "Three up close. Online, I'd say four or five."

"When you say up close, what do you mean? Did you hold the books in your hand? Did you use a magnifying glass or a jeweler's loupe?"

Nora picked up her coffee mug, saw that it was empty, and frowned. "I looked at them with my eyes only. No magnifying tools. Why? What did I miss?"

"Now we're at the fun part." Bobbie was positively giddy. "It wasn't until I cornered a devilishly charming art history professor and author of multiple books on Art Nouveau that I learned that certain book designers from this time period added symbols to their covers. With one exception, these artists were all men. Wanna guess the exception?"

"The designer of Elmer Freeman's books?"

"Bingo! Her name was Sadie Strong. Sadie and her sister, Sarah, started off working for Tiffany Studios. They helped create some of his most famous stained-glass designs."

Recalling the *Miss Daffodil* cover, Nora said, "The flowers on the covers seemed familiar. Is it because they're based on Tiffany glass designs?"

"Yep. Sadie's floral motifs were her signature. She designed dozens of books, and having seen at least fifty photographs of those covers during a three-hour dinner with the same devilishly charming professor, I could now pick a Sadie Strong book cover from a pile of random Art Nouveau covers."

"Three hours? How many courses *was* this dinner?"

Bobbie laughed again, and it occurred to Nora that her friend was even more bubbly and boisterous than usual. "Well, it started out as drinks after work. Simon—that's the professor—wanted to hear the whole story about these old books and where they were popping up in your town, and I figured it wouldn't hurt to tell him." There was a smile in her voice as she added, "Hell, who am I kidding? I wanted to tell him. I also wanted him to do plenty of talking because he's from England, and you know I go weak in the knees for a posh British accent."

"Doesn't everyone?" Nora quipped. "So drinks led to dinner, which led to dessert, which led to . . . ?"

"A digestif and a second date. Simon's taking me to a Renoir exhibit on Thursday and we've tentatively scheduled dinner at Le Coucou on Saturday. Everyone at the library is worried. They think I should take it slow, but I don't. Getting hurt doesn't scare me. Being lonely does. What do you think?"

Nora didn't hesitate. "You're happy, so I think you should go for it. I also think you should tell me more about Simon. That'll have to wait until later because I have to get ready for work now."

"But not before I remind you to get your hands on those Lady Artist books and search the cover for tiny symbols or letters. They'll be camouflaged somehow—in a scroll, a column, or inside one of the flowers. Find them, write them down, and text them to me. Simon and I will work on tracking down the other books in this series. Together we'll decode Sadie Strong's secret message."

"And hope that it will somehow explain why one of the books she designed was found on a dead man."

When she arrived at Miracle Books, Nora called McCabe.

"Why does Sunday feel like it happened a year ago?" he asked after saying hello.

"That's probably how long it's been since either of us had a decent night's sleep."

McCabe listened while she told him about Jack. She shared how hard it was to witness Estella's anguish and her concern for the Pink Lady's employees.

Nora could hear herself rambling, but the way McCabe listened made her want to let everything out. Even over the phone, she could tell that she had his undivided attention. He wasn't shuffling papers or tapping computer keys. His silence wasn't static. It was attentive. He broke it only when he felt it was the right moment for an encouraging noise.

"Enough about me. How are you?"

"Fine. But I'd be better than fine if I could see you today."

Nora smiled. "How about lunch? I don't have time to go to a restaurant, because Sheldon and I have more prep to do for Saturday's party, but we could have sandwiches in your office or hide out in my stockroom."

"I need to stay at my desk because I'm waiting for a call on the owner of the black truck left at the train station, so if you could come here, it'd make my day."

"I'm in, as long as you repeat that last bit in your best Clint Eastwood voice."

McCabe's imitation of Eastwood was spot on, and they were both laughing when someone called the sheriff's name, bringing an end to the conversation.

When Sheldon arrived, he was carrying three bakery boxes instead of two.

"Hester made us a treat," he said.

"How did she seem to you? Her bright and bubbly self? Or was she a little down?"

Sheldon pursed his lips. "Neither. You know that look some of our customers get when a noise suddenly pulls them out of the book they're reading? They're all dazed and confused from straddling two worlds. Hester was like that this morning. I felt like her body was going through the motions in the bakery, but her mind?" He gestured toward the front of the shop and whistled. "It's somewhere else."

Nora untied the string wound around the small bakery box. "Even in a distracted state, she can bake circles around anyone I know. Let's see what she sent us."

Nestled inside the box were a pair of heart-shaped puff pastries drizzled with icing.

Sheldon peered over Nora's shoulder. "She has boxes for Estella and June too. I guess she knew you ladies needed a hit of comfort this morning."

"Does that mean both of these beauties are mine?"

Folding his arms over his chest, Sheldon said, "Only if you plan on walking to the gas station for coffee."

Nora grimaced. "No, no. Here, pick the one you want."

Sheldon deliberated for so long that Nora turned and walked off.

"*Mi amor*, come back! I shouldn't tease you after last night. I'm making the coffee right now and—ohhhh! Nora? Hester put a surprise inside this heart. Don't you want to see if yours has one too?"

Nora did, so she returned to the ticket agent's booth, picked up the remaining pastry, and bit into it. An explosion of tart berries, airy dough, and sugary glaze coated her tongue. She chewed, moaning in pleasure, and looked at the purple jelly threatening to spill out of her pastry onto her sweater.

"Mine's blackberry jam."

Sheldon licked his fingers and said, "Mine *was* lemon curd and raspberry. I would have showed you, but I couldn't control myself."

"I told Grant that I'd bring sandwiches to his office today, but I'll be having salad. I've been eating like I'm about to hibernate."

Rubbing circles over his soft belly, Sheldon said, "I'm just becoming more huggable. And if I could hibernate until April, I absolutely would. I love reading in bed, watching TV in bed, sleeping in bed—but I *hate* getting out of it. I asked June if she'd empty my bedpan if I bought one. She was *not* amused."

"I can't imagine why." Nora grabbed two mugs from the pegboard and passed them to Sheldon. "Let's fuel up and start wrapping our Blind Date books."

Surrounded by books, brown craft paper, and skeins of pink and red yarn, Nora and Sheldon wrapped and labeled hardcovers and paperbacks from every section in the store. Initially they hadn't planned on using any children's books, but when Nora showed Gary Paulsen's *Crush* to Sheldon, he agreed that there wasn't a person on the RSVP list who wouldn't get a kick out of the main character's antics.

When the books were wrapped and labeled with intentionally vague clues, Nora unlocked the front door to a trio of middle-aged men.

"We need help," said the man with glasses.

The man in the black overcoat said, "We need gifts."

The man with the dimpled chin gestured at the red suitcase display. "For our wives."

"For Valentine's Day?" Nora asked.

"Yes," the men answered in unison.

"I'm Nick," said the man in glasses. "And these are my friends Samir and Johan. We've gotten Valentine's Day wrong for the last ten years, and we vowed to get it right this year."

"We've bought them jewelry, flowers, and candy without putting much thought into it," said Samir.

Johan shrugged. "We're all works in progress, but we feel pretty good about ditching all the stuff we see in commercials and doing things our own way this year."

"Yep. We're giving our wives a day off from taking care of us, the kids, the pets, and the house." Nick smiled at his friends. "We got together and decided that breakfast in bed, some books, and a gift certificate to Magnolia Spa for some pampering would be much better than a dozen roses."

Nora had to agree. "Why don't you gentlemen order some coffee and we can all sit down and talk about your wives' reading taste?"

The men followed her back to the ticket agent's booth. While they waited for Sheldon to prepare their drinks, Nora asked them to describe their wives' book preferences. Luckily, this was a question they were ready to answer.

Johan said, "Historical romance and nonfiction."

"Classics and retellings of classics," said Nick.

Samir was studying all the mugs on the pegboard and didn't realize it was his turn until Nick elbowed him. "Sorry, but I've never seen that many mugs in one place. Nadia mostly reads women's fiction and contemporary romance—she loves a good rom-com."

"You're making this too easy," Nora teased.

For Johan's wife, she selected Shaun Usher's compilation of love letters written by famous people. In addition to *Letters of Note: Love*, Nora selected Ada Calhoun's *Wedding Toasts I'll Never Give*. After adding two historical romances, Judith Mc-Naught's *Whitney, My Love* and *Chasing Cassandra* by Lisa Kleypas, Nora delivered the stack to Johan.

"There's a chance your wife has read some of these, but I'll make sure to put gift receipts in each book. That way, she can make an exchange the next time she stops in."

Johan said, "I'll take all of them. Do you gift wrap? Because I'm terrible at it."

Sheldon leaned out of the pass-through window. "We have brown paper and ribbon in the back. I could give you a quick lesson if you want."

The four men headed to the stockroom, and Nora walked to the display of classic romances near the register. For Nick's spouse, she selected Georgette Heyer's *The Grand Sophy* and the Chiltern Classic edition of *Pride and Prejudice* from the table. She added two excellent retellings, Ibi Zoboi's *Pride* and *Ayesha at Last* by Uzma Jalaluddin.

For Samir's wife, Nora picked Talia Hibbert's *Get a Life, Chloe Brown*, Sophie Kinsella's *Surprise Me*, Beth O'Leary's *The Switch*, and Katherine Center's *Things You Save in a Fire*.

By the time Sheldon finished showing the men how to wrap their books, a line had formed at the ticket agent's booth. Nora was steaming milk for a cappuccino when the three men stopped by the window to thank her for her help.

Nick raised his voice to be sure Nora could hear over the gurgle of the steam wand. "When we get back to the office, we're going to tell our coworkers to skip the flowers and chocolate and come here instead. *This* is what real customer service looks like!"

It wasn't until later that Nora realized she hadn't charged the three men for their books. She quickly searched the register log, but there were no sales from around the time they left the shop.

She had to wait for Sheldon to deliver tea and a book pocket to a woman in the Readers' Circle before she could follow him into the ticket agent's booth and whisper, "Please tell me you charged the three guys who were in earlier, because I didn't."

Sheldon was taken aback. "You know I make everyone pay before I even pick out a mug."

"I'm not talking about the drinks. I'm talking about the books."

"Ohhhhh." Sheldon's eyes rounded. "Did they seriously stiff us?"

Nora passed her hands over her face. "Maybe it was an accident. I could just call over to their office—did they mention where they work?"

Sheldon shook his head. "And I've never seen them before. They might not live around here."

Staring at the wall of mugs, Nora began to calculate the total cost of the books, bookmarks, and shelf enhancers the men had carried off.

"Okay, okay!" Sheldon cried. "I can't keep up the ruse when you've got that 'my dog ran away' expression."

He pulled a group of neatly folded bills from his apron pocket. "They didn't stiff us, *mi amor*. They paid in cash and insisted on adding a generous tip. You can use yours on salad. I'm going to treat myself to an afternoon movie and a tub of buttered popcorn."

Accepting the cash, Nora said, "How sweet."

Sheldon put his hand over his heart. "I am, aren't I?"

"You're a piece of work!" Nora grabbed a dishrag and snapped it. The damp end struck Sheldon on the rump.

"Ow! Quit abusing me and get your lunch. If I leave exactly at three, I won't miss a minute of previews."

Nora tossed the dishrag in the sink. "What are you seeing?"

"*Death on the Nile*. I've loved Kenneth Branagh ever since *Chariots of Fire*."

"I liked him in *Henry V* and *Wallander*."

Sheldon made a shooing motion. "Go. We can compare notes about Ken when you get back."

Miracle Springs had limited options when it came to salads or sandwiches, but the deli department at the grocery store had recently expanded to include a decent salad bar and a sandwich station.

After ordering an Italian sub for McCabe, Nora loaded a take-out container with several kinds of lettuce and lots of raw veggies. She added pumpkin seeds and a hard-boiled egg for protein, grabbed a packet of balsamic dressing, and put the container in her basket, along with two bottles of orange seltzer water.

Ten minutes later, she entered the brick building housing the sheriff's department and checked in with the baby-faced desk sergeant. Though she was probably the same age as Lea, she looked like a young girl playing dress up.

"Is the Miracle Springs Sheriff's Department hiring kids straight out of middle school now?" Nora asked as she stepped into McCabe's office.

For a moment, McCabe was puzzled. Then he said, "Sergeant Lassiter must be working the desk. She *is* young, but, boy, does she have a way with our K9 officer. She has lots of ideas about fund-raisers and PR campaigns too. The Luddites are protesting, but I bet she wins them over by Easter."

"I understand why they're resisting," Nora grumbled. "I don't even like updating my website, let alone Instagram. And now, Sheldon wants us to get involved with BookTok."

McCabe was stacking papers on his worktable to make room for their lunch, but he stopped to say, "Am I that old? Because I have no idea what that is."

Glancing around the disheveled office, Nora could see that McCabe had more important things to think about, so she raised a new subject while unpacking the food.

"I talked to Bobbie this morning. She had news about the Lady Artist books."

McCabe held up the container of salad. "Is this yours?"

Hearing mild apprehension in his voice, she laughed. "I was channeling my inner Hobbit and had second breakfast today, so I only need a light lunch. The Italian sub is yours."

"My favorite." McCabe smiled at her with his eyes. He held the look until a loud rumbling came from his stomach.

Nora grinned. "You obviously didn't have second breakfast, and I hate to keep you from your lunch, but is there any chance you have a magnifying glass?"

McCabe went behind his desk and opened a drawer. When he returned to the table, he handed Nora an LED-light magnifying sheet and asked her to repeat her conversation with Bobbie.

Nora was dying to examine the book covers, but guessed that McCabe had eaten breakfast close to sunrise, if he'd eaten at all. Judging by the wrinkles in his uniform and the thick stubble darkening the lower half of his face, he was practically living in this room.

Over the years, Nora had seen McCabe rock a mustache, a full beard, or go completely clean-shaven. But today's five o'clock shadow appealed to her most. His fifty-year-old jaw-line looked chiseled and his close-cropped salt-and-pepper hair gave him an air of rugged, well-seasoned distinction.

Turning her attention to her food before McCabe caught her staring, Nora drizzled a package of balsamic vinaigrette over her salad and recounted her phone call with Bobbie.

"Are the letters hidden in the cover some kind of code? Or do they spell a specific word?" he asked.

Nora knew that he was mostly talking to himself, but she'd asked herself the same questions and was more than ready to find some answers.

She cleared away their trash, while McCabe relocated their drinks, spread a large sheet of white paper over one end of the table, and handed Nora a pair of exam gloves. With these things done, he fetched the three books. Each one was zipped inside a plastic evidence bag.

He removed *Miss Daffodil* from the evidence bag and set it down on the paper. Next he turned on the magnifying sheet's LED lights and placed the sheet over the book cover.

"I'll take the right side if you'll take the left," he said.

Nora scooted her chair closer to his and lowered her elbows to the table. With her chin resting in her hands, she examined the cover. She started at the top corner and worked her way down to the bottom corner. Centimeter by centimeter, she looked for a symbol in the curve of every scroll, the lines of every column, and the delicate curls of leaf and stem. The shadows in the flower petals kept tricking her into thinking she'd found something, but she scrutinized her side three times over without success.

McCabe sat back with a frown. "I've got nothing. Is Bobbie sure about this?"

"She knows more about books than anyone I've met. And what she doesn't know, she can find out from an expert on the subject. She consulted an expert on book designers from this time period and—"

The rest of Nora's sentence drifted away as one of the daffodil bells suddenly caught her eye. She cocked her head, staring hard at the little flower. The difference was minute, but this flower was unlike the others.

McCabe put a hand on her forearm. "You're smiling. Is it my company, or did you find a symbol?"

"Both. But I also remembered how much I loved *Highlights* magazine when I was a kid. It was my job to get the mail after school, and when that magazine showed up in the mailbox, I'd run straight to my room and put on a record. I'd sharpen a pencil to a fine point, flop on my bed, and turn to the hidden-picture puzzle. When I found everything, I'd do the Spot the Difference puzzle next. This book cover is just like those puzzles. One of the flowers is different from the rest. If you look right in the center of this daffodil, you can see a shape."

Nora pointed at the second flower from the left. Peering at it, McCabe said, "Looks like a capital *R*."

"I think so too."

McCabe was still holding her arm. "Anything else?"

When Nora shook her head, McCabe swapped out *Miss Daffodil* for *Miss Delphinium*. It was even more challenging to locate the hidden letter on this cover because it was tucked in a shadowy space between a flower spur and stalk.

"First an *R*. Now a *D*." McCabe jotted the letters in his notepad and reached for the third book.

"Okay, *Miss Rose*. What've you got for us?"

This cover was busier than the previous two. It took twice as long for Nora to point out what she thought might be a letter. "It's hard to tell because it's in the middle of those brambles. What do you think?"

McCabe leaned in, squinted, and let out a frustrated sigh. He then increased the magnification and tried again. "I spy the letter *I*."

"This gives us *R*, *I*, *D*," said Nora.

McCabe looked at her. "I'm glad it's a *D* and not a *P*."

"Why?" Nora was nonplussed. Why did one letter matter

over another? They had only three of a total of eight letters. With five missing letters, there was no telling what the final word might be.

Tapping his notepad with the end of his pen, McCabe shrugged and said, "Call me superstitious, but it would bother me if we ended our lunch date with an *R-I-P*."

Chapter 13

Small towns are like metronomes; with the slightest
flick, the beat changes.

—Mitch Albom

Having placed the three books back in their plastic evidence bags, McCabe stood, staring at them.

When a roar of laughter in the hall brought him out of his trance, he turned to Nora and said, "There are eight books in the series, so we need five more letters. Once we find those, we'll have to figure out which eight-letter words they spell. You any good at those kinds of puzzles?"

Nora shrugged a shoulder. "I'm not bad, but I can't hold a candle to Estella. She's a word puzzle whiz. Scrabble, Boggle, crosswords, the jumble in the daily paper—you name it. The distraction would be good for her too. It would give her a break from worrying about Jack."

"She's worried about him, and you're worried about her. It's a tough situation. Have you heard from her today?"

"I called earlier, but she didn't pick up. I'll try again on my way back to the shop," Nora said. "And if I have any downtime, I'll search for images of the other covers."

McCabe responded with an absent nod, his gaze wandering to the whiteboard attached to the back wall. Several photos taken the day John Doe's body had been found were taped to the left side of the board. There were also photos of his clothes and an overhead shot of his face. His eyes were closed, and his mouth was expressionless. He almost looked serene, as if it had been his decision to lie down on the cold metal table and grab a quick nap.

"We've been calling him Austen," McCabe said.

"After the city?" Nora asked, assuming the stranger had had a connection to Texas.

McCabe waved at the bag containing *Miss Daffodil* and grinned. "After Jane Austen. One of the guys who'd helped recover the body was describing the book to a rookie who hadn't been there. He heard him say, 'The only thing he had on him was this old, girly-type book. One of those English books with lots of tea parties and strolling around in gardens.'"

"Did the rookie get the Jane Austen reference?"

McCabe chuckled. "Nope. And when the veteran officer realized this, he said, 'Son, if you want to impress the ladies, you need to learn about Jane Austen real quick.'"

"Sounds like a smart man."

"He's been married for thirty years, so he's doing something right." McCabe rolled up the white paper he'd spread over the table and got to his feet. As he picked up the bagged books and turned toward his desk, the end of the paper roll knocked a file folder off the table. Glossy photos of a black pickup truck skittered across the carpet.

"Damn," McCabe muttered.

Nora said, "No worries. I've got it."

The photos were all of the truck that had plowed into Lea. Nora studied a series of shots focusing on the truck's damaged hood, grille, right headlight, and bumper. The damage wasn't serious, but the long scratches and paint loss made it clear that the truck had scraped the side of Meredith's minivan in the driver's fervor to send the van careening into a ditch.

"After looking at these, I feel like it's a miracle that Jefferson wasn't hurt," she told McCabe.

She picked up the last two photos off the floor. The first was a side view of the truck. Its blacked-out rims reminded Nora of an insect. Something with an elongated abdomen, like a black beetle or ant. The second photo was a close-up of the truck's license plate.

McCabe said, "As you can see, our hit-and-run driver is from the Keystone State."

"Do you have an ID?"

"We got the owner's name from the VIN number, but we can't say if the owner was involved in the crash or if someone else was driving the truck. We found several sets of prints on the dashboard and steering wheel, but since they aren't in the national database, they're not very helpful. As for other trace evidence, like fibers, hair, or soil, I can't order a range of expensive tests until we rule out the owner. The last round of budget cuts might send us back to the Stone Age."

Leaving the folder on the table, McCabe returned the bagged books to the shelf behind his desk. Noting the time, Nora got ready to leave.

McCabe walked her to his door, but didn't reach for the handle. Instead, he began to button Nora's coat.

"You said that some book designers hid letters or symbols in their covers, but it wasn't the norm. And if I'm remembering this right, you also said there weren't many well-known female designers in the beginning of the twentieth century." At Nora's nod, he went on. "What else do you know about the woman who did the Lady Artist covers?"

"Almost nothing. But I'll have a better answer for you tonight because I have Bobbie." She smiled. "And you have me."

McCabe pushed the last button through the buttonhole. He then slid his hands up her coat to her lapels and stepped closer to Nora. Close enough to kiss.

Nora wrapped her hands around his wrists and looked into his eyes. The warm light she saw there was like a flashlight beam shining out from a dark forest, offering safety and warmth. It was the glow of windows at night. The bliss of knowing that someone was waiting up for you. In that light, Nora envisioned a future with Grant McCabe. Of happy homecomings and nights reading by the fire.

His uniform shirt smelled of coffee, but his exhalations were scented with peppermint. The idea that he meant to kiss her before she left sent a current of heat through Nora's body.

One of McCabe's hands slid up her neck, his fingers tiptoeing along her hairline.

"Thanks for coming," he said. Then his voice dropped to a whisper. "I already know that this'll be the highlight of my day."

Nora's reply was cut off by a succession of quick knocks on McCabe's door.

McCabe steered Nora away from the door before saying, "Come in."

There were two people in the hall, but only Deputy Andrews entered. The other person didn't move.

"Hester!"

Nora hadn't meant to raise her voice, but she was surprised to see her friend away from the Gingerbread House during business hours.

Hester took a step forward and smiled at Nora. "Are you wondering why I'm not at the bakery?"

"Just a bit, yes."

"I had to close early. Plumbing issues in the restroom." She held up her hands. "Don't worry, I won't go into details. But it gave me an excuse to have a desk picnic with Jasper. Now I'm going to the hospital. I have treats for the nurses and some high protein snacks for Estella. She isn't eating enough."

Andrews cast an apologetic glance at Nora and handed a sheaf of papers to the sheriff. "Sorry to interrupt."

Nora waved this off. "You didn't. I have to get back to work."

McCabe put a hand on Nora's arm. "Call me if you find more letters." He then looked over her shoulder at Hester. "Has Jack's condition changed at all?"

Hester had to move into the office to make room for a delivery-man transporting a watercooler dispenser. He called out a friendly "Hey there, Sheriff!" as he passed by. McCabe returned the greeting.

When the merry jingle of the keys hanging from the man's belt receded, Hester answered McCabe's question.

"Jack's in a medically-induced coma. From what I was told, being unconscious will help his body put up its best fight." She pressed her palm to her chest. "His lungs aren't working like they should because of the pneumonia, and he's on oxygen because he can't breathe well enough on his own. They're trying different antibiotics to fight the infection, but it could be days before he responds."

McCabe's eyes filled with sympathy. "Jack's a good man. I hate that he's going through this, but he's tough. He might not look it, but he's got the kind of quiet strength and grit that the rest of us aspire to. I believe he'll beat this thing, no matter how long it takes."

"I wish Estella had heard that. She needs all the hope she can get."

Seeing that Hester was on the verge of tears, Nora said, "You'll tell her, and that'll be just as good. I need to get going, so—"

"Wait. You forgot your phone." McCabe hurried over to the table to retrieve it. He placed it in the bowl of her hand and closed her fingers around it. His lingering touch conveyed many things at once. It said "Good-bye" and "Have a great rest of your day" and "I like being with you." It conveyed a desire to see her again, as soon as possible.

Nora had never been comfortable with public displays of affection. She was perfectly fine with other people demonstrating their affection, but it wasn't something she did. Maybe it was because her parents always said that only attention seekers behaved that way. She couldn't say exactly why, but McCabe's brief hand squeeze made her feel shy and a little awkward.

As Nora headed for the exit, Hester fell into step beside her. She didn't say a word as they walked, and Nora was so caught up in her own thoughts that she didn't notice her friend's silence until they'd reached the main doors. Before stepping outside, Nora turned to say good-bye to Hester. For a moment, she was struck dumb by what she saw.

Hester's face was pale as marble. Her eyes were vacant. She didn't seem to notice that Nora hadn't opened the door. It was as if she'd gone somewhere else, leaving her body behind.

"You look like you're going to pass out! Let's sit down for a minute."

She cupped Hester's elbow, and Hester startled like a frightened pony.

"I'm fine!" she shouted as she burst through the door.

Stunned, Nora didn't react right away, and by the time she made it to the sidewalk, there was no sign of a blonde in a red peacoat.

Hester had disappeared.

On her way back to Miracle Books, Nora tried to guess what had shocked Hester so deeply. How could her reality have shifted in the space of a few minutes?

Nora tried to recall every detail from the time the deliveryman had passed by McCabe's office to the moment she and Hester had left.

Hester had gotten emotional after telling McCabe about Jack, but that wasn't unusual. After all, Hester was an empathetic person. She cried over books, movies, and commercials. News or true crime programs upset her.

Hester's tendency to wear her heart on her sleeve might be considered a weakness to some, but not to Nora. In her mind, Hester's compassion was her superpower. It was the reason Hester was able to send a customer back in time by baking them a customized scone. Guided by instinct, she'd add ingredients to her basic scone mix and put the dough in the oven. Twenty minutes later, she'd serve the warm pastry to her customer.

"Waiting for them to take that first bite is hard," she'd once told the other members of the Secret, Book, and Scone Society. "I never know if the scone will take them back to a cherished memory—or to one they'd rather forget. I always watch them. If their faces light up when they start chewing, I know the flavors brought up a happy memory. If they look crushed, then I feel terrible. I'll spend the rest of the day wondering if I should have used different ingredients."

June's gift was her way with words. After listening to Hester, she'd said, "What if you didn't make a mistake? What if that person needed to revisit that moment because it was still causing them pain? What if they walked out of your bakery and started thinking about ways to heal? Maybe they owed someone an apology. Maybe they needed to grant forgiveness. If a scone convinces them to do the hard work, then they've got better days ahead."

A single tear had raced down Hester's cheek as she smiled in gratitude. Nora had felt grateful too. When it came to friends, she'd hit the jackpot.

If talking about Jack didn't shake Hester to the core, then what did?

Nora remembered how she'd been ready to leave, but had been stopped by McCabe. He'd gone back to the table where they'd eaten lunch to get her phone. If Hester turned to follow the sheriff's movement, she would have seen the array of photos taped to the whiteboard.

Which photo sucker punched her?

A slideshow of images began in Nora's mind. The dead man's clothes. The overhead shot of his face. The Elmer Freeman book. She doubted a stranger's clothes could provoke such an intense reaction, which left *Miss Delphinium* and the death portrait of a stranger.

What if he's not a stranger to Hester? What if she knows him, or she's somehow connected to the Lady Artist books?

Of course, that would mean Hester had lied about the book found in her bakery. She'd told everyone that a customer had left it behind. She'd said that people were always leaving things on her little café tables, like magazines, car keys, or grocery lists. But if *Miss Daffodil* had been left at the bakery on purpose, then it was meant to deliver a message.

"*The Scarlet Letter*," Nora muttered as she opened the back door and slipped inside Miracle Books.

She came face-to-face with Sheldon, who'd been heading outside to toss a bag of trash in the Dumpster.

"Sorry I took so long. I can take that out." Nora gestured for him to hand her the bag.

Ignoring her offer, he said, "You don't look like a woman fresh from being ravished. I thought lunch with the sheriff would have put a twinkle in your eye and a bloom on your cheeks, but you look like you just dropped your ice cream in a puddle."

Nora jerked her thumb toward the end of the hall. "How busy are we?"

"Steady but calm. The elementary school moms and kids should start showing up in the next twenty minutes or so. Why?"

"Come to the front when you can, and I'll tell you everything."

Nora had to pause her narrative twice to ring up customers, but by the time she was done, Sheldon grabbed a stool and dropped down onto it.

"Why would anyone give Hester the Scarlet Letter treatment? She hasn't messed around with a man of the cloth or cheated on her husband. She's all sweetness and light. A grownup Ingalls girl."

Sheldon wasn't privy to Hester's most closely guarded secret, but even if he learned all the painful details of her teenage pregnancy, Nora didn't think his high opinion of Hester would change one bit. He was old enough to know that a person is so much more than their biggest mistake, and he knew a beautiful soul when he saw one.

"Is the jerk who sliced and diced our paperbacks the same jerk who left the old book at the bakery?" he asked.

"Hester's the only common denominator that I can think of." Nora glanced out the window. "You should have seen her today. She reminded me of a tornado survivor who returns to their house to find that it's nothing but a pile of rubble. That's how Hester looked. Completely shell-shocked. Then she bolted. I didn't see which way she ran, or I would've gone after her. She was in no condition to drive."

As he often did when he was distressed, Sheldon began to smooth the silver hairs of his mustache. After repeating the movement for the seventh time, he said, "Hester, Estella, Jack. It feels like our little family is falling apart. Are you going to tell the sheriff that something in his office triggered her?"

Nora shook her head. "Hester's my friend. I need to find out what's going on with her before I say a word. She's scared and needs help. Jasper would do anything to keep her safe, but she isn't confiding in him."

"Well, that's it, then—time for an intervention. Call June. Call Estella. Make a plan. I'll hold down the fort."

Nora threw her arms around him. "I know you're the king of bear hugs, but this time, I want to give *you* one."

That night, the members of the Secret, Book, and Scone Society met for dinner at the Pink Lady. It wasn't the best place to have an intimate conversation, but Estella wouldn't go anywhere else.

Her group text message said: **Jack would want me to make sure everything's running smoothly. And I need to convince Keisha to put someone in charge of the dinner shift. She can't keep pulling ten-hour shifts.**

Nora wrote back: **What about you? You can't run a business, drive back and forth to the hospital, and check on the diner every night. You'll be burned out by the end of the week.**

I'll be fine. See you at seven, Estella replied.

After closing that night, Nora stayed at the bookstore to search for images of book covers from the Lady Artist series. She became so absorbed in the task that her friends were already seated when she showed up at the Pink Lady.

She was able to hang up her coat before a server came over to take their orders. After he wrote everything down, he read what he'd written out loud and promised to be back with their drinks "quicker than a dog can lick a dish."

The women hadn't heard this idiom before, but they found it charming. This led to a discussion on other quirky phrases that meant *quick*.

"Just how long are two shakes of a lamb's tail, anyway?" June asked at one point. "Less than a second? I bet the blink of an eye is quicker."

The server returned with their drinks. His tray held the iced teas they'd ordered and a bottle of Chardonnay as well. While the hostess distributed wineglasses, their server placed the bottle in front of Estella. "Compliments of the Bradshaws. You and Jack have their prayers and support."

Estella swiveled in her seat to blow a kiss at an elderly couple sitting in the middle of the diner. When she turned around again, she was smiling. She poured wine into all four glasses and then raised hers in a toast. "To good people."

"And to Jack," her friends added in unison.

It wasn't long before the server returned with their food.

They'd all ordered a soup-and-salad combo, and as the aromas of chicken and lime tortilla soup and honey-drizzled corn bread wafted through the air, Nora could almost imagine that it was summertime.

Food can evoke so many emotions, she thought, glancing at Hester.

Again she wondered what Hester had seen in McCabe's office. She seemed off tonight. Like she had to remember to smile and to participate in the conversation. Her gaze was distant, and Nora had a feeling her mind was also miles away.

When June started talking about Saturday's Blind Date Book Bash, Nora was sure Hester would become animated. She loved planning her outfits for upcoming events.

"I can't decide what to wear," June said. "Part of me wants to go all out. Put on a red dress and get my hair done. The other part of me wants to wear jeans and a sweater."

"Do both," suggested Estella. "Get your hair done and add some sparkle to your makeup. Didn't you buy a shimmer highlighter stick in December? It's time to bust that out. Put on that red lipstick and wear heels with that jeans-and-sweater combo. What's the official dress code, Nora?"

"Casual. At least that's what we put on the invitations. I don't care if people come in yoga pants. I just want them to have a good time. I'm wearing jeans and a sweater."

Estella grinned at her over the rim of her wineglass. "And heels?"

Nora pulled a face. "Not a chance. You know I have to wear my pink Chuck Taylors. I like the idea of shimmery makeup, but the only kind of highlighter I own is neon yellow."

"That's because you spent years trying *not* to draw attention to your face. You need to get over that. When my life goes back to normal, I'm going to show you a few tricks. We'll have a makeup and pajama party at my house. It'll be like that scene from *Grease.* We'll eat candy and chips and—"

"There's no going back," Hester whispered.

June cupped her ear. "What'd you say, honey?"

Hester turned to Nora. In a voice too world-weary for her age, she said, "Go on. Ask me."

"When you looked at McCabe's board, did you recognize the dead man?"

At the other tables, people continued to eat and drink. The diner was filled with the murmur of voices, the clink of flatware, the movement of servers, and the occasional rumble of laughter.

The cacophony amplified the sudden silence at the corner booth.

Nora stared at Hester, willing her to answer.

Hester bent her head and opened her mouth. When she spoke, each word was a ship's anchor, crashing through the water's surface.

"A long time ago, he was my everything."

Chapter 14

*You can't go back and change the beginning, but you
can start where you are and change the ending.*
                                            —C. S. Lewis

Nora suggested they continue the conversation at Miracle
Books, so the women settled their bill and headed to the bookstore.

They stood in the ticket agent's office while Nora brewed a
pot of decaf. When the coffee was ready, the women filled their
mugs and took their usual seats in the Readers' Circle.

Then they waited for Hester to speak.

"The man in the photo was Elijah," she began. "He was my
everything. And I never told him why I left." She looked at
Nora. "I did what you did. I left it all in the past."

"After your parents took you to live with your aunt, that
was it? You never reached out to him?"

Hester shook her head. "I don't know anything about his
life. I think about him sometimes. I've been thinking about him
more since Jasper proposed."

She looked down at her left hand, where her ring painted her
skin with glimmers of candlelight. Then she slid the ring off her
finger and dropped it in her palm.

"I never told Jasper the truth. It's too late now. They'll connect Elijah to that black truck, if they haven't already, and the second Jasper says his name to me, I'm going to fall apart. I can't listen while the man I love profiles the man I used to love."

Though Hester wasn't crying, waves of grief rolled off her. The candlelight cast long shadows on her face and turned her blue eyes into black pools. Her back and shoulders curved in despair.

June squeezed Hester's arm. "Right now, this feels too big to handle. Let's break it down into smaller pieces, so we know what we can do to help. First of all, did Elijah come to Miracle Springs to see you?"

"I don't know. He wouldn't have any reason to look for me, unless . . ."

Seeing that she was unable to continue, Estella said, "He learned about his daughter."

Hester nodded.

"Did he ever call you or write a letter? Has a man ever made you do a double-take because he reminded you of Elijah?"

Hester turned her dull gaze on Estella. "Never. He's been on my mind because I knew I had to tell Jasper about him, and also because Jasper said that it was an all-black truck that forced Lea off the road."

"Did Elijah drive a black pickup when you were together?" asked Nora.

"Remember how I told you that Elijah was a Mennonite? His sect allowed cars, but they couldn't be flashy. That's why everyone in his community had a black car. Most cars are made with shiny metal parts. Some people thought that was flashy, so they'd cover those parts with black paint. When Jasper said there was an all-black truck with Pennsylvania plates parked at the train station, I thought of Elijah. But it was just a memory.

I didn't think it was really his truck, especially since the man they'd found in the woods wore a neon-orange coat. That's way too flashy for someone from Elijah's community."

The other women quietly processed this information.

"But Elijah didn't try to kill Lea with that truck, so who did?" June's eyes suddenly flew open. "Could it have been your daughter?"

"I don't know!" Hester was angry. "All I know is that I have to tell Jasper that the man who died in the woods is no stranger. Not to me. I have to tell him how I knew Elijah. I'm going to hurt the person who loves me most."

There was no denying the truth in this. Hester couldn't have known that her most painful secret would claw its way out before she'd found a way to share it with the man she wanted to marry, but there was no escape for her now.

Nora's gaze wandered over to the set of shelves reserved for North Carolina Authors. The books with dark covers faded into the shadows, while those with white- or cream-colored spines glowed like a night-light.

"What did Elijah like to read?" she asked Hester.

Though the question clearly surprised Hester, she was quick to say, "Mostly classics. He was a big Steinbeck fan, but his favorite subject was Arthurian legend. He'd read anything he could get his hands on if it mentioned King Arthur, his knights, or Merlin."

Estella's expression turned wistful. "When I was that age, I loved those books too. *The Crystal Cave*, *The Once and Future King*, *The Mists of Avalon*, *The Dark Is Rising*, *Excalibur*. I liked that some brave and noble knight is expected to draw the magic sword from the stone and unite the kingdom, but they all fail. Then along comes this insignificant boy, and he pulls it right out. It's still one of the coolest things I've ever read."

The lift in Estella's voice was wonderful to hear, but Nora had other books to talk about.

"I asked about his reading tastes because of the book found in his coat pocket."

Hester responded with a blank stare.

"*Miss Delphinium*," Nora reminded her.

"I don't think that was his book any more than I think that was his coat," Hester said firmly.

Nora flashed back to the day in the woods—to the sight of a body at the bottom of the gully. She remembered how bright the orange jacket looked in the midst of all the gray and brown hues.

"What kind of clothes would he wear?" Estella wanted to know.

Hester said, "First of all, the Mennonites are different from the Amish. Elijah wore mainstream clothes—jeans and button-downs—in subdued colors. He'd never wear bright orange or anything with a brand name. No Adidas logos on his sneakers or Polo logos on his shirts."

Someone gave Elijah that coat, Nora thought. *That person probably pushed him off the bridge too. Was it Hester's daughter?*

But Lea had seen a man behind the wheel of the black pickup truck.

Lea!

With so much happening, Nora had forgotten to reach out to Lea. The art book she'd meant to give her was still sitting in the stockroom, along with copies of *Girl with a Pearl Earring* and *The Goldfinch*. She'd wanted to deliver these, as well as a few board books for Jefferson, in person. But between prepping for Saturday's Blind Date Book Bash, researching the Lady Artist series, and trying to help her friends, Lea had slipped Nora's mind.

Her private musings were interrupted by Hester, who abruptly leapt to her feet. Her engagement ring fell from her hand and clattered on the glass top of the coffee table. Slipping it back on her finger, she said, "Jasper's on duty tonight and I'm going to tell him everything. All I want to do is crawl under the covers and sleep for three days, but I have to do this now."

Estella looped her fingers through the handles of their empty mugs. As she carried them to the sink, she said, "I'm tired too. But we're women, which means we do what needs to be done, no matter how tired we are."

June stood and tenderly wrapped Hester's scarf around her neck. "We'll come with you."

"You and Nora can come, but not you," Hester told Estella. "Jack needs you. And you can't be there for him unless you get some rest."

"I'm fine."

"This might be the first time in my life I've seen you without lipstick. One of your boots is black. The other one's dark brown. And you're wearing two different earrings."

Estella touched her earlobes and sighed. "I'm a hot mess, aren't I?"

Hester enfolded her in a hug. "Me too. We should get T-shirts printed for the Book, Scone, and Hot Mess Society."

"I like it," Estella whispered.

Nora felt a tightening in her throat. She hated that her friends were hurting and wished she could do more to ease their pain. For now, all she could do was hug Estella good-bye and hold Hester's hand on the short drive to the station.

Nora and June stuck close to Hester as she crossed the lobby, waved at the officer manning the front desk, and made her way to the patrol room occupied by Andrews and another deputy. The other deputy had a phone pressed to his ear and was writing notes on a memo pad. When the women entered the room, he gave them a polite nod and waved at Andrews.

Swiveling in his chair, Andrews caught sight of Hester. His eyes lit up and he started to smile, but when he saw their expressions, he bolted from his chair and was at Hester's side in a matter of seconds.

"What's wrong?"

Hester shot a glance at the other deputy and whispered, "Can we talk in private?"

Now Andrews was on full alert. "Yeah, sure. We can go to the conference room."

He walked to the end of the hall and stepped into the room to trigger the motion sensor lights.

Hester didn't follow him inside. With her feet rooted to the ground, she cast plaintive looks at her friends.

"We'll be right here. If you need us, all you have to do is open the door," said Nora.

June cupped Hester's cheek. "You've got this, honey. Just tell your story. Start at the beginning. That's all you need to do."

Hester drew in a deep breath and entered the room. The door closed behind her with a definitive click.

Nora and June waited until they heard the low murmur of voices before they relocated to the break room. They took seats at the table closest to the hall and tried to tune out the obnoxious ticking of the Homer Simpson wall clock.

The novelty clock was hard to ignore. There was a donut on the end of the second hand, and as the hand circled around Homer's face, his eyes seemed to follow it. The longer Nora stared, the more she disliked the egg-shaped eyes with their pinprick pupils.

June wasn't looking at anything. Her head rested against the wall, her hands were folded in her lap, and her eyes were closed.

Nora decided to use the time to search for the Lady Artist covers she and McCabe hadn't already seen. She'd explored the largest secondhand book databases without finding the kinds of images she needed, but there were plenty of other places to search.

After twenty minutes of squinting at hundreds of thumbnail images on her phone, Nora needed a break, so she sent Bobbie a text. Three dots appeared below her message, and as Nora waited for a reply, she wondered what Bobbie was doing. Was she on her way home after eating at one of the many eclectic restaurants near her brownstone, or had she brought in take-out? Was she curled up on a sofa with a book in one hand and a wineglass in the other?

Nora's phone vibrated, and she hurried out to the hall to answer it.

"What perfect timing!" Bobbie cried. "I finished my book and have nothing else to read. I hate it when I fill the tub, light candles, and put in just the right amount of bath salts, only to be bored two minutes after getting in the damn water."

"I was just thinking about you."

Over the sound of splashing, Bobbie said, "Of course, you were! Which means you have something to tell me about Sadie Strong's hidden letters. Did you find any? Because *I* did! But you have to go first."

Nora felt a welcome surge of adrenaline. "From the three books in McCabe's office, we got the letters *R*, *I*, and *D*. I found another letter this afternoon. *Miss Peony*'s cover was featured in an Art Nouveau book design exhibition catalogued by the Rare Book School at the University of Virginia. It was a large and superclear image, and I was able to see the letter *M* in the veins of a small leaf. Didn't I send you the link?"

"If you did, it's probably sitting in my inbox with the rest of my unread messages. After the budget meeting, I thought it would be a good idea to avoid reading emails for a few days. But I don't want to talk about that now. The water is warm, my wine is chilled, and I found the letter *O* on the cover of *Miss Poppy*. The more I look at these covers, the more I admire them."

"Same here. They really remind me of the stained-glass works from Tiffany Studios."

"Or a William Morris design. Do you still have that scarf with the Strawberry Thief print?"

Nora had her notes application open and was studying the capital letters written next to each Lady Artist title, so she didn't hear Bobbie's question.

Unperturbed, Bobbie barreled on. "*Anyway*, we won't solve the riddle without the other three letters. The head of Cataloguing and Special Editions at The New York Society Library has a copy of *Miss Tulip*. It's tucked away, but if my friend managed to unearth it, images of that cover might be waiting on my computer this very second!" She groaned. "Guess I'll be opening my email after all."

"I wrote an Etsy seller who specializes in books printed between 1880 and 1940. None of his current listings included Sadie Strong covers, but his shop has a subcategory devoted to female binders. I bought an inexpensive book designed by a woman named Alice Morse, and when the bookseller emailed the tracking info, I replied with questions about Sadie Strong's covers. He hasn't gotten back to me yet," Nora said.

She heard more splashing followed by a muttered curse. "I dropped my wineglass in the water and the bottle's on my nightstand. That means it's time to pull the plug. Talk tomorrow?"

" 'Tomorrow, and tomorrow, and tomorrow.' "

Bobbie chuckled. "Good night, Macbeth."

* * *

Pocketing her phone, Nora turned to see Hester heading her way. Her eyes were red-rimmed and her hair was disheveled. Exhausted, she leaned against the wall and said, "It's done. Jasper needs a minute. Then he'll call the sheriff."

June came out of the break room holding a bottle of water. She twisted off the cap and handed it to Hester. "How'd it go?"

"Not well. I told Jasper that I kept this from him because I didn't want him to stop loving me because of what happened in my past. I said I was sorry for not trusting him, but I don't think he really heard me. And when the sheriff gets here, I won't be Jasper's fiancée anymore. I'll be part of the investigation."

Wanting to reassure her, Nora said, "When McCabe sees how much you two are hurting, he'll be as quick and as gentle as he can be."

Hester pointed to the door at the end of the hall. "You should go home now. It'll be harder for me to talk to the sheriff if I know you're both waiting on me. But I couldn't have gotten through any of this without you."

"Are you sure?" asked June.

"Yes. But I'll take another hug before you go."

June told Hester that she was a beautiful person with a beautiful soul and kissed her on the cheek.

Nora hugged her and whispered, "I love you."

"Even if I'm too tired to make book pockets tomorrow?"

Nora dried Hester's tears with the end of her scarf. "Even then."

At home, Nora considered leaving a message for McCabe, but didn't. She was too tired and heartsick to talk to anyone else tonight. What she most needed was a good night's sleep. The kind of restorative sleep that heals every part of the body, including a bruised and battered heart.

Nora burrowed under the covers and closed her eyes. Within

minutes, her breathing turned slow and steady. She was on the verge of sleep when a disturbing image wriggled its way into her mind.

She saw Hester standing on a bridge. Her hands were pressed against the back of a bright orange coat. In the silence of the winter woods, Hester squeezed her eyes shut and pushed.

Chapter 15

There could have never been two hearts so open, no tastes so similar, no feelings so in unison, no countenances so beloved. Now they were as strangers . . .
—Jane Austen

McCabe questioned Hester quickly and thoroughly. After she'd told him everything he needed to know, he drove her home.

"Is Hester a suspect?" Nora asked McCabe when he called the next morning.

"She's a person of interest."

Nora found the term confusing. "Is that another way of saying that she's on your radar because of her former relationship with Elijah?"

"More like standing in a spotlight," McCabe said. "The lab tests came back this morning. Elijah's death wasn't an accident. He didn't commit suicide either. It was murder."

Nora wished she could unhear the word. Like all words, it was a collection of letters. But this one had the power to suck air from a room, cause irrevocable pain, breed distrust, and alter lives.

How would it change Hester's life?

Nora placed her hands in the path of the cornsilk-colored sunbeams illuminating her kitchen counter. Even though it held no warmth, the light was welcome.

"Do the results of those tests point to Hester in any way?"

McCabe hesitated before saying, "Not unless she has a supply of injectable muscle relaxants squirreled away that Andrews doesn't know about."

"Does anyone? I mean, don't you have to get injections like that in a doctor's office?"

"Yes. Years ago, I hurt my back and had to visit a local clinic for daily injections. They helped, but they made me sleepy. Elijah was dosed with enough juice to flatten an elephant."

Faces flashed through Nora's mind. None of her friends had experience with this type of injection. Sheldon would be the most likely candidate, but after a brief addiction to opiates, he shunned prescription-strength pain relievers. Only medical personnel would have access to this kind of drug, and Nora didn't know anyone who worked in a doctor's office or hospital other than Jasmine. And Tyson's girlfriend had no reason to kill a Mennonite man from Pennsylvania.

Is Hester's daughter in the medical field?

Nora asked McCabe if his department was trying to locate her.

"We are. But accessing adoption records isn't a fast or easy process."

Nora wished she could pluck the sunbeams off the counter and wrap them around her like a blanket. "Does Elijah's family know what happened to him?"

"They do." McCabe's voice was leaden. "I've delivered news like this before—the hardest news a person can hear—but not over the phone. I called at seven this morning and his whole family was there. His wife and two children. His parents too."

"Oh, no."

Nora conjured a Norman Rockwell scene of a family breakfasting together. She pictured a farmhouse table, a pitcher of orange juice, a basket of homemade biscuits, and platters of bacon and sausage. She saw aproned women pouring coffee and serving scrambled eggs, while men in flannel shirts passed food to a little boy with a gap-toothed smile and a girl with long pigtail braids.

"Those poor people," she whispered.

McCabe made a noise of agreement. "His parents are coming to identify him. Seeing as Elijah never told his wife or parents that he'd fathered a child when he was younger because he didn't know himself, they refused to believe it. When presented with proof, the truth will only add to their grief."

Nora decided that it was time to mention Candace Heikkinen. After all, Candace could be Hester's daughter. She was the right age. And McCabe should hear how she'd been Jefferson's nanny one moment and gone the next.

"No one knows exactly why she left. For all I know, she's still here," Nora said.

"This is the first I've heard of her."

"I thought Bea—the flea market vendor I love—would know exactly why Candace left, but outside the usual gossip, no one has a clue. I looked around online, but what I found out doesn't help."

McCabe said, "Tell me anyway."

"Well, Heikkinen is a popular surname in Finland. As for Americans named Candace Heikkinen, the ones on Facebook are all over forty. There's probably a dozen Candace Heikkinens on Instagram, but most are private accounts. The public ones don't have enough identifying biographical information or personal photos to let me know the user was a tall, gorgeous blonde in her very early twenties. I don't have Twitter, Snapchat, TikTok, or any other social media platforms, but I did try LinkedIn. No luck there either."

"I'll take a look from my end. Thanks for the tip."

While McCabe wrote down Candace's name, Nora was torn between feeling pleased that she might have provided McCabe with a lead and worried that she might be pointing a finger at an innocent young woman who wished to be left alone.

In search of a new subject, she asked, "How's Andrews?"

"For obvious reasons, he can't be involved in the investigation anymore." His tone softened as he added, "I'm worried about him, Nora, and I want him to talk to someone who can help him process everything Hester told him last night. I've asked him to complete at least one session with a therapist before returning to work."

"I wish Hester would do that too. They're both hurting and could use all the help they can get. Is there any chance her secret can stay a secret?"

Though McCabe promised to do what he could to guard it, his voice held little conviction. After all, his job was to bring things out of the darkness into the light.

"I wish I had more time to talk, but I have a meeting in a few minutes. How's the book cover hunt going?"

Skipping over the details, Nora told him which letters she and Bobbie had found. "I hope to hear from a bookseller today. If I get an answer from him, we'll have our seventh letter. Bobbie has a lead on the eighth. I promise not to stop until I find them all."

"You're a force of nature, Nora Pennington. I'm glad you're in my corner."

Any other time, his sweet words would have made her smile. But like the sunbeams, they lacked the power to chase the shadows away.

When the call was over, Nora headed to the bookstore, where she turned on all the lights and got the coffee started. After that, she went into the stockroom to retrieve the vacuum.

Nora often vacuumed during times of stress. She liked the hum of the motor and the satisfying rattle of dirt being sucked into the machine. As she moved around the store, she felt like she was in control, even if only for a few minutes.

She was using an attachment to clean under one of the

chairs in the Children's Corner when someone touched her arm. Her heart thumped like a threatened rabbit and she whipped her head around to see Sheldon step on the vacuum's power button.

"Don't glare," he scolded. "I called your name, but you were too zoned out to hear me. Would you like a cup of coffee and some good news?"

Nora smiled. "Yes, and yes."

"Then follow me. The good news is on the counter next to the fridge."

It was hard for Nora to abandon the vacuum on the alphabet rug because she'd yet to run it over X, Y, and Z, but curiosity got the better of her.

In the ticket agent's booth, she found two trays of pale pink cupcakes and two trays of mini heart-shaped pies.

"Where'd these come from?"

Sheldon beamed. "June's oven. She went to bed as soon as she got home last night, but her insomnia kicked in around four. She didn't want to walk, so she started making piecrust. I wasn't exactly sleeping the sleep of the righteous, and after flopping in bed like a flapjack for another hour, I joined her. She made cherry pies and I made passion cupcakes. I used a box mix to save time, but no one will be able to tell because the frosting and passion-fruit filling are from scratch."

"Sounds delicious."

"Oh, they *are*. I had them for breakfast. And why not? *Someone* had to eat the mistakes." He laughed. "I saved a few mistakes for you too. There are times when one must have dessert for breakfast. This is one of those times."

"You're a wise man."

Sheldon stroked his goatee as he stared at the treats. "How much can we charge per cupcake? Four dollars? Five?"

Nora shook her head. "We're not price gouging because it's almost Valentine's Day. We'll leave that to the restaurants. But thank you for doing this. Our customers are lucky to have you. I am too."

Sheldon poured her a cup of coffee. "Sing my praises after you try a cupcake."

Nora had never tasted a passion fruit–filled cupcake before, but she loved how the tart fruit offset the sweetness of the vanilla buttercream. After devouring the treat in six bites, she unabashedly licked frosting from her fingers.

"Do I need to call a priest?" she asked Sheldon. "Because you've clearly been possessed by Betty Crocker."

"Not Betty. I'm *much* sexier. *I'm* queen of a culinary empire *and* I hang with Snoop Dogg."

"I never knew you had a thing for Martha Stewart."

Sheldon looked confused. "Um, doesn't everyone?"

The cupcake was wonderful, but the fact that her friends had gotten up before dawn to make treats for the bookstore was even more amazing. The gesture went a long way toward restoring Nora's spirits.

There wasn't much left to do before the store opened at ten, so after reviewing the alcohol order for Saturday's party, Nora sat on a stool behind the checkout counter and powered up her laptop.

There were dozens of unread emails in her inbox. She scrolled through unfulfilled purchase orders from the Miracle Books website, ads from publishing houses touting their new releases, and a notification that the power bill was due, and then she saw what she'd been hoping to see: a message from Connecticut Yankee Books.

She clicked on the attached letter and started reading.

Dear Ms. Pennington,
Thanks again for your order. Your purchase is
already on its way, but I wanted to respond to your
query. I'm very familiar with Sadie Strong's designs

and have seen examples in which her initials have been cleverly concealed on her covers, but I don't remember noticing a single letter in one of her covers. I haven't carried any titles in the Lady Artist series in years, but upon examining Miss Buttercup's *cover, I believe I found such a letter. I've attached images of what I found. To make it easier for you, I circled the second buttercup from the right. If you view the flower as a clock, you'll see what I think is a capital I between the seventh and eighth petals. Unfortunately, the cover's condition makes it impossible to be certain. I'll keep my eye out for other titles in the series and will contact you if I can get my hands on them. If you solve the mystery of the letters, please drop me a line. I'd love to know what Sadie was hiding.*

Sincerely,

B. Gibson

Connecticut Yankee Books

Nora saved the attachments to her desktop before clicking on the first of three images. She carefully scrutinized the second buttercup from the right, but all the flowers had suffered a degree of color loss and the fading was worse on the right half. In addition to color loss, the cover showed signs of rubbing. Green leaves and yellow flower petals had been reduced to ghostly outlines suspended in a sea of dove-gray cloth.

The top crossbar and stem of a letter were visible, but without a side-by-side comparison of the *I* on *Miss Rose*'s cover, she couldn't tell if it was an exact match. After all, if *Miss Buttercup*'s letter had a smaller crossbar, it could just as easily be a capital *L*.

With a sigh of disappointment, Nora closed the email. She'd have to find another image of the cover. Two thirds of that buttercup—including the bottom half of the letter—was just too far gone.

Sheldon rounded the corner of Fiction in time to catch Nora's expression.

"What's wrong? Did the ten million dollars that Nigerian prince promised fail to show up in your checking account? Don't tell me you deleted his urgent email!"

Nora showed him the images of *Miss Buttercup*.

"My eyes aren't sharp enough for an alphabet Where's Waldo." Sheldon took off his reading glasses and squinted at the computer screen. "If these letters spell a word, we'll have to figure out what it is, using either *I* or *L*."

"Even if Bobbie comes through, we're still short one letter."

Sheldon chucked her lightly under the chin. "What would Charlotte say to Wilbur?"

Nora gave him a playful shove. "You're evil. That freaking 'Chin Up' song will be stuck in my head for the rest of the day now."

"Got you to stop worrying about those book covers, didn't I?" Sheldon pinched her cheek before walking around the counter to unlock the front door.

From that moment on, Nora was too busy to think about Hester or Estella. With Valentine's Day fast approaching, customers streamed into the bookshop in search of the perfect gift. Fueled by coffee and a cupcake or heart-shaped pie, they drifted around the shop, plucking books and shelf enhancers off the shelves. Every customer left carrying a Miracle Books shopping bag.

At the tail end of the lunch rush, Nora zipped into the ticket agent's booth to refill her water bottle. Sheldon, who was in the middle of washing mugs and plates, didn't turn around. But when he attempted to put a wet mug in the drying rack, his hand trembled so violently that he missed the counter altogether and the mug fell to the floor with a crash.

"Oh, hell," he muttered darkly.

Nora reached around him and turned off the faucet. She then gently dried his swollen hands with a clean towel. Sheldon's joints were often swollen by the end of a workday, but each flare was different. Pain and inflammation could assault his knuckles, knees, shoulders, ankles, or hips. Sometimes the flares focused on one area of his body. Other times, it attacked several at once.

"Your hands are twice their normal size," Nora said as she studied Sheldon's face. His rippled brow and pinched mouth meant that he was trying to hide his discomfort.

"I'm fine," he snapped.

He bent to pick up the broken mug, but Nora beat him to it. Afterward, she took two gel ice packs out of the freezer and pressed them to his temples. "I think the cupcakes did you in. All that mixing and piping followed by hours of steaming milk and making espresso—it was too much. You're going home, Sheldon Vega, as soon as you can drive. And if you can't, I'll sweet-talk a customer into taking you."

Sheldon rolled his eyes, but didn't argue.

Nora led him to June's purple velvet chair and carefully wrapped his right hand in an ice pack.

An older woman with a Miracle Springs Lodge tote bag hanging from her shoulder approached the circle of chairs. "There you are. I've been waiting and waiting for someone to ring me up. Is this a self-serve business? Should I just leave the money in a box?"

The woman held out a picture book with two polar bears on the cover. It was called *Love Matters Most*.

Nora said, "I'm sorry you had to wait. I'll be with you in just a minute."

The woman huffed in annoyance. "But I'm in a hurry. Can't you ring me up and do whatever it is you're doing *in a minute*?"

The woman's tone rubbed Nora the wrong way, but she refused to be baited. She wrapped Sheldon's second hand as gently as she could, but he still winced in pain.

"I'm sorry. I know everything hurts," she murmured.

Behind her, the woman cried, "You should be apologizing to *me*! But it's too late now. You can play Florence Nightingale for the rest of the week, for all I care. *You* just lost a customer!" She slammed the picture book on the floor and stormed off.

As if nothing had happened, Nora raised Sheldon's feet onto a pillow. After washing her hands, she popped extra-strength Tylenol into his mouth and held a straw to his lips so he could wash the pills down with water.

"Close your eyes," she whispered. "I'll check on you in a bit."

Nora flipped through the picture book as she walked to the Children's Corner. An illustration of a polar bear standing on its hind legs and staring across a vast and snowy landscape gave her pause because the bear looked sad and worried. Mij Kelly's text read: *The wind's full of snow. The air's full of frost. She's looking for something, but what has she lost?*

Something in the bear's eyes made Nora think of Hester. For her entire childhood, Hester had fruitlessly sought her family's love and approval. It wasn't until Elijah Lamb came along that she understood exactly what she'd been missing.

And what about their daughter? Had she grown up the same way? Or had she been raised by loving parents?

Hester had never bothered to check. To protect herself from heartache, she'd denied her daughter's existence. And Elijah never even knew that he'd fathered a child with the girl he met at the library.

Nora couldn't figure out how he'd learned the truth, but she assumed he had. Why else would he come to Miracle Springs? After all this time, he suddenly had a compelling reason to drive hundreds of miles to see an old girlfriend. Only one thing would make him leave his wife and children to seek out a woman he hadn't spoken with for twenty years. And that one thing was a child. Elijah had found out about his daughter. But how?

Hester's name was on the birth certificate, but the father's name was blank. Had their child found Elijah? If so, when and where had father and daughter met? And had their reunion somehow led to Elijah's death?

The cuts in the covers.

Flashing back to those damaged copies of *The Scarlet Letter*, the anger behind the slashes through Hester's name suddenly held new meaning.

"She was here," Nora murmured. "Hester's daughter was in my store."

Her mind buzzed with questions, but there was no time for that now. She spent the next fifteen minutes helping customers and tidying up the ticket agent's booth. Then she checked on Sheldon. His swelling had gone down, so she bundled him up in his coat and sent him home.

The after-school rush was lively. Nora made espresso drinks and offered book recommendations. She looked up titles and pulled books off the shelf. She grabbed inventory from the stockroom and sold the last of the heart-shaped pies and cupcakes.

These activities were an anchor. They connected her to the books in her store and the people of her community. They infused her with purpose and restored a sense of harmony.

Around five, she took advantage of a brief lull to organize the checkout area. Having run out of paper shopping bags, she went to the stockroom to retrieve more. The books she'd set aside for Lea and Jefferson were stacked next to the bags, and when Nora saw them, she let out a guilt-induced moan.

She marched back to the checkout counter and dialed the Comforts' home number. When Lea picked up, Nora apologized for not calling sooner and asked if she could stop by that evening.

"Or another evening. Whatever works for you," she added when her question was met by silence.

"Sorry, I was just asking Meredith to wait for me. She's heading to the grocery store and I'm going to catch a ride. I need something to read. I'm Netflixed out."

"I think I can find something for you." Nora smiled into the phone as she ended the call.

The front door opened to a trio of rosy-cheeked ladies who were immediately drawn to the Blind Date Book display. Leaving them alone to browse, Nora filled in holes on the Literary Lovers table. She was surveying the table with a critical eye when Estella threw open the front door.

Over the clanging of the sleigh bells, she cried, "He's better! Jack's better!"

Nora let out a shriek of joy and ran forward to embrace her friend.

When they pulled apart, Nora said, "What a relief! Is he awake?"

"Not yet, but the new antibiotic is working. If he keeps improving, they'll wake him up tomorrow."

"Then he'll be able to tell you how happy he is that you're his valentine."

Estella's smile was as radiant as sunshine after a raging thunderstorm. "Knowing Jack, he'll ask about the diner first and say 'I love you' second. But I don't care. As long as he's okay, I don't care what he says."

A customer approached the checkout counter with an armload of books, and Estella patiently waited while Nora rang her up.

"Any news from Hester?" she asked after the customer left.

"No, but I haven't called her. I figured she and Andrews needed a little space to work things out. They're both off today, so I hope that's what they're doing."

Seeing that another customer was headed for the checkout counter, Estella began edging toward the door. As she moved, she said, "Their relationship hasn't been put to the test before now. But if they can get through this, they'll be closer than ever. I hope they can get through it."

"Me too."

The bells were still clanging from Estella's departure when the door opened again. Lea stood in the doorway, glancing back at the street.

"You should apologize after knocking someone down!" Lea shouted, cradling the cast on her arm. "Hang up and learn to be a decent human being!"

Nora peered through the window just as a man on the opposite sidewalk flipped Lea the bird.

"I bet your mom's ashamed of you!" Lea yelled.

The man ignored her and strode away. As he passed under a streetlamp, Nora caught a glimpse of a dark coat, beard, and knit hat. The man was big and broad-chested and his wide shoulders swayed when he moved, reminding Nora of the rude man she'd encountered on the sidewalk.

Lea let out a soft whimper and Nora turned to face her. "Are you okay?"

"Yeah," she said through clenched teeth. After taking a moment to recover, she added, "Sorry about the yelling, but he deserved it."

"He did," Nora agreed.

She shut the door and grabbed a shopping bag from behind the counter. "This is for you. It's a belated thank-you for putting me on Meredith's radar. I added a few books for Jefferson and—"

"That's so nice of you," Lea interrupted. "Sorry. I don't mean to be rude, but I have to meet Meredith in front of the hardware store in two minutes. I told her that I was just coming in to see about an order I placed. I'm not sure why I lied—I guess I'm having trust issues because of the accident. I just want to forget about it and move on, but I can't because of this." Lea reached into her coat pocket and pulled out a rectangular object wrapped in a plastic bag.

Book-shaped packages didn't usually set off alarm bells in Nora's head, but bells were definitely ringing.

"The hospital put my clothes from the accident in this bag. When I got home, I stuck it in my closet because I didn't want to think about what happened. But I had to move it to get to my boots, so I decided to go ahead and unpack it. I have no idea why *this* was in with my stuff. I've never seen it before, but I figured you'd know what to do with it."

Lea took the shopping bag from Nora and passed her the plastic bag. After thanking her for the gifts, Lea left the shop.

Nora locked the door and flipped the sign in the window to the SHOP CLOSED side.

Then she reached into the bag and withdrew a book. Even before she saw it, she had a feeling the cover would feature an Art Nouveau floral design.

Holding the book up to the light, Nora whispered, "Hello, *Miss Iris.*"

Chapter 16

Someone once told me that when you give birth to a
daughter, you've just met the person whose hand
you'll be holding the day you die.

—Jodi Picoult

Nora placed the book on a sheet of white craft paper.

For a moment, she stood in the quiet stockroom and admired the beautiful cover. Purple irises bloomed under a starry sky. Seven tall stalks supported seven bulbous flowers. Their petals unfurled like sails in the wind, and their golden signals were the same color as the moon. Narrow trellises flanked the flowers. A metal fence marched across the bottom of the cover.

"What letter are you hiding?" she asked the book. Of all the Lady Artist covers she'd seen, *Miss Iris* was in the best condition. Despite its age, the cover was bright, the spine was firm, and the pages were unmarred by tears or foxing. Two corners were bumped and there was a slight discoloration to the page edges, but those were its only faults.

The book's fine condition made it harder to conceal the letter tucked in the fold of a petal. Nora's breath caught when she saw it.

She immediately called Bobbie and left a voicemail message saying, "We can add a *G* to our letter list! It's up to you now, Wonder Woman. If you can find the last letter, we can start looking for the mystery word. Let me know where things stand, okay?"

Nora wondered if Bobbie was out with her British professor. Were they having cocktails at a cozy neighborhood bar or hopping on the subway to grab dinner uptown? Or was Bobbie stuck at another endless work meeting? Her job was comprised of an endless rotation of meetings, phone calls, and emails. Nora got overwhelmed just listening to Bobbie talk about work.

"It's a good thing I didn't become an academic librarian," she'd told Bobbie a few weeks ago. "You're a natural leader, Roberta Rabinowitz. You were born to compose articulate emails, manage a large staff, and find the money for new acquisitions—all while knowing the exact location of every book, map, and media file in your library's collection."

"I guess we're both exactly where we're meant to be. I only wished the places were closer," Bobbie had replied.

Nora felt that way too, especially right now. She'd love to drop by Bobbie's house and spend an evening poring over the mystery of Sadie Strong's hidden letters. Bobbie would order food and open a bottle of wine. They'd sit in her kitchen and brainstorm while working their way through containers of *malai kofta* curry, *chana saag*, and vegetable vindaloo.

But Bobbie was hundreds of miles away, so Nora went home and opened a can of creamy tomato soup. While the soup simmered, she buttered two slices of marble rye and placed them on a griddle pan. After topping the bread with thin strips of white cheddar cheese, she sorted her mail. Apart from one bill, it all ended up in the recycling bin.

Nora leaned against the counter and made a mental list of the people who had a reason to enter Lea's hospital room. Excluding doctors and nurses, Lea would have seen Miles, Meredith, and Sheriff McCabe. But had anyone else from Miracle Springs gone to see her? Since the hospital was an hour's drive, casual acquaintances were unlikely to visit, but a close friend or concerned church member would probably make the trip.

Why would anyone hide a Lady Artist book with Lea's belongings? Or hide one in the box that came from Meredith's mother? What do these old books have to do with Hester?

An idea niggled at Nora, but she dismissed it as far-fetched and focused on plating her grilled cheese and ladling tomato soup into a bowl. After carrying her meal to her table, she returned to the kitchen for a glass of sparkling water. Her food was still steaming when she sat down, so she decided to call McCabe while it cooled.

Though McCabe picked up on the second ring, he said that he had to put her on hold for a few seconds.

"Are you still at work?" she asked when he came back on the line.

"I am. It's been a long and difficult day. Elijah's parents are here. I stepped out of the room because the ME is talking to Mr. and Mrs. Lamb, but I only have a minute. How are you? How was your day?"

Nora glanced around her cozy space. There was a fire in the hearth, a scented candle on the counter, and a table laid with comfort food. But a few blocks from her tiny house, Elijah's grief-stricken parents sat in a drab conference room, trying to make sense of the senseless.

And then, there was McCabe. He had to sit across from the Lambs and bear witness to their pain as he questioned, consoled, and assured them that he was doing everything in his power to find out what had happened to their son.

"I'm fine, and I don't want to keep you. Give me a call if you want to come over later. I can fix you a gourmet meal of canned soup and grilled cheese."

McCabe let out a soft groan. "You have no idea how good that sounds, but it looks like it's going to be a late night."

Nora heard voices in the background, and before she could tell McCabe about *Miss Iris*, he told her he'd be in touch tomorrow and was gone.

After connecting the phone to its charging cable, Nora dunked a corner of her sandwich into her soup and idly wondered how many times she'd had this meal over the course of her life. She'd always been a fan of soup, though her childhood favorite had been alphabet, not tomato.

Nora remembered pushing the pasta letters around in her bowl, trying to load every spoonful with a complete word. The last few bites were a disappointment because the remaining letters could make only a two-letter or nonsense word.

Memories of alphabet soup reminded Nora of the letters in Sadie Strong's covers, and as soon as she finished her meal, she opened her laptop and searched for an unscrambling site.

There were plenty to choose from, so Nora clicked on the first link and typed the seven letters from the Lady Artist books into the text box. Even though she was short a letter, she hoped that a list of words derived from seven letters would help to shed light on the mystery word.

The results began to appear on her screen. There were a dozen two-letter words and twice as many three- and four-letter words. Nora quickly scanned the list until her gaze was caught by the only six-letter word.

"Milord," she said.

She stared at the word for a moment before clearing the results and retyping the letters. This time, she replaced the *L* with an *I* because she couldn't be sure which of these two letters had been hidden on *Miss Buttercup*'s cover. The search produced only a few words, the longest of which had five letters.

"Rigid. Idiom. Mirid." Nora frowned. "What's a mirid?"

When she clicked on the word, a text box with a definition popped up.

"A leaf bug?"

The definition included a graphic of an oval-shaped bug with spindly legs. An arrow pointed to a needlelike probe on its head and a caption explained how the stylet was used to suck blood from the insect's prey.

"Lovely."

Nora shut down the computer and spent the rest of the evening watching *Call the Midwife*. She was too tired to do much reading, but before drifting off, she got in a chapter of Kristin Hannah's latest release.

Her sleep was disturbed by images of leaf bugs swarming the shelves inside Miracle Books. They crawled over spines and covers, spearing paper and cloth with their probes until the titles and author names were riddled with tiny holes.

As the nightmare continued, the bugs became more and more destructive. They chewed through the chairs in the Readers' Circle and the alphabet rug in the Children's Corner. They made nests in the coffee mugs, the espresso machine, and the refrigerator. They multiplied at a terrifying rate until, finally, the beeping of Nora's alarm clock chased them away.

"Surprise!"

June stood outside Nora's back door, her arms loaded with Gingerbread House bakery boxes.

Nora reached for the boxes. "You didn't have to bring these. I could have picked them up. Will you accept your tip in coffee form?"

"I sure will." As June fell into step behind Nora, she said, "Sheldon's down for the count today, and since my Bible study group is talking about walking in another man's shoes, I thought I'd walk in Sheldon's today. I'm going to try my best to be his substitute. I even borrowed one of his sweater vests. See?"

June unzipped her coat, revealing a maroon sweater vest with a white-and-gray argyle pattern across the chest.

"You look really cute."

"I know, right? I think I'll knit one for myself." June pointed at the espresso machine. "You'll have to show me how to use this thing. Or I can handle the book sales, which means you'll have to show me how to use *that* machine."

Nora shook her head. "Seriously, you don't need to fill in for Sheldon. I can handle things."

"I know that, but I *want* to be here. All the stuff happening with Estella and Hester is weighing on me. Being with you will make me feel better. So don't send me home. Don't tell me I put on this sweater vest for nothing."

"What about your job?"

June shrugged. "I took a personal day. With me out of the house, Sheldon will have the space and quiet he needs. I brought chicken salad for lunch—enough for an army—and I told Tyson to stop by on his way to the theater. See? It'll be great for all of us."

Nora smiled. "You're seriously the best."

"Will you still love me if I admit that I'm scared of that espresso machine?"

"Not to worry. I'll be the barista if you'll handle storytime." Nora wagged a finger. "And no, I don't want the sweater vest. While the coffee's brewing, I'll show you how to work the register. But first, tell me how Hester's doing."

June brushed her fingers over the Gingerbread House logo on the bakery box. "I don't know. She didn't want to talk and I didn't push her."

Looking into her friend's eyes, Nora saw a reflection of the worry and fear she felt.

How can we help Hester if she won't open up to us?

But just like that, an answer came to her. "For years, we've made kindness totes for neighbors in need. I think Hester could use a big dose of kindness right now."

"Yes!" June smiled. "But we're not going to drop it on her

front step. We'll carry it inside and sit with her. Because sometimes, being present is the ultimate act of kindness."

"See? Five minutes together and we're already killing it."

Laughing, the women exchanged fist bumps.

Nora spent most of the morning in the ticket agent's booth, serving book pockets and espresso drinks. When Tyson showed up around noon, June led him to the Readers' Circle.

"Look what the wind blew in," June said to Nora. Her face glowed whenever her son was around, and today was no exception. "Are you hungry?"

Tyson's grin was shy as he mumbled, "Always."

"Sit down, and I'll fix you a sandwich."

"I want to ask Ms. P. something first."

Nora untied her apron and hung it on the hook next to the refrigerator. Sensing that Tyson wanted a little privacy, she asked if they could talk while she reorganized a display or two.

"Sure," he said, following her to the front of the store. While Nora added a few more books to the red suitcase display, Tyson said, "It's the whole valentine thing. I don't get it. I've never done anything about it before, but I'm with somebody now."

The anxious look on Tyson's face told Nora everything she needed to know. Tyson Dixon was in love.

"You want to get Jasmine a gift?" she asked.

At Tyson's nod, Nora asked if he knew what she liked to read.

"Yeah. Books with magic. Not Harry Potter, Percy Jackson, white-guys-with-magic books, though. She wants to read about kick-ass Black women."

Titles rushed into Nora's head. "Tell you what. I'll grab a few for you to look over while you eat. After lunch, let me know if you think any of them will work."

Tyson joined June in the Readers' Circle as Nora headed to the YA section. She pulled J. Elle's *Wings of Ebony* and Tracy

Deonn's *Legendborn* from the shelves and continued her search. Since she didn't want to overwhelm Tyson with choices, she added Namina Forna's *The Gilded Ones* to the pile and carried the books back to where he sat.

Tyson was showing his mother something on his phone, and Nora didn't want to disturb them, so she left the books on a side table and returned to the front.

Seeing Tyson's phone reminded her to check hers for messages. When she glanced at the screen, she was thrilled to find a new text from Bobbie.

The sleigh bells clanged as a woman wearing a leopard print coat and a beanie with cat ears entered the shop.

She took three steps and stopped. "I feel like I just found the end of a rainbow. Can I stay forever?"

Nora grinned. "Will six o'clock do?"

The woman gazed around with the starry-eyed adoration of a true book lover and said, "That *might* be enough time."

Nora knew the woman would be happiest left to her own devices. She'd browse every aisle and shelf, collect a pile of books, and sample dozens of opening paragraphs, leaving Nora free to read Bobbie's message: **Eureka! I managed to get my mitts on an actual copy of *Miss Tulip*. Sneaky Sadie hid the letter *A* inside a finial on the garden gate. Do you know how hard it was to spot that letter on an arrow-shaped finial? Send me the list with all the letters. Better yet, send me the word they spell. I have a hot date tonight and I don't want to be playing word jumble in my head while my hands are busy doing something else!**

Nora grabbed her laptop and viewed her browsing history. She clicked on the unscrambling site she'd used the night before and entered all eight letters into the text box, whispering them like an enchantment as she typed.

"*R, I, D, M, L, O, A, G.*"

The letters spelled a single eight-letter word. Nora stared at an image of a yellow flower for a long moment before reading the accompanying definition out loud.

"'Daisy family. Yellow or orange ornamental flowers. Late Middle English. Comes from *Mary* plus *gold*. Marigold.'"

Nora waited for an epiphany.

The sleigh bells rang again. The sound seemed to be coming from a great distance and failed to break Nora's focus.

"I used to make the same face during algebra class," someone whispered.

Nora looked up from her screen to find the sheriff leaning on the checkout counter.

"I'd like to say that I was thinking deep thoughts, but they're about as deep as a pancake griddle."

McCabe laughed and held up a paper grocery bag. "I thought I'd bring you lunch for a change. Have you eaten yet?"

"Not yet. June and Tyson—"

"Are done with their lunch," June said. "I'm going to wrap Jasmine's books while Tyson washes up, so you two are good to go."

The woman in the leopard print coat was sitting in the Readers' Circle, so Nora led McCabe to the set of chairs in the nook between Sci-Fi and YA. She watched as he placed napkins, cutlery, and several reusable take-out containers on the small table.

"I've got breakfast quiche and a cucumber salad—both homemade—but not by me. The quiche might need a quick blast in the microwave."

Nora didn't want to waste time heating the quiche, so she took a quick bite and said, "Delicious."

"I still want to cook for you. Soon. When we're both free again. Whenever that is."

"I'm hoping Saturday night. How'd you like to celebrate Valentine's Day with a bunch of book nerds? There'll be food, though probably not enough, and booze. Only cheap stuff because we wanted to keep the ticket prices low."

McCabe made a pushing gesture. "Whoa. Ease up on the hard sell, lady."

Nora laughed. "You need to know what you're getting into. I'll be running around the shop like a madwoman for most of the night, but when I'm not, I'd like to be with you."

"Are you sure? I can take the life out of a party just by showing up. People don't always feel comfortable knocking back a few with the sheriff around."

Nora hadn't considered this. McCabe spent what little free time he had at home or hanging out with work friends. His social interactions usually took place at his house or someone else's house. Occasionally he'd go out to eat with his colleagues. Or with Nora. Would his attendance at the Book Bash alter the vibe?

Picturing the faces of the people on the guest list, she dismissed the idea.

"Yes, I'm sure."

McCabe's eyes twinkled with pleasure. "In that case, I'd love to come."

"You'll be right at home with this crowd. Most of us are dying for an excuse to let go a bit."

"After being with Elijah's folks yesterday, I could use a distraction," McCabe said. "I hated having to shatter the image they had of their son. They've known Elijah's wife her whole life too. Everyone thought she and Elijah were a perfect match. They couldn't believe that he'd been with another woman while he was courting his future wife, or that he'd fathered a child with that young woman. They won't waste much time on denial, though. They're practical, down-to-earth people. I liked them."

"I feel so sorry for them. It'll be even harder for Elijah's wife. Talk about adding to a person's grief. I'm not blaming you," Nora quickly added. "I just hate that she'll be hit with so much at once."

"The Lambs don't want her to know. They swear that no one in their circle of family or friends had ever heard of Hester. They're also positive that no one claiming to be Elijah's daughter got in touch with him."

Nora frowned. "He must have given his family a reason for leaving. It's got to be a long drive from their town to here."

"Almost eight hours," said McCabe. "Elijah ran a successful woodworking company with a few friends. According to his parents, he was never very interested in the business side. He loved carpentry, especially furniture making, and would often sell his pieces at festivals or shows. He also liked exhibits on the history of furniture and was planning to drive to Williamsburg to see an exhibit on how different nationalities influenced American furniture design."

"So his absence was expected."

McCabe nodded. "Normally, he'd call his wife at least once a day when he was away from home. But they'd had a big argument before he left, and she assumed he was either still angry or taking time to reflect on his behavior."

"Do you know what they fought about?"

"Elijah had been acting secretive for the past week. He'd been unusually quiet and seemed worried. Since things were good at home, his wife figured his troubles were work related. When she learned everything was fine at the office, she insisted that he come clean. He told her to stop snooping and being suspicious, when he'd never given her a reason to doubt him. From there, the argument escalated."

Nora pulled a face. "That poor woman. It's bad enough that her husband died, but she'll never stop feeling guilty about all the things she said before he died."

"Which is why I won't leave her in the dark. She needs to know that I believe Elijah came to North Carolina because he wanted to hear the truth directly from Hester. Maybe their daughter wanted that too."

"Do you know her name?"

McCabe rubbed his bristly chin. "That's still a mystery. As are those books. We showed them to the Lambs. I sent images to Elijah's wife too. No luck. They've never seen them before."

"Well, thanks to Bobbie, we have all of the letters Sadie Strong hid in the covers. They spell the word *marigold*."

"That's a flower, right?"

"Yes, but it's also a girl's name. One of the characters on *Downton Abbey* named her daughter Marigold."

McCabe gave her a blank stare.

"*Downton Abbey* is a British period drama. I think that's the first time I heard of a girl named Marigold. It'd be an unusual name for our times, but I thought the books might be Hester's daughter trying to tell us her name. She might also go by Mary."

Nora took out her phone and showed him the photo of the *Miss Iris* cover. "Lea brought me this one. She found it in the plastic bag she got from the hospital. Do you think Hester's daughter snuck into Lea's hospital room?"

"Why Lea?"

"I don't know. I think there's a connection to the book collection that belonged to Meredith's mother, but that's just a hunch."

McCabe's expression turned grim. "Lea told us that the person driving Elijah's truck was male. But what if she got that wrong? What if the driver was a female?"

"The book collection arrived almost the same time as Elijah. Now Elijah's dead. And it seems like someone tried to kill the nanny living in the house where the book collection was being kept. Could those two things really be coincidental?"

"I wish I understood where the books fit in." McCabe got to his feet. "I need to get to the station—see if the adoption records have come in."

Nora stood up as well. "What if Hester's daughter was named Marigold by her adoptive parents? What, then?"

McCabe leaned close enough to whisper, "Considering her father was pushed off a bridge and her mother's name was scratched out of a bunch of books, I'd have no choice but to consider her a murder suspect."

Chapter 17

I love the stillness of a room, after a party. The chairs are moved, the cushions disarranged, everything is there to show that people enjoyed themselves.
—Daphne du Maurier

An hour before the Blind Date Book Bash was slated to start, it began to rain.

Nora and Sheldon didn't notice. They were too busy rearranging furniture, queuing playlists, setting up the wine station, and placing three hundred battery-powered tea-light candles around the store.

"Where's the food?" Sheldon asked Nora for the third time.

For the third time, she said, "They'll be here any minute."

"My anxiety is through the roof. Can you call them?" Sheldon pleaded. "If they forgot about our order, or the kitchen caught on fire, or the desserts fell out of the truck and are now scattered all over Main Street, I need to know. Argh! We should have had a backup plan. Do you think Tarheel Pies would make us twenty pizzas at the last minute? Should I ask? Just in case?"

"Okay, okay! I'll call the caterers!" Nora cried.

But there was no need. Her phone wasn't even out of her pocket when the delivery doorbell chimed.

"Hallelujah!" Sheldon raised his hands to the sky and raced down the hall to open the back door.

Minutes later, a man carrying a stack of chafing dishes appeared, and Nora showed him the buffet tables in the Children's Corner.

He put the dishes down and considered how to arrange them, and while he looked at the table, Nora looked at his wet coat and damp hair.

"It's raining?"

"Yeah. It's pretty light right now, but it's supposed to come down in buckets for the rest of the night. I just hope it doesn't freeze. Every bar and restaurant is packed. Lucky for me, my husband is making dinner for us at home. It's a good night to cuddle up on the couch."

A woman holding a bag of serving tongs and spoons and a plate of bite-sized brownies topped with candy hearts entered the room.

"Hiya, Nora. I figured you'd want us to put the dessert aside for later. Do you have a place in mind?"

Nora grinned. "My house is right across the parking lot. But since it's raining, we can use the stockroom. Oh, and I have good news for you. Your special order came in this afternoon. I went ahead and wrapped it because I thought you might be short on time."

"You put the *miracle* in Miracle Springs," the woman said.

To keep the ticket cost down, Nora and Sheldon had ordered off the grocery store's catering menu. As their selections were unloaded from the van and organized on the buffet tables, Nora saw that they'd made the right decision. The food looked and smelled incredibly appetizing, and the catering department had gone the extra mile by adding artistic touches to every platter.

On one plate, lemon slices and shrimp formed a flower with a cocktail sauce center. The caterers used a tiered stand to display vegetarian mini quiche interspersed with dill cucumber–tomato bites. Each cherry tomato was heart-shaped, as were the bell peppers on the deviled eggs and the strawberries on the fruit, cheese, and cracker plate.

Hovering over a chafing dish, Sheldon whined, "I'm dying for a meatball."

Liz, the female caterer, pointed toward the ticket agent's booth. "There's another tray in your kitchen."

"Shouldn't I sample one of everything?" Sheldon asked her. "I mean, what if the guests have questions about the food? Don't I need to be informed?"

The caterer looked to Nora for help.

"Grab a plate and serve yourself from the backup platters," she said. "You should sit down and eat while you can. If you don't chill for a few minutes, you'll pass out before you can say hello to the first guest."

"I might pass out later anyway. Even cheap wine tastes like Lafite Rothschild after a few glasses."

Nora wondered how many glasses she'd have to drink to feel calm. Between the pre-party jitters and the double espresso she'd had that afternoon, she was totally keyed up.

"I hope the rain doesn't keep people away," she said as she fluffed one of the decorative pillows in the Readers' Circle.

Sheldon pulled her down into the chair next to his and held on to her hands. "Stop beating the pillows. The store looks beautiful. *You* look beautiful. It's going to be a magical night. Okay?"

"Okay." Nora drew in a deep breath and let it out again. She squeezed Sheldon's hands and smiled at him, feeling relaxed for the first time in days. "Books, food, and friends. It doesn't get much better than that, does it?"

As if in reply, the sleigh bells jangled. Their first guest had arrived.

Sheldon's eyes sparkled as he looped his arm through Nora's. "Let's get this party started!"

* * *

The rain didn't deter a single guest. In fact, most of them were right on time.

The first guest to arrive was Luca, a member of Sheldon's book club. Luca had volunteered to man the bar and wanted to take a few minutes to get situated before the festivities began.

"The bottle in the gift bag is for you," Nora told Luca as he divided a sleeve of glasses into equal stacks.

"Aw, you didn't have to do that," he said. "Being in this book club has changed my life. I mean it. I used to be too scared to talk to women. But after coming here for a few months, I realized that I didn't have to be a pro athlete or drive a Ferrari to be interesting. You know Prisha, right? She told me I wasn't giving myself enough credit. She also said that I wasn't giving *women* enough credit. She guessed that I was letting the fake people on social media get under my skin, which was totally true. Now that I'm reading more and scrolling less, I'm *so* much happier."

In the front, the sleigh bells rang and Sheldon whooped with excitement.

"Holler at me when you need a break. I want to make sure you have plenty of chances to eat and mingle. I bet Prisha would agree." Nora winked at Luca and turned to say hello to another guest.

She was hanging an elderly man's parka on the coatrack she'd borrowed from Estella when June and Hester arrived.

"Lord, it's nasty out. Feel my nose." June pressed her cold nose to Nora's neck, laughing when she squealed in protest. After giving her a hug, she pointed at the coatrack. "Can we put ours in the stockroom? I parked behind the store and want to sneak out the back when it's time to go."

Nora nodded. "You're always thinking ahead."

Hester glanced around while unzipping her yellow raincoat.

"The shop looks amazing. And something smells amazing too. What is it? The cocktail meatballs you were telling me about?"

"Come on, I'll show you."

Nora led her friends to the stockroom, where they deposited their coats and umbrellas on the worktable and stood back to let Nora admire their Valentine's Day outfits.

Hester was adorable as ever in a red vintage blouse, boyfriend jeans, and red sneakers. A pink scarf doubled as her headband. June wore dark jeans and a winter-white sweater with a red ombré heart in the middle.

"Let's get a glass of wine before we hit the buffet," Nora said. "If we hold out for a bit, we can eat with Estella."

"You know she'll be the last one to arrive. How else can she make an entrance?" joked June.

As they headed to the bar, Hester whispered, "Don't let me drink too much. The idea of getting blackout drunk is pretty tempting right now."

"I doubt you'll be tempted once you try the wine, but I'll keep an eye on you." Nora slung an arm around Hester. "I'm glad you're here."

"Me too."

They waited at the window of the ticket agent's office, watching Luca pour wine into three glasses. He was about to pass them their drinks when he suddenly froze and murmured, "Wow."

Nora knew without turning around that Estella had arrived. She was one of those rare and enviable women who truly took people's breath away. She had an elusive quality that went beyond beauty—a magnetic presence that demanded attention.

At this moment, every eye was on her, though Estella pretended not to notice. When she saw her friends, however, her face lit up with such sincere happiness that the rest of the guests were awestruck all over again.

Estella's black dress had a formfitting bodice and a flirty, tea-length skirt. Its only embellishment was the embroidered red rose on her left shoulder strap. Her hair fell in soft waves and she wore no jewelry. No accessory could compete with her radiant skin and shining eyes.

"Hello, lovely!" June cried, opening her arms for a hug.

Whenever she wore a full face of makeup, Estella preferred loose hugs. But tonight, she held her friends tightly and distributed exuberant kisses on their cheeks.

"Jack must be better. You're walking on air," Nora said.

Estella kicked up a heel. "He's so much better that he threatened to bar me from his hospital room if I didn't come here tonight. And I have to take pictures to show him tomorrow." She looked at June. "Your son has excellent taste. Jasmine is *just* like you. She's a natural when it comes to taking care of people. And she isn't afraid to stand up for what she believes in either. She's your Mini-Me."

June held up a warning finger. "Don't let Tyson hear you say that. No man wants to realize that the woman of his dreams is a younger version of his mama."

Nora saw McCabe out of the corner of her eye, so she waved for her friends to head to the Children's section. "Grab some food. I'll see you in there."

The area around the ticket agent's booth was packed with people, and McCabe had yet to spot her. But when his gaze finally met hers, his eyes filled with tiny stars, each one shining just for her.

He paused to smile or say hello as he made his way over to her, and Nora was relieved to see that no one stiffened at the sight of him. In his merlot sweater and gray slacks, he fit right in.

When he made it to Nora's side, McCabe slid an arm around her back and pulled her against him. Putting his lips to her ear, he whispered, "You're the prettiest flower in the garden."

The feel of his breath against her neck raised her body temperature by several degrees. Nora gave him a soft, sweet kiss on the cheek before easing away from him. She couldn't stand that close to him and still think straight.

"Would you like some of that subpar wine I promised?"

"I'd rather have what's in the fridge."

Nora pointed at the kitchen. "That fridge?"

Lips curved in an inscrutable smile, McCabe watched Nora open the fridge and scan shelves stuffed with food for the party, a variety of milk, and cans of club soda. When she discovered the bottle of Moët & Chandon champagne in the produce drawer, she murmured, "Wow."

"With my job, I've learned to celebrate the good things in life. This"—he motioned between Nora and himself—"is a good thing."

"When did you hide this?"

McCabe started opening cabinets. "I had an accomplice. He was supposed to stash a pair of flutes in—ah, here they are. We don't have enough to share, so I'll try to open this quietly."

Luca glanced at the bottle in McCabe's hands. "Wanna know how to stop the pop in three steps?" He waited for McCabe's nod before continuing, "One, dry the bottle with a towel. Two, cut the foil and loosen the cage. Three, hold the cork in place while you slowly twist the bottle. You'll ease the cork out without making a sound."

"Thanks, I appreciate the tip." McCabe followed Luca's advice to the letter. After filling two champagne flutes with pale pink bubbly, he poured some into a wineglass for Luca.

Luca beamed and raised his glass. "To men who drink pink. And to the fairest bookseller in the land."

The champagne tasted like sun-ripened strawberries with a hint of blackberry and grapefruit. It was elegant and lively, and a lovely surprise.

Nora caught hold of McCabe's hand. "Let's wander over to the buffet. This might be our only chance to eat before Sheldon kicks off the game portion of the evening. Luca, are you hungry?"

"I'm all set. Prisha made me a plate."

Estella, June, Hester, and Sheldon stood in a loose circle between the Cookbook and Gardening sections. They made room for Nora and McCabe and seamlessly incorporated them into their conversation.

Other than Bobbie, everyone I care about is right here, Nora thought.

She reveled in the food, the company, the music, and the laughter. She finished her meal moments before Sheldon called everyone to the Readers' Circle.

Folding chairs had been arranged in the space previously occupied by the upholstered chairs, which were now in the stockroom.

"Squeeze in tight!" Sheldon directed gleefully. "We're playing a party game called Entitled, and yes, I *did* invent it. Two teams will battle to be the first to reach a hundred points. Pick someone to be your team scribe. This person will write down as many *legitimate* book titles as you can think of in three minutes. When the timer goes off, you'll read your titles out loud and every legit title gets you one point."

"What happens if we think a title is bogus?" someone asked.

Sheldon pointed at a woman in the second row. "Good question, Sondra. If you challenge the opposing team and their title is incorrect, you'll get five points. But if their title *is* correct, you lose five points. The losing team is in charge of snacks for our next book club meeting."

Someone called out, "I don't get it. How do we come up with the titles?"

"In this bag are a bunch of incredibly random nouns and a few adjectives just for kicks. Each team will pick two words from the bag. Both words must be a subject in a real work of fiction. My lovely assistant will help me demonstrate."

Sheldon held out a paper bag. June drew the word *boat* and showed it to the crowd. Next she picked the word *monkey*.

"Pretend the clock is ticking! Who has a guess?" Sheldon cried.

Luca leaned over the bar and said, "How about *Life of Pi*?"

The woman named Sondra clapped. "Nice, Luca!"

"*The Voyages of Doctor Dolittle!*" someone else shouted.

A few more titles were put forth before Sheldon signaled for a timeout and said, "I think you've got it. Are you ready to play Entitled?"

Judging by the raucous applause, the participants couldn't wait to start.

The first round went off without a hitch. Nora was impressed by the number of titles each team came up with. The game was a hit, and with every round, the noise level in the shop escalated.

Nora couldn't remember the last time she'd had this much fun or laughed so loud and so often. When she wasn't laughing, she was talking to McCabe or her friends.

Eventually the game ended, and she made her way around the store, collecting empty wine cups and chatting. Every guest made a point of telling her how much they loved Miracle Books, the book club, or both. They raved about Sheldon, thanked her for turning Valentine's Day into something to look forward to, and, of course, brought up their current read.

The desserts were nearly gone, and the wine was running dangerously low when Sheldon called everyone back to the Readers' Circle for another game. This time, individual winners would choose a Blind Date book from the display near the checkout counter.

"You should play," Nora told McCabe. "There are more than enough books."

His smile was as soft as a caress. "I'm not here for the books. I'm here to see you in your element."

Simultaneously pleased and embarrassed, Nora said, "You see me in my element all the time."

"As Nora the Book Cupid. Book Party Nora is new. I like them both."

Nora gave him a playful jab. "Exactly how much did you drink while I was gone?"

McCabe laughed and murmured something about Sheldon and tequila. Nora didn't hear the precise words because her attention was diverted by a dark-haired young woman sitting in the fourth row.

It was Lea, and she was clearly having a ball. Nora was delighted. After what Lea had been through, she deserved to cut loose and enjoy herself.

Glancing around, Nora wondered who'd invited her. Whoever it was must have given her a ride too. Even if one of Lea's arms wasn't in a cast, Nora remembered her saying that she avoided driving at night.

Nora turned back to McCabe and saw that one of his officers, a middle-aged man attending the party with his wife, now had his ear. She gave the men their space and focused on the game. A few minutes later, she felt McCabe's hand on her shoulder.

"I have to talk to you in private. Can we go to the front?"

Based on the gravity of his tone, she knew what he had to say had nothing to do with the party, and as she preceded him through the Fiction section, she wondered if Candace had finally made contact. Would her side of the story cast a shadow over the nimbus of light around Miles Comfort's head? Or would she quell the rumors, once and for all?

McCabe had stashed his coat behind the checkout counter, and Nora wasn't surprised to see him collect it. As soon as he said he needed to speak to her in private, she knew that he had to leave. She just didn't know why.

"There's a fender bender up the block," he said as he put on his coat. "Officers are at the scene, but one of the drivers is inebriated and combative. He took a swing at the female officer and is shouting racist comments at the male officer. Davis volunteered to lend a hand, but he's had three drinks to my one."

Davis was the officer McCabe had been speaking with in the Readers' Circle. Nora knew that he and his wife were also celebrating their tenth wedding anniversary.

Smoothing the front of McCabe's coat, she said, "It's a tough holiday. Not everyone's lucky enough to have Clark Kent as their valentine."

McCabe smiled. "More like Clark Kent's father, but thanks for the compliment."

The winner of the last round, a young woman named Meghan and a member of Sheldon's book club, appeared from the back. Red-faced and giggling, she closed her eyes and picked a book from the Blind Book Date display.

"It's supposed to be a blind date, right?" Meghan let out a snort. "I've been on *one* blind date and that was enough. What a disaster! I had coffee with a guy who thought *The Grapes of Wrath* was a brand of cereal."

McCabe wrapped his fingers around Nora's hand and held it against his chest. In his eyes, she saw all the words he'd say if they were alone.

"Be careful," she whispered.

But he was already out the door, the sleigh bells jangling in his wake.

"Where's your date?" asked Estella when Nora returned to the Readers' Circle.

"Dealing with a drunk driver a block away. He'll be tied up with that until way after the party's over."

Estella held up the paper-wrapped book she'd won. "Most of us have our books and there's hardly any wine left, so I think people will start leaving soon. Normally, I'd stay until the very end, but I want to be at the hospital first thing tomorrow."

Not long after Estella left, a guest who lived on the western edge of the county said that his roommate just called to warn him about the weather.

"Freezing rain is on the way!" he declared.

The announcement spurred the guests into action. With help from June and Hester, Nora cleared the buffet table and transferred coats from the stockroom to the table.

"Isn't that yours?" Nora asked Hester when a young woman grabbed a yellow raincoat from the pile.

"Nope. Mine's reversible. You can see the teal color inside the hood."

June dropped a fresh pile of coats on the table. "There must be five black parkas here. I hope people can tell them apart."

As soon as the last few guests were gone, Nora urged June, Hester, and Sheldon to head home before the roads iced over.

"Give me two minutes," Sheldon implored June. "If I don't clean the kitchen, I'll have nightmares."

June snorted. "Doesn't seem to bother you at home."

"The Board of Health doesn't grade that kitchen. Come on, what's that saying about many hands and light work?"

"It says you'd better hop to it the next time your housemate asks you to take out the garbage."

Nora locked the front door and then she and Hester collected the tea-light candles.

"What a great party," Hester said. "I haven't laughed or eaten that much in forever! It was *exactly* what I needed."

"Me too."

Hester dropped the last candle into the bag hanging from Nora's wrist. "Now I just need to find my umbrella."

"I'll check up front, but it's probably in the stockroom."

There were no umbrellas on the counter, so Nora turned off the lights and returned to the Readers' Circle. Seeing that Sheldon and June were almost done cleaning, she switched off the lamps in the Children's Corner and headed down the hall to the stockroom.

As she drew closer, she heard someone say, "I took the job with the Comforts because of you."

Nora paused. *Why is Lea still here? And what does Hester have to do with Lea's nanny job?*

Hester was obviously confused too, because she said, "I don't understand."

"Look at me. Look at my face."

Lea's tone was brusque and commanding. She didn't sound like the young woman who brought Jefferson to storytime each week. Concerned, Nora edged up to the doorway.

Hester and Lea stood in front of the bookshelves, facing each other. Lea wasn't wearing her glasses and her thick bangs had been swept off her forehead and held in place with a hair clip.

Nora felt like she was seeing Lea's face for the first time. Without the oversized glasses and the curtain of bangs, she looked like a different person.

She looks like . . .

Across the room, the color leached from Hester's face. She stood stock-still, staring at the other woman.

"You see it, don't you?" Lea's eyes flashed with defiance. "Seeing is believing, right? It's true. I'm your daughter."

Chapter 18

Everybody trusts a guy in a raincoat. I don't know why. It's just one of those mystery facts.

—Stephen King

The silence stretched like a rubber band.

Lea was the first to break it.

"I don't want anything from you," she said. "I just wanted you to know. In case you ever wondered about me, the way I wondered about you."

When Hester still didn't reply, Lea released her bangs from the hair clip and put her glasses on.

Nora didn't want Lea to know that she'd witnessed such an intimate scene, so she slowly backpedaled. She made it to the restroom when she heard Hester call out, "Lea, wait! *Please!*"

A shadow darkened the stockroom's doorway. Lea was inches away from coming out to the hall.

"Did the people who . . ." Hester stopped herself and tried again. "Growing up, were you okay?"

The pause that followed was so long that Nora was able to reach the other end of the hall. As she rounded the corner, she bumped into Sheldon. June was right behind him.

Nora put her fingers to her lips, pointed at the hall, and frantically shook her head.

At that moment, they heard one word. A resounding *"No!"*

Sheldon looked at Nora and mouthed, "Who is that?"

The slamming of the back door prevented her from answering.

June whispered, "What's going on?"

There were no more noises, but even though it was quiet, Nora couldn't reply.

Words circled in her mind, like sink water being sucked down a drain. The speed and velocity kept increasing, making her breathless.

Hester, Lea, Elijah, mother, daughter, father, Hester, Lea, Elijah.

Unable to speak, Nora grabbed the lapel of Sheldon's coat and tugged. Understanding that he was meant to follow her, Sheldon gave Nora his hand to hold instead of his coat.

The three of them hurried to the stockroom, where they found Hester on the floor, hugging her knees to her chest.

June rushed over and knelt at her side. "What's wrong, baby?"

"Baby," Hester repeated in a wooden voice. She looked at June through dull eyes. "My. Baby. She . . . was here."

June shot Nora a frightened glance.

Hester kept talking. "I didn't think I had the right—to look for her. To know her story. I didn't think I deserved to know her name." She smiled to herself. "It's a pretty name. *She's* pretty. She has his eyes. I didn't see them past her glasses. And I think she covered her freckles with makeup. She got those from me. Her hands too. But the rest of her is Elijah."

"Your daughter? Is that who you're talking about?" June asked.

Sheldon gasped, but it was too late to hide anything from him now.

A sigh burst out from deep in Hester's chest. It was heavy enough to sink a ship. "I want to go home."

June nodded. "Okay, honey. We'll take you. Sheldon?"

Sheldon extended his hand to Hester. "On your feet, *cariño mío*. June's got your coat, Nora has your umbrella, and I've got you."

At the back door, June passed her key fob to Sheldon. He walked Hester to the car, covering her head with the umbrella until she was safely inside. Ice pellets bounced off the umbrella's canvas and skied down the slope of June's windshield.

"You're white as a sheet," June said to Nora. "Who went out this door a few minutes ago?"

Hester, Elijah, Lea. Mother, father, daughter. Hester, Elijah, Lea.

"Lea."

June put her hand over her heart. "*She's* Hester's child?"

"Hester and Elijah—Lea's their daughter."

"Oh, Lord, Hester. The father of your child is dead and your grown daughter has been living in the same town as you for months. That's too much for anyone to bear." June pulled her hood over her hair and hugged Nora. "If Andrews isn't waiting for her at home, I'll stay with her tonight. She shouldn't be alone."

June scurried to her car. As soon as she drove out of the lot, Nora locked up and went home.

The metal stairs leading to her deck were covered with a skein of ice and her WELCOME mat crunched under her weight. As she got ready for bed, her bedroom lamp flickered. It would be no surprise if the power went out while she slept, so she put a flashlight on her nightstand and plugged in a portable phone charger.

As she listened to the snare drum rattle of the freezing rain, she wondered if McCabe was home, or if he was still at the station. She'd love to hear his voice right now, but she wouldn't call him. Even though Hester's secret had a direct bearing on McCabe's investigation, Nora wouldn't share it with him. Even though it might kill the thing growing between them—the warm, tender homecoming thing—she would stay quiet.

Hester was more than a friend. She was family. And Nora would go to the ends of the earth to protect her family.

She put her phone on silent mode and crawled into bed. When she closed her eyes, a collage of images began forming in her head. Lea and Hester in her stockroom. Lea holding Jefferson. Lea in the bonus room of the Comforts' house. Lea locating Miracle Springs on a map. Lea standing outside the Gingerbread House, waiting for that first glimpse of her mother.

She found out the names of her biological parents. She found out where they lived. She made a life in her mother's town. She watched and waited until she was ready to reveal herself. She told Hester that she hadn't been okay growing up.

What does it all mean? What does she want?

Nora pictured the ruined copies of *The Scarlet Letter* and remembered feeling the anger behind each gash—the desire to obliterate a name.

Her last cohesive thought before sleep came was *She wants revenge.*

June stopped by Nora's tiny house on her way to church. She wore a floral shawl over a pale pink dress with a full skirt.

"You look like springtime," Nora said while pouring her friend a cup of coffee.

"Except for the black rubber boots. But I'm not going to wear good shoes. It's a mess out there." June took a grateful sip of coffee. "If I didn't have so many prayers to raise up to the rafters, I might have stayed in bed all day."

Nora added another splash of cream to her coffee. She always made it strong, but she'd overdone it this morning and it was more bitter than strong.

"Sorry I didn't call to say I was coming. I just drove here without really thinking about it. I guess my car knew I needed to see you."

Nora said, "Your car must have known that my coffee tastes like Quaker State coffee."

The two friends laughed.

"How's Hester?" Nora asked.

The humor left June's eyes. "She didn't want to talk. Not last night or this morning. She was going to clean the house, make a nice lunch for her man, and tell him about Lea. She's going to do it too. I could see it in her face."

"Oh." Nora pushed her spoon around in her mug. "Do you think Estella's at the hospital?"

"Probably. We should call her."

Estella picked up on the second ring, greeting June in a bright, upbeat voice.

"I'm with Nora, and I've got you on speaker. Are you with Jack?"

"I am," said Estella. "He's doing even better today than yesterday. They're moving him to a different floor today. He'll be eating regular meals and watching bad TV in a few hours."

Nora and June smiled at the phone.

"Keisha visited last night," Estella chattered on. "She and Jack got a bunch of work stuff straightened out, which means Jack might actually listen when the nurses tell him to rest."

June said, "We're so happy for you. And for Jack. Tell your man that I won't stop praying for him until I see him in his apron, cooking the lightest, fluffiest pancakes in the South."

There was a murmur in the background and Estella laughed. "Jack said you should put that in a Yelp review."

After promising to add it to her to-do list, June said, "Honey, can you step out of the room for a sec? Something happened after you left the bookshop last night, and it's for Secret, Book, and Scone Society ears only."

"Got it," she said. Then, "Jack, I'm going to talk to the girls on my way to the cafeteria. I'll be back in a few."

"I'll be waiting."

It was wonderful to hear Jack's voice. It sounded a little weak, but he was awake and talking.

Nora and June exchanged joyful smiles. One of their friends, at least, was coming out the other side of a terrifying ordeal.

"Okay, I'm in the hall," said Estella. "What's going on?"

June looked at Nora and pointed at the phone. Nora nodded and said, "Hester's daughter was at the party."

"*What?*"

"That's what she told Hester—that she was her daughter. And when I saw them standing together in the stockroom, I knew she was telling the truth. She has Hester's nose and mouth. And her freckles. She got Elijah's brown hair and eyes. Maybe his height too because she isn't as tall as Hester."

When Estella didn't respond, Nora wondered if the call had been dropped, but following a slam and a *whoosh* of air, Estella said, "Sorry. My brain went all fuzzy and I had to get outside. I can't believe this! She was at the *party?* Wait—do we know her?"

"It's Lea Carle."

"*No!* It can't be! *Lea?*" She blew raspberries into the phone. "It's going to take a hot minute before this sinks in."

June grunted. "I'm still waiting for it to sink in."

"Why did Lea tell Hester last night? Because it was Valentine's Day? Because she was almost killed? Is that what finally prompted her to introduce herself?" Estella spat out questions like they were watermelon seeds. "How did Hester react? And where is she right now?" After a quick intake of breath, she asked one more. "Does Andrews know?"

Nora chose to answer the last question.

"Hester and Andrews are having lunch at her house today, and she's going to tell him that her daughter is here, in Miracle Springs. I'm counting on Andrews to contact McCabe afterward. He needs to know about last night—just not from me."

"Yes." Estella turned the word into a sigh. "Someone scratched Hester's name out of a bunch of books around the same time Elijah's body was found in a ravine. I'd say our sheriff definitely needs to know that Hester and Elijah are Lea's biological parents."

June frowned at Nora. "Do you think Lea did those things?"

"Maybe she wanted to punish them for giving her up for adoption. I think Lea's angry at Hester because she never tried to find her."

"But that doesn't explain the Lady Artist books or the name hidden in the covers," June argued. "After you told us about that at the party, I kept wondering what made that flower so important. I still don't see it. There are no Marigolds in this story—unless Lea's middle name is Marigold. And let's not forget the man in the black truck. Lea didn't force herself off the road. How does he fit in?"

Whatever Estella said next was drowned out by sirens. "Hold on!" she yelled.

In the seconds it took June to put her coffee cup in the sink, Estella was back.

"This place is such a circus that I don't know how anyone gets better here. The noise is nonstop. If, by some miracle, a patient is able to fall asleep, they can't stay asleep. Between the checking of vitals and the parade of carts, the alarms and talking—I can't wait until Jack is well enough to go home."

June said, "I hope that's soon. I need to run, or I'll be late for church, but give Jack a big hug from us."

"I will. And if you hear from Hester, call me. I hope she and Andrews will be okay." After a pause, Estella added, "You're going to pray for them, right?"

"I pray for everyone I care about, and not just on Sundays."

After June left, Nora started a load of laundry and did her weekly dusting and vacuuming. While her clothes tumbled in the dryer, she tackled the bathroom and made a grocery list. She didn't mind doing household chores, because they gave her a chance to catch up on her current audiobook.

Listening while working wasn't usually a problem, but she was so captivated by Colson Whitehead's *Harlem Shuffle* that she added eggs to her list three times. She'd also written certain words so close together that it looked like she needed to buy green-bean ice cream.

By the time she was ready to venture out, the sun was shining in a winter-blue sky. It was too early to hit the flea market, so Nora decided to walk to the grocery store.

She crossed the wet parking lot, heading for the narrow lane running behind the block of shops. Water dripped from the eaves and pooled at the base of the buildings. At the mouth of the alley that would take her to Main Street, she paused.

Something was on the ground near the trash bins pressed up against the wall of the hardware store. There were four bins in all, and in the space between the garbage and recycling bins, Nora saw a flash of yellow.

Because the alley was a blend of muted grays and browns, it was hard to miss the pop of color. It was like seeing a canary perched on a leafless tree.

As Nora approached the bins, she recognized the particular shade of yellow. It was the color of ripe lemons, of the brick road in *The Wizard of Oz*. It was raincoat yellow.

"HESTER!"

Nora ran to the gap between the trash bins.

When she had a clear view of the body on the dirty ground, she screamed Hester's name again.

Inching closer, she took in more details. A red ankle boot, the lower half of a leg clad in acid-washed jeans, and the curve of a pale cheek. The yellow hood had fallen back, revealing a cloud of curly, dark hair.

Nora let out a sob of relief. It wasn't Hester.

Her relief quickly gave way to shame. A woman was dead.

She was one of two women who'd worn yellow raincoats to the Blind Date Book Bash.

Nora unslung her backpack and removed her phone from the front pocket.

It felt heavy in her trembling hand, but McCabe's voice helped steady her.

"Take a breath," he soothed. "That's it. A big breath in. Hold it. Now let it out slowly. Good. Okay, let's start over. Where are you?"

"In the alley between the florist and the hardware store. There's a woman—her body's here. She's in Sheldon's book club. She was at the party."

"I'm on my way. Keep your distance from her, and if anyone else tries to get close, tell them I'm seconds away."

Nora stared at the woman's profile. "Her name's Meghan. She likes YA and contemporary romance. She loves hot chocolate with extra marshmallows."

"What else?" McCabe sounded breathless, like he was running.

"Her umbrella's on the ground. It's still open. Her mouth is too. But her eyes are closed. She's in a fetal position, and . . ." Nora leaned forward to see if Meghan had dropped a purse or a set of car keys. What she saw instead was a purple line encircling her neck. The skin surrounding the line was marred with bruises or mud, Nora couldn't tell which.

She backed away, darting fearful glances at either end of the alley. No one was there. No one was coming.

"I'll be there in two minutes, Nora," McCabe panted. "What else can you tell me about Meghan?"

Nora tried to slow the rapid-fire beat of her heart.

Focus, she told herself. *Focus on Meghan.*

"I think . . . I think someone choked her. There's a mark on her neck." Nora scanned the ground for a length of wire or thin rope.

"Is she wearing gloves?"

Reluctantly Nora looked back at Meghan. "Yes. They look like the ones June knits. They have pink, blue, and yellow stripes."

"I'm pulling up to the alley now. Do you see me?"

Nora heard an engine and then a sheriff's department SUV came to an abrupt stop at the mouth of the alley. The car was still bucking in protest when McCabe's door flew open and he vaulted out.

Other vehicles joined McCabe's and soon there was a handful of officers at the end of the alley. Equipment was unloaded. Officers pulled on jumpsuits and booties. The quiet was broken by shouts, radio noise, and the slamming of trunks and car doors.

The activity had a calming effect on Nora. McCabe and his team would take care of Meghan. They would examine her and document the scene. They'd collect clues and place markers on the wet ground.

Eventually they'd pick her up, lay her on a stretcher, and cover her. She'd be protected from the cold and shielded from prying eyes. Her dignity would be carefully guarded.

Right now, McCabe cared more about the living woman in the alley.

Moving to her side, he put a supportive arm around her waist. "Come on, let's get you out of the cold."

Nora glanced at the dead woman. "Someone killed her, Grant. Because of that raincoat. Hester wore a yellow raincoat last night. It was so dark. And there was rain. Whoever followed Meghan into this alley wouldn't have known they made a mistake until it was done."

"I want to hear everything, but not until you're in the car."

With Nora safely relocated to the passenger seat of McCabe's SUV, his team began cordoning off the alley and taking photographs.

McCabe handed Nora a bottle of water. "I wouldn't make a very good Saint Bernard, but it's all I've got. Take a few sips."

After draining half the bottle, Nora told McCabe all she knew about Meghan.

"She moved here after Christmas to work as a speech pathologist in our schools. The last one quit without warning, and Meghan was ready for a change of scenery. She lived in a small town outside of Winston-Salem and was thrilled to be closer to the mountains. She joined Sheldon's book group, hoping to make friends, which she did. She was outgoing and sweet. Everyone liked her."

"Did you see her leave last night?"

"I didn't see her walk out the door because I was moving coats from the stockroom to the Children's Corner at the end of the party, but when I saw Meghan grab a yellow raincoat off the table, I thought she'd taken Hester's coat by accident. But Hester's was still in the stockroom. It was a bit different from Meghan's because it was reversible. The other color was teal. You could see it in the inside of the hood," Nora said, demonstrating on her own coat.

McCabe wrote in his notepad. "Any idea what time that was?"

Nora gave him her best guess and went on to add that Hester, June, and Sheldon had stayed to help clean up. "We all left together. That would have been thirty minutes or so after Meghan left."

"Do you remember seeing other cars in the lot?"

"Not counting June's and Hester's, I'd say two or three. There were no people around. The cars probably belonged to party guests who drank too much and had to catch a ride home." Nora remembered seeing her friends hurry out to June's car. "The weather had turned really nasty by that point. I don't think any of us looked around. I know I didn't. I left the store and hurried home as fast as I could."

McCabe nodded. "Did you know everyone at last night's party? In other words, if I showed you the guest list, would you recognize all the names?"

"Yes. They're all regulars."

"Did anything surprising or unexpected happen at the party? Arguments? Rumors? Dirty looks or whispering in corners?" Nora shook her head and McCabe grew pensive. "Did anyone seem detached or look like they felt out of place?"

Nora remembered the small clusters of jovial people scattered throughout the bookstore. "Everyone talked to everyone else. You were there. Did you see anyone *not* having a good time? Because I didn't. Nothing unusual happened the whole night except—" She stopped before she said too much.

"Except?"

How can I tell him what he needs to know without spilling Hester's secret?

She could feel McCabe's eyes on her. He knew how to read people. He'd been doing it for decades. If she didn't give him something tangible, he'd question her until he was certain she'd told him everything.

"It was Lea Carle. She wasn't on the guest list and she didn't buy a ticket. She just showed up. I don't even know when. I noticed her during the first book game." Nora raised her hands. "Don't get me wrong, I'm glad she was there. I'm glad she had a chance to take a break from the Comforts, and I wish I'd invited her to the party. After all she's done for me and all she's been through, I should have asked her to come."

"Hm. I wonder how she got to the party and who drove her home. She doesn't drive after dark."

Nora thought back on her conversation with Lea. "I don't know how she got home, but she was one of the last people to leave."

McCabe's gaze sharpened. "Was that around the time Meghan left?"

"No," Nora said firmly. "A small group of people lingered for ten of fifteen minutes after the rest of the guests made a hasty exit. They were all worried about getting home safely, but the guests who stayed till the very end lived in town. They wanted to see which Blind Date books their friends had gotten. After that, they helped tidy up a bit before heading out."

McCabe's pen raced across the paper. When he was done writing, he closed the notepad and tapped the tip of his pen against the cover. "I'm sure I'll have more questions as things develop." He gestured at her backpack. "Where were you headed when you found her?"

"The grocery store."

Nora glanced at the alley through the window. It was surreal to see it buzzing with movement and noise. It no longer resembled the quiet, shadowy place where she'd noticed a splash of yellow.

"You usually hit the flea market first, but I guess the roads weren't clear enough for your moped," said McCabe. "They still aren't, but I can run you over there if you want."

Nora gave him a weak smile. "Honestly, I don't know what I want. I don't want to go home, but the flea market is too people-y. I'd have sensory overload in five minutes. I'll stick to my grocery store plan. Walking sounds good right now. I think it'll help me process this."

"I think so too." McCabe covered her hand with his. "Anytime you want to talk today, give me a call. If I see your name on my phone, I'll answer. Okay?"

"Okay."

He squeezed her hand. "We're going to figure this out. Elijah, Meghan, the old books—all of it."

Nora heard the conviction in his voice and saw resolve burning in his eyes. There was strength and warmth in his grip.

Turning his hand over, she laced her fingers through his and said, "I believe you."

They sat in silence for a long moment, and though Nora didn't want to let go of McCabe's hand, she knew she had to get out of the car. If he kept gazing at her so tenderly, she'd tell him everything, and she couldn't do that to Hester.

She pulled away and reached for her backpack. "What's your next step?"

"After I spend time with Meghan, I'll have a chat with Lea."

Nora's fingers moved to the door handle. "Why? Because she wasn't on last night's guest list?"

"Partly, but there's another reason. Elijah's mother said that he didn't wear contacts or glasses, even though he probably needed them. I need to call and have her clarify what she meant by that."

After wishing him luck, Nora got out of the car.

As she walked away from the alley as quickly as she could, she remembered Hester saying, "Lea has Elijah's eyes."

Chapter 19

*He who has no Fools, Knaves, nor Beggars in his
Family, was begot by a Flash of Lightning.*
— Thomas Fuller

Nora had no choice but to wait for events to unfold. In the
upcoming hours, Hester would tell Andrews the identity of her
daughter. Andrews would then immediately share this information with McCabe. And even though the connection between
Hester, Elijah, and Lea would be revealed, plenty of unan-
swered questions remained.

After unpacking her groceries and putting her sheets in the
washing machine, Nora sat down with a cup of tea and made a
list of all the things that still had to be resolved.

> *What do the Lady Artist books mean?*
> *Who's Marigold?*
> *Who drove the black truck?*
> *Who killed Meghan?*
> *Was the killer at the party?*
> *Is Hester in danger?*
> *Is Miles Comfort involved?*
> *What inspired Lea to find her parents?*
> *What does she want?*

*   *   *

Nora sipped her tea and stared at the list. When no insightful revelations or brilliant ideas came to her, she wandered through her tiny house, searching for something to clean. And while emptying her refrigerator, wiping the shelves, and reloading her foodstuff was productive, she still didn't know how to help McCabe find answers. And if she couldn't help McCabe, how could she protect Hester?

The washing machine beeped, and as she moved her sheets to the dryer, a line from *The Guernsey Literary and Potato Peel Pie Society* ran through her mind.

"'We clung to books and to our friends,'" she said aloud.

Nora shook her head. Why had she been trying to solve these issues by herself? She knew better than that. Books and friends were her magic weapons. Always had been. And it was time to rely on them again.

She called Sheldon.

He answered by saying, "What a night. It was all so glorious until . . ." He didn't bother finishing the sentence. "I can't believe Hester's been carrying that secret around all this time. I just want to wrap her up in a hug and never let her go. And Lea? What are the chances that the child she last saw twenty-plus years ago ended up in the same town?"

"I'd say they're slim to none," Nora replied. "I was calling to ask if you've eaten yet. I'm making grilled cheese and tomato soup for lunch if you'd like to join me."

"That would be perfection, but my chauffeur is having lunch with Tyson and Jasmine and it's too cold to hoof it— wait! Mrs. Lassiter's walking to her car. Let me see if she's heading your way."

Nora heard Sheldon holler at his neighbor. A moment later, he said, "I'll be there in ten. With bread."

The soup was simmering when Sheldon arrived. He handed

Nora a loaf of Cuban bread, draped his coat over a chair, and followed her into the kitchen.

"Why is the alley roped off? Wait, wait! Let me guess! The raccoons were partying in the trash cans again."

Nora buttered four slices of bread and laid them on the warm griddle. Next she turned the burner to the medium-low setting and covered the bread with white cheddar cheese. She'd already put napkins and glasses of water at the table, so she steered Sheldon to a chair. When he was seated, she took his hand.

"When I cut through that alley this morning, I found a woman's body near the hardware store. I'm sorry to be the one to tell you this, but it was Meghan."

Sheldon reared back. "*My* Meghan?"

"Yes."

He shook his head. "That can't be right. She was at the party, having the time of her life. She's young and healthy. You must be thinking of someone else."

Nora didn't argue. She just held his hand.

After a long moment, he pressed his napkin to his wet eyes and said, "Tell me everything."

Nora did. She told him about the marks on Meghan's neck and how two women had worn yellow raincoats to the party.

"I think someone targeted Meghan because of that raincoat. If it had been another color, she'd probably be alive right now."

Sheldon paled. "*Hester* has a yellow raincoat. *Ay, Dios mío,* the books! The person who scratched her name out of the books—do they want to kill her?"

"Maybe. I don't know. I told McCabe about all of it, just in case I'm right, but I hope I'm not." Nora released Sheldon's hand and went into the kitchen to flip the sandwiches.

"I was in the shower when June got home from Hester's house this morning and was gone again before I got out. So where's Hester right now?"

"With Andrews."

Nora ladled tomato soup into two bowls and carried them to the table. Next she slid the sandwiches off the griddle and onto a cutting board. She sliced each sandwich into four triangles— the perfect size for dipping—and plated them.

She served Sheldon first. He murmured his thanks, but his eyes were on his phone. "Should we call everyone from the party? Maybe someone saw Meghan leave or knows something we don't—some detail we missed because we were too busy hosting."

"I think Meghan's killer saw Hester in her yellow raincoat. That would have been at the beginning of the party. She and June left their coats in the stockroom, which is where Hester was around the time Meghan left."

Sheldon watched Nora's spoon move through her soup, raising wisps of steam with every pass. "We need to know who saw Hester show up in her yellow raincoat and *also* saw a woman in a yellow raincoat leave hours later. Was this person watching from a parked car? Or from inside the bookstore? No. It can't be one of our book friends. It just *can't*."

"I don't know your book club members like you do, but we have to take a close look at all of them." Sheldon opened his mouth to protest, but she kept talking. "Elijah was found dead in the woods. Meghan was found dead in an alley. I don't want Hester to be found dead, do you hear me? If we really want to keep her safe, we'll help McCabe find out what the hell is happening."

"Okay!" Sheldon shouted. "I want to help! Of course, I do. I just *hate* this. I *hate* that someone took Meghan's life. I *hate* that someone wants to hurt Hester. And the idea that someone in my book group might be responsible—*it's too much*."

Nora nodded in understanding. "Then let's work on ruling them out. Let's figure out who was in the bookstore after

Meghan left. Which guests carpooled? Who walked home together? Who left alone? We'll call everyone. As we talk to people and compare stories, we can start crossing them off the list."

Sheldon picked up a grilled cheese triangle and took a bite. "I
shouldn't be able to eat, but I want to. What kind of person can
eat at a time like this?"

"The kind of person who needs to convert food into energy,"
Nora soothed. "We both need to eat because we have work to
do. And while we're doing that, you can look at the guest list
and tell me things about your book club members that I probably don't know."

By the time they finished their meal, Nora learned that most
of Sheldon's book group only knew Hester from the bakery.
Some were regular customers, while others rarely patronized
the Gingerbread House. None of them had cause to dislike her.

"That didn't get us anywhere," Sheldon said, gazing at the
guest list. "What about Lea?"

"McCabe might be talking to her right now."

Sheldon's forehead creased. "Why? Didn't you say that she
was one of the last people to leave?"

"She was also the only person at the party whose name wasn't
on our guest list." Nora stacked their plates. "McCabe wants to
know if she was invited by another guest or if she attended on a
whim. She couldn't drive with that broken arm, so he'd also
like to know how she got to the bookstore."

Leaving Sheldon to mull this over, Nora carried their plates
into the kitchen. She washed the griddle pan by hand and
loaded everything else into the dishwasher. When the sink was
empty, she filled the electric kettle. Contacting all the guests
from last night's party would require caffeine.

She placed two mugs on the counter. "I'm making tea," she
called out. "I have Earl Grey, Cinnamon Spice, a floral relax-
ation blend, or Decaf Breakfast. Do you have a preference?"

The kettle's gurgle drowned out Sheldon's reply, but Nora thought he said something about flowers.

Moving closer to the table, she asked, "Did you say you wanted the floral blend?"

Sheldon's phone was in his hand. "Is Lea a nickname?"

Nora was overwhelmed by the feeling that it was important to learn the answer to this question. Ignoring the kettle's agitated rumbling, she sat back down. "I don't know, but I think we need to know."

Sheldon pointed at the list. "I just added her name and the question popped in my head."

Nora grabbed her laptop and typed "Lea" and "nickname for" into Google's search box.

"According to this baby name site, Lea can be short for 'Leann, Leandra, Cecilia, Lorelei, Amelia, Cornelia, Ophelia . . .'" After reciting more names, Nora added, "There's also Leah with an *H* and an *L-I-A* version."

"This site has most of yours, plus 'Julia, Leila, Eleanor, Leonora, Linnea, and Ileana.'"

"Never heard those last two before."

Sheldon squinted at his screen. "Am I supposed to hold my phone under a microscope to be able to read this? Can you see what it says?"

The font was so small that Nora had to zoom in three times before she understood what she was looking at. "It just says that Ileana is similar to Eileen or Aileen and means, 'God has answered.'"

"*I* want to be God's answer," Sheldon huffed. "Talk about bragging rights. Do you know what Sheldon means? I'm a 'valley with steep sides.'"

Nora couldn't stop herself from grinning. "You're God's answer to bighorn sheep?"

Sheldon scowled. "I hear your kettle calling. I'll have Earl Grey, please."

Nora made the tea and set the mugs on top of fabric coasters infused with the scent of cinnamon. As soon as she sat back down, Sheldon pointed at his screen again. "I can't read this one either."

"'Linnea. Scandinavian origin. A lime or linden tree. Or a flower.'" Nora clicked on the thumbnail of a pink bell-shaped flower. "'Linnea is a member of the honeysuckle family. It's also known as the twinflower, owing to its paired, pendulous flowers.'"

Caught off guard by the sudden and intense ghost tingling in her pinkie, Nora dropped Sheldon's phone. It skittered off the table and landed on the floor with a soft thud.

Nora was relieved to see that it wasn't damaged.

"Sorry," she said, covering her right hand with her left. "I guess flower references are freaking me out right now. It's the Lady Artist books."

"When you mentioned the floral tea, I said that I wasn't in the mood for flowers. And here we are, figuring out that Lea could be short for Linnea, a pink bell-shaped flower."

The prickly sensation was subsiding, but Nora kept her right hand balled in a tight fist while she typed a brief message to McCabe.

Sheldon cocked his head. "I thought we were calling people, not texting."

"I was asking McCabe how Lea's name was spelled on her driver's license. He would've seen it on the paperwork from the accident."

Sheldon tapped his temple. "Smart."

"He probably won't text back until—" She was cut off by a *ping* from her phone. "Her name is Linnea Carle."

"Linnea. The twinflower." Sheldon was studying a close-up photo of the pink flower. "Is Lea a twin? Is Hester?"

Nora shook her head. "Not Hester. Her brother's a few years older. I've never talked to Lea about her family."

"I have. Just once." Sheldon's eyes turned sad. "That girl was passed around foster houses and group homes like she was a hot potato. She tried to hide it, but I could tell she had it rough. Still, she told me everything turned around when she found some organization that helps former foster kids get jobs. That's how she ended up with the Comfort family. In another year, she'll be able to pay for art school."

"I thought the Comforts hired her through a program run by their church." Nora's fingers moved over her laptop's keyboard. "Did Lea mention a name? Of the organization?"

"It was Hope something."

Having brought up the church's homepage, Nora navigated to the Resources header. She clicked the Family Resources link from the drop-down menu and saw a listing for HopeStart Youth Initiative. She read the short paragraph describing the service and blanched.

"What'd you find?" Sheldon demanded.

Bemused, Nora said, "HopeStart was founded by a woman named Marigold Wright."

"Holy shit. Is that *our* Marigold?"

Nora couldn't take her eyes off the name. "It has to be."

"Hurry up and Google her!"

Snapping to attention, Nora typed in Marigold's name. She made a mess of it, but the search engine had no trouble delivering results.

"'Marigold Strong Wright of Harrison, New York...'" Nora's voice trailed off as her eyes raced ahead.

Sheldon waved his hands at her. "Hey! Sharing is caring."

Nora's words poured out like water as she paraphrased what she was learning.

"Marigold is Sadie Strong's daughter. Sadie had an affair with a married man and became pregnant. After three months in a home for unwed mothers, her baby was born. The adoptive parents were given a letter Sadie had written, begging them to name the little girl Marigold. She included a drawing with the letter, which later became the logo of Wright Publishing House. The company was founded by Marigold's husband, Sebastian Wright, but the couple ran the business as equal partners. Sebastian was in his prime when he died of a brain aneurysm, but Marigold remained at the helm after her husband's death. In 1956, she sold the company to a large publishing firm. The following year, her biological father died, leaving Marigold a substantial sum in his will. With the sale of Wright Publishing and the legacy bequeathed by her father, Marigold became a member of the decamillionaire's club."

Sheldon whistled.

The next paragraph focused on Marigold's philanthropy. She'd supported a number of organizations striving to improve the foster care system. She'd also established scholarships and grants for female artists. The Wrights had no children of their own, and when Marigold passed away in 2007, a press release stated that her considerable fortune would continue to serve foster children and female artists well into the future.

"She gave away all that bling-bling? Every penny?" asked Sheldon.

Swiveling her computer around, Nora pointed at a map of New York State. "Here's the town of Harrison. It's about an hour north of the city. Marigold lived most of her life there, and I need to see what her house looked like."

"Why?"

But Nora had already opened a new window and was furiously typing. She drew in a sharp breath when a Victorian mansion filled the screen.

"*Espléndida.* Oh, look. There's a slideshow."

The lakefront Queen Anne mansion was a blend of historic craftsmanship and modern convenience. The slideshow featured images of the state-of-the-art kitchen, three-car garage, and game room. The front parlor, dining room, and living room had fireplaces, crystal chandeliers, and floor-to-ceiling windows. When an image of the library appeared, Nora hit the pause button and grabbed Sheldon's arm.

"I think this house belonged to Hester's great-aunt. Her name was Mary. Hester described this place to us in detail, especially the library."

Sheldon's jaw went slack.

Staring at the screen, Nora tightened her grip. "I think Hester's aunt Mary was Marigold Wright. Marigold *Strong* Wright."

Nora released Sheldon and began a search on Marigold's biological father. The teaser for an article with the headline CEO OF WRIGHT PUBLISHING LEARNS THE IDENTITY OF HER FINANCIER FATHER seemed promising, so Nora clicked the link.

"Look, it says here that when Gerald was diagnosed with incurable liver cancer and wanted to make amends before he passed, he confessed his affair with Sadie Strong and tracked down the daughter he'd never met. Marigold. She was accepted by the rest of the family and was at her father's bedside when he passed and attended his funeral service."

This time, Sheldon clamped a hand around Nora's arm. "Gerald Winthrop is Hester's grandfather?"

"Or great-grandfather. I'm not sure. Family trees can be so complicated."

"You don't have to tell *me*. I'm the son of a Cuban father and a Jewish mother. My tree has more branches than the Amazon River."

Nora handed him a piece of paper and a pen. "We should try to make Hester's family tree. It'll help us get a sense of who's who."

It wasn't hard to find a short biography on Gerald Winthrop. "At twenty-two, he landed a job at a major Wall Street

investment firm. At twenty-three, he married the only child of
the firm's owner. Gerald and his bride, Wilma, bought a house
on Long Island. Their son, Richard, was born in 1908. Marigold, Gerald's daughter by Sadie, was born in 1915. Marigold
didn't have children, but her half brother, Richard Winthrop,
had two. Alexander was born in 1932 followed by Lee in 1937.
You with me so far?"

Sheldon made a noncommittal noise and Nora gave him a
minute to finish what he was writing before she continued.

"Okay, let's look at the next generation of Winthrops. Lee
died in his late twenties. No children there. Alexander had one
son. Lawrence was born in 1955. He married Shannon and had
two kids." Again, Nora gave Sheldon a moment to catch up.
"Lawrence Junior in 1981 and sweet, lovely Hester in 1983."

"Our girl has some rich relatives," Sheldon said. "I know
her parents treated her like dirt the whole time she lived under
their roof, but did they cut her off financially too? Unless the
money was mismanaged, some of it should have trickled
down to Hester."

Outside the stories Hester had shared with the Secret, Book,
and Scone Society, Nora didn't know much about the Winthrops. And even though she and Sheldon had found the connection between Hester and the Lady Artist books, Nora was
no closer to understanding the message the books were meant
to convey.

"Okay, Lawrence and Shannon. It's your turn."

Nora never imagined that her search would lead to an obituary.

"*Dead?* Both of them? Oh, Hester." Sheldon tugged his
mustache as he gazed at the screen.

After scanning the obituary from *New Castle News*, Nora
found an article explaining why Hester's parents had died on
the same day. "It happened in December. They were driving

home from a Christmas party when they hit a patch of black ice. Their car went into a creek. It was found a mile away the next morning. Cause of death was hypothermia."

Sheldon crossed himself. "Who does Hester have left?"

"Her brother, Lawrence. According to the obituary, he goes by Junior. He owns a chain of sports therapy centers called Game Time. He's married and has one stepson. No mention of Hester in the article or the obituary. It's like she's been erased."

They both stared at a photograph of a black sedan sitting in the middle of a creek. A policeman stood on the bank with his hands on his hips and his back to the camera. It was an unsettling image.

"Why wasn't this all over the news?" asked Sheldon. "The Winthrops must have been the richest people in the whole county—maybe even the state. Hester's father probably inherited two fortunes. Even if he had to share it with foster kids and lady artists, he must've been worth a few mil. What about that house? Let's see if it really was Marigold's."

The Register of Deeds confirmed that the Victorian mansion had belonged to Marigold. It became the property of the Bright Star Trust following her death.

Sheldon frowned. "Why the slideshow? Is it for sale?"

"It's an event space. Wedding receptions and the like. But if it *was* for sale, here's the estimated value according to Zillow."

"Damn! If that house is worth five million and Marigold was worth ten million when she died, Larry Senior must have been rolling in it. Why wasn't he retired? Why wasn't he taking a limo home from that Christmas party? Where's all the money? And who are the beneficiaries of the Bright Star Trust?"

Junior? Hester? Nora wondered. Then she had a more chilling thought. *If something happened to Junior and Hester, Marigold's only living descendant would be Lea.*

Sheldon pointed at Nora's phone. "This is too big for us,

mija. We're booksellers, not forensic accountants. It's time to
call the sheriff."

Nora was reaching for her phone when a text message appeared on the screen.

"It's from McCabe. He wants me to come in."

Sheldon leaned back in his chair and exhaled. "Good."

Nora pocketed her phone. She didn't want Sheldon to see
the entirety of McCabe's message: **Hester's not doing well. She
needs a friend. Come right away.**

Chapter 20

Secrets are things we give to others to keep for us.
—Elbert Hubbard

Nora threw on boots and a coat and drove her moped to the station.

The short drive did little to calm the noise in her head. Thoughts rolled around like balls in a bingo cage. Her chest felt tight, and despite the cold, she was sweating.

Inside the lobby, she was hit by an unexpected wave of dizziness and had to sit down. She closed her eyes and tried to breathe deeply. Knowing Hester needed her and was waiting at the other end of the building only increased her respiration rate.

Suddenly an image came to her. It was as bright and clear as sunshine burning through the fog. Nora saw herself in the Readers' Circle with June, Estella, and Hester. Plates of food and several copies of *Miss Benson's Beetle* sat on the coffee table. Her friends were laughing over a passage from Rachel Joyce's novel. Hester was nearly doubled over, Estella clutched her side, and June was stomping both feet.

Nora could hear the music of their laughter over the roar of thoughts in her head. The sound eased the tightness in Nora's chest. It opened up her lungs and coaxed air in through her nose. The dizziness abated.

After waiting a few more seconds, she opened her eyes to find that she was okay.

She called June.

She called Estella.

Then she approached the front desk. The officer on duty waved her through.

Nora knocked on McCabe's door. He immediately opened it, but instead of inviting her into his office, he slipped into the hall and closed the door behind him.

"You knew." His voice was low and gravely. He wore a wounded expression.

"Yes."

McCabe pointed at the door. "She's the common denominator I've been looking for since Elijah's body was found. Hester and her daughter, Lea. You knew information pertinent to an ongoing investigation, yet you kept it from me."

Nora's ire rose. "I gave Hester my word—so did June, Estella, and Sheldon—that I wouldn't tell a soul about Lea until Hester had a chance to tell Andrews. I'd never betray her trust. Not for an investigation or any other reason."

"Not even for justice?"

"I only found out about Lea last night, Grant. Hester asked for a little time and I gave it to her." Nora pointed at the door. "Is Andrews in there too?"

McCabe shook his head. "He's in a patrol car parked in front of the Comforts' house. I thought he could use a little alone time."

"Look, I don't blame you for being mad at me, or disappointed in me, or whatever. In your shoes, I'd probably feel the same way. But I'm asking you to table this discussion for later. Sheldon and I have been trying to figure out why anyone would want to kill Hester, and we've learned some important things this afternoon."

"Like rich relatives?"

Nora's face lit up. "Yes! The only two people to benefit from

Hester's death would be Junior or Lea. One of them must be a murderer."

"Not Lea. Her alibi for the time leading up to Elijah's death checks out and several Book Bash guests saw her run to a car across the street from Miracle Books. Meredith Comfort was in the driver's seat and Lea waved to the group with her good arm before getting in the car."

Nora's shoulders drooped in relief. "I am *so* glad to hear that. I didn't want her to have done these horrible things. I've seen her with Jefferson. She loves that boy and he loves her. I don't know her well, but I like her."

When McCabe didn't respond, she jerked her thumb at his office door. "Is Hester in there? Can she go home now?"

"She shouldn't be alone. That's why I called you." McCabe's tone softened. "I had no choice but to question her. She heard about her parents from me—I never imagined I'd be the first person to tell her they were dead."

The agonized look in his eyes told Nora the whole story. Hester had sat in one of the stiff chairs facing his desk and spoken the name of the child she gave up for adoption all those years ago—the child who may or may not have come to Miracle Springs for nefarious reasons. And just when Hester believed she couldn't feel more pain or grief, McCabe raised the subject of her dead parents.

Only she hadn't known they were dead until that moment. No wonder she wasn't okay. She was moving through a waking nightmare. She needed comfort, quiet, and safety.

Nora didn't wait for McCabe's permission to enter his office. She pushed open the door and went in before he could say a word.

At first, she thought the room was empty because none of the chairs were occupied, but she found Hester sitting on the floor next to the worktable, her gaze fixed on Elijah's photo. Her face was ghostly pale.

Nora rounded on McCabe. "How long has she been like this? Go get water and a blanket."

McCabe rushed down the hall. He returned less than a minute later with a bottle of water, a fleece blanket, and a package of crackers.

Nora, who was already kneeling on the floor next to Hester, draped the blanket around her friend's shoulders.

"It's all over now, honey. You don't have to do anything else. You can rest." Scooting closer, Nora put an arm around Hester. "You can rest."

Hester put her head on Nora's shoulder. Her glassy-eyed stare remained locked on Elijah's photo.

Nora stroked Hester's hair and told her how brave she was and how much she was loved. Over and over, she murmured, "I'm proud of you. You're so strong. You are *so* loved."

Finally she said, "Are you ready to go home?"

Hester's nod was an infinitesimally small movement, but McCabe saw it. After giving Nora a hand, he used both arms to lift Hester to her feet.

"I'll drive you."

Nora helped Hester into her coat and slid her mittens over her cold hands. She and McCabe supported her weight as they left the building. As soon as they got Hester settled in the backseat of McCabe's SUV, Nora spread the fleece blanket over her friend's lap. She held Hester's mittened hand the whole way.

When they reached Hester's house, the kitchen lights were on and smoke curled from the chimney. Estella's car was parked on the street.

As soon as McCabe turned into the driveway, the garage door began rising. June stood inside, beckoning McCabe forward. He pulled in and cut the engine.

June opened Hester's door and smiled at her with such tenderness that Nora knew she'd done the right thing by calling June and Estella.

June touched Hester's cheek. "I bet you didn't expect a welcoming committee, but here we are. Estella made your cozy room even cozier. It's like a nice, warm, sweet-smelling nest. Come on, sweet girl. I'll show you."

As soon as June led Hester away, McCabe pivoted in his seat and said, "She wasn't like that when you knocked on my office door. She was in a chair. She wasn't talking and she didn't look right, which is why I called you. I tried to help, but I knew I couldn't reach her. She needed your kind of comfort."

"What about Andrews?"

McCabe let out a sigh. "He's been hurt and confused since Hester first told him her secret. Learning that her daughter is living here has rocked his world all over again. It might take a little time for him to come around, but I hope he does."

Nora fought back tears. "Hester's already lost so much. She can't lose him too."

McCabe got into the backseat with Nora.

"Elijah's mother calls me twice a day. She's desperate for answers. Her son is dead. I can't bring him back. All I can do is help her find closure, and that can only happen when the important questions have been answered. And they haven't. Elijah's killer has yet to be identified. Meghan's killer hasn't been identified. We don't know who ran Lea off the road." He studied Nora's face. "You gave Hester your word, and I admire you for keeping it, but *I* gave Elijah's parents *my* word. So, where does that leave us?"

Nora slid her hand across the seat until her fingertips were barely touching McCabe's. "I'll always be honest with you. But if I make a promise to Hester, June, or Estella, I'll keep it, no matter what. If that's a deal breaker for you, I'll understand. I'll hate it because I think all of my roads have been leading me to you—but I'll understand."

Just then, the door to the kitchen opened and Estella pushed the illuminated button on the wall. She waited until the garage door was closed and went back inside.

"It's cold. You should go in too," McCabe said. "We can talk more about us later. I'm not going anywhere."

Nora had no idea what he meant by that, but she said, "I'll go in, but first I need to ask if you've seen a copy of Marigold's will."

McCabe was puzzled. "Marigold? You found her?"

"Yes. Let's go in and I'll tell you her story. It's complicated, but I have a cheat sheet."

"What kind of cheat sheet?" he asked as they got out of the car.

"A family tree," said Nora, stepping into the warm, coffee-scented air of the kitchen.

Estella put down the carton of milk she was holding and opened her arms to Nora. "There you are! And you're half-frozen. Sit in the chair next to the heat vent while I make you a coffee. That goes for you too, Sheriff. You look like a man who could use a strong cup of coffee."

"I sure could."

June swept into the room and put her finger to her lips. "She's asleep, and sleep is the only thing that'll help right now, so we're going to be very quiet."

Nora asked her friends to have a seat. When they were settled, she placed the family tree in the middle of the table and pointed at Sadie Stone's name.

"The story begins with Sadie. The letters hidden in the covers of her books spell a name. Marigold was Sadie's illegitimate daughter. She was given up for adoption. After Marigold's birth, Sadie stopped designing covers."

She moved her index finger down the tree, explaining how

Marigold had married, run a publishing house with her husband, and become a very rich woman after his death. She then told him how Marigold's biological father had sought her out before his death, which led to her becoming a legitimate member of the Winthrop clan.

June brushed Hester's name with the side of her thumb. "Marigold was Hester's great-aunt. Aunt *Mary*. I never put two and two together."

"Me neither, but I think that's because of how Hester described her. She rarely left the house or invited people over. She wasn't close to Hester, her parents, or anyone in her community. I guess money didn't buy Aunt Mary happiness," said Estella.

Nora pictured Marigold wandering the empty rooms of her Victorian mansion, lost in memories of better times. She probably missed her husband and her work. Despite having more money than she could spend, her Golden Years were marked by loneliness. With Hester's arrival, Marigold was suddenly sharing her home with a pregnant teen she barely knew.

"Over time, Marigold and Hester grew close. Hester said they'd read together at night and that she learned to cook because she wanted to please her aunt. Aunt Mary's home became Hester's home. They became family in the truest sense."

"And Aunt Mary gave Hester the money she needed to start a bakery," June added.

Nora glanced down at the tree. "Marigold's millions. Did the bulk of it go to charity? Did she make provisions for her descendants? I don't know. But with the death of Hester's parents, there are only three living descendants."

"Junior, Hester, and Lea," Estella whispered.

When Nora had called her friends earlier that afternoon, she'd told them about finding Meghan's body, and how Meghan and Hester had worn nearly identical yellow raincoats to the Book Bash. She'd told them how Hester was with McCabe and would need every ounce of support she could get. Finally she'd shared the news about Hester's parents.

Nora finished by asking them to meet her at Hester's house. She knew they'd drop everything to make that happen and would use the spare key hidden in the birdhouse by the back door to let themselves into Hester's home. While she was at the station, they started a fire, cleaned, and lit candles. They turned down Hester's bed and made coffee.

McCabe's cup was nearly empty, and as soon as Nora took a sip, she understood why. The coffee was smooth and strong. It warmed her from the inside, and she smiled gratefully at Estella over the rim of her cup.

Suddenly June jumped up. "I forgot the cookies!" she stage-whispered. "Jasmine made Italian breakfast cookies for her coworkers and she doubled the recipe so Tyson and I could have some too. They're meant to be dunked in coffee."

She returned to the table with a plate of cookies shaped like rectangles with rounded ends. She passed the plate, and everyone but McCabe took a cookie. He reached for the piece of paper covered with the names of Hester's relatives instead.

"I was in the middle of reading Marigold's will when Andrews showed up with Hester. As soon as a will is filed, it becomes public record." McCabe looked at Nora. "While you were tracing Marigold's bloodline, I was tracing the money. But we were working in opposite directions. I was working backward from Hester. Her lifestyle didn't raise any red flags, but that wasn't the case with her brother or parents. The photos on their Facebook pages made it pretty clear that they lived high on the hog. I didn't think their chain of PT centers could be as profitable as all that."

Estella waved half a cookie at McCabe. "When you say 'high on the hog,' do you mean British royalty or tech tycoon? Castles, servants, and priceless jewels or the kind of money where you take one of your private jets to one of your private islands because the weather forecast is better there than it is at your Italian villa, penthouse in Singapore, or mansion in Malibu?"

McCabe stared at her for a moment before saying, "No crown jewels or private jets, but both the parents and the brother own multiple homes and a handful of luxury cars. Lots of vacations too. On Lawrence Junior's page, I saw photos of him scuba diving in the Maldives, golfing in Scotland, touring vineyards in France, and taking a dip in Iceland's hot springs. All in the same year. Hester's parents were into cruises. They didn't cruise on big party boats either. Their ships were small with two-story cabins and top-rated chefs. The cruise they took to Antarctica starts at sixteen thousand per person."

"Dang. I'll have to raise my prices if I want to travel in style to see penguins and lots and lots of ice," Estella said.

"And seals. Mrs. Winthrop had dozens of posts about them."

Nora broke off a piece of her cookie and popped it in her mouth. Other than a hint of vanilla, it didn't taste like much, and she could see why people dunked it in coffee, tea, or milk.

"Hester's parents inherited a lump sum of one million dollars," McCabe continued. "In addition, they received the dividends from a trust fund Marigold set up before she died. The trust was supposed to be turned over to Hester when she turned thirty-five, but Hester's parents hired a legal team to prevent that from happening. The case has been tied up in probate court for years."

"How much money is in this trust fund?" asked Nora.

"I won't know that until I hear back from the attorney representing Marigold's estate, but I assume years' worth of legal fees have reduced its capital. And you'd think the death of Hester's parents would've put an end to the legal battle, but Junior picked up the baton." McCabe held up the family tree. "If something happened to Hester, the money would pass to her living children. After them, it would pass on to the next closest blood relative."

Staring at the paper in his hand, Estella said, "Junior."

Nora felt such a violent ghost tingle in her right hand that she dropped her cookie. Hiding her balled hands under the table, she looked at McCabe. "Do you know where he is?"

"According to his wife, he and a few friends had gone to the movies. After that, they were going out for drinks and dinner. She didn't expect him back until late tonight."

June grunted. "Doesn't the man have a cell phone?"

"He does, but he never set up his voicemail. I left messages on his office phone and told his wife that I wanted him to call me back tonight, no matter the time," replied McCabe.

"Junior," Estella hissed. "That piece of shit told Hester she was a waste of space. He called her ugly, stupid, and useless. Said she was a loser and that no one liked her. Their parents only put up with her because they had to. They didn't love her. That's what he said. The whole time she was growing up, he told her no one would *ever* love her."

June touched Estella's hand. "In her own way, I think Aunt Mary did. I think she wanted to make up for everything Hester didn't get from her family, but she ran out of time. She found another way to tell Hester that she cared about her—by leaving her enough money to live like a Kevin Kwan character."

"Wait a sec. Lea inherits before Junior," Estella pointed out. "Is she a suspect?"

McCabe said, "No. She didn't kill Elijah or Meghan. We want the person who forced *her* off the road."

"What kind of person pushes a man off a bridge, doesn't care about killing an innocent child, and strangles a woman from behind? A coward. A bully. Someone who couldn't look his victim in the eyes. That's Junior," Nora said with conviction.

"What does he look like?" June asked McCabe.

The sheriff pulled up an image on his phone. The round-faced man with the receding hairline and practiced smile was completely unremarkable. He could blend in with any crowd, and that made him even more dangerous.

"Deputy Andrews is parked at the Comforts' house. I'm going to send another officer here because I need to get back to the station. I'm waiting on trace evidence from the truck and a call back from the sheriff of Junior's county. It's tough to make headway on a Sunday, but we can't wait until Monday for answers. We've had to wait too long already."

While McCabe stepped into the garage to communicate with the station, the women stayed seated. No one talked. They gazed at their coffee cups, turning over everything they'd learned in their minds. It was easier to focus on facts over feelings, but a single emotion refused to be ignored.

Estella was the first to give it a voice. "I'm scared. Hester needs a team of bodyguards—not a single officer sitting in a patrol car."

"I wish Andrews would stay with her. He's upset—of course, he is—but I know he loves Hester and would do anything to keep her safe," said June.

Nora wanted to take action. "We can't sit around and wait for her to be a victim. The whole town needs to see Junior's photo. If we can stop him before he has the chance—"

Hearing a thump from upstairs, the rest of her sentence went unsaid.

June raised her eyes to the ceiling. "I didn't think we'd hear a peep out of her. She was snoring before I left the room."

"Maybe she had coffee at the station. The older you get, the faster it runs through," said Estella.

But Estella didn't feel pins and needles in a part of her body that was no longer there, like Nora did.

"I'll check on her," she said.

June must have seen something in her face because she also got to her feet. "We'll all go."

The women climbed the stairs as quietly as possible. They'd been to Hester's house so many times that they knew where to plant their feet to avoid creaks or groans. Part of Nora felt silly for creeping down the hallway leading to Hester's bedroom, but she'd rather be silly and have her hunch proved wrong than proceed with caution only to find that she was right.

Hester's door was closed. Nora put her ear against the wood and listened for several seconds. She couldn't hear a thing, which was no surprise. Hester's house had been built in the 1950s. Everything about it was solid, including the doors.

After a backward glance at her friends, Nora wrapped her hand around the knob and turned, inch by excruciating inch.

Without releasing the knob, she cracked the door a tiny bit and peered into the room. No lights were on and the curtains were closed, so Nora couldn't see anything at first.

Then she saw the bed. She saw the shape of legs under covers, but as her eyes moved up the shape to the torso, she saw another shape standing next to the bed.

Except standing wasn't the right word. The man-sized shape was leaning over Hester, blocking Nora's view of her friend's face.

Nora burst into the room just as Hester whimpered and the man clamped a pillow over her face. Screaming in rage, Nora launched herself at the man, knocking him off balance. He fell sideways, but didn't go down. As Nora swiped the pillow away from Hester's face, she heard June and Estella cry out in terror.

The man stood between the bed and the doorway. His right arm was raised. In his hand, there was a gun.

"Get in here." He waved the gun at June and Estella. "Go stand by the window."

His voice rumbled with anger, but he didn't shout. He waited until June and Estella were clinging to each other on the far side of the room before aiming the gun at Nora.

"Pick her up," he said, pointing at Hester with his left hand.

"I don't care if you drag her by her hair—just find a way to move her. We're going for a ride to this nice bridge I know. In the woods."

June and Estella started pleading for him to leave them alone.

"One more word, and I'll shoot the three of you right now. Is that what you want? You two move, I shoot. Say another word, I shoot. Do anything I don't like, and Nine Fingers gets a bullet in the brain. Let's go, Nine Fingers. Move my useless sister."

He's seen me up close. He's seen my hands, Nora thought as she folded Hester's comforter back.

Hester was so still. A sob rose in Nora's throat, but when she felt the warm skin of Hester's hand, she choked down the sound.

She's not dead. She's not dead. Not dead.

Nora focused on this truth as she slipped her arms around Hester's back and pulled. Once Hester's upper body was resting against hers, Nora tried to get under her friend and raise her in a fireman's carry, but she wasn't strong enough.

The man growled in annoyance. "Come on! Grab her from behind and drag her."

Nora did as she was told, wrapping her arms around Hester's waist and stepping backward. The sudden shift of weight as Hester's body came free of the bed almost toppled Nora, but she clenched her teeth and held on. Then she shuffled toward the door.

She got Hester into the hall, but when the man came out after her, she looked at him and froze.

He was the man from the street. The man who'd shouted an obscenity after bumping into *her.* Now that she was this close to him, she saw that his beard and brows were too dark. He'd dyed them, of course, to conceal what was probably honey-blond hair streaked with white.

"Junior."

She spit out the name like it was curdled milk.

He grinned. "I guess she talked about me, huh?"

Nora tightened her hold on Hester. "Only once or twice."

Junior preened. "What'd she say? That I picked on her? I made her cry?" Seeing Nora's reaction, he laughed. "Once a whiner, always a whiner."

Nora knew Junior wouldn't let her live. She knew she should feed his ego—should keep him talking. She should drag Hester as slowly as she dared, holding out hope that McCabe would come out of nowhere, weapon drawn like a sheriff from a pulp Western, and drop Junior with a single shot.

Nora was scared and tired. Any plan she came up with was likely to fail. She had no weapon or fighting skills.

She assumed June and Estella had called 911 or sent McCabe a text asking for help as soon as Junior left the bedroom—and help was right in the garage—but Junior still had the advantage. He'd killed two people and was about to murder a few more. Everyone was dispensable to that arrogant, entitled jackass.

For a single moment, fury eclipsed Nora's fear. She lowered Hester to the floor and raised herself to her full height. "You're a cardboard character made of toxic masculinity and an inflated ego. You still see Hester as a doormat, but she's always been stronger than you. She had Matilda and Nancy Drew, Lizzie Bennet and the March sisters in her corner. She had Aunt Mary. And us. No matter what you take from her, she'll always be better than you. She's like a star. She shines her special kind of light on people and is loved by this whole town. But you? You're as common as a penny."

Nora's voice carried a quiet power that shook Junior. He gaped at her for several seconds before his lip twisted in a snarl.

And then he lunged.

He stretched out his free hand to grab her, but with Hester's body between them, his lunge fell short and his fingers grasped empty air. He was so surprised by this that he unintentionally lowered his gun.

Nora kept backing away, inch by agonizing inch, until she reached the top of the stairs.

The house was silent.

Where are you, McCabe?

Nora didn't want to lose her life to a man like Junior. She couldn't stand the thought of him railroading one person after another and continuously coming out on top.

But there was no escape. No hope of overcoming him.

Flooded by feelings of desperation and rage, Nora released a primal scream.

Of all the possible reactions, Junior hadn't expected this. Stunned, he paused for a moment in the doorway to the second bedroom.

It was a moment that would change everything.

There was a flash of movement and a broom handle arced out of the darkness and slammed into Junior's neck.

He dropped like he'd been struck by lightning. His head hit the floor hard and bounced once. After that, he didn't move again.

McCabe threw the handle down and knelt to check Hester's pulse. He looked back at Nora and nodded. Hester was alive.

After repeating the motions with Junior, McCabe stood and reached out for Nora. He touched her cheeks, her shoulders, and her upper arms as if they were playing a strange version of Simon Says.

"Are you okay? Did he hurt you?"

Nora sagged against him. "I'm okay."

He held her so tightly that the buttons of his uniform shirt dug into her face, but she didn't care.

In the distance, she heard sirens, and the sound broke through Nora's shock. Terror and relief hit her like a rogue wave, and she started crying.

McCabe didn't shush her. He didn't speak words of comfort. He simply held her.

To Nora, he felt as tall and solid as a mountain. His cheek was rough and the stubble on his chin was sharp. But the kiss he pressed to her temple was infinitely tender.

Loosening his hold the slightest bit, McCabe began to hum into Nora's hair. His voice was so low that she felt the music more than heard it.

It wasn't until much later, after a nurse announced that Hester was awake and ready for visitors, that the song came back to Nora.

Nora's heart was full as she fell into step behind the nurse.

Softly—too softly for anyone else to hear—she started singing what McCabe had hummed into her hair.

Smiling to herself, Nora sang "The First Time Ever I Saw Your Face."

Chapter 21

At some point in a woman's life, she just gets tired of being ashamed all the time. After that, she is free to become whoever she truly is.

—Elizabeth Gilbert

To Nora, it felt like years since she'd stood in Hester's kitchen. But it also felt like she'd been here seconds ago. In reality, it had been three days.

Since then, Junior had been placed under arrest. A battery of lawyers had materialized to sort out the laundry list of charges against him, and it wouldn't be long before the media descended on Miracle Springs.

At least they'll spend money, Nora thought.

Mid-February was the slowest time of the year for area businesses, Miracle Books included, and while Nora wasn't going to talk to strangers about the events leading to Junior's arrest, she'd happily sell them bags of books and cups of coffee.

As she unpacked the groceries she'd bought on the way over, she wondered if the influx of visitors would have the opportunity to patronize the Gingerbread House or if the bakery would remain closed.

Hester had completely recovered from the high dose of muscle relaxants injected into her body, but it was clear to her medical team that she was far from well. She wasn't taking in enough food or fluids. All she wanted to do was sleep.

The first day, they let her rest. On the second day, they called for a psych consult. Hester wouldn't say a word to the first psychiatrist, a middle-aged man who bore an unsettling resemblance to her father, but after coaxing from her friends, she agreed to speak with a female psychiatrist.

After several sessions with a patient and soft-spoken psychiatrist called Doctor Deborah, Hester finally got out of bed. She showered, ate a full meal, and wrote down detailed instructions on how to make a working volcano cake because one of her nurses wanted to make it for her son.

That was yesterday.

Today she was being discharged. Sheldon would be driving her home in June's car, and Nora, June, and Estella would be waiting for her when she arrived.

Nora was trying to decide which of Hester's mixing bowls to use when Estella banged on the back door and called out, " 'Little pig, little pig, let me in!' "

Startled, Nora dropped the entire stack of metal bowls. She scowled at Estella and said, "You scared me."

"That's what bad wolves do. Aren't these gorgeous?" Estella smiled down at the flower arrangement in her hands.

"Gorgeous. All the hot pinks and oranges have a Caribbean island vibe." Nora pointed at the container. "Where'd you find the tin?"

Estella placed the arrangement in the middle of the kitchen table and turned it so that the lettering on the old Domino Sugar tin faced forward. "One of my clients. We started talking about retro signs while I was coloring her hair and I happened to mention Hester's collection of vintage advertising tins. My client went straight home after her appointment, got this out of her attic, and stopped by the salon to give it to me. She said that she wanted the sweetest person in town to have her mama's sugar tin."

Nora wagged her finger. "Don't you tear up. We're on a mission, and if you start crying, *I'll* start crying."

"Nobody's crying!" June commanded as she strode into the kitchen. "I have my smudge sticks and we're going to cleanse this place with smiles on our faces and joy in our hearts. You hear me?"

Estella saluted. "Yes, ma'am!"

"But first, we need to make our dough. It can chill in the fridge while we get our smudge on," Nora said.

"I'm still nervous about baking for a baker." Estella slipped one of Hester's many aprons over her head. "I think a distraction would help. Why don't you let us in on what the sheriff told you at the diner last night? Yes, the whole town knows you two were there."

June washed her hands and selected an apron with a purple-violet print. "I can't concentrate if we talk about anything too complicated, so how about telling us when Junior had the chance to cut up all those copies of *The Scarlet Letter*?"

"He didn't. That was Lea."

While Nora cubed cold butter, she explained how Lea had called her to apologize for ruining the books. One of the picture books Sheldon had read during storytime that day was *A Mother for Choco*. A twist on *Are You My Mother?* the book tells of a little bird finding a home with Mrs. Bear and her other adopted children. While the children loved it, Lea found it painful.

"Lea told me how the story made her angry, so she lashed out at Hester the only way she could at that moment. She took scissors from Sheldon's storytime craft cart and attacked those paperbacks. But that wasn't the only time her anger came out. Lea helped Meredith sort her mother's books, and when she came across the Lady Artist books, she hid them in her room. There were so many books that Meredith didn't even notice. Lea left one at the bakery, stuck one in a box heading to Miracle Books, and pretended to find one in her hospital bag."

Estella paused in the middle of scooping flour into a measuring cup. "Did she know that she was related to Sadie Strong? Or that Sadie's daughter was über rich? Wait. Does this mean Hester's about to be über rich?"

"Eventually, yes, I think she will be."

The realization that their friend stood to inherit millions rendered all three women speechless for a moment. Nora was the first to break the spell.

"We could talk about the money all day, but let's get back to Lea. She'd never heard of Sadie Strong. But—and this will sound too crazy to believe—when she was nine, Lea *met* Meredith's mother."

"*What?*" Estella and June asked in unison.

Nora gestured for Estella to finish measuring. "We need to mix the butter in while it's cold."

"I'm scooping. Keep talking."

"Hester's great-aunt lived in Harrison, New York, which wasn't far from the town where Lea was born. She was adopted by an affluent couple from Stamford, Connecticut, who gave her everything a child could want. Four years later, her life totally changed when the cops came to arrest her dad for running a Bernie Madoff–level Ponzi scheme. He wasn't home because he'd already fled the country with his mistress. After their assets were seized, Lea's remaining parent fell into a deep depression. When she later died from an accidental overdose of sleeping pills, no one petitioned the court for guardianship of Lea. A person had been named custodian in her parent's will, but since that individual had recently been diagnosed with Alzheimer's and couldn't take care of a child, Lea became a ward of the state."

June sighed as she added baking soda to the flour mixture. "That poor baby."

"Fast-forward another five years. At nine, Lea spent her

summer break helping her foster mom clean houses. One of their clients was an elderly woman who used to work at the publishing house founded by Marigold and her husband. This lady, a Mrs. Fairfax, was an avid book collector. You with me so far?"

Her friends nodded. Nora scraped the cubed butter into the flour and used a pastry blender to work the butter into the dry ingredients.

"Mrs. Fairfax saw how much Lea admired her books and guessed she owned very few of her own. Every week, she'd give Lea one or two children's books. These were special editions with beautiful covers and illustrations. At the end of the summer, Mrs. Fairfax gave Lea a copy of *Miss Iris*, telling her that she could also become a lady artist if she worked hard, went to church, and believed in herself. As soon as Lea was back in school, Lea's foster mom sold her books and used the money to buy makeup. Not long after, she was texting while driving and crashed the company car. Without a job, she couldn't be a foster parent anymore. Luckily, Lea kept *Miss Iris* in her book bag, so her most prized possession went with her from one foster or state-run home to another."

Nora rinsed her hands in very cold water and finished blending the butter and dry ingredients with her fingers.

"If you tell us that Mrs. Fairfax was Meredith's mother, I'm going to turn into a Regency romance character and swoon," June said.

"You don't have to swoon. When Mrs. Fairfax died, many of her books were donated to the local library to be sold at their annual book sale—and Meredith's mother never missed that sale. She and Mrs. Fairfax shared similar interests, and Meredith believes that her mom bought the Lady Artist books—and many more—from that sale."

Estella pushed a bowl of beaten eggs closer to June. She

poured cream into the bowl and continued mixing. "So that's how the books got to Miracle Springs. How did Lea get here?"

"Lea listened to Mrs. Fairfax's advice. She worked hard in school, attended church, and believed in herself. When she turned eighteen, she signed up for the HopeStart Youth Initiative—the foundation created by Marigold. Small world, right? That same year, Lea also learned the name and location of her biological mother."

June said, "Ah, so she didn't become Jefferson's nanny by coincidence."

"Not at all. Lea had to wait a year before she had a chance at taking Candace's place. Candace was the perfect nanny. Until she wasn't. One night, she packed her stuff and wrote a note to the Comforts saying that she was flying to Vegas to marry a man she'd met online."

"*That's* where she went?"

Nora bobbed her head and went on. "Lea was the first to apply for the job. On a video chat, she told Meredith and Miles about the foster siblings she'd helped care for and how she'd give anything to be a part of a family. She had glowing recommendations from her youth pastor and a dozen teachers, but it was her love of art and of children's books that won Meredith over. Lea reminded Meredith of her mother. She also liked that Lea seemed too young and shy to elope with someone she met online."

Estella held up a finger. "Wait. Did we add the honey?"

"We've got flour, baking soda, salt, lemon zest, butter, honey, eggs, cream." June looked at Nora. "Are we good?"

After consulting her notes, Nora said, "We're golden. The dough can chill while we cleanse the house."

"You should tell us about Junior first. I don't want to speak that scumbag's name after we're done."

"I want to turn on some lights too," Estella said.

Just as they had the last time they'd used Hester's spare key to enter her house, the women lit a fire in the hearth and created a path of light from the kitchen to Hester's bedroom. Nora assumed her friends were equally unsettled to be doing the same things they'd done before they found Junior in Hester's room. Despite their discomfort, Nora knew they had to talk about him. They had to summon him like an evil spirit and then cast him out of Hester's house and their lives.

Once they were in the bedroom, Nora said, "Everything that happened to Elijah, Hester, and Lea happened because of money—a number with more zeroes than any of us will ever see on our bank statements. Junior knew about Marigold's money because he and his parents were contesting her will. All three wanted a bigger piece of the pie."

"Didn't they have enough?" June asked.

"I guess not. Not only were they all big spenders, but the sports therapy chain Lawrence and Junior ran wasn't very profitable. On top of that, Junior convinced his dad to invest heavily in the bitcoin market. For a few months, this looked like a brilliant move. But when the cryptocurrency market crashed, the Winthrops lost a ton. Hester's parents were months away from having to sell their house, vacation condo, and all four cars."

Estella let out a grunt as she tugged on Hester's comforter. "How sad."

"Because of their tenuous financial situation, the police are taking a very close look at their deaths. McCabe said they're leaning toward foul play or a double suicide owing to the amount of muscle relaxants in their bodies."

June gasped. "Was it Junior?"

Nora piled Hester's pillows back on the bed. "He's definitely a suspect."

"How nice to be under investigation in two states. Hester's

brother has always been popular. I bet he'll be popular in prison too," Estella said.

After exchanging a quick grin with Estella, Nora continued. "Junior was desperate. It didn't look like he'd get Marigold's money through legitimate means, and with his parents gone, there were only two people standing in his way: Hester and Hester's daughter. Junior knew where Hester was, but he had no idea how to find her daughter. However, he was one of the few people who knew the identity of the baby's father, so he contacted Elijah."

"How? Did he show up at his door?"

"Based on Elijah's phone records, McCabe thinks Junior used a burner phone to make initial contact. Elijah received several calls from an untraceable number, most of which happened the day before Elijah was scheduled to be out of town. Elijah also placed calls to Connecticut's Vital Records Office and the Office of Foster Care and Adoption Services. Since his name wasn't on the birth certificate, I doubt he was given any info about Lea, but Junior must have shown Elijah a copy of that birth certificate and told him that his daughter was living in the same town as Hester."

June clicked her tongue. "I can't blame the man for wanting to see with his own eyes. I would've done the same thing."

"But this is all circumstantial!" Estella cried. "Will the charges against Junior hold up in court?"

Nora smiled. "Junior thinks he's so clever, and while he managed to cover most of his tracks, he made some mistakes. First, he hired a private detective to locate Hester's daughter. Second, Junior drove his own car to the campground where he and Elijah agreed to meet. The cops found a vial of the same muscle relaxant used on Junior's parents, Elijah, and Hester under the driver's seat of Junior's car. Not only that, but the dog hair found in Elijah's truck came from Junior's car. Junior has an Akita. Elijah doesn't have a dog."

Estella sat on the corner of Hester's bed. "I just want Junior to go away for a long time. It's only fair that his sentence is equal to all the years he bullied Hester. Though I'd be fine with more."

"Don't worry. Junior's going to prison," Nora said. "Whether he's found guilty of all or some of the charges, I can't say, but he'll be an old man before he drives a car, eats in a restaurant, or accosts someone on the sidewalk."

"I still can't get over how fast the sheriff moved once he heard the rumbles of a man's voice coming from this floor. Or how lucky we were that Hester left a broom in the spare room after using it to get a cobweb off the ceiling fan." Estella grinned at Nora. "He showed great restraint by not shooting Junior clear off his feet, especially seeing how he was threatening you."

Nora said, "I'm glad he did. I want Junior to stand trial. I want him to face justice. And then I want him to have lots of time to think about his actions."

June opened the curtains a little wider, inviting every particle of the afternoon light to enter the room.

"Maybe he'll change," she said. "Like Tyson did. All of us too."

After taking a moment to think about the second chance they'd been given, the women returned to the kitchen. Estella set the oven to preheat, Nora took the scone dough out of the fridge, and June searched Hester's drawers for a pizza cutter.

Nora washed her hands. Next she overturned the dough onto a baking sheet lined with parchment paper and pressed it into an eight-inch circle. As she touched the dough, she pictured Hester in the bakery. She saw the pride and pleasure Hester took in watching her customers drool over all the tempting goodies in her cases. When Nora was done, she moved aside, giving June a turn to handle the dough.

June took great care cutting the circle into eight triangles. Next she arranged the triangles until they were an inch apart. She then motioned for Estella to complete the last step. Estella brushed the scones with egg wash and slid the tray into the oven.

Nora set a timer on her phone. "Twenty-five minutes."

"Speaking of time, Sheldon just texted. ETA is forty minutes." June pointed at Nora's notes. "What's next?"

"Can you find Hester's mesh strainer and a bowl? Estella, we need more sugar and lemon juice."

The women took turns using the back of a wooden spoon to press thawed frozen blueberries through the mesh strainer.

"This is cathartic. Maybe I'll make scones with Jack when he gets out of the hospital," Estella said.

"That sounds fun. And I could invite Tyson and Jasmine over for a scone-baking date. Sheldon would be into it too. He's been wanting to test a *pico de gallo* scone recipe he found online."

June put the mesh strainer in the sink and placed the bowl in front of Nora. She whisked in confectioners' sugar and lemon juice until the glaze was smooth.

"Time to smudge?" she asked June.

Estella held up a finger. "One more question. If Lea had the Lady Artist books, then how did one end up in Elijah's coat pocket?"

"She meant to put *Miss Delphinium* in the pocket of Andrews's coat. Back in January, Andrews and a few coworkers went to lunch at the Pink Lady. They hung their coats on the hooks on the wall next to Keisha's office. Junior must've been there too—he'd probably come to scope out the hiking trails. Flo had counter duty that week and remembered serving a man with too-dark facial hair. It was her birthday, and she wasn't going to let some stranger's bad manners bring her down. She had no problem picking Junior out of a lineup."

"Where does Lea fit in?"

Seeing June take three smudge sticks from her purse, Nora kept her answer brief. "She and Jefferson met Meredith for lunch that day. The event was on both of their phone calendars. Andrews remembers the date because he was covering a sick coworker's shift. Lea told McCabe that she put the book in the pocket of Andrews's coat. I guess Junior took it and, assuming it meant something to Hester, or to Hester's boyfriend or daughter, put it in the coat he bought for Elijah."

"No more, okay? It's time to focus on light and love." June distributed the smudge sticks and lit them.

Hester came home to a cleansed house, hot tea, and a warm scone.

"What's this? You baked?" she asked after hugging her friends.

Nora said, "A lemon scone with a blueberry glaze. The lemon is for your sunny outlook and bright smile."

"But this lemon isn't subtle. It's tart because you're strong and hardworking and will stand up for what you believe in," said June.

"And we used blueberries because you're such an important part of our community. You bring people together using kindness and empathy," added Estella.

Hester stared at the pastry in awe. "You made me a comfort scone."

"We did. And some for ourselves too." Nora gestured at the table. "We're having a midwinter tea party. No need to get dressed up. Just no hospital gowns, please. That's a bit too casual. Not to mention airy."

Hester sat down with a laugh and waited for June to pour tea before breaking off a piece of scone and putting it in her mouth. As she chewed, a look of bliss came over her face.

"Wow," she breathed. "This takes me back to the first cookies I made for my aunt Mary. They were supposed to be lemon thumbprint cookies filled with strawberry jam, but all she had was a jar of wild blueberry jam. I made the cookies super tart by accident, but my aunt loved them. She said they tasted like a summer day by the lake. She told me that I had a gift and that she couldn't wait to see what I'd make next. Those words woke something in me. I began to wonder if there was more to me than what my family tried to make me believe. This little seed of hope sprouted in me that day."

"Damn, we're good," exclaimed Estella.

Hester elbowed her. "Do I have to worry about you poaching my customers?"

"Not a chance. I'll leave the cooking to you and Jack."

"I stopped by to see him before I was discharged," Hester said. "He'd just gotten off the phone with his sister and looked pleasantly surprised. I saw Jasmine too. She's such a sweet person. She checked in on me whenever she had a break. *And* I had a visit from Meredith."

Her friends waited for her to mention Lea's name.

When she didn't, June said, "You look good."

Hester chuckled. "The silver lining to being drugged by my psychotic sibling is that I finally took some time off. But seriously, Dr. Deborah is a godsend. My family said that people who needed therapy were crazy or weak. They couldn't have been more wrong. I feel so much better now that everything's out in the open. Whatever happens from here, I can handle it. I have her and, more important, I have the three of you." She gave Nora's hand a squeeze. "My heroes."

"That's McCabe's role. I had no idea how to save anyone, but he swung that broom handle like it was a Louisville Slugger."

Hester rubbed her right shoulder. "I'm sorry I missed that. I really am."

"Is that where he injected you?" Nora whispered.

"Close. The needle actually went into my armpit. He did the same thing to Elijah. And because Elijah had hair there, it was hard to see the needle mark. I guess that's why my brother needed to dress Elijah in a new shirt. As for that stupid coat—I think he wanted Elijah to be found." She shrugged. "He wanted me to know that my first love was in Miracle Springs, and that he was dead."

The silence that followed her words was weighted down with grief, but no one tried to dispel it. They let it sit between them as a way of honoring Elijah's memory.

Eventually June broke the quiet by saying, "I take it Lea didn't visit."

"No. She's been getting counseling from their pastor. She's been through so much, I'm glad she has someone to talk to." Hester splayed her hands. "I wrote her a letter and Meredith promised to give it to her in a few days. The whole family leaves tomorrow for Puerto Rico. Meredith and Miles are going on a dental mission trip and have rented a house right on the beach. It'll be good for all of them. After that, Lea's staying with Elijah's parents for a few weeks. That'll be good for all of *them* too. She'll write me back when she's ready. I hope she does. I'd like to be part of her life if she'll let me."

Hester carried her plate to the sink. Without turning around, she said, "Jasper's here. It's already dark, but I know that's his truck."

"Time to go," Estella whispered to Nora and June.

The three women cleared the table and put on their coats.

Hester glanced out the window again. "He's coming down the driveway. How do I look? Be honest. Do I need lipstick? How's my hair?"

Cupping Hester's face in her hands, Nora said, " 'Shall I compare thee to a summer's day? Thou art more lovely and more temperate.' "

June said, "Want the CliffsNotes version? You're beautiful. Through and through. Your man thinks so too."

After a quick round of hugs, the three women headed for the door. When Nora opened it, Andrews stood on the other side, his balled fist frozen in midair.

"I was just about to knock."

Nora smiled at him. "We didn't want you to wait outside for another second because *we* made scones."

"And they're amazing!" cried Estella.

Andrews stepped aside and the women smiled and touched his arm on their way out. The gestures were so full of kindness and support that Deputy Jasper Andrews's heavy heart was instantly buoyed.

The women walked to the end of Hester's driveway and stopped.

"It's so dark," June griped. "It's not even six and I can see Orion's Belt."

Gazing skyward at the Milky Way's billowy arm, Estella said, "Do you think he still loves her?"

"I know he does," Nora replied.

June and Estella stared at her.

"Wanna know how I know?" Starlight reflected in Nora's eyes. "Because he had a book sticking out of his pocket. A book wrapped in a white ribbon. No one buys books for people they don't care about. We buy books for people we love. A book wrapped in a ribbon says, 'I *love* you'."

"Did you see the title?"

"Nope. I don't think it came from my store, but that doesn't matter. What matters is that one person wanted to give a book to another person. Sounds like the start of something, doesn't it? A new story? Or the next chapter in an ongoing story? Something like that."

Looking at the starry sky once more, Estella said, "I'm glad you stopped before 'and they all lived happily ever after.' "

June smiled at Estella. "We've had our share of hardship, but the happiness I've known since meeting the three of you is much bigger than anything I've ever felt. I guess we're all old and wise enough to know that real magic is what happens when you finally find your people."

"You're my people." Nora slipped an arm around each of her friends. "And even though I'm freezing my ass off, I'm happy."

Estella whispered, "You should put that on a throw pillow."

"Or a mug," added June.

"I need new friends," Nora muttered.

Their laughter burst skyward, bright and beautiful as a comet.

Epilogue

You can't forgive without loving. And I don't mean sentimentality. I don't mean mush. I mean having enough courage to stand up and say, "I forgive. I'm finished with it."

—Maya Angelou

Weeks later, when the crocuses had begun to bloom, the Secret, Book, and Scone Society met to discuss George Eliot's *Middlemarch*.

Nora, June, and Estella were in the Readers' Circle, chatting away while shooting furtive glances at the food on the coffee table.

"Has anyone heard from Hester? She's never been this late before," June said.

They all checked their phones, but no one had missed a call or text from Hester.

Estella reached for the pie server. "I'll just take a tiny sliver of crustless quiche. Just to make sure it's good."

June glowered. "Oh, it's better than good. I made it for my knitting—"

"I'm here!" came a cry from the back hall.

Estella pumped her fist and whispered, "Yes!"

"I'm here!" Hester repeated as she trotted into the ticket agent's booth. "I'm *so* sorry. I got distracted."

Seconds later, she appeared in the Readers' Circle carrying a bowl of chopped salad and a basket of cheese rolls.

"Was it an X-rated distraction?" asked Estella.

Though Hester's cheeks flamed, she smiled and said, "That was *last* week. Jasper's on duty tonight, so I'll be going to bed with my book. Any other guesses?"

June pursed her lips. "What could've distracted you? Let's see . . . were you baking something?"

"Nope. Nora? Last guess."

Nora caught the flash of joy in Hester's eyes. The more she studied her friend, the more she seemed to glow, as if sunlight were trapped beneath her skin.

She whispered, "You heard from Lea."

Hester nodded so rapidly that the curls framing her face danced.

As one, the other women jumped to their feet, shuffled around the coffee table, and threw their arms around Hester. There, in the gap between the bookshelves housing Local Authors and Contemporary Romance, they held each other, bouncing up and down and whooping with happiness.

In a voice that was half sob, half laughter, Hester cried, "I got a letter from my daughter!"

The Vanishing Type:
A Secret, Book, and Scone
Society Mystery
Reader's Guide

1. In the beginning of the novel, Nora and Sheldon are creating a window display featuring film adaptations of famous books. Which book-to-film adaptation would you like to see in the window?

2. What are your thoughts on Deputy Andrews's marriage proposal? Do you think Andrews and Hester will make it to the altar? Why or why not?

3. Despite the saying, it's almost impossible *not* to judge a book by its cover. Have you ever walked into a library or bookstore and ended up leaving with a book because its cover spoke to you? Is there a book in your personal collection with an especially beautiful cover?

4. Blind book date displays are becoming more popular. Have you ever read a book from one of these displays? If the purpose is to encourage readers to try a genre they never or rarely read, which genre would be your blind date?

5. Pretend you're Nora Pennington. Which fiction or non-fiction books about adoption would you recommend to your customers?

6. *The Vanishing Type* takes a close look at the meaning of family. How do the members of The Secret, Book, and Scone Society demonstrate the idea that friends are the family we choose for ourselves?

7. Nora and Jed or Nora and Sheriff McCabe? Do you have a preference? Or do you think she'd be better off on her own?

8. At the end of the novel, Nora, June, and Estella make a custom scone for Hester. If you had to do the same for a close friend, what kind of scone would you make? What would you want your friends to make for you?

9. Which of the chapter quotes was your favorite? How did the quote relate to the action or theme of that chapter?

10. After reading *The Vanishing Type*, did you add any books to your wish list? If so, which ones?

Bibliotherapy from
The Vanishing Type

Sci-Fi Classics Made into Films
Ray Bradbury, *Fahrenheit 451*
Orson Scott Card, *Ender's Game*
Arthur C. Clarke, *2001: A Space Odyssey*
Philip K. Dick, *Minority Report*
Robert A. Heinlein, *Starship Troopers*
Frank Herbert, *Dune*
Andy Weir, *The Martian*
H. G. Wells, *War of the Worlds*

Women Seeking Promotions or Raises
Angela Duckworth, *Grit*
Roger Fisher and William Ury, *Getting to Yes: Negotiating Agreement Without Giving In*
Sheryl Sandberg, *Lean In: Women, Work and the Will to Lead*
Jen Sincero, *You Are a Badass*
Barbara Stanny, *Secrets of Six-Figure Women: Surprising Strategies to Up Your Earnings and Change Your Life*

Book to Movie Adaptations Worth Watching
To Kill a Mockingbird
The Godfather
L.A. Confidential

Like Water for Chocolate
The Color Purple
Crazy Rich Asians
The Maltese Falcon
Pride and Prejudice
Lonesome Dove
The Namesake
Remains of the Day
No Country for Old Men
Silence of the Lambs
The Wizard of Oz

Cookbooks for Families
America's Test Kitchen, *The Complete Cookbook for Young Chefs*
Mark Bittman, *How to Cook Everything* and *How to Bake Everything*
Yolanda Gampp, *How to Cake: A Cakebook.*

Literary Valentine's Day Gifts
Ada Calhoun, *Wedding Toasts I'll Never Give*
Katherine Center, *Things You Save in a Fire*
Uzma Jalaluddin, *Ayesha at Last*
Georgette Heyer, *The Grand Sophy*
Sophie Kinsella, *Surprise Me*
Lisa Kleypas, *Chasing Cassandra*
Judith McNaught, *Whitney, My Love*
Beth O' Leary, *The Switch*
Shaun Usher, *Letters of Note: Love*
Ibi Zoboi, *Pride*

Books About Young Lovers
Becky Albertalli, *Simon vs. the Homo Sapiens Agenda*
John Green, *The Fault in Our Stars*

Jenny Han, *To All the Boys I've Loved Before*
Rainbow Rowell, *Eleanor and Park*
Nicola Yoon, *The Sun Is Also a Star*

Bromance Books

Lyssa Kay Adams, *The Bromance Book Club*
Khaled Husseini, *The Kite Runner*
S. E. Hinton, *The Outsiders*
John Knowles, *A Separate Peace*
Madeleine Miller, *The Song of Achilles*
Evelyn Waugh, *Brideshead Revisited*
Colson Whitehead, *The Nickel Boys*

Don't miss the next Secret, Book, and Scone Society novel from *New York Times* bestselling author Ellery Adams. . . .

PAPER CUTS

Miracle Springs, North Carolina, is famed for its healing springs. But bookstore owner Nora Pennington has a tendency to land in a different kind of hot water. Though she loves to practice bibliotherapy by finding the perfect books for her customers while listening to their secrets, she also likes to bury her nose in the occasional local crime . . .

Nora escaped her past a decade ago. So it feels like a visit from another world when Kelly Walsh—the woman her ex-husband left her for—walks through the door of Miracle Books along with her son, a sweet, serious boy with a talent for origami. Kelly hasn't come to gloat, though. As it turns out, she's been dumped too. She's also terribly ill, and all she wants from Nora is forgiveness.

Shockingly, however, this woman who's been the victim of so much misfortune is about to become a murder victim. Who would do such a thing? Certainly not Nora, but that doesn't stop the gossip and suspicion—especially after Kelly's brother claims that he saw the two women arguing.

In seeking justice for Kelly, The Secret, Book, and Scone Society joins forces with the sheriff's department, but they've barely begun their probe when life throws another wrench. After serving a twenty-year sentence, Estella's father returns to Miracle Springs. And when *his* past comes back to haunt him, it might be more than the four friends can handle.

Coming soon from Kensington Publishing Corp.
in May 2023

Chapter 1

What is better than wisdom? Woman. And what is better than a good woman? Nothing.
　　　　　　　　　　　　　　—Geoffrey Chaucer

"I loved this book." Hester Winthrop stroked the paperback on her lap as if it were a cat. "I underlined a bunch of passages, but my favorite line was when A-ma said, 'Always remember that food is medicine, and medicine is food.'"

The perfect arch of Estella's left brow rose a centimeter. "Your food is more like therapy than actual medicine."

Hester laughed. "Come on. Does broccoli make you feel better when you're down? No, it doesn't. Certain times call for donuts and chocolate cakes and pecan pie with ice cream. If comfort food isn't medicine, then I don't know what is."

"Maybe I should shelve a few baking books in the Health section," said Nora Pennington, proprietor of Miracle Books.

June Winthrop, guest experience manager at Miracle Springs Lodge, a high-class resort frequented by guests from all over the world, peered at her friends from over the rims over her reading glasses. "All I can say is that I'm glad to be living in this era of body positivity. When I was in school, back in the Stone Age, girls were always trash talking other girls. I don't know why, but we all did it. From the top of our heads right on down to our toes, we were too big, too small, too pointy, too wide. No one wore the right clothes. And don't even get me started on hair. You don't know nasty until you hear what some folks say about Black hair."

"That kind of thing doesn't stop when girls become women either," said Estella. "Every time I put two ladies of any age, race, or class under the blow dryers together, they start picking apart the celebrities in *People*. I don't know what's wrong with our sex. Why can't we just be happy when other women succeed? Why can't we tell another woman they look good without worrying about how we look?"

Hester smiled at Estella. "You *always* look good. And June? You're channeling Etta James with that new do."

June passed a hand over her head. She usually kept it close-cropped, but Estella had convinced her to rock a teeny weeny, icy blond afro. "Which tea would Etta order?" she asked as she studied the paper menu on the table before her. "Beau-tea-ful or Feeling Flir-tea?"

Nora removed her copy of Lisa See's *The Tea Girl of Hummingbird Lane* from her bag and placed it on the table. She was ready to order and get their book discussion going.

"I'm going to try the Flir-tea," she said. "I've never had tea with hibiscus and apple before."

"I've never even heard of flowering tea. You'd never know I was in the food bus—"

Hester was unable to finish her sentence because Estella suddenly grabbed her by the hand and said, "You're not wearing your ring. Did you forget to put it on?"

Color rushed to Hester's cheeks, and she lowered her eyes. "It didn't feel right to wear it because things are weird between us, so I gave it back to Jasper. It's his grandmother's ring, which is why he should hold on to it."

"But you're still together, right?"

"Yeah. We're just . . . taking a step back. Being engaged put too much pressure on our relationship. It's easier to tell people that we decided to put off the wedding than to explain that we're in couple's therapy because I nearly lost the man I love over my trust issues. Luckily, no one's asked me why we postponed the wedding. Without that ginormous event hanging over our heads, we can focus on us without feeling like a clock's ticking."

Nora searched her friend's face. "Are you okay?"

Hester see-sawed her hand. "I'm getting there. This is going to sound awful, but I feel lighter without that ring on my finger. Our couple's counselor asked us to pretend like we've just met, so that's what we're doing. We're going out on dates and getting to know each other all over again. It's strange and super awkward at times, but it's also kind of sweet. Last night, Jasper walked me to my front door and kissed me good night. He seemed almost shy."

"Maybe you can bring him here for a lunch date. Everything on the menu sounds good, but Tastes like Royal-Tea was made for me, don't you think?" Estella tossed her auburn hair and cupped her chin in her palms.

"Yes, Fergie, it does. I'm getting A Cuppa with my Best-tea." June put her menu down. "Looks like we order at the counter. Is everybody ready?"

The four-woman group maneuvered around tables and potted trees on their way to the counter. It was their first visit to Tea Flowers and there was so much to take in. The newest business in Miracle Springs was an eclectic blend of café and garden shop. The large space was divided into sections with the tea shop of the left and the garden shop on the right. A checkout counter sat in the middle.

The limited menu offered flowering teas, sandwiches, and a selection of macaroons. After ordering at the counter, customers could sit at one of the tables in the dining area. The tables were laid with chintz cloths featuring pink roses on a field of pale blue. The floral centerpieces, which were in teapot-shaped vases, were all for sale, and the salt and pepper shakers looked like real blossoms.

The dining area made up most of the tea shop side of the business, but most of the building was dedicated to gardening. The front section was full of waist-high tables featuring potted herbs, houseplants, flowering plants, and hanging baskets. The shelf space in the back half of the store was stuffed with whimsical pots, gardening tools, bird houses and feeders, and a selection of small statuary. Spinning racks stood like sentinels at the end of every aisle, their pockets laden with seed packets, work gloves, and plant labels.

All the potted trees and plants in the café side were for sale, and as Nora and her friends got in line, they heard the customers ahead of them debating over whether to buy the plant on their table—a maidenhair fern in a Ruth Bader Ginsburg face pot—or the snake plant in a llama pot from a neighboring table.

"Can we really pick a llama over RBG?" one man said to the other.

"We can't. So, let's get both. RBG for us and the llama for your boss. Remember the Christmas party? She was spitting mad when I stole that White Elephant gift."

The first man put his credit card on the counter and gave his partner an affectionate nudge. "She *still* talks about that! Yes, I'm going to give her the llama, and I'll think about *you* every time I'm in her office."

"We should come here more often. Tea makes you extra sweet."

According to her nametag, the middle-aged brunette behind the counter was Val. She was short and apple-cheeked with blue-gray eyes and a quiet manner. After telling Nora and her friends that she'd be with them in a moment, Val began packing the men's plants in a small box.

Nora handed June some money. "Will you order for me? I want to check out that Language of Flowers display."

Scooting behind the two men, Nora examined the baskets of blooming flowers on a tiered display stand. Each basket came with a detailed label and a satin bow. The Sympathy basket was made of marigold for grief, mint for consolation, and chrysanthemum for condolences. The Friends Forever basket had crocus for cheerfulness, ivy for loyalty, and zinnia for friendship. Other baskets were called Love Me Tender, Happy Home, and Let's Celebrate. But Nora was most intrigued by the I Will Survive basket.

Leaning closer, Nora read the label to herself, "Carnation for heartache, yarrow to cure a broken heart, rue for regret, and lily of the valley for happiness in the future."

"Interesting?" June asked when Nora rejoined her group.

"Very. I never think about what flowers mean when I buy them at the grocery store—I just grab the colors I like and plop a bouquet in my cart. Who knows? All this time I might've been buying flowers for the shop that mean, 'I wish you'd drop dead,' instead of 'please spend lots of money here today.'"

June laughed. "I want a bouquet that says, 'Stop leaving your dirty dishes in the break room sink when the dishwasher is a foot away.'"

Having finished ringing up their tea and sandwich orders, Val gave Estella a number flag to put on their table.

While they waited for their food, Nora told her other friends about the basket of flowers. Like June, Hester was interested, but Estella was lost in her own thoughts. She stared at the number in the center of their table and didn't say a word.

"What's wrong?" Nora asked.

By way of reply, Estella opened her copy of *The Tea Girl of Hummingbird Lane* to a passage marked with a pink sticky tab. "Want to hear my favorite quote? It feels like it was written for us."

"Go on," Hester prompted.

" 'One mistake can change the course of your life. You can never return to your original path or go back to the person you were.'"

The women exchanged meaningful looks. They'd all made mistakes. Big ones. The kind of mistakes that turned family into strangers and made homes uninhabitable. Each woman had done something they deeply regretted. Their mistakes had left deep scars, and though the pain had lessened with time, it would never fully disappear. They could not think about the past without being pricked by cactus spines of regret.

Nora would forever feel shame over what she'd done. She'd gotten behind the wheel after drinking way too much and had crashed into another car. The occupants of the other car had been a mother and child. Their car had caught fire and Nora had been burned pulling the woman and toddler to safety. After a few months, both victims had completely healed, but Nora was burned from her right hand to her hairline. She lost half a pinkie finger and gained lots of shiny, shell-smooth scars. A few years ago, a plastic surgeon had worked wonders on her face, magically erasing her scars. He'd offered to repair the rest of her damaged skin, but she'd refused. The scars on her neck, arm, and hand reminded her that she'd come very close to killing two innocent people.

Before June began working at the hotel, she cared for seniors at an assisted living facility in New York. During her fifteen-year tenure, she'd seen to the needs of hundreds of people and treated each and every resident with compassion and respect. But when the facility was acquired by a national chain, things changed. The grade school kids who came once a week to play boardgames with the residents were no longer allowed to visit. There was no more animal therapy. The beautiful gardens were neglected, and outings became more and more infrequent. Seeing how depressed the residents had become, June sough to cheer them up by bringing them to a carnival. Unfortunately, a gentleman in her care suffered a fatal heart attack that day. When his family sued June for damages, she lost her life savings and the money she and her husband had saved for their son's college tuition. In the aftermath, her husband filed for divorce and she and her son became estranged.

Hester, the youngest of the four women, faced an unexpected pregnancy as a high schooler. After degrading her and imprisoning her in her room, Hester's parents sent her to a home for unwed mothers. The moment the baby was born, Hester's daughter was whisked away into the waiting arms of her new parents. Hester never had the chance to hold her. Traumatized by the experience, she never told the baby's father about the pregnancy or searched for her daughter. Twenty years later, her daughter tracked her down. What could have been a joyful occasion was marred by violence and grief, and now, Hester's only communication with her child came from a weekly letter.

Estella was the only Miracle Springs native of the Secret, Book, and Scone Society. Hers had been a hardscrabble childhood. Raised by a negligent mother and an abusive stepfather, Estella had known the hunger and humiliation of poverty. What she'd never had was a loving parent. And when her biological father, a man who'd been absent for most of Estella's childhood, returned home to find the new man in the house assaulting his daughter, he drew a gun and killed the man on the spot. Estella had always dreamed of escaping Miracle Springs, but with her father imprisoned nearby, she could never leave. She felt somehow responsible for his incarceration. That guilt had manifested in a series of flings with rich, handsome, well-traveled strangers. The dalliances, which left Estella feeling hollow and tarnished her reputation, ended when she fell in love with a local man named Jack Nakamura.

Now, Nora saw tension in the fine lines around Estella's mouth and brows.

"I liked that quote too," she said. "It reminded me of why we became The Secret, Book, and Scone Society. We've always trusted each other with our secrets. We tell each other things we'd never tell anyone else. So, tell us what's going on. Whatever it is, we've got you."

Estella touched the number card. "Fifteen. That's how many years my daddy's been in prison. He's served his time, but it's done. He's being released next week."

"That's a good thing, right?" Hester asked.

"Yes, yes, of course, it is." Estella unfolded her napkin and spread it over her lap. She smoothed the white cloth over and over. "We talked about how it would be when he got out. You know, which foods he'd want and how he couldn't wait to go to a barbershop, take a walk around town, or have the bathroom all to himself. But we've never talked about the nuts and bolts. What's he going to do for money, for example? How is he going to adjust? This is a very different world from the one he used to live in."

June murmured in agreement. "Listen, honey, I know a bit of what you're going through. Tyson was in rehab for a long time, and you remember what it was like when he got out. He had to spend months in the halfway house before he was ready to live and work on his own. He's come a long way, but he's still shy around strangers. He still looks over his shoulder, half-expecting to see the dealers he stole from when he was using. My boy is in his thirties, but he lost years to those damned drugs. In some ways, he's still a kid.

In others, he's an old man. Time didn't stand still for your father, but it didn't move as fast as it did for you. The pace is going to be hard for him to handle at first."

"People weren't glued to their cell phones fifteen years ago. They didn't drive electric cars or fly to space just for kicks," said Nora. "He doesn't need to adjust to any of that, but I imagine it'll be a shock to see how different the town is now. And the people he knew before he went inside—they're going to look pretty different too."

Estella said, "I've brought him the local paper for years, so he's not totally in the dark about our area. And he's going to live with me until he finds his feet. I don't know what he'll do for work, but all the articles I've read say that a job is super important. It's the one thing all former prisoners need to have to feel like they're back in society. They need the routine and the responsibility. Earning money is important. Working gives them a sense of pride. It'll help Daddy from getting depressed."

"Has he had any vocational training?" asked June.

"Just food service. He cooked for the inmates whenever he had the chance and even developed special menus to build morale. Super Bowl meals and things like that. I bought him a few cookbooks so he could make some stuff in my kitchen. I figured it would be a good idea for him to putter around at home for a few days and get used to his freedom before he goes looking for a job."

Nora cocked her head. "Would Jack hire him to work in the diner?"

"I don't think that's a good idea," Estella said. "He'll find something, but in the meantime, I'd like some books focusing on reentering society after prison. I have a week to do whatever I can to help him transition, and I can read at least two books by then."

June smiled at Estella. "You're a good woman."

"Don't tell anyone. I have my bad girl reputation to protect."

Their conversation was curtailed when Val appeared with their orders. She distributed four small glass teapots and four plates of sandwiches. Finally, she put a plate of flower-shaped macarons in the center of the table. "On the house," she said with a smile. "And since this is your first time dining with us, let me tell how your flowering tea works. Each teapot has a bulb made of tea leaves and flowers. In a few seconds, the bulbs will expand and slowly unfurl. Once it blooms, you'll see the flowers inside. Let your tea steep for a few minutes before you drink it."

Hester said, "Do you mind if I take a video?"

"Not at all. Enjoy."

Val started to turn away when her gaze caught on Nora's right arm.

Strangers were always fascinated by the burn scars that floated like jellyfish over the back of Nora's hand and her arm, her incomplete finger, and the faint lines on her face where the skin had been grafted. They couldn't help but stare, and Nora really didn't mind.

Most adults gave her a good once-over before eventually turning away in embarrassment. Children had no such compunction and would often ask why her skin was bubbly or why she was missing the top half of her finger. She always told them she'd been in an accident and that her scars no longer hurt but she had to put sunscreen of them every day, even in the winter.

Though Nora felt the weight of Val's stare, she was too enraptured by her flowering tea to care. The bulb of tea leaves slowly unfurled, and a centerpiece of dried flowers floated in her glass teapot.

"That's the coolest thing I've ever seen," Nora said to Val.

Finally tearing her eyes away from Nora, Val saw customers waiting at the counter and hurried off.

Nora and her friends resumed their discussion of *The Tea Girl of Hummingbird Lane,* bouncing back and forth between scenes from the book and anecdotes from their own lives. They also talked about the upcoming Honeybee Jubilee.

"For the next two weeks, my bakery will be stuffed to the gills with honey-flavored treats and flower-shaped cookies." Hester plucked a daisy macaron off the plate and examined it with a critical eye. "This is beautiful work. I'm glad it's the only dessert item on their menu. You know I like being the only baked goods game in town."

June bit into a sunflower macaron. "Oh, yum. Mine's lemon and strawberry."

Estella took a nibble out of her tulip-shaped cookie and grimaced. "Ick. Coconut."

"The rose is red velvet," said Nora. "You picked the winner, June."

Hester chewed her cookie thoughtfully. "They're pretty, but I think they were baked somewhere else and shipped frozen."

"I'm going to bring some back for Sheldon," Nora said. "That man needs a treat because even though he pretends he's not, he's still tired from yesterday's story time. He read *Where the Wild Things Are* and made monster crowns with the kids. The whole children's section was covered in glitter and feathers—including Sheldon! His mustache was twinkling like a disco ball."

While her friends cackled with glee, Nora headed to the counter to order a sampler box of macarons. Val was taking a phone order and didn't see Nora, so she ambled over to a display of low-maintenance houseplants. She was immediately drawn to a Chinese money plant in a hedgehog pot. The hedgehog wore glasses and was too cute to ignore.

"That plant will bring you luck," said a man holding a pricing gun.

"I could always use more of that."

The man moved closer. His nametag, which read Kirk, was pinned to the front pocket of his khaki work shirt. Of average height, he had a thick torso and hands as wide and square as a slice of bread. His brown hair was graying at the temples, his brows were bushy, and he had the weather-beaten skin of an outdoorsman.

"The luck is specific to money," Kirk said. "See how the leaves look like coins?"

"I could really use that kind of luck. I'm trying to save up for a car. And as much as I'd like to put this on the checkout counter in my bookshop, I have a brown thumb."

Kirk's brows twitched. "The bookstore on the corner? That's you?" At Nora's nod, he gave her the same overt assessment Val had given her. The only difference was, he was quicker to break eye contact.

Gesturing at the plant, he said, "Here's all you need to know to care for it. Don't overwater. Let the soil dry out between waterings. You'll know when it needs a drink because the leaves will look droopy. It doesn't like direct sunlight, but if it gets indirect light and you rotate it once in a while, you won't kill it. If you need a plant medic, you know where to find me."

"The man I work with keeps saying that we need a store mascot. What could beat a ceramic hedgehog with glasses?"

As Nora carried the potted plant to the checkout counter, she could feel the weight of Kirk's stare on her back.

Val rang her up, packed the macarons, and lowered the plant into a box, shooting glances at Nora's face the whole time.

Nora had had enough, so she said, "Ten years ago, I was in a fire. My face used to be much worse, but I had surgery. There's nothing I can do about my finger but having half a pinkie didn't stop me from eating that curried egg salad sandwich in record time. Do you make all of the food here?"

Pink splotches appeared on Val's cheeks. "Not the macarons. We order those from a bakery in Brooklyn. I do the tea and the sandwiches. Kirk, that's my husband, takes care of the plant side of things. We're new to town."

Val was talking a mile a minute and her movements were jerky. Nora couldn't understand why she was so flustered.

Get over it, lady. I'm not exactly the Phantom of the Opera.

Kirk appeared from the back room and began looking through some papers on the desk directly behind his wife. When he didn't find what he wanted, he touched Val's shoulder. She startled so violently that she swept the box with the potted plant right off the counter. It crashed to the floor in front of Nora, flinging soil and bits of broken pottery everywhere.

"Oh! I'm so sorry!" she cried.

Kirk pivoted his wife around until she faced the back room. "I'll clean it up. There's another hedgehog pot on the third shelf in the storeroom. Go get it and I'll fix the plant right up."

Clinging to his arm, Val whispered, "I'm sorry. I got nervous when I saw her."

"Go on, Val. I'll sweep up."

Nora was tempted to take her macarons and go, but she'd already paid for the potted plant and didn't want to wait around for Val to refund her money. She didn't want to interact with Val at all. The woman was too fascinated by Nora, and not in a good way. She had no interest in being studied like a specimen under glass.

Kirk came around the counter with a broom and dustpan. "The good news is the plant's fine. Give me just a minute while I add a little soil to a new pot."

Leaving him to clean up the mess and repot the plant, Nora returned to her friends.

"Are you causing trouble?" Estella teased.

Nora pulled a face. "Do I have lettuce in my teeth or

something? I'm used to people giving me the once-over, but that lady is making me feel like a circus attraction."

"You think everyone's grossed out by your scars, but she's probably staring at you because you're beautiful," said June. "People do it all the time. You still see yourself as the woman with the scarred face, but no one else does. You need to say goodbye to her once and for all."

Though Nora knew Val hadn't been admiring her, she let the subject drop. Since it was a Monday and Hester was the only one who didn't need to get back to work, Nora told them to go ahead and leave.

June slipped her crossbody bag over her head and wiggled a finger at Nora. "Tell Sheldon not to eat those macarons right before dinner. I'm making lemon chicken and butter beans tonight."

"I'm having a big salad. All these diner meals are catching up to me," said Estella.

Hester eyed Estella's trim waist. "You never gain weight."

"That's the power of an A-line dress." Estella said, glancing at her watch. "I need to run. The mayor is coming in at four. She's decided to go silver and is going to look so amazing. She's ditching her French manicure too. She wants fuchsia on her hands and navy on her toes. Oh, I love helping a woman transform!"

Estella bustled out of the shop to several admiring glances.

"She's a force of nature. I wish I was like that," Hester said with a sigh in her voice.

June waved her comment aside. "You have your own gifts. We all do. Estella can't conjure memories with her baked goods, I can't give people the perfect book recommendation, and none of you can knit worth a damn."

Hester laughed. "That's true. Maybe I don't want to be a force of nature, either. Maybe I want a transformation like the mayor's getting."

"You want to go silver?" Nora joked.

Hester twirled a strand of honey-colored hair around her finger. "I want to get out of bed and not have to deal with these curls. I've worn my hair in a headband or ponytail since I was in high school, but when your workday starts at five a.m., being stylish is the last thing on your mind."

June ran a hand over her head. "You could shave it all off. It's incredibly liberating."

"That's a bit too liberating. How about a shag?"

"Is that a haircut or a proposal?"

Hester and June headed for the exit, laughing as they walked.

Nora returned to the counter where Kirk had her potted plant ready to go.

"Hope to see you again soon," he said, pushing the box across the counter. His smile was perfunctory. He suddenly seemed eager for her to leave.

Nora bristled. She dealt with rude, impatient, and self-centered customers all the time. Because of this, she went out of her way to be polite to those in the service industry. If this is how Val and Kirk were going to react to her burn scars, how would they treat other customers with obvious physical differences?

Knowing she had no chance of getting through to them by being hostile, she took a deep breath and spoke in a casual but direct manner.

"I'd like to come back here again, but I'm not sure if I will. Your wife seemed uncomfortable being around me. I'm used to people staring at my scars, but they usually get over it after a few minutes."

Kirk flapped his hands like a pair of agitated birds. "No, no! It's not that at all. The truth is, we never planned on moving here. We came to be close to my sister and to help out with her son." His eyes clouded with sorrow. "She's sick, you see. She's tried everything, including the hot springs. Now, she's just trying to manage her pain and live what little time she has in peace."

When Kirk turned away to compose himself, Nora said, "I'm sorry. That must be really hard."

Hundreds of years ago, the Cherokee traveled to the hot springs to experience the healing properties of mineral waters. Over time, the waters attracted more and more people. As hotels, shops, and eateries were built to cater to these visitors, Miracle Springs became known as a retreat for those grappling with physical or emotional illness.

The hot springs weren't magical. The waters couldn't cure cancer, undo trauma, or fix a broken heart. They could offer rest and hope, and if these failed, the beautiful scenery, kind residents, and charming shops and eateries could still provide comfort.

Most visitors found their way to Miracle Books, lured in by colorful window displays and the promise of a good read.

Over the years, Nora had heard some sad stories. She knew that people could act when they were scared, and if Kirk's sister was gravely ill, it was no wonder he and Val were on edge.

Nora picked up her box and said, "This is a good place to find peace. I hope that's what your sister finds."

Another customer was approaching the counter. Kirk darted a glance his way as he murmured softly. Though it made no sense, Nora could have sworn he said, "That depends on you."

Visit our website at
KensingtonBooks.com
to sign up for our newsletters, read
more from your favorite authors, see
books by series, view reading group
guides, and more!

BETWEEN THE CHAPTERS

Become a Part of Our
Between the Chapters Book Club
Community and Join the Conversation

Submit your book review for a chance to win exclusive
Between the Chapters swag you can't get anywhere else!
https://www.kensingtonbooks.com/pages/review/